THE 480

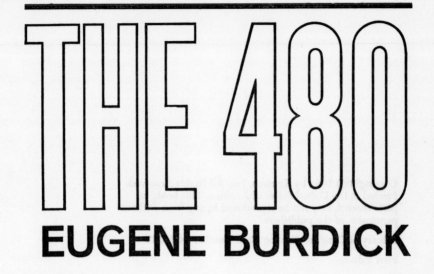

THE 480
EUGENE BURDICK

McGRAW-HILL BOOK COMPANY
NEW YORK TORONTO LONDON

A KAMIMA, INC. PUBLICATION

Library of Congress Catalog Card Number 64-20515

First Edition

08932

For Katie, Maggie, Michael, Ballantine
—And An Old Royal . . .
All Steady, Provocative and Honest

Preface

There is a benign underworld in American politics. It is not the underworld of cigar-chewing pot-bellied officials who mysteriously run "the machine." Such men are still around, but their power is waning. They are becoming obsolete though they have not yet learned that fact.

The new underworld is made up of innocent and well-intentioned people who work with slide rules and calculating machines and computers which can retain an almost infinite number of bits of information as well as sort, categorize, and reproduce this information at the press of a button. Most of these people are highly educated, many of them are Ph.D.s, and none that I have met have malignant political designs on the American public. They may, however, radically reconstruct the American political system, build a new politics, and even modify revered and venerable American institutions—facts of which they are blissfully innocent. They are technicians and artists; all of them want, desperately, to be scientists.

The American public believes that it "chooses" the Party candidates for the Presidency and then makes a free and sovereign choice between the two candidates. This is hardly an accurate description of what happens. The American public believes it is sovereign. It is not. The American public believes that its views "trickle up" to the halls of the Congress and the White House and become law. This is rarely so. The American public believes in some vague and undefined way that its opinion is a fundament of our democracy. Too often this is not the case.

This situation is not evil. There is no conspiracy against the American public. There is only a great gap in knowledge. A few know a great deal, the great mass know very little. The few that know decide the shape and character of American politics.

The Presidential candidate will say, publicly, often, and with a profound hypocrisy that he believes in the "common man" and is appealing to him. It is a form of Plato's Royal Sie: there are plenty of common men about and all the candidates know them well. They will vote out of habit for the party they voted for at the last election, and the one before. The "uncommon man" is the person the candidates are trying to find, identify, analyze and appeal to. The victorious Presidential candidate is the one who is most successful in appealing to the uncommon voter.

The "uncommon voter" is not, alas, always a superior person. His "uncommonness" sometimes consists of being bloody minded, hostile, ignorant, frightened and prejudiced.

The Presidential candidate will make the form appearances before the "bosses" and the political rallies, but he knows these are not important. Political dinners at $100 a plate will not affect the election. The Presidential candidates this year care very little whether the major newspapers or *Time* or *Newsweek* indorse them. They will be courteous to editors and publishers, but they know that newspapers and magazines comment significantly after an election not before. Most of the newspapers opposed F.D.R. each time he ran and it did not hurt him. It would appear that the American voters do not necessarily trust the political views of their newspapers.

Who will the Presidential candidates listen to? They will attend most carefully to the views of their invisible, underworld, usually quite small. There is every reason to believe that President Kennedy defeated Vice-President Nixon in 1960 in great part because President Kennedy had put together a perceptive, quick, and "scientific" group from the new underworld. Nixon tried but was not as successful as Kennedy in his recruiting.

Every Presidential aspirant must say "I believe that the American people when they have all the facts will make the right decision." But he knows it is not true. The average American voter has neither the interest nor the information to make a rational decision between the two major Presidential candidates. The average voter votes the way his father did. He tells his wife to vote the way he does . . . and usually she obeys. Furthermore, these American voters are exposed to words and slogans which have been carefully researched to make sure they have exactly the desired effect. The candidates listen to these expert, a-political, neutrals much more closely than to any boss from Boston or Chicago or the Far West.

Why the phrase "new underworld"? Because these people operate in happy anonymity. This underworld, made up of psychologists, sociologists, pollsters, social survey experts and statisticians, cares little about issues. That is one reason the candidates keep them invisible. The *romantic* heart of politics is partisan rather than neutral and deals with issues rather than statistics.

There is nothing un-American in all of this. On the contrary, it is in the best American tradition to use new facts, new discoveries, new insights. But there is a potential here which is ominous. First, the existence and mode of operation of the new underworld should be made known to the people. Much of the information given to President Kennedy in 1960 was handled at the time as if it were "top secret" classified information. Copies of reports were numbered and the information was seen only by those who had to see it. This was not casual reading, this was armament for a major battle.

Slavish adherence to such advice might mean the end of statesmanship. Candidates often do not say what they believe: they say what they know the people want to hear. And if farmers want to hear something which is contradictory to what trade unionists want to hear, two speeches will be written. One will be delivered in Des Moines and the other in Detroit. The new techniques could make a science out of this hypocrisy.

"The public temperature" is taken. If the pulse is feverish, the public is told "fever is good. I support it." The "public pulse" is taken and if it is low the public is told "passivity is good. I stand four-square behind it."

This may or may not result in evil. Certainly it will result in the end of politics as Americans have known it in the past. While I do not intend this novel to be a moral tract, it is nevertheless based on what I believe are the political realities of today and the political hazards of tomorrow.

The Simulmatics Corporation is a real company. It formulated the concept of "the 480" and was employed by and gave advice to the people who directed Senator Kennedy's Presidential campaign in 1960. Where statements in the first third of this novel are attributed to Simulmatics, they are based on reports prepared by the company or factual articles written about their work. I am indebted to officers of the Simulmatics Corporation for supplying me with these reports and for allowing me to print their 480 categories in the back of the book. However, the interpretation of their work and its implications are entirely my own.

What I have written concerning simulation in the 1964 campaign is not based on the work of Simulmatics Corporation. This is entirely a projection by the author. Simulation Enterprises is a fictional corporation.

Some public figures in the political background of the book bear a reasonable resemblance to living individuals. If they do not, it is my literary failure. The foreground characters in the novel are fictional and to my knowledge bear no resemblance to persons living or dead.

Eugene Burdick

THE 480

The road was a thin streak through the rain jungle. It looked like a lancet wound which went deep and ran even. It cut through huge trees, hills, solid rock, tiny glades, over rivers and never deviated. It was unnaturally straight. The surface of the road was an old red, scabbed over and gray, but the subterranean red, fresh and wet, showed when the sun was right.

As the jeep went squarely down the road John Thatch glanced at the geologic slice the bulldozer blade had exposed. At the bottom there was a thick layer of hardened ancient compost, the slime and rot of generations. Above this a layer of dead matter and then the living top. Here bizarre and tiny animals, in uncountable billions, waged an endless and soundless war.

The boles of the trees shot up straight and colorless, as if carved from a neutral shade of marble. Vines, lianas, creepers swung between the trees in the strange bleached world of the parasites. Orchids dangled, pale and exquisite, their mouths flecked with gold and orange. Great clots of air-feeding plants grew until they were the size of a small house, and a boy could carry one in his hand. On the ground nothing was green.

The green started high, where the vines began. The vines curled tightly to the trees, exerted a desperate grasp, clawed toward the sun. The new branches and leaves of the tree and the tops of the vines fought for space, writhing and twisting, shooting out new growth, smothering one another, exploding in greenness toward the air and sun.

Thatch looked up at the narrow slit of sunlight far above. Although it was ten in the morning the jeep's lights were still on for the morning mist hung in thick streaks across the road. The mist was an unhealthy color; a dirty white. Each time the jeep shot through a roiling mass of the stuff Thatch stopped breathing. He knew the odor too well, beyond time and yet flecked with a death-smell that was fresh. Thatch disliked this night gas.

It would stay dark on the jungle floor except for a few moments at noon. Then down the deep, narrow cut in the trees would come sunlight . . . brief, dazzling, unbelievable. It was the sunlight, abrupt and novel, that congealed the ancient corruption of the jungle floor into good road topping.

"How many more miles, Gujral?" he asked the driver.

"Five, maybe six, sir."

Thatch hummed an old song. It was once a workingman's song of protest against working on the railroads for the British. During the hard years of the revolt, it had been considered subversive by the British. Now it was humorous, sung by the Indians who had to work as hard as ever on survey and road-building gangs in the jungle. Gujral smiled his tight ex-sergeant-major's smile.

Then the smile vanished. Gujral jammed on the brakes, arching his graceful body forward, and with his right hand turned off the ignition. The silence settled in. Gujral cocked his head and listened.

Then both heard the sound, like small steady thunder. It was growing.

"Are we in a high place?" Thatch asked.

"No, we are in a low place, sir."

Gujral's body slammed against the seat, the engine started and the jeep jerked ahead. They shot through a thick bank of mist and Thatch automatically held his breath and caught only a whiff of the odor of death, enough to make his throat work. Gujral came through the mist without having deviated from the center of the road by an inch. Their speed was dangerous. So was the threat.

"How far to high ground?" Thatch asked.

"One mile."

They would make it, Thatch knew. He remembered others who had not. Jim Colby was one, an experienced engineer who had never worked in the rain jungle, but only in the desert wastes of the oil countries. Colby had not left when the Indians started running out of the wide deep bowl through which they were putting a survey line. He laughed as one Indian hurriedly explained what the distant thunder meant. It was impossible to rain that fast, he said. He would stay. Five minutes later the water was at his knees. Ten minutes after that he was drowning, his hands slashing with rage at the brown frothing lake which had sprung up about him. They picked his body out of the mud, his face a muddy mask of anger. Before they burned him they chipped the mud off and an old woman massaged the dead face into a smile. It was bad to face God with anger on one's face.

Thatch felt the road rise. His gut eased. They could hear the thunder again, nearer. Gujral stopped. They got out ponchos, drew the canvas curtains of the jeep shut. The air turned evil. Thatch knew it was the refracted light thrown ahead by the low storm clouds. Still it turned the air evil. The next half-hour would be a hot soaking misery.

"Sahib," Gujral said. His voice was part whisper, part warning, and part fear.

Thatch hated the sound of *Sahib*. Gujral used it only when he was shocked back into the old British Army jargon. Gujral was pointing ahead and to the left. Thatch felt a queer spasm jerk through his body and his fingertips trembled. Words formed on his lips. Reassuring words—it's only jungle stuff, imagination, maybe malarial vision, the old fever.

The upper half of a man's body hung a few feet above the ground. The man's hands pointed a rifle at them. On his head was an antique British helmet and he wore a uniform. He had the face of a Gurkha, mustached and taut. One eye was closed. But the bottom part of the body was missing.

Who did it, and for what purpose? Even in this jungle he knew so well, Thatch had never seen such a thing . . . the half-body of a man slung in the air, to dangle, swing, be spoiled by morning mists and finally assaulted by the crawling things. How many billions of bites, gnaws, snaps, nips had it taken to devour the lower half of the man?

Then the one open eye blinked. The face grinned. The half-body moved toward them.

Gujral giggled with relief. The Gurkha had been standing in a low jungle mist and the evil light had made the mist dun-colored and therefore invisible. In a few steps the man was whole.

"Get in the jeep, friend," Thatch said in Nepali. "Standing in the rain is unhealthy."

The Gurkha climbed into the back seat. Thatch opened three cans of boneless chicken, a tin of English biscuits, and a jar of hot peppers and unfolded a napkin of cold *chaputtis*. He handed the Gurkha and Gujral each a tin of chicken. The Gurkha was sweating slightly.

"You are a fool of a corporal," Gujral said, using the peculiar Gurkha accent, his voice unmistakably that of a sergeant. "To stand in the open while a rainstorm comes. It is bad for the rifle. Is the rifle greased? No. It does not look it. In my regiment we would have known how to take care of you."

The attack by Gujral cheered the corporal, but he still held the tin uncertainly in his hand.

"The chicken holds up well in such a climate, Sergeant Gujral," Thatch said.

Instantly he heard the slight pinging sound of the Gurkha's knife go into the tinned meat.

The damned Gurkhas and their pride, Thatch thought. The Gurkha was afraid the can might contain pork, but he could not bring himself to ask. That would be offensive to the gift-giver.

"Soon there will be plenty of water for those that are thirsty," Gujral said. "Just stand out and open thy mouth and into it will fall all the water of heaven."

"And one will drown before he can close his mouth," Thatch said quickly.

Gujral was teasing the Gurkha, knowing the Gurkha was fearful of the rain jungle.

It made Thatch weary, the endless tiny stabs of provincialism, the barbs between different sects, the veiled insults of different language groups, the gestures of insolence and distance toward others only slightly different. He had seen the joking words and gestures suddenly explode into the ugly reality of knives, pistols, clenched fists, gushing blood, and eyes rolling in heads that did not yet know they were dead.

Thatch turned and looked at the Gurkha. The man was sweating less and the muscles beneath the dark skin were relaxed.

"Why dost thou close thy left eye?" Thatch asked.

"Because there is something in it that pains," the Gurkha said. "It is best to close the eye."

"Open thine eye, please, and let me see."

The Gurkha opened the eye slowly. Thatch reached for the flashlight.

The thunder of the storm was not more than a hundred yards away. Tons of water, driven by the wind, made their assault. Rain hit solidly the huge leaves at the top of the jungle. Fragments of water slashed like shrapnel and it occurred to Thatch that it was not natural for liquidity to rip so sharply, make such hard sounds.

The Gurkha's eyeball was inflamed. The arteries, now visible in the white fluid of the eye, were red threads that jerked spasmodically. Then Thatch saw the pricker.

"The eye is pierced by a pricker," Thatch said. "To close thine eye permits the pricker to work itself deeper. It will kill the eye."

"Blind the eye?" the Gurkha asked. He was listening to both Thatch and to the storm. His eyeball was huge in the darkness. The storm was no more than a few seconds away. He feared the storm more than the pricker.

"Most surely," Thatch said. He sought a phrase the Gurkha would understand. Thatch had seen the prickers, endless varieties of them, under microscopes. They were one of nature's weapons, designed for an unknown enemy. They were tiny and exquisitely formed. "It is like a corkscrew which the English officers use to open wine bottles."

"Can one take it out?" the Gurkha asked.

"Perhaps. Not surely, but perhaps," Thatch said. "It will hurt. It is worth the effort."

He brought the flashlight closer, tilted the man's head. A black dot, no larger than the point of a pin, was still out of the eyeball.

"I would not like to lose the eye," the Gurkha said. Thatch understood that it was consent. The Gurkha would never make a direct request.

Thatch put out his free hand; Gujral already had the first-aid kit open. He placed an aseptic bandage in Thatch's hand. Thatch gently rubbed the swab over the Gurkha's eyeball, holding the man by a firm grip on the back of his head. The Gurkha did not blink, although each pass of the swab pulled dozens of invisible barbs back through the mucuslike substance of the eyeball. The butt end of the pricker came out a bit. The liquid of the eye leaked and flowed onto the lower lid.

Then the storm hit them. The Gurkha's throat quivered. The small muscles, inured to physical pain, could not control the fear of this unbelievable assault of nature. The Gurkha wept, both eyes wide open.

The water came in a solid wall. All three men gulped for air, sharing the claustrophobic fear of suffocation. The jeep lifted to one side. Water, in fine jets, found every opening. Now they were inside the noise. From a distance of even a few yards, the storm had been menacing, but no more than that. Now it was a presence which gripped. It was an assault, compounded of trees creaking, vines snapping, breaking, stretching to the outer limits, giving way.

"I have always thought it was like the sound of soccer balls," Gujral screamed calmly, "made of rock and rolled down a great river."

Thatch felt the neck muscles under his fingers tense with pain and fear.

"The pricker is coming out, but it will take time," Thatch said. "Thou art a good patient."

He bent close. The pricker was a third out. The eyeball was collapsing, but not badly. No worry. The eyeball, Thatch had learned, was a marvelous object. It protected itself by the fluttering eyelid; it replenished itself, resisted destruction. Next to his testicles, a man protected his eyes most carefully.

"Why art thou on this road?" Thatch asked. "There have not been soldiers on it before."

"I am not sure," the soldier said. His right eye blinked for the first time. He was troubled. He was not certain he should talk. The swab caught the butt of the pricker, pulled a few more barbs loose.

"It is to prevent the completion of the bridge," he said. "To stop the last gap from being closed."

"Why is it necessary to prevent the last gap from closing?" Thatch asked.

"It is the enemy across the bridge," the Gurkha said. "When the bridge is completed they will cross it with troops."

Thatch held his hand steady, but with an effort. He concentrated on the Gurkha's eyeball, caught in the circle of light.

He listened to the roar of the storm, felt the spray of water lace across his body.

"Who says they will cross the bridge?" Thatch asked.

"Our commander. Who tells him I do not know," the Gurkha said and a faint smile crossed his lips. "But that is all I am told."

"Then the bridge is not completed?" Thatch asked.

"No. The workers have been forbidden to complete it," the Gurkha said. "It will become a bridge for invasion."

"For you to invade Pakistan or for Pakistan to invade you?" Thatch asked.

The Gurkha hesitated.

Gujral willed the Gurkha to be quiet. Gujral knew this white man well. You are in the presence, Gurkha, of a calm angry one. Be quiet. Gujral watched the white swab move evenly across the eyeball, listened to the din of the storm. He is one who is full of rage, Gujral thought.

"I only obey orders," said the Gurkha, sensing Gujral's mood.

Thatch gave one more swipe and the pricker came out.

"Get out of the jeep," he said.

"I will get out, Sahib," the Gurkha said, his voice startled. "But you are forbidden to go past this point. It is an order."

"Get out. I am going past this point," Thatch said, his voice calm, almost detached. "If you stop me I will run you over."

The Gurkha got out of the jeep. He did not look back as the jeep moved slowly forward. Its headlights made an aureole of light, like a firebrand able to burn under water.

"Pick it up, Gujral," Thatch said. "Move out."

Gujral put the throttle down and the jeep shot ahead. He would not quarrel with Thatch.

Abruptly the jeep moved into clear sunlight. The road and jungle steamed.

"We are close to the turnabout," Gujral said. He drove ahead a hundred yards to the circular cut in the jungle where pieces of heavy equipment could pass one another. The turnabout was at the edge of a cliff which gave a long clear view of the valley.

Thatch got out of the vehicle and walked to the edge of the cliff.

Below was the long sharp line where the mountain range had been torn by ancient catastrophe, ruptured by some vast convulsion. The result was a valley with almost vertical walls.

Centuries of plants and trees had inched their way into the cliffs, found a footing, sent down root systems, and finally smothered the raw marks of the seismic rip. Now the valley walls were green, soft, searing, implacable and an obstacle to travel. Somewhere along the floor of the valley was the unmarked boundary between the two countries.

Thatch could see the spidery shape of the bridge, its filigree of struts and cables blurred by the morning mist.

"Bring the glasses, please, Gujral," he called over his shoulder.

Gujral got the binoculars from the jeep, removed them from the case, and handed them to Thatch. Then he shaded his eyes from the sun and tried to make out the bridge.

Thatch swore. It was only five or six words, but they were hard and bitter and formed no sentence.

"Not yet?" Gujral asked.

"Not yet," Thatch said.

He handed Gujral the glasses and his face was distant, his eyes focused on some faraway object. His lips made a slight smile. Actually Gujral knew that it was the black rage, the rage so great that it was the rage of nobility. Lesser men had lesser rages. Gujral wondered for a moment why Thatch was so frightened of his own rage.

Gujral moved his glasses along the bridge. He knew what to expect when he came to the middle. He felt a powerful sense that the two soaring, marvelously cantilevered, jungle-bred, balanced and contrived arcs should come together and be fused. But he felt it only in the body. He knew with his head what to expect. His head was correct.

The gap was slight. No more than twenty feet. But it was twenty feet of empty blue air, broken only by the soaring of a pair of vultures hovering and enormous in the middle distance. They made slow black circles in the sky, their bare pink necks hanging down, holding their cruel ripping beaks far below their bodies.

"It is not right," Gujral said.

Thatch smiled. He got into the jeep. Gujral got behind the wheel and they moved.

"I know what you think," Thatch said, his voice flat. "You think, Oh God, if it were the old days and I had the power behind me of the Rajputana Rifles, the Bikaner Camel Corps, the

Mahratta Light Infantry, Hodson's horse, the smart field guns, the sabers, the pistols, the machine guns. Oh God, then I would sweep these Pakistanis into the abyss and the vultures would eat for a month."

Gujral did not dare look at at Thatch. The sahib, as usual, had cut too close.

2

"He's in, Mr. Bookbinder, but he's on the phone," the secretary said. "He said go right in. He said—"

"I know, Miss Brighton," Bookbinder said. "He said 'Tell him anybody's welcome. Everything I say is public. But throw out reporters and Democrats.' Right?"

"Right, Mr. Bookbinder," she said. Bookbinder made her uneasy. He was friendly enough, but he had a reputation for being rich and he was not "regular" and that kind was hard to handle.

Bookbinder looked around the room, part of the Republican Party National Headquarters, with its orderly rows of typewriters and stenographers, files, addressograph machines, its flow of *In* and *Out*. He turned and walked into Bertrand A. Kelly's office.

"Look, Oscar, we didn't send you to L. A. to find out if they've got any money," Kelly was yelling into the phone. He waved a chewed cigar at Bookbinder. "We know that already. We sent you there to *raise* money. To be precise, about seven hundred fifty thousand. . . . They say what?"

Kelly held the phone away from his ear, the crackling voice went like a thin scream through the room. Kelly looked at Bookbinder, shook his head, waved a hand toward a table which held part of the famous Kelly Distinguished American Glass collection.

Today on the tray was a bottle of twenty-five-year-old Maryland rye, a Kentucky corn whiskey, a pre-Prohibition pint of medicinal whiskey with a faded label on it, a dusty quart of Old Granddad. The bottles were surrounded by heavy crystal glasses and a Steuben pitcher of tap water. Bookbinder poured himself a finger of the Old Granddad.

"Look, Oscar, don't be stupid," Kelly yelled abruptly. The thin scream died. "If they all want to be ambassadors and they think Hollywood is due for some of the diplomatic gravy, give it to them." He paused and then broke in. "Keep it general so they'll think you've guaranteed them the Court of St. James's. Put the bite on them and run."

The room was, as always, chaos. It smelled of old cigar smoke. And whiskey. One wall was covered with signed pictures of celebrities and politicians. The ones in the left-hand corner were starting to yellow, those in the lower right were crisp and new, but all of them were in identical cheap frames.

The rest of the room was a shambles. There were stacks of letters on the floor, a box of telegrams on Kelly's desk, books were canted on shelves and in heaps in the corners. In front of Kelly's desk was a paper box with the words *Del Monte Fruit Cocktail* on the side; it was full of telegrams which were covered with a fine film of cigar ash.

"Oscar, if you're so damned dumb I have to tell you step by step, then we'll send someone else out there," Kelly was saying. "Look, if you want to get Hedda Hopper to mention the drive, get John Wayne to talk to her." He paused, let the mechanized voice squawk for a few seconds, then cut in, his tone corrosive. "Don't wail, just do it."

Bookbinder, bored, looked at a huge wall map covered with pins of various colors. Someone had barely rubbed out the obscenity which had been scrawled across three Midwestern states which had gone Democratic in the off-year 1962 election. Bookbinder looked at Kelly—the mushy cigar, the silver chain across his belly, his coat off, his feet on the table, his eyes half-closed. He had a brutal job.

How many people noticed how small Kelly's feet were? And how many knew there was a Phi Beta Kappa key at the end of the silver chain? Bookbinder remembered meeting Kelly before World War II when Kelly had just graduated from Princeton and wanted advice about where to go to law school. He had been a thin, sallow, very unconfident boy.

Some people discover an image of what they would like to be, Bookbinder thought, and then work, fight, eat, drink, smoke, and talk themselves into that image. He thought of Saltonstall, white-thatched, lean, patrician, gentle, proper. Could Saltonstall have willed his hair white and his body lean?

Maybe a man saw the spot, the job, the role, the position and worked his way into it, clipping away at what would not fit, changing this mannerism, picking up a new one, gradually losing his original self and becoming a creature of the image perceived. Sam Rayburn, Stevenson, Dirksen, Kennedy, Nixon, Goldwater. Original creatures? Impossible.

Bookbinder saw it clearly. Acheson cultivating the mustache and brisk manner; Goldwater becoming bluff and open and so honestly conservative; Stevenson puckish and witty as a Presidential candidate and then pious and even pompous as UN ambassador. No one could have been born with a voice like Dirksen's. . . . Maybe it hurts, Bookbinder thought, to cut away little parts of the original you, and then like a plastic surgeon build a new man of borrowed flesh.

Kelly had been a skinny retiring boy from a wealthy Episcopalian family in Vermont. He had been sent to Groton, where he did not make the debating team, and to Princeton, where he had joined one of the lesser clubs. He remained a gray memory to most of his classmates, the one in the class picture they could never identify. He had been commissioned an ensign in the Navy during World War II and during that time the transformation had taken place. He came back hard-drinking, cigar-smoking, thirty pounds heavier, and utterly dedicated to politics. Now in his early fifties, he was the most powerful single member of the National Committee. He continued to take on weight, to talk tough, to give the impression of being city-bred. He deliberately created the disorder around him, drank great quantities and was never seen drunk. He was, and everyone said it with delight, "a character." He had developed a reputation for remembering names; knew the precinct, ward, and borough leaders of almost every state in the union; could rattle off the names of Congressmen and Senators for the last twenty years; knew the products and chief industries of every city over 20,000, although he had visited few of them. Kelly had power, but he used it quietly.

At Princeton Kelly had collected butterflies. They were now

long gone, replaced by the collection of bottles which, Kelly said loudly, contained every whiskey manufactured in the United States.

Kelly finished the conversation, swung his feet to the floor and came around the desk. "Well, Book. Been months. Weeks anyway. You're just in time for lunch."

"No. Bert, I don't have time," Bookbinder said. "I just dropped by to ask you a question."

"You can ask it when you're eating," Kelly said. He spoke to his secretary on the phone. He held a glass up to the light, noted it had a hardened residue of whiskey in the bottom, shrugged and poured it half-full of the twenty-five-year-old rye. "Confusion to our enemies. My God, there are more of them every day. Better drink deep."

"Who are you going to back at the Convention?" Bookbinder asked.

"Me? I don't back anyone," Kelly said with exaggerated innocence. "I'm just a wheelhorse. I'm the obedient servant of the Party. Forget you asked me an improper question."

"I mean it, Bert," Bookbinder said.

There was a sharpness in Bookbinder's voice that caused Kelly to shoot him a hard look as he sat down in his chair.

The phone rang and Kelly shrugged, picked it up and began to talk. It was a Senator with a grievance, but easy to handle. He studied Bookbinder as he talked.

Bookbinder must be almost seventy, Kelly thought. Book was an insider's legend. He had come out of Kansas, ham-handed, muscular, wearing a suit which he said had been made from a horse blanket, burning with a sense of "social justice," and possessed of eighty-five dollars which he had made shoeing horses. He presented himself for admission at Harvard Law School. There was a famous story, repeated often by Dean Pound, that the Admissions Officer looked at Bookbinder's big hands and wrists extending six inches beyond the cuff and denied him admission on the spot. Bookbinder had drawn out an envelope with a list of his high school grades, and although he had attended on and off for ten years, they were A's. The envelope also contained a fluent, somewhat arcane, very forceful explanation of how Bookbinder wanted to "end oppression in the United States and everywhere else it appears." It was a letter of recommendation Bookbinder had written for himself.

Bookbinder in law school was raw, defiantly poor, unpolished, ambitious, and he mingled with Socialists on week ends and got drunk on beer and red wine. He should have plowed his first year. But he had a raw intelligence that was formidable, he worked prodigiously, and he had a fierce integrity which made even the most cynical of his professors pause for a moment. By the end of his second year at Harvard no one, except the very stupid, took Bookbinder as a joke.

"Sure, Senator, if you're opposed to foreign aid get up and make a speech," Kelly said. He sipped his whiskey carefully. "Oh, come on. We can't get the whole Party to back you. Ike's for more aid. He told Kennedy that."

Kelly did not listen to the Senator's complaint. He merely waited for the noise to end.

Bookbinder, Kelly remembered, had once run for office in New York and lost. He loved politics, but he had been born in the wrong state at the wrong time. And, so, the rumor went, he decided that to be influential he must become wealthy. He became both.

Bookbinder had made his name, established his reputation for integrity, and dug his political grave all at the same time. Kelly was vague on the details, but the story was enough to make him careful whenever he dealt with the man. Book had been appointed chairman of some obscure finance committee. It was obscure because a great deal of money in cash passed through it. Traditionally this money had been carefully not counted, not recorded, and dispensed without receipts. Some question was raised when after the election a great deal of valuable waterfront property in Manhattan was sold by the state to an uncle of the successful candidate. The Democrats made the usual cry for the usual inquiry and expected the usual result. But there was a hitch: Bookbinder had kept a careful record of all the cash received. When subpoenaed he read from a broad meticulously kept ledger the interesting fact that most of the cash had come from the uncle and gone to the successful candidate.

Both parties were horrified and the hearing was quickly quashed. Every other witness contradicted Bookbinder's account

—including several Democrats. The ranks drew solid. Anonymous cash, Bookbinder learned then, was the invisible glue which held the political complex together.

Bookbinder had listened without expression as his testimony was torn to shreds. He made no protest when he was accused of seeking to advance his own career by false testimony. A reporter, making a crude play on his name, labeled him "Open Book" and occasionally it was still used, but not to Bookbinder's face.

Bookbinder came back with an abiding distrust of party organizations but an even firmer, almost obsessive, concern with politics. He was a Republican, but the Party regarded him as unnaturally flawed by either innocence or compulsive honesty. In turn he distrusted the Party hierarchy but was intrigued, almost obsessed, by the apparatus of power. Over the years the Party had used Bookbinder in only very special ways.

He was an expert on Latin American law and counsel to a number of American firms in South America. He sensed, long before others, that the income tax would be a permanent part of American life and he published one of the first books in the field. *Bookbinder on Taxation* was in its twelfth edition.

He had been appointed by four Presidents to serve on those powerful but anonymous commissions where high policy is worked out. Never elected but often appointed, he wrote long cool letters to the various Presidents that over the years had several times become policy. Bookbinder never claimed credit. It was enough to be involved in that mysterious process of governing.

Kelly, barely listening to the Senator's familiar complaint, inspected the old man and saw that he was still in good shape. And he still had that precious reputation for blunt honesty. And Kelly still disliked him.

"Look, Senator, let me level with you," Kelly said abruptly. "You count up the judicial appointments that have passed through your hands. You are doing about twice as well as most of your colleagues." Kelly laughed—the great, booming, acquired laugh. Bookbinder knew the Senator had yielded.

"Of course, Senator, you have every right to ask. It is your duty. But it could look like hell in Drew Pearson."

Gently Kelly put the phone down. He faced Bookbinder with real pleasure. Bookbinder was a worthy opponent.

The door opened and a waiter from a nearby delicatessen staggered in with a huge tin tray.

"Oh, Good Lord, I forgot about the Kelly lunch," Bookbinder groaned.

The waiter put the tray on the table. Kelly untangled a five-dollar bill from the debris of pencils, matches, notes, and penknives in his pocket, handed it to the waiter. The tray was loaded with huge slices of cheese, thick salami, a steaming platter of sausages, three kinds of bread, a large bowl of potato salad with two forks stuck in it, six bottles of German beer, jars of mustard, a wooden bowl of unsalted butter. Kelly picked up a sausage, put it between his teeth and with a sharp pop the taut skin broke.

The lunches were famous, both for the people who ate them and for the huge quantities of food. Everything was double-thick, heavily spiced, almost deliberately crude. Halfheartedly Bookbinder took a slice of cheese and put it on half a piece of pumpernickel bread. Part of the tradition of the lunches was that no one was given a plate or an individual fork. Everyone ate directly from the bowls and plates and the delicatessen was merely told how many forks or spoons to include.

"Just suppose that I did have a candidate," Kelly said, a forkful of potato salad in front of his lips. "I don't need to try and fool you, Book. The real job of the National Committee is to win the election. We try for a candidate with a chance to win. Anyone on the Committee who says he is neutral during a Presidential nominating convention is a liar or a damned fool. We have to put on a good show. It has to look lively; the delegates have to think they're participating in a combination circus, horse race, and true-blue American brawl." He paused, scanned the tray, placed a thick wedge of Swiss cheese on a piece of bread, covered it with salami, put on two kinds of mustard and a circle of red Bermuda onion, and slapped another piece of bread over it. He crushed it in his fingers, reducing it to an inch-thick mixture. "Of course the Committee also has to give every reasonable candidate a fair shake. Not the best shake, but a fair shake."

"But there is one who gets a little better shake than the others," Bookbinder said. He looked away as Kelly's teeth came down into the sandwich.

"Right," Kelly said, his face broadening into a grin. His

voice was muffled. "The one I support. He gets things better . . . but not so much that it shows."

"Who is that man going to be when you get to San Francisco next year?" Bookbinder asked.

"Why do you want to know?" Kelly asked.

Bookbinder was prepared. He just waited.

"Book, you're a regular, but just barely," Kelly said. His eyes had narrowed above the sandwich. "Mostly you're with us, but sometimes you sit on your hands. Once they tell me you said 'Vote No for President.' "

"Right. I didn't like either candidate."

"Book, if that was the standard I'd never vote," he said. "But it happens to be a stupid attitude. What is important is the Party. You have to support a party, work with it, make it as good as you can, weed out the crooks and the phonies, hammer out a platform, build a machine. Yes. Build a machine. That horrible word you and all your independent friends sniff at is the thing that keeps America going. When you've got the Party as hard and trim and mean as you can get it, you send it in to fight with the other party and somehow out of all the dust and low blows and hurrahs something like political virtue emerges. But it doesn't emerge in persons. It emerges through the Party."

"All right. I'm a loner in politics," Bookbinder said. "But I also happen to back my choice with money and some energy."

"That you do. We got over a hundred thousand from you and your friends in fifty-six," Kelly said. "We could use it again. But I still want to know why you're interested."

"I haven't got a candidate," Bookbinder said. "But I've got an idea."

"You've got an idea," Kelly said. He put the remains of his sandwich down and picked up a dill pickle. Subtly, in a dozen little motions which another man would not have noticed, Kelly came to full attention. Bookbinder could feel the man's intelligence, his sensitivities, his perceptions come to life. In a way it was offensive, for it meant that Kelly had really not been interested before. "An idea. And what might that be?"

"I'm not going to tell you," Bookbinder said.

Kelly's eyes did not flicker, his jaws chomped on the food, he sucked on the beer bottle. But excitement ripped through him:

The old man wants it himself. Now, after all those years of being the honest, inconspicuous, humble man, Book rides out like a knight. He had credentials ten pages long, white hair, self-made wealth, the respect of the moneyed people and a reputation for being right on the big issues. Kelly felt the low-pitched ecstasy that came so infrequently: He could stop this man dead in his tracks.

Without looking up, Bookbinder could feel a change. This hit close to where Kelly lived. Kelly could endure anything, but not the denial of information. He could listen to long speeches, to drunken splutterings at cocktail parties, to the tearful confidences of a Congressman's wife, to the half-spiteful chatter of a Secretary's secretary . . . and remember what was politically relevant. He never showed boredom. He tolerated endless dinners in search of a single clue, made fifty phone calls and was rewarded if one gave a solid piece of information. Kelly was valuable because he had information: in his head and in the rumored journals in a safe in his house in Georgetown. The information in his head he treated with absolute discretion, and this assured him of more information. The journals in Georgetown would, years after he was dead, be published as the finely etched, magnificently detailed chronicle of an age. Kelly was a Boswell, Bookbinder knew, but he saw himself as a Boswell to a Johnson who was protean, vast, sweeping, plural: the Party.

It was for this he had forced himself to become fat . . . everyone trusts a fat man. For this he had forced himself to learn a thousand jokes by heart . . . don't trust a man in politics who doesn't have a sense of humor. For this, he had not taken a wife . . . people confide in a bachelor.

"Book, I've developed a reputation for loving dogs and kids just because anyone who loves dogs and kids can't be all bad," Kelly said. "He's a man you can confide in."

Bookbinder looked up at Kelly and at once he knew he had made a mistake. Kelly's eyes were lumed with a hard curiosity, blank and unconcealed.

"I didn't put it well," Bookbinder said, carefully keeping anything like apology out of his voice. Now he had to be very precise. "I've got a young partner. Bright fellow. Name of Madison Curver," Bookbinder said. He went slowly. "Mad believes that the incumbent can't be beaten. Any incumbent. When we elect a President, we elect him for eight years. If he wants to run the second time."

"And you don't like it?" Kelly asked.

"I don't like the President becoming a commodity we buy for eight years," Bookbinder said. "Our whole system depends on it being a real horse race every time."

"You can't beat somebody with nobody," Kelly said. "Your friend Curver got any suggestions for what horse will run strong against Kennedy?" Kelly asked. Things were not as clear as they had been. He had a feeling he had misjudged Bookbinder.

"No. He doesn't think anyone can beat Kennedy," Bookbinder said. "But he has a few ideas about what kind of man will give the President a tough race. First, he has to be a hero. A real believable hero. In some other field than politics." He looked squarely at Kelly. "Or law."

Kelly's certitude had vanished. Book didn't want to run. He had something else going for him. And Bookbinder, his friends, and his money could be helpful in the next eighteen months.

Kelly decided not to tell the complete truth.

He made the decision coolly and without remorse. He had a reputation for truth of a sort. But he knew that there were times when one simply could not tell the entire truth. This was one of them.

"I'll level with you," Kelly said. "This just isn't our year. So I don't really care which good man gets our nomination. Kennedy will beat whoever we put up. We'll go through the formalities but our boy isn't going to win. Kennedy has got everything going for him. He and his family have their faces on the cover of every slick magazine on the stands, they are on TV every week, and the Democrats have built up a pretty good machine around the country."

So far, Kelly thought, that's the truth. Our man doesn't have a chance. He was lying only around the edges: He did have a candidate, for 1968. And Kelly wanted Book's discovery—if he made one—nominated because he would lose to Kennedy. Then in 1968 Kelly could run a winner.

Kelly smiled behind his sandwich. Book would come up with a good man, honorable and a credit to the Party.

"What you need, Book, is a new Messiah," Kelly said, feeling his way carefully. "The Willkie type. A hero with no enemies." Easy now, make it sharp, but not completely accurate. Book was no fool. "In a sense I agree with Curver. What ruins us this year is the President's power. And our boys seem to be killing one another off. The Millionaire quick-draws on the Flyboy, the Flyboy skulks around the pass and shoots from ambush, the Rambler acts like a maiden, the Loser goes for the pastures where middle-aged lawyers grow fat."

Book enjoyed Kelly's nicknames. Kelly used them when he wanted to say something frank or cruel about a man in his own party. The Millionaire was Rockefeller (sometimes Kelly varied the routine by calling him the Banker, which wasn't quite accurate); Goldwater was the Flyboy (also Tom Mix); Nixon the Loser (coined after that disastrous press conference following his 1962 California defeat); and Romney was, of course, the Rambler.

"There aren't many Messiah types around," Bookbinder said. He watched the merged faces of the old heroes blend in the refraction of the sun against many pieces of cheap glass. "They just don't pop up every day."

"Book, I agree. But why don't you look? Because if you find one I'll support him to the hilt."

The two men turned slightly and looked at each other. In one sense they trusted one another: they were far past examining one another's motives.

They both felt refreshed.

Book made a token sandwich and took it with him from Kelly's office. On the sidewalk he looked for a trash basket.

3

The jeep moved at a careful high speed. Gujral had a sense for potholes and slippery mud.

"The Pakistanis have been unreasonable," Gujral said abruptly. "They agreed the two halves of the bridge should be exactly the same length. Both countries signed a paper. Now they say the boundary is the middle of the river at the bottom of the gorge. The middle of the river is actually ten feet east of the exact middle of the bridge."

"So?" Thatch asked.

"So now they say that India is invading ten feet of Pakistani air space," Gujral said. "This truly is the talk of children. Yes?"

For a few moments Thatch did not respond. He seemed not to hear. He stared ahead at the bridge.

"What would Gandhi say of this?" Thatch asked. "Would he say that the side that has the greater length of bridge is the better? What would Bhave say? Would he say that the owner of the longer part of the bridge had proved himself superior?"

Gujral felt the logic tighten around him. His mind blanked except for a kind of pink haze of sentiment. He kept his voice even.

"Injustice should be fought wherever it exists," Gujral said. "That is what Gandhi meant. That is what Bhave means."

Thatch considered.

"Is ten feet more of bridge justice?" he asked. "Bhave asks that he who has much land should give it to those who have little. Gandhi said that from violence only evil can flow. Gandhi would say that *satraghya* would lead you to give the ten feet of bridge to your friend and with love. From that could come friendship. And now around that bridge there are gathering commandos of Indians and Pakistanis who will hunt one another out like animals."

Gujral hated Thatch. He wondered if he could rejoin his regiment. Would they take a man so old? No, they would say his stiff left wrist, which contained only a small fragment of German steel, made him unfit.

Gujral looked over at Thatch and, quite suddenly, his own anger was gone. Thatch was rigid in the seat, his eyes closed tightly. His hand fumbled out for support toward the dashboard. His breathing was shallow.

"All is well, sir," Gujral said in Urdu. It was a joke between them.

"No, all is not well," Thatch said, but his eyes cleared, his hands stopped groping. He had a thin but real smile on his face. He spoke Urdu. "I am . . ." he sought for the word. He shook his head. "There is no word for it in your language." He spoke in English. "I am mad."

"We have such a word," Gujral said with pride. "It is *taish*. It means an excess of anger."

"No. We have that word. It is not the same," Thatch said. "Very occasionally I am mad"—he paused—"technically."

They both laughed. *Technically* was spoken in English, for there is no Urdu equivalent. It sounded funny after the flow of Urdu.

"I understand, Sahib," Gujral said gently. He did not, really. The word *technically* meant steel and welding torches and motors. *Taish* and *technical* did not mix.

The jeep swung around a huge gulmahar tree. They could see the bridge. Gujral hit the brakes lightly, brought the jeep to a feathering halt. The bridge was durable but not massive. It was made of iron, steel, paint, miles of cable, chrome undercoat, rivets, vision and skill. It was an artifice. But it soared with an inherent beauty. The lines were clean and swinging. Where strength was needed it had it. It was not bulky or muscular. Its cantilevered length and the long loops of the cables came together at precisely the point at which a man's viscera told him the support was needed. It was harmonic, spare as bones and, in some maddening way, the most beautiful man-made thing Thatch had ever seen.

And when the eye reached the gap, there was nothing but blue air, and *it* was somehow unnatural. Thatch did not understand the chemistry and metabolism by which a view of something could be felt like a blow, but for a moment he opened his mouth as if he were going to gasp. The sight of the gap hurt him.

He had built warehouses, roads, quays, factories, causeways, tunnels, houses. Nothing had gripped him as had this bridge. The bridge was different; soaring up out of the green jungle, marvelous in its symmetry, a symbolic joining, and difficult to build—oh God, how difficult to build! But it was right. For months he had waited and watched and something inside him had unfolded with pleasure as the spans and cables and buttresses fell into place. Now it was stopped. It hung there unfinished.

Thatch growled. The jeep moved ahead. Gujral looked at him and grinned behind his beard and mustaches. Somehow there was going to be victory today. Gujral inhaled deeply. He had always been able to smell victory. Defeat was a mystery, unpredictable. No one knew when it would strike. But victory he could smell.

People milled around the head of the bridge. Some of them Thatch recognized. There was a group of Nationalist students carrying banners which said in Urdu, Hindi, and English that the bridge was an indecency to India. There were Communists, somewhat older, who attacked the United States for building a bridge when thousands starved. Both groups had picketed the bridge since the day it began. The Nationalists picketed because they opposed a bridge link with Pakistan. The Communists picketed because the bridge was being built by an American contractor.

There was a *guru* who had wandered to this bridge and found it a satisfactory place. He had locked his arms over his head when he was a boy and stared into the sun. Now he was gray-haired and his arms had fused together and the sun had burnt his eyeballs a deep sightless yellow. He could not feed, bathe, or care for himself, but others could. He had an uncanny sense of guessing the politics of the person to whom he was talking. He gave wise advice in a very low voice and to one person at a time. Even the Communists listened and put *chaputtis* or a bit of rice into his mouth or covered him with leaves when it rained. The *guru* slept sitting upright. His upraised arms, neck, spine, and the supporting muscles had hardened into an unbending fossilized cage.

Two new Land Rovers and the men around them were unfamiliar. From one of the Land Rovers a thick rattail antenna waved blackly and Thatch knew it was a transmitter. Thatch guessed they were reporters. Then, as the jeep came to a stop, he saw the glint from half a dozen camera lenses. He tensed.

The pickets were marching in regular lines, sweating, lifting their feet high, slapping them to earth, jerking their banners up and down, their eyes on the photographers. With the jeep engine stilled Thatch could hear them chanting. The usual slogans. Nothing different today except that their voices seemed louder. The native workers were lounging on the bridge, drawing their pay although there was no work to do—welders with their masks lifted off their faces, painters with their helmets on, "high" steel men wearing heavy boots. They liked their company-supplied uniforms and did not take them off even in the hottest weather. Sweat poured down their faces. The handful of American workers were drawn together in a knot at the entrance to the bridge. Thatch could not tell if they were blocking the bridge or merely standing there.

He swung out of the jeep and walked toward the bridge. The eyes of the cameras followed him. Cowell, Thatch's foreman, short, burly, quick, and dependable, broke from the group of Americans. The reporters came after him, but the photographers stayed back, anxious to shoot Thatch with the bridge as a background.

"Hi, Boss," Cowell said, talking fast. "We're in a hell of a spot. A light plane flew over this morning from the Pak side. It circled the bridge, apparently taking pictures. Someone began to fire at it from the Indian side. I guess they hauled up a forty-millimeter gun. They hit the plane and it went down in Indian territory spang in the middle of a village and apparently killed seven people. Or that's what the Indians say. We offered to give them transportation or first aid, but they had someone up from the capital already and they wouldn't let us near the spot. Both governments are ordering troops up to the bridge. The Indians say the body of one of the Paks has been identified as a general in the Pak Air Force. The Communists are raising hell because it was a plane supplied by the US to the Pak Government. The Indians are claiming their air space was violated. That's as far as I can make it out and some of that is rumor.

"I saw a sentry back on the road," Thatch said.

"He must have been part of the advance guard, sent out to keep the road open," Cowell said. "The troops are supposed to arrive in late afternoon. Nice, huh? Troops at each end of the bridge with howitzers and mortars and recoilless cannons all ready to go. The first trigger-happy bastard that pulls a lanyard will probably shoot half the bridge away."

"They aren't going to bivouac at the ends of this bridge," Thatch said in a low flat voice.

A lean handsome reporter came toward them. Cowell made the Communist clenched-fist sign. Thatch nodded. He knew the reporter. He was called Rajput because he was the son of a rajah. He had repudiated his family and in addition to writing for a Communist paper was a correspondent for Tass.

"Mr. Thatch, what do you think of American planes being used for raids on India?" Rajput asked. He had a casual manner and an Oxford-accented voice. Thatch had argued with him before. Rajput was no lightweight.

"I did not see the plane or the incident," Thatch said. "Therefore I have no comment."

"It is well known that the Pakistani planes were given them by America," said Rajput with soft sarcasm. "Logically, therefore, it had to be an American plane. Now that we have cleared away any ambiguity, what is your response?"

"Mr. Rajput, you have a fine collection of suits made in Bond Street, London," Thatch said quietly. "Every time you wear one are you a servant of English imperialism? Don't be an idiot. America sells, leases, loans and sometimes gives planes all over the world. She is not responsible for what happens to them when they are out of her hands." He paused. "Or that would seem to me logical, even to a Magdalen man."

The other reporters laughed. A man from a progovernment newspaper said "Hear, hear." Rajput, unruffled, snapped back with a question, but Thatch had turned away and was answering another reporter. Seeing he was ignored, Rajput's voice went high and shrill.

"Please, Mr. Rajput, common courtesy," Thatch said over his shoulder. "Kindly repeat your question, Mr. Kandirit."

"It looks as if your bridge will be used as a scene of battle before it is ever used for transportation," the reporter repeated. "Both governments have ordered their troops to move to the 'outmost limits of their legal boundaries.' Which means the troops will be looking at one another across the twenty feet of empty space at the middle of your bridge."

Thatch looked at the clever eyes in the dark sweating face, watched a drop of sweat roll down and disappear into the soft fold of the collar. He turned and looked at Cowell.

"Is that true?" he asked.

"That's what the USIS broadcast said," Cowell replied. "They expect the troops to go to their 'legal boundary.' That would take them onto the bridge. Apparently the UN is worried about it and has asked both governments for a conference."

"There is going to be no fighting on that bridge," Thatch said stolidly. He had no idea what he would do, but the decision had been made.

Thatch turned and walked out onto the bridge. He was followed by the Americans, then the Indian workers, and finally by the reporters and photographers. At the other span of the bridge he could see figures moving toward the center, probably the same people as on this side, reporters, workers, some Americans. When he arrived at the gap he would do what was necessary.

He looked up at the cables, casting an appraising eye on the steelwork, looking for imperfections. There were none. It was beautiful work. He heard Rajput's voice, lofting over the quiet shuffle of feet.

"Thatch works for the Central Intelligence Agency, of course," Rajput was saying. "Why else would an American know Hindi and Urdu? Why else would he build a bridge which is so obviously provocative?"

Thatch laughed. He glanced sideways at Cowell and shook his head. Cowell was nervous.

They got to the gap. The end of the bridge was unprotected and the edge made razor-sharp by the enormous emptiness beneath it. Thatch walked to the gap, stood with his feet only inches away from the edge. He did not glance down. Across the gap a group of Paks were gathered. He saw faces of workmen he knew, several Americans who worked for Thatch Inc., men in city clothes and others with cameras.

Both groups shuffled to a halt. The gap, with its morbid and persistent fascination, silenced everyone. They looked up at the big sweep of the cables and the arched span of the bridge and then back at the gap. The two groups stared at one another, the cameramen making a few adjustments but not shooting pictures. Each man seemed to sense his own smallness against the stark reaches of the towering bridge.

"*Bhai,*" Thatch said across the gap. The word anywhere in Asia meant almost the same thing: brothers. It hung in the air. Some of the Paks began to move their hands, bringing their palms together. The silence deepened.

"Cowell, man the crane," Thatch said.

He pointed at a small movable crane ten yards back from the gap. Its cable circled a twenty-foot span of chrome-colored steel, the keystone girder that would close the gap. It had been forged at Bhilai with Thatch and three Indian engineers observing, machined so that it would fit perfectly into the huge slots on either side of the gap, where explosive rivets would then be inserted and detonated. It would, Thatch knew, be a ticklish fit, for the temperature could expand the girder slightly and throw the rivet holes off by a fraction of an inch. But he had anticipated fitting the girder when the sun was high.

For four months the girder had been on the site. For three weeks it was all that was needed to close the gap.

Cowell started the crane engine. It fired, hesitated, started erratically. Quickly Cowell made adjustments, his head cocked to one side, listening. The engine smoothed out.

Thatch walked over to the girder, stepped onto its smooth chrome surface, wrapped his arm around the cable, and with his left hand gave a thumbs-up signal. Cowell stared at him. Thatch still held his thumb up. Cowell nodded. The winch tightened and the girder lifted. Thatch adjusted his weight slightly so the girder was straight. His hand went flat and the winch stopped. He was five feet above the bridge. The crane moved forward. Thatch's finger dropped when the girder was precisely over the middle of the gap and had swung perpendicular to it.

Now the photographers began taking pictures frantically. Some merely shot Thatch from the edge of the gap. But one imaginative Pakistani, a small wiry man, ran back down the bridge, scrambled up a cable, ignored the empty space beneath him, and climbed. He kept climbing until he had everything in perspective—the gap, the two groups, the crane, Thatch on the girder, and the thread of the river. The thread of the river was the ultimate touch which made the photograph famous. The river was so distant and minute that Thatch seemed to be suspended in space, dangling casually over an abyss. Like any great news photograph, it was partly accident. The sun was at an angle which caught the water in the gorge and turned it a deep red. It gave the picture a solemnity, a kind of raw symbolism which no one could miss. Later, the picture was reproduced everywhere and it won many of the prizes given for news photography. The little Pakistani photographer became a celebrity, but he never again shot such a picture.

"Friends, I want to tell you a story," Thatch said. He was no orator—God! he had reason to know he was no orator—but suddenly he knew what he was going to say. He knew the words which could close the intolerable gap. The only competing sound was the distant roar of the river. His voice carried easily to both groups. He spoke in English. "Many years ago a group of patriots protested the British salt tax and made a march toward the sea. They did not call themselves Hindus or Muslims, Pakistanis or Indians; they did not quarrel about Urdu or Hindi or Bengali or Pharsee. They were like all of you, they were your fathers and mothers. They were marching to the sea to take their own salt from the ocean. And that was against the law of the British. They marched not because they were hungry for salt, but to show their defiance to an unjust law."

Thatch stopped. He looked from one group to the other. They were silent, their faces looking up at him. Even Rajput was listening, his face blank.

"The British sent a message that the next morning they would barricade the road the salt-marchers were taking," Thatch went on, his voice more certain. "It was hot when the marchers came to the barricade. A double line of British soldiers was drawn up across the road. The first line of soldiers held *lathis*, the second line rifles. The marchers stopped a few hundred yards from the barricade and, without instructions, each man's family gathered around him. They bathed him and dressed him in clean clothes. They said good-by to him. And then between men there were good-bys; Hindus said farewell to Muslims, Christians to Sikhs and Parsis, Brahmins to Untouchables, poor men to rich men. And in all the languages—Urdu, Hindi, Bengali, Tamil, English, Gujrati, Marathi, Telegu, Malayan. Then the men walked forward to the ege of the barricade and sat down, spacing themselves so that the British with the *lathis* would have room to swing. The British officer in charge of the soldiers ordered the marchers to disband and to clear the public thoroughfare. Those men, your fathers, did not speak and they did not move. They were brothers. Their wives and children crouched a hundred yards behind them and waited."

A sigh, a single haunted sigh, went up from the Pakistani

side of the bridge. It came from an old man Thatch recognized as a skilled painter. Perhaps, Thatch thought, he had been on the march as a child. People aged quickly in this climate. Unself-conscious and delicate, the painter's sigh was a sound of hard recollection and of suffering. It lingered in the air. Thatch knew it resounded in the heads of his audience.

"The British soldiers stepped out with their *lathis* and began to beat the marchers. The marchers put their hands over their heads, but did nothing more to protect themselves. The blood poured down their arms and soaked into their *dhotis* and made puddles on the ground. When they fell over unconscious, the *lathis* bit into their faces and chests and stomachs. The British soldiers whipped until their arms were sore and then they switched hands and whipped again, for their officers walked behind them. One marcher lost an eye, whipped out of his face like a marble and as it rolled on the road he turned to watch it with his remaining eye and then the *lathi* tore out the other eye. There were moans, for they were only human. But no one ran. No one shouted. They listened to their families mourn for them . . . for all of them. Not just the ones who were Muslim or Hindi or Bengali-speaking or Episcopalian. Brahmins sat in the shadows of Untouchables and waited their turn. The flies came first. Swarms of flies. Black, frantic for blood—"

A voice, perhaps that of the old Pakistani painter, uttered a single word: *"Enough."* Thatch turned, the girder swung like a pendulum. Expertly Thatch regained control. His eyes looked for the speaker.

Thatch was not aware of the girder and his weight shifting. Much later when he saw the films and heard the gasp from the audience he felt a shock of surprise, for he could only remember his vague sense of triumph that he was reaching them. Rajput's face had changed. It had lost its bland and artificial toughness and was younger, like that of a child listening to an adult. Thatch felt something rise in him.

"Not enough," Thatch said calmly. "Not yet. Not until the vultures came and perched on the trees and waited. Ants swarmed over the fallen bodies, covering them like a moving red *dhoti*. And the British sweated through their uniforms, but continued to swing the *lathis*. Some *lathis* broke but the officers had been careful. The soldiers were handed fresh *lathis* and sent back to work. And the marchers were silent.

"Enough? Not yet. For there is an ending."

Thatch stopped and looked down at the gap. The river was a small thing, far away and unreal. He almost forgot his audience. When he looked up, he sensed that all their eyes were on him. Again he felt something new prickle inside his head. It was a strange itch of pleasure, blended with a fugitive sense of something illicit. They listened so *carefully*.

"And how did it end? A daring vulture made a pass at the road and plucked up a human eyeball. The vulture was seen by a young soldier who vomited. Then the British were seized by an epidemic of vomiting. They looked up at one another, at their blood-soaked *lathis*, at their uniforms red to the knee, at the spray of blood in the air, at the ants and the flies and, one after another, they began to vomit. Finally the soldiers staggered away from the strange heaving mass of men and insects. With their eyes bulging they crawled out and refused to lift the *lathis* again. And so it ended. Not a marcher had fled! Your fathers . . . all castes, all tongues, all colors, all religions, from all regions . . . not one had fled."

He paused. The story of what he had seen himself as a terrified little boy was over. But he had to go on, to speak further, to forge the final link.

"After that day something happened to the British. The end of their Raj was known to every marcher there . . . whether he was Muslim or Hindu or Christian. They knew it in their hearts and in their comradeship. They had won. And why? Because all men, under the skin, are made the same and when skin and muscle are ripped the same blood flows. They learned that day, that day under the sun and the vultures, what a cause means."

Thatch paused. He sought the eyes of the old Pakistani painter. Their eyes locked for a moment. The man sighed and said, "It was like that. I was there." He held up his arms and the cloth fell away and on both sides of the gap they could see the dull patchwork of old *lathi* scars. "I was young and therefore in the last rank of marchers. I was scarred only on the arms."

There was a long moment of waiting. Thatch listened to the

silence carefully. He watched the postures of the listeners until he noticed a wave of little motions, a shifting. The moment had come.

"This gap between the two halves of this bridge is a sign of the meanness and the evil and suspicion in men," Thatch said. "It was this gap between humans which the salt-marchers closed. It was their unity, the absence of any gap which made them prevail." He paused. Then he asked the question slowly: "What should we do?"

"Close the gap."

It came as a whisper, first from one mouth, then several. It was repeated and this time many voices, even those of the photographers, repeated the three words.

Thatch maneuvered the girder with his feet so that the ends swung toward either end of the bridge. He looked at Cowell and turned his thumb down. The girder lowered slowly. A few inches above bridge level it was seized by a half-dozen hands on each side. Bodies leaned over the gap, oblivious of the height. Slowly, with infinite care, Cowell eased the girder down. There was a click on one side. A moment passed and Thatch felt sweat start up between his shoulder blades. Then there was the second click and a low cheer rose from the workers. Rivets were slipped in. The girder fit. There were several sharp explosions and it was locked into place.

Thatch took in the slack of the cable, eased pressure on the hook and freed it from the girder. For a moment Thatch stood alone on the girder. He was very tired. Maybe, he thought looking down, I really am afraid. He lifted his head and without looking at his feet walked to the Pakistan side of the bridge.

He heard footsteps behind him. When he was on the bridge he turned around. It was Rajput. He had tears in his eyes and the antagonism was gone from his body. He said nothing, but he nodded his head. Then he walked to the old Pakistani painter and put his arms around the man and held him for a moment. The painter's scarred arms came up and touched the shoulders of the son of a rajah lightly. They separated.

"The bridge is finished," Rajput shouted. "We must send the soldiers home. There is no need for them here. And if they do not go we will sit down on our bridge and bare our backs as the salt-marchers did."

Thatch sensed rather than saw feverish activity on both sides. Other girders rose on the crane and were riveted into place. He leaned against a railing, his body weary beyond anything he had ever known.

Such an event on a far-off frontier might have gone unnoticed and unremarked except for three things. First, both India and Pakistan had intended to use the bridge as an excuse to start general warfare against each other and every major power in the world and the staff of the United Nations knew this. Second, every word and gesture had been photographed. Third, a sophisticated Oxford-educated Indian Communist had been converted back to a faith in his country.

4

Eve Wilder was the thin, hyperthyroid wife of a USIS officer in Delhi. She was also a stringer for AP, and when she heard about the trouble at the new bridge she took off on the train. She traveled third class and listened. She had learned the language in the States when her husband took language training. By the time she reached the village railhead nearest the bridge she realized from the scattered conversations that something close to a revolution or mutiny had occurred at the bridge.

At the railroad station three Europeans got out of first class. Eve Wilder knew them. They were all correspondents. They began to negotiate with the stationmaster for a taxi. Eve looked around the village and decided she could beat them to the bridge by walking.

She struck off down the road, swinging a knobby cane. She stopped at a few villages to buy soda pop and to gossip. At each village the bridge incident became clearer. When Eve got to the bridge her seersucker dress was dark with sweat around the shoulders. The American workers drifted toward her; a white

woman was a rarity here. She was no beauty but they joked with
her anyway. She fished for information. Finally she walked over
to Thatch's tent and introduced herself. He was curt and brief
in his answers. She was surprised, for his shadowy reputation
through the countryside was that of a gerat orator.

"What did the workers do when the troops came?"

"The troops didn't get to the bridge," he said abruptly. He
got up and left the tent.

"Why not?" Eve said, following.

Thatch did not answer. They were walking toward the middle of the bridge, toward the gap so recently closed. The concrete topping was fresh and white. At one edge of the cement
there were some words in Hindi and Pakistani. Eve Wilder
stopped and knelt down.

"They are names," she said, looking up at Thatch. He was
surprised. "The names of the workers?"

"You speak the language," Thatch said and for the first
time he smiled.

"Not well, but enough to get along," she said.

He walked back and forth on the fresh cement. Occasionally
he looked over the railing, down at the river and then up at the
great sweep of the bridge.

"I heard about the salt-march speech you made," she said.
"That was an ingenious idea."

"Ingenious?" Thatch said. He looked surprised. He stopped,
watching a bicyclist emerge from the rainforest on the Pakistan
side and weave out onto the bridge. The bicycle was overloaded
with a huge bundle of spiky limbs used to start the dung fires
when the weather was wet. "I saw that massacre. I was in India
with my father, a missionary, and he wanted to join the salt-
marchers. My mother talked him out of it, but we went down
to see it. The marchers would not have allowed a foreigner in
the march anyway, but my father always felt guilty. We dressed
wounds for the marchers. No, it was not ingenious of me to use
the episode. It just came to mind."

They stood for three hours on the bridge, greeting the people who walked or bicycled past. Occasionally someone would
get off his bicycle and approach Thatch and say *"Darsan,* Sahib,"
and without self-consciousness Thatch would reply *"Shanti."*

"Why do they ask your blessing?" Eve asked.

"It's just courtesy," Thatch said. "It would be impolite to refuse. It's really for the bridge."

Eve, like many women who are not attractive, had developed an acute sensitivity to other women's reactions to men. She noticed that the women who passed had a curious boldness toward Thatch; when they had passed their remarks floated back, clear and distinct and flattering. Thatch was unaware of them. Later she had an impression of Thatch which she did not wish to identify.

When they returned to the Indian side of the bridge the three reporters had arrived in a jeep. They converged on Thatch. Thatch's face hardened. Eve Wilder walked over and in slangy Hindi persuaded the jeep driver to take her for a ride. The ride was to the village and was nonstop. Three hours later she filed a wire to New Delhi.

STRAIGHT COLLECT AP DELHI STOP THATCH SPEECH ON SALT MARCH MASSACRE LED TO SPONTANEOUS COMPLETION OF BRIDGE GAP STOP HE SAW MASSACRE AS SON AMERICAN MISSIONARY STOP WORKERS BOTH SIDES AFTER COMPLETING GAP AND POURING CEMENT FANNED OUT INTO COUNTRYSIDE AND TOLD STORY ALL VILLAGERS WHO WEPT AND THEN THREW SELVES FRONT MILITARY CONVOYS STOP RAJPUT'S ABDICATION COMMUNISM AND FIERY SPEECHES VERY INFLUENTIAL STOP FOR THREE DAYS COUNTRYSIDE CLOSE TO PEASANT AND WORKER INSURRECTION STOP NO ARMED FORCES WITHIN FIVE MILES OF BRIDGE STOP MY IMPRESSION BOTH GOVERNMENTS FORCED CHANGE POLICY BY UNEXPECTED MILITANCY OF BRIDGE WORKERS AND RECOLLECTION OLD SOLIDARITY AGAINST BRITISH BUT CHECK YOUR END STORY STOP RUMOR PAK TIMES HAS MARVELOUS PICTURE CLOSING GAP RECOMMEND YOU BUY STOP BIOGRAPHY OF THATCH FOLLOWS BY MAIL STOP ALL GOVMUTE
        EVE WILDER

Ed O'Reilly, head of the Delhi AP bureau, had managed news bureaus in a half-dozen world capitals and he wasn't easily excited. He had already checked with the Indian government and knew, off the record, that they had called off "military operations" around the bridge. But until he received Eve Wilder's wire he had not known the reason. The words ALL GOVMUTE was shorthand for government suppression of the story. He knew that the Indian government information officers were angry. The gen-

erals in charge of the Air Force and Army were demanding that
Thatch be thrown out of the country. It was a long time since a
foreigner, or for that matter an Indian, had defied the government on so big an issue. He filed the story to New York and told
Karachi to get the picture Eve mentioned. He stated, in careful
language, that he thought Thatch's action had forestalled possible
war between the two countries.

Tom Gulligan, the head of AP in New York, put the pieces
together. For two weeks there had been signs of rising tension
between India and Pakistan, emergency meetings at the UN,
talk of a "fact-finding mission," and the President had sent W.
Averell Harriman on a special mission to Southeast Asia. It looked
like an old pattern . . . it had happened in Korea, Laos, Viet
Nam, the Congo and Algeria and at least half a dozen other
places.

But now, Gulligan thought, some innocent engineer named
John Thatch whom no one had ever heard of had blundered into
an international incident and come out smelling like a rose. No,
it was more than that, Gulligan thought; the man had, in a way,
shaped history. This man Thatch had done something and said
something that generated a kind of solidarity, rekindled some old
memory. The bridge workers on both sides suddenly began to
act like professional agitators. Clearly the Pakistani military were
disappointed, but also frightened by direct action among the
peasants and the workers. Gulligan's Karachi man had picked
up rumors of action centering around the slogan "Remember the
salt march."

Something flickered at the edge of Gulligan's mind. Once
every decade a real story broke, one that his apathetic readers
didn't forget tomorrow. Maybe this was it, or maybe he just
thought so because he was bored. Everything was so dull. Politics, the baseball season, the stock market, Hollywood, Congress.
He looked down at the slight bulge of his belly, soft from too
many years of sitting in a chair and looking at teletype messages
and picking up the phone. He felt resentment. He was tired of
the same old mothball heroes and weary of his stomach and he
decided to do something. He was not quite sure what.

Gulligan authorized Karachi to pay up to three hundred
dollars for the picture that had appeared in the Pakistan *Times*.
He set a rewrite man to putting together a story under the head-

line AMERICAN ENGINEER MAY HAVE PREVENTED WAR. He wired
New Delhi to get as much of Thatch's speech, word for word, as
possible.

The AP release went out and was picked up by about 50
per cent of the subscribers. The next day the picture arrived
from Karachi with a note that it had cost only fifty dollars.
Gulligan sat looking at the picture, at the tall powerful American, dangling on a girder high above a river bed miles below.
In the middle distance were the faces of the two groups of
workers and the grainy detail was fine enough to see that they
had a look of absorption or, you could imagine, something deeper
. . . rapture or the look of men hungering to believe. Far below
was the streak of water . . . pure red.

It was a masterful picture. It combined symbolic value with
clarity and balance. The physical danger to Thatch made it arresting. But the look on the faces of the workers and the red
thread of river and the knowledge that the man on the girder
was defying two sovereign nations while troops were hurrying
toward the bridge gave it added dimensions. Gulligan sensed
that the picture was fated. He was right. AP finally earned over
fifteen thousand dollars on sales of the picture, including rights
to use it on a post card and a calendar advertising a soft drink.
Gulligan felt a mild regret that the color contrast in the picture
would be lost in a black-and-white mat.

The tape recording of Thatch's speech which the Delhi AP
man had borrowed from an Indian TV man and played over into
his own tape recorder was blurred and rough in spots. Gulligan
sat in his noisy office not fully understanding what was said. But
at the moment when he heard a voice cry *"Enough"* the hair on
his neck rose. Suddenly, this pot-bellied, tough, and cynical
newsman felt in touch with the stuff of history. It made Gulligan
uncomfortable. He was used to fast analysis, to putting things
into their correct categories, to resisting emotion, to a quick de-
tection of the fraudulent, to a distaste for the sentimental. At the
end of the speech, as the tape flapped on the spool, Gulligan
was moved.

"Bowman, come over here," he yelled at his assistant. "Send
out a notice that we are having a follow-up on the Thatch story
at the bridge and that we consider it one of the big ones of the
year. Will supply photos as well as text of speech Thatch gave.

Have this stuff worked up into a thousand words. Get some more biography on Thatch. His company must have an office in the States . . . but don't put in too much bio. Hit the drama at the bridge."

Bowman was staring at the photograph. He turned it over, looked at the credit quite reflexively. "This is quite a picture, Boss." He hesitated. "I mean it's got moxie, but something else." He clearly was not up to defining the "something else."

"Get going now," Gulligan turned away. "And head the story this time 'The Man Who Shaped History.' "

When Bowman was back at his desk Gulligan picked up the phone and dialed a number. He got the executive offices of CBS and asked for the director of news. It took a few minutes to get through.

"Frank, this is Tom Gulligan at AP," Gulligan said. He had no sense of making an ordinary business deal; somehow he felt as if he were on a reckless mission. "We've got some more stuff on that Thatch guy on the bridge and one wonderful photograph. I just have a feeling, Frank, that it's going to be one of the big stories. I'd like you to see the picture and listen to a tape. I think this is the stuff you can make a documentary out of. 'Course I could be wrong . . ."

Frank came by two hours later, looked and listened. Without leaving Gulligan's office he called New Delhi and talked to four different people. He then phoned his own office and sent a young producer off on the next PanAm flight to Delhi.

"The Indian government has confiscated copies of the TV footage shot at the bridge," he told Gulligan. "Apparently one independent Delhi producer who took some footage wasn't hit because he doesn't have contracts with any wire services or television outlets. We'll get his stuff."

The story and the pictures went out that afternoon. For some reason Gulligan hung around the office after dinner waiting to see if anything would happen. By midnight he felt slightly drunk, although he had had nothing except one martini before dinner. It was not just that he had been right about the appeal of the picture and the story, but he felt somehow evangelical. As the teletype started to chatter off requests for more copy, with the afternoon papers almost frantic for something fresh to compensate for the morning release, Gulligan realized that the story was going to be picked up by close to 100 per cent of his subscribers.

AP dominated the story for more than four days, partly by luck and partly by hard work. It was luck plus Eve Wilder's skill that they got a picture of villagers, led by one of the bridge workers, lying in front of a huge tank. They were on their backs, their eyes staring up at the great moving thing above them and their faces showing no sign of fear. Children lined the highway, looking at the tank with curious opaque faces. The exhaust of the tank showed clearly, black and thick. The tank looked like some powerful but very puzzled animal out of the primordial past. The bodies of the villagers seemed frail and tiny, but they puzzled the big metal beast and it knew it could not pass.

It had been taken with a cheap Kodak by a fifteen-year-old girl in a village close to the bridge. Eve Wilder had paid five dollars for it.

On the fourth day AP sent out a story asking if John Thatch was completely safe. Rumors were widespread in Karachi and Delhi that both governments intended to arrest Thatch on the grounds that he had "engaged in domestic politics, encouraged insurrection among the people, used his position to support anarchy." The story, a reliable one as it turned out, was what exploded the whole episode. It was no longer an AP beat; it was a national issue. Dozens of papers spontaneously ran editorials stating that if John Thatch were punished for his courageous act the United States Congress should cut off all foreign aid to both countries. As if written by the same pen, they talked about the resurgence of American individuality and resourcefulness, the courage of the "common man" of India and Pakistan, and castigated the ponderous bureaucracies of the two countries.

Time scrapped the cover story it had planned and ran an artist's conception of Thatch on the girder over the bridge. Its story was studded with facts about Thatch's background, reporting that he was a self-made millionaire who had heavy construction contracts all over the world, that he had gone to college for three years but possessed no degree, that he had enlisted in the Navy during the war and had wound up as a warrant officer.

In a boxed editorial *Time* demanded that the President of the United States take steps to assure Thatch's physical safety. "It would be the supreme irony if this young man, who has become a symbol of individuality and courage and who has the support of the masses of South Asia, should be punished by petulant governments outraged that their sovereignty has been challenged."

Thirty-two senators, sixteen Democrats and sixteen Republicans, signed a statement to the President urging him to use the power of his office in assuring the safety of John Thatch. The President said he would comment at his news conference the next day. He could act so promptly because he had already received a top-secret cable from his Ambassador. It stated that the Indian government had, in fact, proposed taking steps against Thatch for he had aroused the first popular demonstration against the government by using principles of *satraghya*, a form of nonviolent resistance developed by Gandhi to oppose the British. It had a subtle, but powerful, appeal for Indians and there was something about the bridge episode, the cable continued, which had aroused old memories. The military, a proud and sensitive group, were especially angered that their troops had been blocked by the actions of an American. The Prime Minister was not the least frightened by American threats of cutting off aid as long as he could turn to the Soviet Union for help. In fact, the Ambassador went on, for he was a brisk and honest man, there is nothing to be done diplomatically. Technically Thatch had broken the law of the land.

However, there was nothing to worry about. Somehow the government's plans to arrest Thatch had become known, largely through a young Communist named Rajput who had abandoned communism after hearing Thatch and, using his father's enormous financial resources and political contacts, had made speeches and sent out letters to thousands of village leaders. The result had been rumors of a march on Delhi by outraged peasants from the provinces and, while the government chose to ignore the threat, the marchers did in fact materialize. By the second day observers estimated that more than a hundred thousand people were already on the move toward Delhi. Clearly the mob would be immense in numbers by the time it reached the city. They chanted a slogan—"Remember the salt march." The government quickly stated that it had never intended to arrest Thatch and sent emissaries out to tell this to the marchers, who promptly dispersed.

The Ambassador closed with the usual crisp and elegant paragraph which the President had come to enjoy. "Although our diplomatic officers are hopeless in such a situation, our technical inability to act was countered by the thin nerve of India's politicians and the hysteria of its soldiers. I should hope that more such confrontations could take place in the future." The government had finally become so panicky over Thatch's safety that they had temporarily arrested all known Communists and extreme nationalists or possible assassins until Thatch was out of the country.

The President had an exquisite sense of timing. That night he saw the CBS documentary on John Thatch. During the morning and the afternoon the telegrams poured into the White House demanding action to guarantee his safety. The Press Secretary told the President that he thought the telegrams were genuinely spontaneous and not an elaborately framed campaign.

At the news conference the President used several minutes to describe the situation regarding Thatch. Then he stated that while the United States government had intervened forcefully, Thatch's release had really been accomplished by the energies of "countless thousands of the nameless masses of India and Pakistan rallying to the support of an American friend. It is an inspiring episode. America can be proud of John Thatch.

"I pledge you that wherever an American acts in a manner which is in the best American tradition and in the American interest he will have the full support of this office," he said and then added, looking squarely into the camera. "And, I sincerely believe, the support of the entire American people."

That, officially, closed the matter of John Thatch and the episode at the bridge. The City of New York toyed with the idea of a civic welcome, with a parade up Broadway, but the metropolitan papers did not follow up on Thatch and the idea was dropped. Besides, he had not responded to the cable sent him by the Mayor of New York. The White House staff discussed the possibility of having John Thatch down for lunch with the President. They discarded the notion after a call to the Indian desk at State: the knowledgeable young man on that desk thought it might be considered a slight to the Indian government.

Senator John Reddick of Kansas asked permission to read a brief laudatory statement into the *Congressional Record* entitled

"The Americanism of John Thatch" and handwritten by the Senator over the week end. His style was somewhat old-fashioned but his statement was nonetheless effective. It talked of Thatch's devotion to the highest ideals of Americanism, his defiance of arbitrary government, the courage he displayed in making a direct appeal to those most concerned: the citizens of the two countries which the bridge would link. "One might hope," the statement concluded ambiguously, "that the act of this young engineer would be not only an inspiration to the youth of America, but it might also serve those in various branches of the government as a model by which to measure themselves."

The Congressional reporters read the statement closely, especially the last few lines. Senator John Reddick had a reputation for being one of the men in Washington most sensitive to the mood of the country and was very powerful in the Republican Party. In the end the reporters decided unanimously that the statement did not rate a write-up. The Thatch affair, they agreed, was over.

John Thatch watched the outlines of San Francisco Bay come into focus. He had made the PanAm polar flight from London to San Francisco so often that he no longer looked down until the plane was close to the Bay. All one could usually see was cloud cover or occasionally the glitter of a city's lights. But the Bay always brought him to the edge of his seat. Partly it was the pure symmetry of the Golden Gate Bridge, which he loved; partly it was the Bay Bridge, the San Francisco half of which he admired while the Oakland side irritated him, and partly it was the horror of the San Rafael-Richmond bridge, humpbacked and ungainly. Some day they'll learn that you can't put a dollar sign on beauty, he thought.

Ten minutes later he was walking up the airport ramp. He knew where Terry would be. She always hid behind an abutment at the top of the ramp, only her forehead and one eye visible. He ignored her, looking away. There was something about the ritual which pleased Thatch. Terry said it gave her a few seconds to see if he was the same man and also to keep her from crying in public.

Terry stepped out from the abutment and said *Mabuhay,* emphasizing the middle syllable so the "Boo" was loud. In the few steps it took Thatch to reach her he sensed how unlike this little game Terry really looked. She was a tall girl, but she had retained the smallness of bone, the kind of Malay fragility which was undefinable, but seemed like something just behind the skin.

In other ways she did not look like a Malay, and, in fact, Thatch did not know how much Filipino blood she had. It was probably a small amount, for Filipinos often thought her French or Spanish, even though she spoke Tagalog perfectly. A palmist in Hong Kong had once said she was one-thirty-second Filipino and Terry had laughed and said she would ask the doctor the next time he took a blood sample. Hong Kong palmists are not used to laughter, for theirs is a responsible profession and this one had frowned his displeasure.

Her eyes were huge and brown. She dressed very simply, but the unconscious grace with which she walked often made people mistake her for a model. She added to the illusion by a kind of aloofness which was really shyness. At a party she would often stand coolly in a corner, watching, listening carefully to whatever was said, but saying very little herself. It unnerved people who didn't know her. Thatch would bring her out of the corner and into the flow of conversation. They did not go to many parties.

He kissed her full on the mouth and, as always, felt the low-pitched surprise at the sweetness of her breath and the softness of the mouth which looked so small. Terry was a beautiful girl and as he pulled his head back he had a sharp, angled, exaggerated glimpse of her face: a rounded face which escaped being pure Malay because of a strong and finely wrought nose; great brown eyes that would have been almost too much in a pure-white skin but against the soft brown complexion were perfect; hair so black that it glistened steel-blue; and a long Malay neck.

But this morning there was tension in her. He felt it under his hands and saw it in the tightness of her smile.

"Thatch, the famous man," she whispered. "Thatch and his bridge." She hid her fright and laughed and blew warm air into his ear.

Thatch released her and they walked toward the entrance. She held his arm tightly, and watched him as he searched the big caverns of the dismal airport with his eyes.

"If you're looking for reporters," Terry said, "I told them you were coming on the TWA plane which gets here in three hours."

"Good girl," Thatch said. "You a good Pill-a-pino girl," he said, imitating the Tagalog dialect with its inability to aspirate the *f* sound.

Later, when they were in the car and making the short drive home Terry sat with her arm along his leg, the fingers touching the back of his knee.

"How was it, John?" she asked quietly.

"Not as bad as the papers made it out," John said. "I don't think I was ever in danger of being arrested."

"I didn't either," Terry said quietly. She had lived through a war and years in a concentration camp. She did not panic easily. "But did you really make that speech? The one at the bridge?"

"Yes," he said slowly. "It was me all right." Terry's fingers tightened.

Terry laughed. "People said you sounded like a combination of Billy Graham and FDR. It didn't sound like you, but in a strange way it was you." She hesitated. "But when you got to the salt march it was like a part of you talking that I thought belonged only to me."

"And it scared you," John said, no question in his voice.

She sighed.

The house was a mile back in the hills from El Camino Real. It was set on five acres with a corral, a barn, and beyond that a small guest house. The buildings were made of adobe bricks. The house was not large. Their guests were usually overseas friends whom they knew well and who were content to stay in the guest house and manage for themselves. The main house was dominated by a large living room clearly not done by a professional decorator . . . it contained too much. There were chairs from Thailand, Indonesia, India, and Egypt and in front of the fireplace a Japanese rug. The lamps ranged from Siam brass to a gimbal lamp from an old whaler. From the low rafters hung a variety of objects . . . a sextant, an old rusted plumbline, the scrimshawed tooth of a whale, a Buddhist prophesy written on a beautiful piece of Thai silk in dark bold calligraphy, a Douba aborigine arrow with tiny

kangaroos racing down the side. The objects changed from time
to time; were given away, stored, moved to make room for new
things. The room had a kind of pleasant disorder about it.

Today in the center of the room on a table there were several stacks of letters, each over a foot high.

Thatch stood before the table, eyeing the mail.

"Letters," Terry said. Her voice was uncertain. "I guess you
call them fan mail. After the first news story they started coming
in, maybe twenty or thirty a day. Then after the TV thing they
started coming by the thousands."

"Thousands?" John asked.

"It's kind of crazy," Terry said. "The letters just came ad-
dressed to John Thatch, San Mateo. Three times the Post Office
drove a special truck out here and dumped the mail in the front
room."

"They'll stop," Thatch said. He walked cautiously around the
stacks of mail.

"I'm not sure, John," Terry said. "The last news story was
four days ago and today over a thousand letters arrived. I stuck
them in the guest house."

One letter, as if it had drifted away from the others, lay alone
on the floor. It was partly held down by a dictionary. Thatch
moved to pick it up.

"I'll take care of them," Terry said. She intercepted him, and
they both knew it, before he could reach the letter. She smiled
and took his hand. It was only inches from the letter. "I put that
one aside. It has some dirty words in it I want to look up in the
dictionary."

She walked over and stood close to him. "These people—
they want you for something, John—I don't understand. Today's
letters, those I read, a lot of them said that you shouldn't give
up your fight just because the government and the newspapers
blacked you out. They were from all over, but they sounded the
same . . . as if you were the leader of a crusade."

Thatch felt something that he could not identify for a
moment. And when he did, he was instantly angry with himself:
The sight of the stacks of letters gave him pleasure.

"Well, I'm not leading any crusade," he said, and his voice
was flat and harsh. "Why do you have them in stacks?"

"Well, I started to sort of classify them," Terry said. Her slim body circled the table, her hands moved slowly over the paper. "Letters from kids, those from schoolteachers, requests to make speeches, demands that you run for public office. There were also some crank letters . . ." her voice shook a little ". . . written by people with bad handwriting and made up of swear words, the four-letter ones. Do you want to read one?"

"No," Thatch said. "Maybe later, but not now. I'd like a corned-beef sandwich and some beer."

John walked around the stacks of mail. Curious little erratic mounds of paper, all shapes and sizes; some on elegant bond; some on cheap ruled paper; some typed and some written in a large scrawl. There couldn't be thousands, Thatch thought. Thousands of people scribbling notes to him? It was silly. Why would they?

He picked up the letter under the dictionary. The handwriting was very steady, small and intricate.

Engineer Thatch:

I felt very sluggish this morning. Like a snail. More like a dirty pig. The sheets in the bed were messy with slime or something.
It's been like that a long time. Since my brother died. I try to be brave and kill myself. I think about the razor and the pill bottle or renting a room in a high hotel and jumping out. But that wouldn't bring Brother Julius back. And still I want to do it.
Then I read about you and I don't feel so bad. You are a hero. A real one. Maybe if we talked I wouldn't take up all my time trying to think of ways to kill myself. I'm sorry, I don't want to worry you. But I hate to go to work. I'm a stenographer but since Brother Julius died I know that *they*, the ones at the office, know I can't work very well. I DON'T HAVE ANYONE. Except maybe you.

Thatch heard Terry moving in the kitchen. He put the letter back on the floor. No wonder she didn't want him to read this one. Yet there were no dirty words. He looked at the rest of the letters warily.

He felt again the odd mixture of curiosity and some kind of excitement. It had happened before . . . on the bridge, looking down at the faces of the workers and the reporters. He was shamed by it, somehow sullied. Vanity can mask as duty, his father had preached long ago.

On top of the pile which Terry had said were this morning's "angry letters" was a large expensive sheet of bond paper with a name and address embossed at the top. The writing was a steady Italianate hand, done with a nib, using very black ink.

Thatch bent over and picked it up.

Dear Mr. Thatch:

I have never before written to a stranger. That is for the cheap adulators of movie stars or the frenzied and pathetic who pursue distinguished people.

I write you, however, for what I hope are much better motives. Sir, you are the first American of our times who has stood up and told foreigners that America will not forever put up with every kind of idiotic provocation.

You have let the citizens of two nations know that they need not be slaves to the Machiavellian manipulations of their inept governments. For the first time in memory an American has acted in the tradition of Decatur.

As you are fully aware the American government, led by President Kennedy and his Harvard eggheads, the newspapers and the mass media have decided to black you out. You are paying the price of outspokenness. I write only to let you know that I, and a group of my friends, are deeply affected by your courage. Keep up the good work.

Respectfully,
Allen Trowbridge, III

"Interesting?" Terry said.

Thatch jerked around. Terry was holding a plate with a sandwich on it, a bottle of San Miguel beer in the other hand. Thatch smiled slowly. He felt an unidentifiable irritation.

"Do you think this is a crackpot?" Thatch asked.

Terry glanced at the letter.

"I don't know. Maybe half crackpot," she said. "All that stuff about Kennedy and the press plotting a 'blackout.' You don't believe any of that, do you?"

"Hell, no," Thatch said at once.

Terry smiled, but tightly.

He drank the beer from the bottle, enjoying the flow of the cool liquid. He brought the bottle down and smiled at Terry.

"Do you want to see the boys?" Terry asked. "They're at school, but I could get them to come home for lunch."

"No," Thatch said. He looked at Terry. His shoulders hunched. She noticed and her eyes clouded. He had never seen this look on the face of an American or European woman. It was frightened and provocative and laden with a childish curiosity. Though he had known her for eighteen years, still she retained this kind of innocence.

He went to her. For a moment her lips curled and she almost laughed. But then the timidity, the trembling fragility came back.

It was an act and yet not an act, for each time Thatch felt the brutal reversion, the sense of being *juramentado*. His fingers tightened and were strong and curious. He shifted his weight, aware of her hair and scent, aware of his own blood going thick, his heavy single-mindedness.

For so long it had been like this. So slow in beginning but quickening with the secret knowledge that later on Terry would scream with excitement and scratch an arc across his back.

But today it was not to be. She wept against his chest, her slim body shaking and her words almost incoherent. He listened, not understanding. "Don't let them take you away." His not-quite white-skinned wife he'd found in a foreign prison—she needed him more than they needed him.

He mumbled his assurances and patted her back, all the while wondering who "they" were and when he would meet them.

5

The door to Bookbinder's study opened and Madison Curver came in. He was tall, almost too thin, and he walked with a slight stoop. He is fit, Levi thought. He looked like the squash or handball type. His narrow face was as intellectual as Levi had expected, but it also had a quality of curiosity which showed when he swung his head around the room.

"You must be Mr. Levi," Curver said. He walked over and shook hands. "Book has told me about you. Classmates at Harvard."

Levi had never seen such self-assurance in so young a man.

It was the very opposite of glibness. It was a certitude, an easy way of walking, an absolute absence of shyness. As Curver bent over him, Levi could see that that young man dressed well . . . he was wearing a handmade tweed suit which was not new but was beautifully put together. His shoes were old, creased by hundreds of wrinkles, but the leather had a deep fine glow. Levi smiled. Even after forty years in finance he could not escape the old days, when he had worked in the garment district.

"Good of you to join us, Mad," Bookbinder said. His voice grated.

"Sorry, Book," Curver said. "Long-distance call. Urgent." He shrugged gracefully, slid into a chair. He lit a small green Filipino cigar.

"Well, Mad, if you're comfortable enough and it's no strain and your cigar is well lit, then I might just ask you a few questions," Bookbinder said.

"But of course, Book. Feel free," Curver said, exaggeratedly tapping ashes into a crystal ashtray.

"Oh, Christ. Levi, I should have fired him a year ago," Bookbinder said. "No respect for age and authority."

"I would have if it were my firm," Levi said. Curver shot him a glance. Levi's face was smiling but his voice was firm. Curver knew Levi was no one to joke with. He and Book were not only classmates; they were friends, widowers, self-made rich, politicians to the bone and anonymous.

Curver looked easily at Levi. He took out a pad of 3-by-5 cards and began to write on them with a pencil.

"Don't start that doodling, Mad," Bookbinder said. "It makes me nervous."

"It's not doodling, Book," Curver said. "It's my form of shorthand; you get used to it in a few minutes."

"It's what?" Levi asked. He felt a slight irritation. Curver interested him and at the same time was somehow offensive.

"It's a kind of shorthand I worked out," Curver said. He leaned forward and showed Levi a card. It was covered with unfamiliar signs with a few letters showing and one word *Levi*.

"With dictating machines and tape recorders," Bookbinder said, "I think shorthand for a lawyer is a waste of time."

"Some people freeze when a tape recorder goes on," Curver said. "But they think I'm just a compulsive doodler."

"What does the card say?" Levi asked. He disliked asking the question, but he could not resist.

"It just gives today's date, the names of those present . . . your name is short so I put it down once and after this I'll just use my sign for *L*. And a proposed agenda."

Levi straightened in his chair. Book had told him about Curver before, but this was not quite what he had expected. Book had taken Curver into the firm three years ago, straight from Columbia Law School. He was old-rich, old-Midwestern rich, but he never talked about it. He carried one of the heaviest work loads in the office and still had time to go off to seminars on things called "systems analysis," "statistics in the behavioral sciences," and "SES indicator use by interviewers."

Such a boy should be married and have a family, Levi thought. Book had mentioned Mad was interested in women, but never talked of marriage. The girls in the office were silly over him.

"You've got an agenda?" Book asked.

"Why not? It never hurts," Curver said. "Only three items on it. First, can the incumbent President be beaten? Second, Dr. Cotter's work. Third, discussion of Simulmatics Corporation."

"Let's skip the first one," Bookbinder said, "and go right to Cotter. Does Cotter know what he is talking about?"

"No."

"Then why the hell did you give me his report to read?"

"Because Cotter is the best of the pollsters, that's why," Curver said. "He has no imagination, no flair, he hates guesses, lacks intuition. That's what you want in a pollster. Also his results are usually better than those of the politicians. And the Simulmatics people are way ahead of Cotter."

Bookbinder and Levi both swung their heads. Curver laughed.

"Any time some kid Ph.D. has more political know-how than Jim Farley or Whitaker and Baxter or Joe Kennedy or Dirksen I'll pay your bar bill at the Club for a month," Bookbinder growled.

"Okay, Book, you want some evidence?" Curver asked. "Nineteen sixty is a good year to compare. The pollsters were getting a lot of problems ironed out. Out in California Teddy Kennedy was running the campaign for JFK in the eleven Western states.

Every week he got reports from the pros. From the pot-bellied boys with the big cigars who hung around the pool halls and the courthouses and talked to precinct captains and made deals on government contracts and raised money for the Democratic Party and said they had their finger on the pulse of the people. They all predicted victory in their areas. I saw the reports. They kept talking of "good party morale," "peaking the campaign," "tough precinct organizations." It was all crap. A smart guy named Lou Harris was running a confidential poll for Kennedy. His reports went to Teddy too. Harris indicated that Kennedy might lose *all* the Western states, including California."

"Kennedy won only New Mexico and Nevada," Levi said drily. "For a total of seven electoral votes."

"That's right. Seven electoral votes," Curver repeated. "The point is that the pros honestly believed the Democrats were going to win big. All of them. And Lou Harris and Teddy Kennedy knew the Democrats would lose small. The simple fact is that the polls are better than the pros if you're trying to guess who's going to win an election."

"Just a minute," Bookbinder said. "What about all the polls indicating that Dewey was going to lick Truman in 1948?" His eyes lit up, recalling the event. He grinned at Levi. Levi had supported Dewey, Bookbinder had supported Truman.

"The pollsters made a mistake," Curver admitted calmly. "They were new at the game. Polls were only eighteen or twenty years old and there wasn't enough money behind them yet. They stopped polling during the last month when a lot of people switched over. Most pollsters were dinosaurs in 1948. They made mistakes, like phrasing the questions incorrectly. Also, and Book won't like this, they assumed that the undecideds would split evenly. They ignored the fact that the incumbent President has a grip on people. They hate to turn him out. So most of the undecideds voted for Truman."

"I don't see that the polls are any better now," Levi said.

"That's because you don't read them and perhaps don't understand them when you do," Curver said. There was no insolence in his voice. "Both Gallup and Roper are up out of the primeval slime and galloping around pretty fast these days. Some of the younger people are doing even better."

"Why do we need Cotter?" Bookbinder asked.

"For just one purpose," Curver said. "To tell us *what* the voters are thinking about. He's already suggested something, Book, that has you in a spin. His results indicate no one can beat Kennedy next year. Read the rest of the polling literature and the thing becomes even clearer: we're electing a President for eight years these days."

"I don't believe that for a minute," Bookbinder said quickly. "And if we are, it's unconstitutional." He hesitated. "I don't really mean that, but it's unhealthy."

"Can Cotter tell us *why* the power of the incumbent President is so great?" Levi asked softly.

"He doesn't have a clue and if he did he wouldn't dare breathe it," Curver said. "This man believes he is as precise as a physicist and physicists don't go around predicting how experiments will work out. But there is a way to find out why voters vote the way they do."

"I don't want to hear it again," Bookbinder said. "But go ahead; let Levi know what is happening to politics."

"You get the services of an outfit called Simulmatics—which also thinks it is very scientific—and then you combine that with the reports from some shrewd psychiatrists and you have just about as much as we are going to know about the *why* of anything going on inside one hundred and eighty million different heads."

"Go on," Levi said.

Curver hesitated. It was so difficult. He knew Levi and Bookbinder would oppose whatever he said. They would disbelieve it, would think he advocated it, would distort it. And the whole damned thing was so fugitive, so hard to catch, so difficult to say easily . . . and so incredibly important.

"It's not easy, but I'll try," Curver said. "Take a group identified as Southern, wealthy, urban, professional, third-generation." Curver paused. "How would they vote?"

"Oh, Christ, Mad, that's easy," Bookbinder said. "They're either Democrats who vote like Republicans or recent converts to the GOP because they hated Roosevelt so much."

"The *why* is not so difficult, Curver," Levi said. "I think Book caught it pretty well. They'll vote for the Republicans or a states' rights party just because of the Democratic position on civil rights. Or Bobby Kennedy. Or high income tax."

Curver smiled. He inhaled the cigar, watched it shrivel a quarter of an inch.

"You didn't give me time to add the last adjective," Curver said. "It was *Negro*."

There was silence in the room. When Bookbinder spoke it was in a soft wondering voice.

"Southern, wealthy, urban, professional third-generation Negroes," he said. He reached in his desk, took out a box of cigars and offered it to Levi. Levi took one and the two men began the small diverting ritual of rolling, tipping, smoothing, snipping, and lighting their cigars.

"Mad, are there enough such people to influence a Presidential campaign?" Bookbinder said. "I doubt it."

"And you would be wrong, Book," Curver said.

"Which would not be a new thing," Bookbinder said.

"First, because winning the undecideds is what the campaign is all about. The party regulars turn out in just about the same numbers, but the undecideds may or may not come out on Election Day. So you pick up a tenth of one per cent here and half a per cent there and pretty soon it amounts to something. So those wealthy Negro professionals in Southern cities are important. First, because they vote. Second, because they get out the Negro vote wherever the Negro can vote. They influence others."

"How do you know how these people are going to vote?" Levi asked.

"You go out and ask a few of them and you take their behavior on past issues and you run this through a computing machine and you come up with an analysis of where they stand on various issues," Curver said. Levi started to interrupt and Curver lifted his hand. "That is what the Simulmatics group does. But we can take their information and give it to the psychologists and psychiatrists who have really studied Negroes in the group and finally you tease out *why* they think the way they do."

"Curver, how many of those Negroes have gone to a psychiatrist?" Levi asked.

"Maybe damned few. If they haven't we send the psychiatrist to them," Curver said and slumped lower in his chair.

"How many groups do these Simulmatics people have?" Bookbinder asked.

"For analyzing a national election they have four hundred

and eighty groups. They didn't just invent those groups, Book. People don't even know they're in a group so don't act like your precious democracy is being raped on the street. They went through every poll worth looking at and after a lot of work came up with four hundred and eighty groups which seem to react and vote the same way. And now they know a lot about each of those groups, so much, in fact, that they can simulate how the group will act before the group has even heard of an issue."

"That's what I object to," Bookbinder snapped. "Even if the groups exist it's wrong that people don't know they belong to such a group and, shut up a minute, Mad, if you know that much about a group you're going to start to manipulate it."

"Book, I don't think Curver is suggesting that," Levi said. He had a softly persuasive voice. "These people have just developed a new tool. Now maybe they can use the tool in an immoral way, but we have to wait and see."

Levi paused and then went on slowly. "I'm always interested in individuals. Now, as they change jobs and locations and income their vote is going to change, isn't that true?"

"That's correct," Curver said. He had sunk down so far in the chair that his knees were higher than his head. He chewed on one pencil and with the other he wrote on his cards.

"Take a Jew in 1920 and tell me how he would vote," Levi said, and Curver knew he was dealing with a shrewd man used to cutting to essentials. And also someone who did not especially like him.

"Tell me his age in 1920, where he lived, how much he made a year, and his occupation," Curver said.

"But you don't understand about Jews," Levi said. "There are Russian Jews, German Jews, the old aristocratic Sephardic Jews, Polish Jews. They were, and still are, all split up, don't communicate much with one another. You don't know a thing about that."

"The fact is I do, sir. But it's also a fact that I don't need to," Curver said. "Can you answer the questions I asked?" He glanced down at his cards. "Would you like me to repeat them?"

"My memory is good," Levi said. "This Jew was twenty-five years old in 1924, he lived on the East Side; he made, let us say, four hundred and fifty dollars a year, and he worked as a coat presser."

"Anything else?" Curver said. He was not taking notes now.

"Maybe he is a college student. Maybe planning on law school," Levi said.

Bookbinder realized Levi was describing his own background. They had met at Harvard Law School and had been among the oldest students in their class. Levi had never practiced law because courtroom appearances made him nervous. Instead he had gone into finance and was now in a web of operations which he ran easily, anonymously, and at enormous profit. His second love was politics.

"And in 1928?" Curver asked. "His income and occupation."

"Let's say around five thousand and he is associated with a brokerage firm," Levi said.

"Let's skip to 1936. What's his income then and his job?"

"Maybe thirty thousand and he's in general finance. That close enough?" Levi asked.

Bookbinder leaned back in his chair, grinning. It was Levi's career and probably Mad knew it, but that wouldn't help him much. Mad had worked himself into a box.

"You told me once that it was silly to make guesses about how individuals would vote," Bookbinder said. "You're only interested in groups. Now here you go trying to guess how one single Jew voted in four different elections."

From the depths of the chair an arm waved. Curver took the sharp pencil from his mouth, tossed the dull one on the rug.

"In 1920 our subject voted for Eugene Debs, the Socialist," Curver said. "In 1924 he voted for Robert La Follette, Progressive and Socialist candidate. In 1928 he voted for Alfred E. Smith, Democrat. In 1936 he voted for Landon. Since then he voted for every Republican candidate except in 1952 he voted for Stevenson. That should be right with the possible exception of the Stevenson vote."

Levi looked at the cards in Curver's long fingers. They were somewhat dirty. The man must work with soft-lead pencils a lot. Bookbinder was looking at Levi, a grin on his face.

"That is correct," Levi said. Bookbinder's grin faded. "Even to the 1952 vote for Stevenson. That's quite impressive, Curver."

"Not really, Mr. Levi. The most important determinant of voting behavior is income, then occupation, then where one lives. Jews, whether they are Sephardic or Polish, tend to vote Democratic when their income is low and then switch to Republican as it gets above ten thousand dollars a year. If the voter's social-economic position remains the same, so does his vote."

Bookbinder moved his big bulk in his chair. He forced himself not to chomp on the cigar.

"Anybody ever use this Simulmatics outfit in an election?" Levi asked.

"Kennedy did in 1960. Then the group was in its infancy, but Kennedy gave them some problems to work on. He was interested to see how much of Ike's popularity would rub off on Nixon. All the pros were saying 'Don't worry about the Negro vote. It will come back to the Democratic Party once Eisenhower is off the scene.' The Simulmatics people got out their tapes and fed them into the computer. They found that the Negroes had shifted not just to Eisenhower, but many had transferred their allegiance to the Republicans.

"Why?" Bookbinder asked.

"I told you that the Simulmatics people don't know why, but they can make some damned good guesses," Curver said. "Earl Warren, a prominent Republican and an Ike appointee, had written the first big desegregation judgment. The white Democrats in the South were keeping Negroes from registering and maybe the dissatisfaction with those Democrats started to drift up North. Maybe they started to distrust people like Fulbright who was a good pious liberal Democrat on everything under the sun, but the moment the civil rights thing came up he was strangely silent."

"What did Kennedy do with the information?" Levi asked quietly.

"First of all he believed it," Curver said. "Oh, he kept patting the pros on the head and telling them they were doing great, but he had learned long ago the pro with the longest experience is likely to be the most out of touch. Second, he started, with what seemed a great burst of spontaneous enthusiasm, to be very, very strong on the civil rights question. Remember that phone call Kennedy made to Martin Luther King's wife when King was thrown in the Southern jail? Remember the speeches in which he kept hitting for civil rights?"

"Anything else?" Bookbinder asked.

"Sure. Take the fact that Kennedy was a Catholic," Curver

said. "Everybody had a different answer. Most of the pros, the old experienced hands, remembering Al Smith, told Kennedy to play it down. Others said it had already been ventilated enough . . . forget it. What would you have recommended, Book?"

"I'd have told him to forget it," Bookbinder said. His voice was truculent. "Don't heat up an unpopular subject."

"Remember it was August of 1960," Curver said. "The Gallup Poll had Nixon leading with fifty per cent of the votes, Kennedy trailing with forty-four per cent, and six per cent undecided. The Simulmatics people 'simulated' how their four hundred and eighty groups would react if the Catholic issue was raised."

"Deliberately raised?" Levi asked softly.

"Use your own words. We agree on the *raised*, anyway."

"Who would do it deliberately?" Bookbinder asked.

"Kennedy," Curver answered. "Nixon had laid off the subject and the tons of crackpot fundamentalist literature going around only circulated among people who were already so anti-Catholic they wouldn't vote for Kennedy. So the only person who could use the issue effectively was Kennedy."

"That would be very close to cold-bloodedly fomenting intolerance," Levi said.

"Or it might be putting a reverse twist on intolerance," Curver said. Levi wished suddenly that the young man would sit up straight. His head was almost invisible. It was disturbing to have the sharp words come from a mouth one could not see.

"The Simulmatics report ran something like this, leaving out all the technical stuff:

1. JFK was trailing Nixon.

2. JFK had already lost as much as he probably would on the Catholic issue, although if it got hotter he might lose a few more Protestants in the Bible Belt and Southern California.

3. But if the anti-Catholic issue got any more bitter—and here listen carefully, Mr. Levi—there would start to be a reaction. A lot of Protestants would feel that the anti-Catholic thing had gone too far. They would drift back toward Kennedy because although they might be suspicious of a Catholic in the White House they feared religious intolerance even more.

4. Any more embitterment of anti-Catholicism and the Jews would be solid behind Kennedy.

5. If the Catholic issue kept coming up it would consolidate the Catholic vote behind Kennedy."

There was a long silence. Bookbinder got up and went to his small bar, swung it open, and mixed them each a Scotch and soda.

"This could become a nightmare, Levi," Bookbinder said. "That's why I wanted you to hear it. Let a madman or just some very ambitious power-seeker start to use stuff like this and the whole game is changed. He would be getting at people in a way they are not even aware of."

"That's possible," Curver said. "But let's take a look at politics before the computer came along with its big stack of tapes. It was pretty damned irresponsible then. Pretty much of a nightmare. Remember the cute stories they used to pass around about FDR? He had paresis, colored mistresses, was given half of Bermuda as a gift in exchange for giving Britain the fifty destroyers. And the sweet things they said about Eleanor. That was decency in politics? And then McCarthy with his handful of lists and ranting accusations against whoever crossed his path. Nice and clean, eh? Ever read about the ditties they made up about 'Cleveland's little bastard'? Look, a big part of politics has always been an underground of wild rumor, fantasies, filthy jokes, stories about corruption and boozing in the White House and dipping into the public trough."

"Those old politicos were playing on prejudice and irrationality," Book said, "but they did it haphazardly, just making wild stabs and hoping they'd hit the public nerve."

Levi stood up and walked toward the bar. He glanced at Curver as he passed. The boy had not moved since he had sat down. He seemed nerveless, like an Indian or Asian who could squat endlessly in one position.

"If you could use this kind of approach to learn how to 'embitter' an issue, you could also use it to take the bitterness out of an issue," Levi said. "Book, maybe the way to reduce anti-Semitism is to bring it into the open and have it discussed. Maybe we could also find out why people become anti-Semitic."

Bookbinder stared down at his glass. His whole posture rejected what Levi said. Finally he shook his head.

"Levi, part of our protection in politics is the fact that no one really knows how it works. If one man can refine it to a science he or the next guy won't be able to resist temptation. And if he was the wrong man, that would be the end."

"But if everyone knows what is going on, then they all have the same advantage," Curver said.

Bookbinder ignored the comment.

"Did the Simulmatics people tell Kennedy how to act during the TV debates in 1960?" he asked.

"They did," Curver said. "Keep in mind that all they really do is make a kind of 'symbolic imitation' in advance of how these four hundred and eighty groups might react. Kennedy would have been silly not to try and find out before the debates how the groups looked at both him and Nixon."

"What did he find out?" Bookbinder asked.

"First that Nixon was regarded as being 'super-cool.' Kennedy was regarded as more 'friendly.' More people thought Kennedy was 'trustworthy.' Among Jews only four per cent thought Nixon was the 'most trustworthy.' On almost anything that affected personality, Kennedy came off better than Nixon. Only on 'competence' did the voters give Nixon the nod," Curver said. "So the Simulmatics group told Kennedy to stay away from Nixon's super-cool position. They said that Kennedy could make use of his more personal traits—including a range of emotions such as fervor, humor, friendship, and spirituality—and thus cause Nixon to 'lose' the debates."

Levi sensed, with a slight shock, that Curver was quoting the last sentence from memory from a report.

"Maybe that's why the debates were such a farce," Bookbinder said. "Lot of damned foolishness and no one learned a thing. That's not politics. Politics is knowing what you believe and going out and trying to persuade the people to go along with you. But this damned pollster approach means taking the pulse of the people and if they get a fever you stand up and say 'Fever is great.' I'm for fever and motherhood and against men who sweat on TV screens."

"Book, listen to me a minute," Mad said. Bookbinder's voice faded. "Listen, because I think it means something. How did we get into this? Because I told you that not in our lifetime would an incumbent President be licked for a second term if he wanted to run. Right? You said I was crazy. But Hoover was the last incumbent to lose and it won't happen again. If the incumbent acts, he gains support . . . even if he makes a whopping mistake."

"What about someone who comes in with a reputation as big as the President's?" Bookbinder asked. "Someone like this Thatch fellow in India? He's been on every TV program, in every magazine and newspaper for the last month."

"Book, it's possible," Curver said. "But do you know what this challenger would have to be? For example, he'd have to be 'sincere.' Meaning that people believe he is above avarice, ambition, and pride. Book, the most sincere person in America in recent times has been Kate Smith. Ike beat Stevenson on sincerity, among other things. Ike looked more sincere. Ike wasn't as sincere as Kate, but more than Adlai. Second, your man has to be a hero. A shrewd old observer named Frazer who wrote *The Golden Bough* once said that people want their leaders to 'belong to a higher order of humanity than themselves.' It's possible to find someone like that, but usually he is the incumbent President."

Levi waited a good long minute.

"I think that's right, Mad," Levi said. "But I'm old. I remember listening to Debs. That's how old I am." He pulled his long thin body to its feet, walked over and stood beside Curver at the window. "My father was sick but I got him out. We went down to Central Park and my father stood there with a handkerchief to his mouth drenched with some patent medicine that was supposed to cure TB. I remember we were in the middle of a group of Italians who stank of garlic and red wine. They chanted agreement with Debs as he spoke and I don't think they really understood a word he said. My father listened, sniffling at the handkerchief and eyeing this wild stranger. At the end of the speech he put his hand up and Debs looked down at him like a hawk about to pounce. 'Do you believe that a forty-hour week is desirable and possible?' my father asked. Debs slowed down, smiled, spread out his hands and said, 'It is possible, desirable and, comrade, inevitable.' The crowd went wild. My father sniffed at his handkerchief."

"And your father voted for Debs," Bookbinder said.

"He never spoke to me about Debs as a personality," Levi said, "but he voted for him. My father was for a forty-hour week because it was humane, not because he loved Debs."

Curver looked at the two men. They were not weak; they had principles. But now they seemed to sag. Maybe, Curver thought, it was an accident of light, the passing of a cloud's shadow over the window, a sudden need for blood sugar, a protective gesture. He had seen the posture before. Not nice. It came when a man got the word he was going to be punished . . . and no one had told him why.

Levi recovered first. When he spoke his voice had its usual soft and precise quality.

"Book, let's don't fool ourselves," he said. "The young man has just described a technique, a tool, an instrument. We're here because we believe some things are more important than techniques. One such thing is that the President should not just automatically be re-elected. So we are going to back the best men running against him and if there aren't any good ones we'll find one." He smiled. "Or we'll try like hell. Could we talk a minute, Book?"

Instantly Curver uncoiled himself from the chair. The excellent cloth of his suit was wrinkled, but that was the only indication he had been through a long conference. He shook hands languidly and left the study.

"Book, if this Thatch person you've mentioned measures up and we've got any chance of getting him interested, we'll have to try the new ideas Curver described to ever get him to the Convention," Levi said.

"I'm opposed to it," Bookbinder said.

"I gathered that," Levi said. "But you've been around long enough to know this thing will take a lot of doing. So let Curver go ahead and try. We can watch him closely and we'll still have control over the campaign. I'll get five people to put up ten thousand each just to see."

"I didn't think you would," Bookbinder said.

They walked to the door. Just before Bookbinder opened it, Levi said, "Did I ever tell you that one of the last things my mother did before she died in 1952 was to vote for Eisenhower. She was ninety and she loved Ike. Also she insisted he must be Jewish."

Bookbinder had heard Levi's story before but he liked hearing it again.

"You watch that Curver boy, Book. Smart kid. Probably Jewish."

Bookbinder shut the door and leaned against it, laughing. Levi always left him feeling better.

6

Emily, encoder third class, looked across the window and saw the Rolls Royce come in the driveway of the big old restored colonial house.

"Visitors," she said to Stern, also encoder third class, who sat across the table from her.

"Hurrah," Stern said.

He did not even look up. Emily could not make out what was wrong with his glasses. They made Stern's eyes huge, almost froglike, while the rest of his face was thin. But the distortion was so great that she could not possibly see how they helped Stern *see*. She watched as he took a card and, setting it in the encoder, started to punch keys.

He worked hard. Emily gave him that. He worked hard and he was square. He was working for a Ph.D. in sociology and was devoted to Dr. Cotter. He had once told Emily, "Dr. Cotter is the first scientist of opinion. He is as scrupulous as Pavlov and his influence will be as great." Emily had almost become hysterical with laughter. Since then they had talked very little.

Emily did not like silence. This had forced her to become a liar; it produced something close to a compulsion to talk. She lied about the fact that she was taking a Ph.D. at Columbia. Dr. Cotter insisted that all of his staff work on advanced degrees. Emily, who was working her husband's way through law school, simply took a Columbia transcript, inked in straight *A*'s for herself in courses she took from the catalog and sent it along to Dr. Cotter at the end of every semester.

Emily took an envelope, glanced at the postmark *Pasadena, Calif.*, and ripped it open. She took the questionnaires out and slid an IBM card into place on the encoder.

"I finished my M.A. thesis," she said as she started to work.

It gave her a sharp pleasure that her accuracy rate was somewhat better than Stern's. She averaged about 1½ per cent of error in encoding the material from the questionnaires to the IBM cards and Stern's error was around 2¼ per cent.

"So fast?" Stern said, and the big watery eyes in the handsome face looked approximately in her direction. His mouth was open. Maybe it meant envy. "What were the results?"

Oh Christ, Emily thought. What did I tell him my thesis was about? She coughed and took a Kleenex out of her purse, trying to remember.

"I changed it at the last moment," she said. She could not remember her last story. "It's on newly arrived Puerto Ricans and the frequency with which they visit supermarkets," she said. "The other hypothesis didn't give a big enough N to make it feasible."

"Enough N? I thought there were enough illegitimate Negro-white paired children to keep you busy for a year," Stern said.

"Not when you correct for social-economic status and hold education steady," Emily said, thinking fast.

Stern's lower face expressed concentration, interest. He finally nodded.

"Not if you hold education constant, I guess," he said. "What is the hypothesis on the Puerto Ricans?"

"That going to a supermarket represented breaking away from the little neighborhood stores and the Puerto Rican ghettos. Might correlate with outward social mobility, acculturation, socialization, and fading of color chauvinism."

"That's a hell of an idea," Stern said. He took off his glasses and Emily realized the boy was tired. If she had a million she would buy him leisure and some contact lenses.

"Thanks," Emily said.

She knew she had a reputation at the Institute for being imaginative. If only they knew, she thought.

The door opened and Dr. Cotter came in. Stern didn't recognize him until he spoke. Instantly Stern clapped his glasses back over his eyes.

Acolyte schmuck, Emily thought.

She looked at the three men who came in with Dr. Cotter. The big man was familiar—not famous-familiar, but familiar. In law. The Jew (My God, why do all thin Jews look like Oppenheimer?) was not familiar. The younger man looked at Emily and for a moment she was pleased and then she sensed that he was watching her fingers. The flush of pleasure died. He was waiting to see how good she was on encoding. He had been around.

Her fingers flew over the keys and she knew Stern was getting tense. It gave her a vagrant knowledge of superiority. And then the inevitable sense of competing with Jews. And the inevitable guilts. She jammed a card into the encoder.

Long ago Emily had given up reading the questions. They were so damned dull:

Do you intend to buy a major appliance in the next year?

	Yes	No
Refrigerator	_____	_____
Stove	_____	_____
Air conditioner	_____	_____

Do you approve of Elizabeth Taylor's rumored divorce?

Do you send your child to the movies more than once a week?

Have you changed coffee brands in the last year?

From what brand?

Do you prefer whole-wheat bread to white bread?

With Curver's eyes on her Emily worked fast. She put in sex, age, political registration, region, estimated SES, occupation, race (not asked of the subject but guessed by the interviewer), marital status, religion.

"What does SES mean?" a voice asked. Emily looked up. It was the big husky man.

"It's social-economic status," Emily said.

From the corner of her eye she saw Dr. Cotter coming toward them. It was a rule for employees not to speak to clients, but what the hell, the man had asked, Emily thought.

"Social-economic status?" Bookbinder said. "Come on, young lady, don't leave me there. What does it mean?"

"It means the estimated position of the subject in the total population in terms of his social position and income," Dr. Cotter said firmly.

Emily hated Dr. Cotter. He was square and knew it. He used it. He deliberately dressed in boxlike suits and heavy brown shoes and starched collars and held onto his Minnesota manners. Emily hated him because it worked. In a city where everyone dressed Ivy League, Dr. Cotter was a walking antique. And it made him more believable.

"How do you know someone's SES?" Bookbinder asked. "Do you slip up alongside and ask 'Come on, buddy, tell me your SES'? Sounds like a dirty word."

Emily started to laugh and stopped. She needed the job.

"It's not as ambiguous as it sounds," Dr. Cotter said. "First of all the interviewer is told precisely what neighborhoods to go into. He is told to skip the corner house and start with the next one."

"Why?" Bookbinder asked.

It was not the kind of *why?* that was heard around the Institute very often. This old boy is tough, Emily thought.

"Because corner houses are usually occupied by higher-income families," Dr. Cotter said. He gave his solid unaffected Minnesota laugh. "We don't know why, but it just works out that way. But before we send the interviewer his packet we already know whether it is a working-class, blue-collar, white-collar or high-income-type area, or a slum. So that takes care of the economic thing. You don't find a ten-thousand-dollar-a-year man living in a working-class neighborhood."

"What if you find a Negro in one of the houses?" Bookbinder asked. Emily felt excitement grow in her. She liked the old boy. "What does that do to his social-status ratings? I mean if you find him in a high-income neighborhood?"

"We mark him low on social status," Dr. Cotter said. "Several studies by Warner and the Lynds and others have indicated—"

"I don't care what those studies indicated," Bookbinder said. "Why do you automatically put a rich Negro in a low social status?"

Stern's face lifted. His lips were set in a thin line. The refracted eyes swam. He was impatient.

"Because that is where his neighbors and peers put him," Dr. Cotter said. "Through an elaborate scaling technique we have discovered how people rank one another. Any person of color—

Negro, Filipino, Chinese, anything—falls in the lowest social status."

"As judged by their neighbors?" Bookbinder asked.

"Of course. What other standard could we use?" Dr. Cotter asked.

Emily watched Stern. Stern was bewildered and unbelieving. He seemed to regard the big husky man as a student in a seminar who was not getting the word.

"What about using your own judgment about his social status? Say he was the Negro doctor who discovered how to make blood-plasma transfusions?" Bookbinder said. "Why wouldn't you give him a high social status?"

"Mr. Bookbinder, that would be a subjective evaluation on our part," Dr. Cotter said and his voice grew calm and pedantic. "Very unscientific."

Emily watched the big man's fists dig deep into his pockets.

"Book, knock it off," Curver said quietly. "We're not here to argue about the thing. We're here to find out how Dr. Cotter runs his poll."

"Listen, Mad, no one ever thought that majority rule meant you could just ask someone's neighbors where he stands and then stick him in that . . ."

"Book, Mr. Curver's right," Levi said, his voice low, but not so low that Emily did not hear it. "Just listen for a while. Get your adrenalin up later."

Bookbinder hesitated. His hands came out of his pockets, big and open, nicely manicured. He smiled.

"Dr. Cotter, did you know that the blood-plasma technique was developed by Dr. Charles Drew, a Negro?" Bookbinder asked. His voice was friendly, easy, open. Curver knew the symptoms. Bookbinder was charming this poor vulnerable bastard. The knife would flick in a moment.

"No. That's surprising," Dr. Cotter said. "I never knew that."

"Why surprising?" Bookbinder asked. Curver winced. "Oh, you'll enjoy this piece of irony. Dr. Drew died outside a Southern hospital after an automobile accident opened one of his major arteries. 'White only' was the hospital policy. Dr. Drew couldn't get any of the plasma he had developed. Odd, isn't it?"

"Very odd," Dr. Cotter said. His face was blank. "I mean

a terrible tragedy. But understand. As a scientist I cannot concern myself with *abstract* theories of social status. That has been the pitfall of classical scholars. They invented what they thought were important elements in social status. Very unscientific. I get out and find what social status really is. That doesn't mean I approve of it. Some of my best friends . . ."

"Could we go on," Levi said. His soft voice was cold.

Oh, poor Dr. Cotter, Emily thought with pleasure, you just got shot. Like with a machine gun from forty feet.

"I'll continue with the explanation of our technique," Dr. Cotter said.

And you don't even know it, Emily finished her thought.

He walked over and picked up one of the envelopes of completed questionnaires. He ripped it open, talking out a long slip of paper and glancing at the envelope.

"It's from Los Angeles," he said. He looked at a card in the envelope. "The interviewer, a woman, had instructions to cover three square blocks in the Long Beach area. She took every other house, ignoring the corner houses, and from noon until six o'clock she only talked to women. After that she only asked for men." Dr. Cotter cleared his throat. "You see, Mr. Bookbinder, we've worked these techniques out over a long period of time, checked and rechecked them. Just on a random basis, we come up with a good cross section of the American public. For example, we know this Long Beach area is retired, Republican, very conservative, lower-middle-class people. We know from the census reports how many such people there are in the country and so we include a precise percentage of them in the sample."

"No one has ever interviewed me for a poll," Levi said.

"A very common question," Dr. Cotter said. "In a good solid sample we might take only fifteen hundred people. So you can see that the chances are very heavily against your ever being interviewed."

"But, presumably, enough people like me will be included so that you can conclude that I would react the way they would," Levi said.

"Exactly, Mr. Levi. You've got it," Dr. Cotter said. "That's the science part. You don't have to take all the blood out of a human to know what it's like. You take a single hypodermic and that's enough to tell you about the rest. Well, groups in society are like that. We don't have to take all the blood out of every subject."

"No; Christ, no!" Bookbinder said. "We'd have all sorts of pale bloodless people running around. Or not running around. Just slumping down and dying."

Dr. Cotter eyed Bookbinder. Then he spoke slowly.

"Science is a method of generalizing from small samples to larger units."

Emily suddenly loathed Dr. Cotter.

"Dr. Cotter, I've got a question," Emily said. Stern's head snapped up, so sharply it seemed inhuman, toylike. A mood compounded of anger and boredom and humiliation made her go on. She also sensed there was something unusual in the questionnaires she was encoding.

"Yes, Emily," Dr. Cotter said. He was not irritated. He was never irritated.

"I've done about a hundred of these questionnaires and on at least five there have been written-in responses to the Presidential-preference item," Emily said.

"The procedure is just to make a separate note of the written-in names," Dr. Cotter said. "They never amount to anything significant in a statistical sense."

He turned and started again for the door. Emily waited until he had his hand on the knob.

"But, Dr. Cotter, these five names are the same person," she said.

Dr. Cotter's hand came away from the knob with a jerk. Emily felt a stab of pleasure and knew it was malice. It was the first time she had seen him jerk like that.

"All five were the same name?" he asked.

Emily cultivated the malice deep inside her.

"What does all this mean?" Levi asked.

"It's all very simple," Dr. Cotter said. He went over to a shelf and picked up some blank questionnaires and a card.

"Every so often we have a name-identification question. We throw in all sorts of people . . . movie stars, businessmen, sports figures, politicians, maybe even a Nobel Prize winner," Dr. Cotter said. "The subject is asked to identify the person."

He handed Levi the card. Bookbinder looked over Levi's shoulder. The names were in large bold type.

1. Nelson Rockefeller
2. Elizabeth Taylor
3. John Steinbeck
4. Barry Goldwater
5. Marlon Brando
6. Charles de Gaulle
7. Richard Nixon
8. The President
9. Sandy Koufax
10. Doctor Clark Kerr

11. Jonas Salk
12. Edmund (Pat) Brown
13. Kate Smith
14. Frank Sinatra
15. Robert Kennedy
16. George Romney
17. Laurence Olivier
18. James Hoffa
19. Juan Trippe
20. James Roosevelt

"The subject is asked, number by number, if he has heard of the person," Dr. Cotter said. As he spoke he glanced at Emily's cards. She knew he could never imagine a person cheating. He was frightened of the eccentric cards.

"What do you take as a reasonable answer?" Bookbinder asked.

"That was a problem at first because the interviewers tended to want a very precise answer," Dr. Cotter said. "For example, for Dr. Clark Kerr it is not enough to say he is in California and an educator, but they want him identified as the president of the University of California. That is unreasonable. We recorded a lot of conversations between our interviewers and subjects and analyzed them. We discovered the interviewer was discouraging the subject, breaking down rapport by asking for too much information.

"For example, if the interviewer says 'Oh, come on. You've got everything right about Goldwater except what state he comes from,' the subject freezes," Curver added. "After that he just mumbles, or wanders away, or says he has an appointment."

"You ought to start them out on the President and Elizabeth Taylor," Bookbinder said. "They can't miss there."

"That's not exactly so," Dr. Cotter said. He had, quite deliberately, no sense of humor. Humor conflicts with reality, he had once said to Emily. "If we insisted on a strict identification of the President, fewer than fifty per cent of the people could speak his given name."

"John Fitzgerald Kennedy?" Bookbinder asked. He tilted his big head. "Guess that puts me in the good fifty per cent."

"The accurate fifty per cent," Dr. Cotter said.

"You mean that there is anyone abroad in this land who

doesn't know the name of the President?" Bookbinder asked. "You must have included kids, illiterates, or hermits in your sample."

"No, we did not include juveniles or nonliterate persons," Dr. Cotter said. His voice had a heavy authority. "But literate Americans, over twenty-one years of age, of all races, all degrees of social-economic status, all religions, and all regions include one person out of ten who cannot identify the President's name."

"What about Elizabeth Taylor?" Bookbinder asked. Levi glanced quickly at him. "How does she do?"

It was obvious to Emily that the older gentleman who looked like Oppenheimer could not quite place Elizabeth Taylor.

"Better than the President," Dr. Cotter said. "She has a name-recognition percentage of about ninety-five per cent."

Bookbinder, old in the ways of adversary trials and the matching of wills, knew that Cotter took satisfaction in the figure. Bookbinder did not. It wilted something in him . . . a vision of America, a view of human intelligence.

"What happened when you asked the item the way you have it here, 'The President'?" Bookbinder asked.

"The figures are in my office, but the President dropped from ninety per cent when his name was on the card to forty-eight per cent when only his title was mentioned," Dr. Cotter said.

"You mean that if you tell the subject the President's name nine out of ten people can identify him as the President," Bookbinder said, "but that if you just give his title less than half of the people can supply his name?"

"Precisely."

"I don't believe it," Bookbinder said. "If people were that dumb we wouldn't be a republic. We wouldn't have anything like popular participation in politics."

Levi cut in as softly as a razor through suet.

"Book, give a lecture on your own time," he said. "I take it that Dr. Cotter has a very low opinion of the level of citizen information on politics."

Dr. Cotter looked genuinely puzzled. Emily felt a sensation which was familiar but buried and very elusive. Then she knew. She had felt this way whenever she passed a wreck on the highway, with the flares out and the police-car lights blinking, traffic slowing, the white form of the ambulance, the glitter of broken glass, the smear of oil and the climactic thing: the human forms doll-like and twisted on the black asphalt. Thank God, not me, she thought.

"I have no opinion on such matters, Mr. Levi," Dr. Cotter said. "The task of the Institute is to reduce attitudes and opinions held by millions of different people to a quantifiable level. If I were to hold deep opinions it would surely influence the way in which I proceed. Scientists have hypotheses and they test them and then they either verify a law or a norm or they do not. But opinion has nothing to do with it."

"But surely politics is a matter of opinion," Levi said. "That's what it is all about. Who is right and who is wrong."

"I suppose so," Dr. Cotter said slowly. "Politics is concerned with right and wrong, but that is not what we are concerned with here at the Institute. We are measuring attitudes about politics, breakfast food, nylon tires, contraception, attitudes toward cholesterol . . . really almost anything. But the right or wrong of any one thing is something else. That's out of our field."

"What about those five people who gave the same name?" Bookbinder asked.

Oh Sweet Jesus, Curver thought, if this poor jerk Cotter ever knew how much he had just been put down. But he didn't. His face was bland and professorial. And he didn't even know he had alienated two of the most influential anonymous men in America.

"It just doesn't happen that way," Dr. Cotter said. "Probably a person has made an impact on some group in one area and they all volunteer this name. For example, if that U-2 pilot . . . you know the one that came down in Russia . . . Powders."

"Gary Powers," Curver said quickly.

"Thank you. If we were polling his home town, maybe five people would volunteer his name rather than one of the list names," Dr. Cotter said. "But overwhelmingly, in a broad geographical sampling, people stick to the names on the list. Emily, what area are the five write-ins from?"

"Ohio, Southern California, Massachusetts, Washington, D.C., and Kansas," Emily said.

She was almost faint with pleasure. Dr. Cotter had led her into it. She was just doing her job—and giving him a clout behind the ear.

"Did you recheck it?" Dr. Cotter said. His face was pure astonishment.

"Yes, sir," Emily said.

She fanned out the five questionnaires.

The Presidential-preference item was the last one on the list. Bookbinder, Levi, and Curver moved over and looked at them. In the blank labeled *Other* the first questionnaire said "That Thatch guy, an engineer type or high man, who finished the bridge in India." The next one said, "That cat who told those Indians to go to hell. Built a bridge, I think. He's good."

"The interviewers put down as accurately as possible the exact words the subjects say," Dr. Cotter said. His finger hovered over the remaining three forms.

"John Thatch. That's who. He stands up to all those damned bureaucrats. Those Hindus or whatever they are," the third one read. "That man would make a good President."

The last two were much the same, except they were somewhat more illiterate.

"This is most extraordinary," Dr. Cotter said. "Usually the write-ins are supplied by obvious paranoids. They will put in Abraham Lincoln or Jesus Christ or Buddha or some local religious revivalist."

Emily was euphoric. Dr. Cotter didn't know what in hell to say.

The group of visitors left the room, Dr. Cotter leading the way.

"How many subjects, Dr. Cotter, do you think would have preferred this Thatch person if his name had been on the list they were handed?" Bookbinder asked.

"I don't have an opinion," Dr. Cotter said. Curver noticed sweat against the white skin on Dr. Cotter's neck. "We've never had a reaction like this. I'm sure it's a clerical mistake or just a local enthusiasm." He paused. "Well, not local. Not with that wide geographical distribution. But it's very irregular."

"Do you know this Thatch person?" Bookbinder said.

"No. I never heard his name before today," Dr. Cotter said. His face brightened. "Maybe he isn't a real person at all. Sometimes when a popular novel or big movie comes along people will get confused and take the name of a fictional character as their preferred choice for President or governor or whatever. We had some people who preferred James Bond as the most qualified man to head the FBI when Mr. Hoover retires. And another time—"

"Thatch is a real person," Bookbinder said.

Dr. Cotter invited them into his office for coffee, but Bookbinder did not even hear him. He turned the corner and headed for the parking lot.

7

"How would you describe your professional qualifications?" Bookbinder said.

He walked to the window so he could take his eyes away from the tall woman Mad had brought into the room.

He was unaccustomed to women in his study, and she made him uneasy. Mad leaned against a bookshelf. He was smiling. The smile irritated Bookbinder. One of the things he had to discover was whether or not this girl was one of Mad's casuals, a professional, or just what.

"I am thirty-three. Ph.D. in mathematics, advanced research in statistics, psychology, and sociology. Special training in psychoanalysis but have never practiced it. M.D., but have never practiced."

The cloth and the tailoring of the suit gave her the appearance of elegance, but her face was severe. Something about her seemed slightly skewed to Bookbinder . . . not unpleasant, but like an object seen in a light which makes matter shimmer. He was not sure he saw her accurately.

He waited for her to go on.

She did not.

She is tough, Bookbinder thought. And the guts to be silent came from experience.

"Anything more?" she asked. Her voice was cool and very slow.

"You did not add what your profession was, Dr. Devlin," Bookbinder said. He swung around but saw immediately that the tall young woman remained completely calm.

"I'm sorry," Dr. Devlin said evenly. "I thought the qualifications described the profession. I'm a behavioral scientist."

"What does a behavioral scientist do?" he asked.

"I study the behavior of humans," she said, and smiled.

Mad laughed and his lean frame seemed to fold against the bookshelf.

"Did Mad tell you what we are interested in?" Bookbinder asked.

"Yes. The possibility of an incumbent President being defeated for a second term."

"Let me narrow it a bit," Bookbinder said. "Not *an* incumbent President, but President Kennedy. I don't know if you are aware that the Twenty-second Amendment to the Constitution makes it impossible for a President to serve more than two four-year terms."

"Unless he has acted as President for less than two years of a term to which some other person was elected President," Dr. Devlin said. "Then, he could serve one year, three hundred and sixty-four days and then decide what to do."

She had recited the exact language of the Amendment and had also made a quick calculation. Bookbinder was impressed.

"So he might, under some circumstances, serve a term of one year, three hundred and sixty-four days and two more four-year terms," Bookbinder said.

"He might and probably would, Mr. Bookbinder," Dr. Devlin said.

"Why?"

"Because the incumbent President occupies a virtually unassailable position," Dr. Devlin said. "He has every advantage. If he is not mentally incompetent or ideologically rigid he will win."

"Did you get this opinion from reading polls, Dr. Devlin?" Bookbinder asked. "Like Mad here?"

The woman leaned back in her chair and smiled at Book-binder.

"Mr. Bookbinder, you have a reputation for being open-minded," she said. "Many new forms of scientific knowledge are developing at breakneck speed, using terms which are strange to you. Some fields which I knew well five years ago are now a blank to me. That is the price of progress. But I gather almost none of my opinions from polling. Excuse me just a moment," she put up a small hand because Bookbinder was leaning forward to talk. "Polling is not a science. Science is concerned with etiology: What is the true cause of an event? Now all the pollster does is take a portrait of the American people . . . the scabs showing, the ignorant stares, the sneers of the intellectuals, the cowlike look of the party hacks, the busy League of Women Voters. The portrait then can be labeled *Republican* or *Democrat*. But why? The pollsters don't have a clue."

"So Mr. Curver tells me," Bookbinder said. "But do you have a clue?"

She smiled, a pleasant smile, not cocky, and nodded her head.

"Yes. I have had training in a number of fields. I know that none of them is a science. But each produces some facts. Verifiable facts," she said. "I take the most reliable facts from all of these fields and apply them to a given problem. If there is no relevant data I tell my clients so. I also tell them how to interpret my reports. If they wish to take flights of imagination or fanciful projections, I never restrain them. I simply dissociate myself from romanticism."

"Dr. Devlin, I take it you agree with Mr. Curver that President Kennedy cannot be defeated for re-election. Tell me why."

"A lot of reasons, Mr. Bookbinder. Part of it is that the incumbent is surrounded by over four years of honorific words and rituals. He seems as though he ought to be President. He assumes the mantle."

"Dr. Devlin, Mad may have told you that I think very little of this kind of approach," Bookbinder said. "But that's not the point. We need someone to keep my old-fashioned notions from becoming encrusted."

"One question, Mr. Bookbinder? What do you want—other than to prove an idea?"

"That's all. Is that so strange?"

"In this day and age, yes, sir. Most people aren't interested in ideas, only in verifying their prejudices."

Curver knew what Bookbinder saw: a plain woman, perhaps thirty-five, in fine clothes, with eyes wide apart, no make-up, a profile that was beautiful, almost perfect, but seldom exposed. Dr. Devlin faced people squarely but somewhat too deliberately. When one was very close to her the pureness of her skin, the delicate blue-white color of the veins around her temples and on her hands became apparent. But few people got that close. That was the way Dr. Devlin wanted it.

He had met her two years before at a meeting of psychoanalysts and behavioral scientists at the home of a very wealthy woman who gave a few million a year to what she called the "psychic research area." Her lawyers were very scrupulous and no one had a free ride. Her salon was sometimes interesting, more often tedious.

The people present knew that the wealthy woman was entirely unaware of what was happening in psychic research, psychoanalysis, or psychiatry. But they all indulged her. Except one.

"Your belief, Mrs. Andrews, that psychoanalysis and ESP will eventually merge is extravagant," a slim inconspicuous woman had said. She happened to be sitting next to Curver.

The room froze. The patroness wheeled slowly away from a bearded man who had taken peyote, LSD, smoked marijuana, sniffed heroin, never ate flesh, had slept four nights in subzero weather, and was very talkative.

"What?" the fragile woman said. She wore a flowing gown of pure silk so white that it glowed. She was confused. "Why not?"

"Because neither is a science and their results are quite contrary," the woman said.

The thirty people in the room knew their duty. They did not let the discussion go on. They flowed in around Mrs. Andrews and floated her to the bar and Curver was left alone with the heretic.

"Would you like me to take you home?" he asked out of kindness rather than interest. She must be embarrassed.

"That would be nice," she said. "No one is going to learn

anything here." She smiled. "They are very happy, though, aren't they?"

Dr. Devlin shook hands with Mrs. Andrews. She gave no indication that she recognized her hostess' frozen mood. She left with neither gaiety nor solemnity. She merely left. Curver felt he was a mechanical accessory, suddenly called into duty.

They got in Curver's car and rode for a few blocks through the upper Fifties.

"It's a four-day holiday, starting today," Curver said.

"I work every day," Dr. Devlin said pleasantly.

They drove a bit more. Curver drove to his apartment and left the car with the doorman and Dr. Devlin stepped out without a question.

Curver's apartment was big and open and very well furnished. It had a nice combination of antique furniture, modern paintings, Swedish crystal, and a very elaborate but easily managed high-fidelity set. Curver pushed a button and a record fell and music came into the front room.

Dr. Devlin was neither cautious nor enthusiastic. She looked at his books, listened to the music, and took a light Scotch and soda.

"Tell me an obscene story about your childhood," Curver asked.

"I have no recollection of my childhood," she said.

"A selective loss of memory," Curver said. He did not know whether to believe her. "Fenichel." Now he was tensely aware of her every move.

"Have you read Fenichel?" Dr. Devlin said.

"Yes," Curver said.

For two hours they went through a gentle, subtle, and quite attentive dialogue.

"You are a lawyer?" Dr. Devlin finally asked.

"A lawyer."

"Why are you interested in these other disciplines?" she asked.

He shrugged, "I want to know why you cannot remember your childhood."

"Because nothing worth remembering happened to me until I got to college on a scholarship," she said, and smiled. "It was the first time I could think of things in an abstract sense. Abbott and Morehouse did a study on chronic amnesia of the adolescent. It is not so exceptional. Perhaps three in a thousand subjects experience it."

Curver paused and looked closely at her. He was still unable to tell whether she was pretending. He was startled and very much interested.

"You literally have no memory of your childhood?" he asked.

"I have no memory of anything that happened before I went to Radcliffe on a scholarship."

"But you must be a little curious about your childhood, your parents, your siblings."

"I have no curiosity at all. It was a dreadful childhood or I would not be reluctant to probe it. Right? So, my amnesia is a form of health."

"The psychoanalysts say that you cannot know yourself fully . . ."

"I happen not to believe completely in analysts. Analysts suffer from pluralistic ignorance. They have specialized so much they have no knowledge of other fields. Osborne and Cabot demonstrated that psychiatrists and analysts are the most ignorant of medical specialists," she said. She looked at Curver. Then she smiled. "I'm joking about remembering my childhood. I could if I tried. I just don't want to. Most childhoods are boring and mine was worse. Look, you have to pay someone $25 an hour just to listen to all that drool about childhood . . . Eysenck showed that analysis doesn't cure a patient any faster than the mere passage of time."

"'Do you always cite a monograph for any statement you make?" Curver asked.

"You know about monographs," she said, and her pleasure was genuine.

"Yes. You are a snob about such things and find that unbelievable, don't you?"

She waited and pondered. Calmly she looked at her drink, then back at Curver.

"Yes I do. I don't believe you really understand the monographic literature of the behavioral sciences," she said. "A study by Thorndike and Muscatine indicates that professionals are very limited in their span of knowledge."

"You mean the *other* Thorndike," Curver said easily. "And the study showed that about five per cent of accredited specialists have a solid knowledge outside their certificated fields." Curver waited a moment, enjoyed her look of surprise. "You are a very boring person. Did you know that?"

She glanced at him and then, for the first time, she looked away and showed her profile. The room was dim and the bones, flesh, and shadows of her face were caught by light from the city. Curver knew what she was doing.

"The exposure of one's most favorable aspect is an infantile regression to Oedipal realities," Curver said.

Dr. Devlin flushed.

"A study by Modect on exposure of the face shows—" she began.

"That you are very afraid of something and are trying to bury it," Curver said. He laughed. "But just what? That would be interesting to know. A mechanical way of life is the surest sign of deeply buried guilt."

"I do not lead a mechanical life," she said. To prove it she swallowed off the rest of her drink. She held out her glass for more.

"You cite a source for everything you say," Curver said. "But now I tell you about your mechanical life and you hold out your glass. That is the only citation you can offer."

She sighed and turned toward him. She put down her glass. Her eyes seemed oddly unfocused, but something had happened to her body. The muscles seemed to have relaxed, there was a melting of her posture. Whatever had happend to her, it was exciting. She moved toward him and it was the most sensual gesture he had ever experienced. It was like an unfolding, a gentle attack.

Curver was actually frightened.

They went to bed quietly. Dr. Devlin was hesitant, fragile, waiting at the edge of the loom of the light.

Hours later, with Dr. Devlin's hands still moving over his back, feeling out the weary bones at the bottom of his spine, he realized what had happened. He had been manipulated, and by an expert. He was under the distinct impression that she had looked at the watch on her left wrist, its hands glowing in the dark, even as the fingers of her right hand had flickered over his body in some carefully timed pattern of arousal. She had arched her slim body in a big strategic move above him, her small breasts larger as she leaned forward. When she twisted and reversed position, Curver, always proud of his potency, was suddenly an accessory. But the words she spoke into his ear told him he was really dominant.

No sexual experience had ever excited him so much, exhausted him so completely, or left him so mystified and frustrated. He had sought, without any success whatsoever, a repeat performance. She had never again so much as taken off her severely tailored suit coat in his presence.

"Simulations Enterprises," Bookbinder looked out the cab window at Madison Avenue, "is a dreadful name."

The cab came to a stop before a window which held a huge array of technical equipment. Dr. Devlin led the two men toward the entrance. In Bookbinder's office she had suggested this trip to inspect a computer at work, jokingly calling it "the second stage of your indoctrination." He was uncertain what the first stage had been.

They walked into the room and looked at the lines of cabinets. Most of them bore the letters *IBM* followed by a number. Some were obviously operating. The air-conditioning was so powerful that it made conversation difficult.

"What are we going to do? Buy an IBM machine?" Bookbinder shouted.

"This is not a sales room," Dr. Devlin said, looking at him with surprise. "This is an actual operation."

Bookbinder found it unthinkable that a business would be carried on behind huge plate-glass windows on the street level where any passer-by could observe. A half-dozen people had their faces pressed against the window. One extremely old woman, a ratty furpiece hanging almost to her knees, was staring with the bright incomprehension and delight of senility.

"This is the IBM seven-oh-nine-four Computer," Dr. Devlin said. "Isn't it beautiful?" She moved her hand to indicate six gray boxes, each about the size of an upright coffin. Four identical boxes were on the right, and in front of them a console of levers and lights blinked occasionally. Below the lights was a series of buttons. At the top of the coffin-shaped boxes was a large window and behind it two large rolls of tape. The tapes jerked spasmodically. The tapeholders were colorful plastic . . . red, blue, yellow, gray, or white. The twelve spools within the six machines were mesmerizing. A red tapeholder spun. Its tape passed over a reading head and whipped into a solid-blue holder. The colors blurred before Bookbinder's eyes; then the two round holders clamped to an instant stop. Two other boxes started, their bright holders blurring and then coming to a startling halt. At the console, horizontal columns of small lights glowed, went off, came on again. The brilliant buttons, each neatly labeled, popped up.

A young man in shirtsleeves, his face studious, self-conscious, inserted an IBM card in a small machine to the right of the console. Instantly, all six of the machines at the left began to whir. Bookbinder realized he had been staring at the machines for several minutes. He felt a kind of pleasant dizziness. There was something carnival-like about the machines, as if they belonged on a pier at Coney Island and would, at some point, ring a bell or drop jellybeans down a slot into your hand. Quite unconsciously he looked around for the end of the machine, the funnel from which something must flow.

"Nothing drops out," Dr. Devlin said, and smiled.

Bookbinder did not reply.

"What does that card do that the man just stuck in?" he asked.

"That card gives an order to the tapes on the left, the ones behind the console," Dr. Devlin said.

"I expected someone to sit in front of the console," Bookbinder said.

"Oh, no. He might be tempted to touch something, and human interference could be costly. This machine rents for around six hundred and fifty dollars an hour. Any mistake the machine might make it will catch itself."

"What does all this do?" Curver asked. It was clear that Bookbinder was not going to ask for an explanation.

"It solves a problem. Say we want to know how people in Midwestern cities feel about 'getting the US out of the UN and the UN out of the US.' Isn't that a position Goldwater has taken?" Dr. Devlin asked.

"Something close to it, but not exactly," Bookbinder growled.

He shifted his feet, glanced at the whirling plastic tapeholders. "How would the machines give you an answer?"

"First, we'd look at the census tables and get the raw social economic facts of, say, a typical group of one thousand people in a Midwestern town. We'd need the age, sex, education, income, and neighborhood of our theoretical thousand people. That's all the original work we'd have to do. Then we'd put that information on these cards, which have to be key-punched by a machine which looks like a typewriter. Say we know that there are fifteen Catholics in our sample. We put the information about them on a card . . . how many are children, average ages of others, occupations, and so forth. That's a Fortran Statement." She walked to a wastebasket and picked out a rejected card. It was a typical IBM card except that across the top it said FORTRAN STATEMENT in large letters.

"All that means is 'formula translation,'" Dr. Devlin said. "That constitutes an order to the bank of machines on the left. Now we load those machines, called 'periphery memory units,' with tapes. Each of the tapes has thirty thousand of what we call 'words,' but each word is really a tiny magnetized spot and each spot is a piece of information."

"It's *what?*" Bookbinder said. He could not keep either the disbelief or the interest from his voice.

"A bit of information. Like 'How many Protestants in the Midwest read the Chicago *Tribune.*' Another bit might be 'What fraction of Catholics in Midwestern towns belong to country clubs.' Now on each of the tapes there are thirty-two thousand 'words,' each containing thirty-six 'bits,' so you multiply that and get somewhere around one million, one hundred thousand bits of information on a single tape."

"It would be too much information to use," Bookbinder said suddenly.

"No, that's one of the virtues of the seven-oh-nine-four." Bookbinder watched her face grow more animated. Obviously she loved these damned machines. "Those six machines are all busy scanning bits of information on the tapes at a speed of two hundred fifty thousand bits a minute, or one million every four minutes. Most of the bits it rejects because it has been 'ordered' by the Fortran card to select only things relevant to

Catholics among our fictitious thousand. Most of the 'bits' it passes over, but whenever anything about Catholics in Midwestern towns is scanned it is promptly transferred to one of the tapes on this bank of four machines to the right.

"I won't bore you with the details, but we very quickly gather the bits which Fortran has ordered and they are accumulated on the tapes at the right. There they are grouped into categories. For example, we will know which newspapers these Catholics read and whether they are pro or con the UN, who they talk to about such things as the UN, their orientation vis-à-vis Red China and the UN and how much they tend to accept or reject arguments . . . the same argument made in *America* or repeated by a priest might be believed, while if it appeared in *The New York Times* it might be automatically discounted. In a few minutes we would have run through all the recorded bits of information which bear on how Catholics in a typical Midwestern town feel about the UN . . ."

She had stopped for several seconds before Bookbinder realized he was leaning forward as if she were still talking. She had said a great deal and it had affected him both physically and mentally. His mind had raced ahead: after the Midwestern Catholics were explored, then another block of one thousand, say, Protestant, professional, sales, Democratic would be punched into a Fortran (God, that word has a ringing authoritative sound to it—like *sergeant!*, or *Snap to!*, or *Attention, men!*) card and new millions of bits would go flowing through the machine, be scanned at a fantastic rate and the useful items would go spinning off into the accumulator tapes.

Then he remembered that the thousand did not really exist. They were imaginary, fictitious, used like zero is used in arithmetic. Yet real flesh-and-blood people would respond like—like automatons? It was this thought that gave him a sense of light-headedness along with a kind of deep sullen rage. A shrug of protest ran through his thick muscular shoulders. And yet he knew it was silly to feel this way.

"Where does the information come out?" Bookbinder asked.

Behind the machines there was still another machine which looked like a huge teletype writing on light-green paper with white lines alternating down the page. It was a pleasing arrangement. The machine wrote furiously, as if the dammed-up information from the tapes was generating a pressure. Bookbinder bent forward and looked at some of the typing.

IF (N–1) 69, 26, 38
GO TO 150
INTEGER VARIABLES . . . I, IFS, IPL, J, K, L. SWINE
NEEDS NEW CONFIGURATION . . . DEVELOP NEW STRATEGY

There were twenty more entries and then the words:

STRATEGY UNFEASIBLE . . . DEVELOP STRATEGY USING VITAMIN SUPPLEMENT
GO TO (9, 71) IIPL (1, L)

"I guess the computer rejected one strategy," Bookbinder said. He felt bleak. "Wonder what it was? What does that vitamin-supplement stuff mean?"

"I'll try and find out," Dr. Devlin said.

She walked over to a man leaning against a chair and watching the console. He did not take his eyes from a horizontal line of lights. He talked to her from the side of his mouth.

"What are they up to?" Bookbinder said. He could see she was tight-lipped.

"They wouldn't talk much, but I could see the over-all strategy," she said. "It's for a drug company with a new contraceptive pill. The competition is tough so they're trying a couple of new approaches. First, they're seeing if it's possible to get into the hard-core Catholic group by adding vitamins, iron and a few other things to the pill and then promoting it as a fertility pill."

"A what?" Curver said, laughing.

"It's not so odd," she said. "The pill actually does increase fertility among sterile women after they take it for a while and then stop. The other problem they have is to get women to take the pill regularly and then stop every 24 days. Very common problem with low SES groups. So they are trying two simulations. The first is to test the reaction to a box which would have 24 pills in slots and the woman would have to turn to a new slot each day to get a pill. When the box is empty, she stops taking the pills for four days then starts up again. The second simulation is to see how high SES women will respond to the box . . . they might think it means they can't read and would refuse to buy it."

Bookbinder was staring away, slightly embarrassed at the conversation.

"Dev, I've got a better idea. Have them try rhinestone boxes for ladies past the menopause. They could flash them around, give the impression of being real sexy and make their husbands look potent," Curver said. "Good?"

Dev looked at him levelly. "Not bad," she said. "Just a little dishonest."

They left the big tasteful room and the silence after the air-conditioning made their voices loud. Dr. Devlin explained that the machines generated a great deal of heat so the air-conditioning was many times more powerful than that in an ordinary room.

"Let's walk," Bookbinder said. "It's a nice day."

They walked down Fifty-ninth and then up Park.

"Dr. Devlin, tell Mr. Bookbinder how Simulations Enterprises relates to Dr. Cotter's operation," Curver said after they had gone a few blocks.

"Most professionals are reluctant to criticize their colleagues," Dr. Devlin said. "They do it all the time, but in oblique ways. I don't have any hesitation in pointing out what I consider the inadequacies of a technique or, even, the performance of a colleague."

"That's refreshing," Bookbinder said.

Dr. Devlin laughed.

"Dr. Cotter runs a straightforward and quite orthodox poll," she said. "He goes out and asks people to give answers to questions. He tries to eliminate as much error as possible. The questions are written clearly and so as to avoid bias. But all he can do is ask one-dimension questions and only a few at a time. The pollster taps only a small fragment of the subject's mind, attention, background, family influence, and habits. The Simulations thing, just because it can consider thousands of elements influencing the subject, even things he may not know himself, gets much better results."

"And one further thing, Book," Mad said, "Simulations Enterprises can predict what people will do in a situation which they have *never heard of before.* That was the whole point of the UN in the Midwest example. No one has gone out there and asked them to vote on whether we should get out of the UN, but Dev outlined a procedure by which you can predict how they *will* react . . . if they ever do have to vote on it."

Again Bookbinder had the sharp sense of unreality. Unreal people were being asked invented questions and a result came out on green, white-lined paper . . . and when you got around to the real people six months later with the real questions they would act the way the computer had said they would.

They walked quickly along the Avenue, Bookbinder's pace acquired long ago and maintained over the years. Today he felt it a bit too much and so he increased it, refusing to believe his body had weakened.

"Book, Dr. Devlin uses Cotter's stuff and Simulations' stuff, but she also uses the information from the psychoanalysts and the psychiatrists," Mad said.

"The psychiatrists' material is more disorganized and, compared to Simulations Enterprises, chaotic, but it does give some insights into individual motivation which Simulations Enterprises can't provide," Dr. Devlin said.

They walked for a few more blocks. Bookbinder didn't want to hear any more. He had made up his mind. He'd let a detailed description of the psychiatrists' part in all this wait for another time.

"I'd like you to work with us, Dr. Devlin," Bookbinder said, "on this Thatch matter." They were at the office door. "Work out the financial details with Mad." He disappeared into the building without shaking hands, without saying good-by, almost as if he were in flight.

8

Kelly felt the thin layer of sweat build up between the flesh of his ear and the phone. He delighted in the sheer sensuous pleasure of the phone, a few ounces of black plastic, smooth and molded to the hand, that plugged him into the world. He thought of the marvelous mechanisms which received and translated the dialings, the thick trunk lines running out of New York and Washington and Chicago, thinning out into smaller lines and finally becoming merely the single strand which led to the ear of the person you wanted.

Ten per cent of phone subscribers were unlisted. In New York that meant over one million unlisted phones. Part of it is vanity, but a good part of it is fear, Kelly thought. Most people were fearful of their phones, afraid of what dreadful word might come through the mechanism. But Kelly loved his telephone the way a rifleman loves his weapon.

"Does Book have anybody?" Kelly said. It was too brusque, a discourtesy which could cost the National Committee $50,000, but this was the third phone call he had received from Levi in two weeks.

"What do you think about this fellow Thatch?" Levi asked.

"That character who built the bridge in India or someplace?"

Levi controlled his irritation. Kelly knew damned well who Thatch was. They'd talked about him only a few days before. But this was Kelly's way.

"Do you think it's possible to take Thatch and make him a Presidential candidate?" Levi asked.

"We did it with Willkie. The Democrats did it with Stevenson. But it's tough. Instant candidates don't come easy."

"You mean he would need money and important backers?" Levi said.

Kelly hated things put so flatly.

"That's what I mean."

They sat in the front room, not looking at the stacks of mail. They were having cocktails.

"The letters have dropped off a bit. Most of them want you to speak," Terry said. "Chambers of commerce, universities, Rotary clubs, American Legion posts. They all assume you are a conservative. They keep talking about 'debating with a liberal' or 'giving the conservative point of view.'"

"I'm not going to speak anywhere," Thatch said.

Terry saw his eyes glance at the stacks of letters. He was pleased, she knew. His pleasure made her a little afraid. She walked over and poured gin into her glass. She ignored Thatch's silence and recalled another time of much greater fear, when they had first met.

She remembered John coming into Santo Tomas in 1945 looking like a Greek god, only because he was not undernourished. She remembered his asking about his parents and not blinking when he was told they died of malnutrition.

And she remembered John taking her out of the camp into the still-smoking city and giving her a K-ration chocolate bar. She chewed at it for a few moments and then gulped down chunks of the rich matter. When she threw up she was horrified at the loss. She apologized and said she must look terrible and soap was a good thing . . . she could eat it or wash with it. John did not act puzzled. He knew she was begging for soap and the next time he brought two big bars of Ivory. He waited while she showered and then took her out of the camp.

"Someone said that no woman is as beautiful as when she is in mortal fear, terrible danger, or very very sick," John had said. "Nietzsche or Schopenhauer or someone. I don't remember. Anyway, you look beautiful. Skinny but beautiful."

In three years she had not had a compliment about her personal appearance. Everyone was too hungry, too desperate, too preoccupied with survival. And this big awkward man had found the only compliment which was believable.

She felt dizzy with her own prescience. She could feel everything, know everyone's motives, see strange things that the healthy rational mind did not see. This Thatch man was flawed. He hurts someplace. These things one learned in a prison camp. The camp first strips the fat off, then manners, then strength, then concern for others, and at last one dies. But if one lives the body becomes a kind of sensitive perceptor, marvelously attuned to what others feel and say. No one wastes energy speaking. One has to sense others' meanings.

He said her eyes were huge and beautiful and starved and her hair was very black and she was shapely. But it was just the padding of the suit, for she was bony.

She knew she had to protect herself against involvement. He was safe, he walked with a calm assurance; he did not have the disappearing quality which everyone else had, he was durable. He would last. She looked at him and knew he clung to the earth, would not float away, would always be there. But it might be an illusion. Something bothered her eyes, but it was somehow inside her head; she hated all of her family for dying so quickly. Her fingers flicked across her eyes. Mommy had gone with malaria in Zamboanga seven years ago. Then Flora, her big kind sister, had wilted down into a walking skeleton and then a thin frame under the sheets and only her eyes glowed and when even they dimmed the Filipinos took the whole bed out, crying as they went. Her father, a slim nervous man, had snapped back at the Japanese when they came into Zamboanga and that night her friends told her he was dead.

This man would not be like that.

She told him her flaw very quickly, before he should find out from someone else. Life in the camp had gone well for a while. Then they had realized they were going to be starved to death. The Japanese guards knew, the prisoners knew, the Filipinos knew. None of them could avoid it. They all watched with fascination as the caloric arithmetic calculated in Tokyo was implemented in Manila.

The Filipinos could help only their friends. Some had been shot sneaking rice in to their friends and their blood leaked from their bodies and flies gathered and the guards watched, the whole thing forever brilliant in the floodlight instantly trained on any break in the fence.

"I was the first one who put out for the Japanese," she said as they walked down the smoking street.

"Put out?" Thatch said, as if it were a joke.

"Put out. With one of the Japanese guards," she went on. She glanced at the familiar but ruined buildings. "The Japs had food and chocolate and beer. We had only one thing to barter with. We women, I mean. I don't know what the men offered. But I was the first one."

"Was it . . . did they force you?" Thatch asked. "Christ, what I mean is did they hurt you?"

She did not even hesitate.

"No. They didn't force me. I approached one of them," she said. "Other people in the camp had things to trade. They were Americans and had prestige or they were rich Filipinos with family connections outside the camp. But a *mestiza* from Mindanao? I was alone. So I put out for a guard, the gentlest one. No, he never hurt me."

They walked a few blocks. A woman carrying a basket of books in her hand came out of the bowels of a building that was still smoking.

"But afterward, back in my bunk, I'd feel like a snail. Like I was slimy. And a slime that would not wash off. Maybe if I killed myself . . ."

"Don't talk like a nut," he said. He was final. The world was mending itself before her eyes.

She wavered with relief.

She looked sideways at the American. He looked straight ahead. He shrugged his shoulders, knowing she was looking at him.

"What do you want me to do?" he asked. "Run screaming through the streets?"

She started to say something, she could not remember what. He went on. "You wanted to tell someone? Isn't that right?"

She wavered slightly and his hand came under her elbow.

"And I happen not to care very much why you did it," Thatch said. "I am just pleased that you survived."

He said a lot more as they walked toward the waterfront.

They were on Dewey Boulevard. Manila Bay was going molten in the sunset and the triangle of a Moro boat was black and fast-moving. And she remembered the smells. The smell of the city's debris, the uncountable tons of fish scales and discarded bones, tar from the pilings of the waterfront, and the plankton and small fish and seaweed which were exposed to the sun by the falling tide. The odor from the big gray US Navy ships was heavy and rich. It was the smell of coffee, bacon, hot bread, roast beef. It was heavy enough to hear. By breathing she felt she could stay alive. She swayed and John held her steady. He had a brown bag of food which the ship's doctor had given him. He passed the bits to her slowly, insisting she chew everything thoroughly.

"You worry," she said—out of gratitude, relief, the cessation of pressure. "You worry very hard about a few things."

"I do," he said. "I worry about rage. It comes on me like an attack. Like an epileptic seizure, where the poor bastard writhes on the ground and bites his tongue." He waited as he unwrapped a small candy bar. "I think I might be crazy."

Then he told her, because it seemed like the natural thing to do.

It had happened at Stanford. He had never before associated with a group made up entirely of whites his own age. Always it had been mixtures of Indians, half-castes, Chinese, Filipinos, Africans . . . varying only when his father's mission was changed.

At Stanford everyone was white and they said things he did not quite understand. "Niggers have a funny smell," they said; Thatch thought they were joking and then realized they were not. "A good personality, that's what you got to have to get ahead," they said. "A loyal fraternity brother is the best friend you'll have in this world, Thatch," they said.

His mother had taught him by the Calvert method and he had never connected knowledge with personality or fraternity or color.

For a while he felt his vision was faulty. He had his eyes checked. Perfect. He had his hearing checked. Perfect. Once, after the fraternity brothers talked about miscegenation and "bad blood," he felt dizzy. He went to the health service again. His "kinesthetic sense" was perfect. Between himself and the others a haze grew and thickened so he felt impeded in his movements, grotesque, like a bear walking on its hind legs.

In his sophomore year his fraternity ticked him off to run for class vice-president. One of the dormitory boys from the "tribe," a Southern California Jew boy, was running for the office and the fraternity felt called upon to beat him.

Thatch memorized a speech. He got to the auditorium, looked down at the five hundred faces, and was struck by a sudden paralyzing fear. Somehow the class, mostly unknown to him, looked ominous. He glanced at the other candidates. The boy from the "tribe" had a tough assured smile on his face. The girls running for class secretary were chatting and laughing with one another . . . and the fear deepened.

It's in the bag, he told himself. That's what they said at the frat house. But he could not remember a word of the speech. A part of his brain had been seared, the words burned away. Phrases tumbled senselessly through his mind, odd phrases. . . . "A well-memorized speech will always return at the time it is needed," from a book by Dale Carnegie or someone. "Student self-government builds early character and preparation for later activity in politics," said a voice in a political-science class.

He heard his name spoken. He got up and walked woodenly to the podium. Now he waited for it to happen . . . for the synapses to relink, for the magic to work, for his tongue to talk. There was nothing in his head except the memory of a day . . . a day when the channel between Zamboanga and Basilan was a deep blue, ruffled by a slight wind which took the *caïque* along at over six knots and he and Joe Camote, a skinny Moro boy with long thin muscles, hauled in one fish after another. He smiled at the memory. The boat moved out of the lee and sea swells caught it, made the outrigger shiver. They came about and headed back.

Far away, as distant as a surf, he heard a strange sound. It was the sound of laughter. His eyes focused. The five hundred faces were contorted with an expression which must have been laughter . . . rows of white teeth, red faces, crew-cut heads, lipsticked mouths.

He stood smiling. And then he was not smiling. The faces before him suddenly had canine teeth, the red on the girls' lips was hardened blood, the sound was a hunting howl. He felt in mortal danger, felt a sense of sliding . . . he was going to pitch forward into the maw of faces. And they were laughing, but with a hyenalike quality. They were as deadly, as thin and hungry as dingo dogs. His body bent backward, his shoes tilting on their heels. He was falling backward. He came sharply to a dead balance. Then carefully, like a man running from a bull he does not want to provoke into charging, he moved across the stage. The howl deepened and he felt feet stamping in unison.

While he ran something inside his head, as loose as a ball of black mercury, took form: rage. He almost turned and ran back. Rage overcame fear. But then he realized how awful were the things he wanted to do to the crowd . . . rip, gouge, scream, make blood flow, dismember, wade through torn flesh.

He ran five miles. Panting like a dog, legs tired, heels moist in his shoes and the slow knowledge it was blood, lungs heaving, aware of passing the old Stanford barn, a violent stitch in his side, then the golf course and he could smell the wet night grass. He slowed his pace and swung his arms high. The sound, regular and clopping, was his feet on black asphalt. He could not have stopped if he wanted. He was a neutral observer of his own body, which had to sweat out some vile thing. Every bush, tree, plant, blade of grass, roadside pool had an odor, and he sucked in the air of these natural things. Sweat, welcome and hot, ran down his back.

The car followed him for several minutes. He was not aware of it, for he heard and felt only himself and his jarring contact with the earth. A voice spoke and he glanced sideways. A black car moved beside him and a big friendly face was saying something. Thatch could not hear the policeman. Thatch shook his head and trotted along.

The car suddenly pulled over in front of him. Thatch trotted up to it, put his hands against it and kept his feet pounding. Two policemen got out of the car and spoke, but he could not hear them. One of them opened the rear door. Thatch could see a wire screen, and the sound of a radio blared suddenly in his ears.

"Get in," a voice said and the elbow in his ribs told him he was spoken to.

"No. Not tonight, thanks," he said and kept jogging. The inside of the car, full of sound, with its wire coop was enough to make him dance backwards.

Two bodies nudged him simultaneously, pushed him toward the car. Thatch roared and struck back with both his hands, felt his elbows go into soft bellies. He turned as they came for him and tried to tell them why he did not want to get into the narrow noisy space, but they came swinging and he chopped at them, speaking all the time, begging them to let him jog along the road. But the noise of the radio and the gasping and the blows (he did not feel a blow, his body seemed narcotic) drowned his breath. He felt a row of teeth crumple under his fist, the snap of someone else's bones, his fists thudding into soft blue uniforms. He knew he was screaming with rage now, but he could not stop. He bounced off the car, felt the thin metal crunch, swung at the big targets. Then something hard caught him on the side of the head and he knew it was final even before the blackness came.

The next morning he was in an institution and his body hurt. He talked to an endless series of faces. The last one, a tired man who identified himself as a psychiatrist, was helpful. He told

Thatch he could not go back to Stanford but that he was not really sick. Rest, the psychiatrist said. And exercise.

"So I spent a year in a mental hospital," Thatch had told an emaciated Filipino girl that day in 1945. "They never gave me a diagnosis. I don't believe they were positive themselves what it was. But they assured me I had a potential."

Now Terry looked over her martini glass at Thatch. In all the years they had been married he has never spoken before a crowd . . . until the time on the bridge.

"I'd like another drink, John," Terry said. She was surprised.

"The lady is a lush," Thatch said. "Me too."

He walked over and put ice cubes in the glasses.

It was preposterous that a childish fear of crowds could linger still in a man so strong. Yet she hoped that it was so. She hoped that it was so!

"Oscar? Fella, it's good talking to you," Kelly said. "How goes the money-raising?"

Kelly did not listen to what Oscar said. No one ever raised as much money as they anticipated on a fund-raising trip. But it didn't hurt to keep them worried.

"No, no. Don't take that attitude," Kelly said when the voice stopped. "We know it's tough." He hadn't listened to what Oscar said, but it was said in a whining voice. So he knew the money-raising was not going well. "How did the sale of an ambassador-ship go?"

The voice picked up enthusiasm. Kelly listened.

"No, Oscar," Kelly interrupted. "Don't ever let them bargain with you. This crap about five thousand now if they get the Court of St. James's in 1964 is dangerous. Remember how Bobby Kennedy handled that Democratic Convention in 1960. He just told everyone 'You're for us for just one reason: we're going to win.' Well, that's what you've got to do. Make 'em believe victory is inevitable and they'd better be with us—and *now*. Not the day after the election, but *now*."

He heard the voice wheedle on for a few moments.

"Oscar, I've got a little job for you," Kelly broke in. For jobs like this he wished he had a quill pen, heavy parchment paper, a shaker of sand, and a black messenger. "Run up to San Francisco and check on a guy called John Thatch. T-H-A-T-C-H. That's right. Lives someplace on the Peninsula."

The voice broke in.

"You used to be a gumshoe," Kelly said patiently. "You know the kind of thing I want. Women, drinking, college record, source of income, any convictions, general reputation, what kind of wife, how many kids."

He paused and listened. He laughed.

"Of course you can do it on an all-expenses rather than per-diem basis, you damned fool," Kelly said. "Just make sure you send the expense account to me at my home. Also a single and only copy of the report. No carbons."

He hung up. He was disgusted for a moment. Someday it would not be like this. Someday he would operate in a manner appropriate to the Republic. Then his language would revert and he would be . . . he sought for the word . . . he would be *gracious.*

Five days later Oscar's report on Thatch arrived, along with a package, special delivery, airmail and registered for Kelly. The package was four inches thick and the shape of a large book.

Kelly read the report before he opened the package. He had his secretary duplicate a paragraph and sent it along to Bookbinder.

The paragraph said: "Thatch's competition such as Bechtel Corp. and Utah Construction rate him as one of the toughest negotiators in the business. He appears, however, only infrequently at negotiations, usually making his views known through a half-dozen assistants thoroughly familiar with his views and always in telephone contact with Thatch. His own organization is said to be efficiently run. Mostly an overseas business. Thatch seems to operate a lot by telephone from his home. Likes to drop into headquarters at night and run over files, reports, etc. Well liked by his executives, who say he gives them complete instructions and then turns them loose and judges only by results. They seem not to resent his absences. Thatch spends approximately half of his time traveling to inspect overseas projects. Difficult to get accurate figures on gross business as firm is not public but would estimate $20 million per year for last four years and growing steadily."

Kelly opened the package. Several hundred pages of cheap old paper, waterstains on many of the pages, gave off a musty tropical odor. The pages were written in longhand and at the top of each page was a date and the words *S. T. Camp.* It was a diary, kept obviously by a woman.

Oscar had inserted markers in five different pages. Kelly opened the diary to the first marker. He read it once. Then he went back and read it more slowly. A spot of nausea started in his stomach and spread rapidly.

He closed the diary, rewrapped it and put it in the big old-fashioned safe in his office. He sat down and wrote a telegram to Oscar:

IF ANY OTHER COPIES DIARY BUY THEM. CHECK WITH ME IF PRICE GETS TOO HIGH. MENTION TO NO ONE. REPEAT NO ONE. MOVE FAST. KELLY.

Three hours later he had a reply:

YOUR COPY ONLY ONE. PROCURED UNDER CIRCUMSTANCES WHICH MADE DUPLICATION IMPOSSIBLE. WRITER LONG DEAD. OSCAR.

He held the wire in his hand and looked at his safe. He hoped that he would never have to take that diary out and look at it again. Bert Kelly was a decent man. There was no reason why he should even bother Bookbinder and Levi about it. The information would remain his alone.

9

There was no direct outside phone line to the Thatch house. All calls came to the Company switchboard and only those from personal friends or from a small number of Thatch's executives were passed through. He had a reputation for being very abrupt and curt on the phone.

"Thatch, it's Tom Carroll," the voice said. Carroll was combination general manager, public relations, and troubleshooter. He was tough and independent and consulted Thatch only a few times a month. Every time he made a mistake he sent Thatch a short unapologetic memo on the matter. There were not many such memos. "I'll make it quick. Two things. A guy named Bookbinder from New York is trying to get you."

"The name's familiar," Thatch said. "What does he do?"

"He's a lawyer with a big practice, a lot of it in South America. Wealthy, dabbles in politics, had a number of appointments on commissions and special investigations."

"What does he want from me?"

"He won't say and he's not the kind of a guy you play footsie with. Call him." Carroll gave Thatch the New York number.

"Second item?" Thatch asked.

"It's the Zamboanga cement-factory contract. We've got the skeleton of the building completed and it's ready to take the machinery from Japan. But we're having a hell of a time on the pier. Crane keeps breaking down; supplies don't arrive; and yesterday an underwater explosion threw the pile driver off the pier."

"You mean someone is sabotaging the job?"

"That's what I mean. Today I got a cable from Ferguson and he said the pile driver was in fifteen feet of water. None of the workers will touch it. He wants you to come and have a look. If we don't get that pier finished, we're going to start paying out a penalty of a couple thousand dollars a week."

"You really think it might be Huks?" Thatch said.

"Sounds crazy; everyone thought the movement was broken up for good. But you hear rumors of stragglers holding out in the hills, waiting for aid from mainland China. I'd feel better if you took a look."

"Okay, Tom. Terry and I will go out. Have the office get us space on a flight leaving tomorrow. We'll fly right to Manila and take PAL to Cebu City. Ferguson can meet us there with the company plane."

Thatch put the phone down and walked into the kitchen. Terry was sitting on a stool gossiping with the old Filipina cook. They spoke Tagalog—precisely the way women gossiped in the Philippines . . . endlessly, in a circle, coming to no conclusions, careful never to offend anyone. Gossip was to be taken seriously. Thatch listened for a moment and realized that the subject was the merits of freeways in and out of San Francisco.

"They build only to take the bribes," the cook said in her assured voice. "It is always that way with politicians. The freeways will collapse from the overload. It is common knowledge."

Terry clucked her outrage.

"Pardon, pardon the interruption of your important business," Thatch said in Tagalog. "But if you wish to go to Zamboanga you must begin to prepare at once."

Terry swung around, her face delighted.

"When do we go?" she asked.

"Tomorrow. I won't know the flight until later today."

Terry came to him with that exciting walk. It was the walk of the very young and Thatch marveled that she was old enough to have two sons in high school.

"All right, stop there," he said in English. "I have to make a phone call. Then I'll come up and help you pack."

She walked by him without replying, a slow smile on her lips. He realized she hadn't smiled that way in weeks.

In five minutes he was talking to Mr. Bookbinder in New York.

"Mr. Thatch, I won't take much of your time," Bookbinder said. "I have been for years very much interested in politics . . . all kinds. It's a hobby or a curse or a duty depending on how you look at it. This year I happen to think that the Republican Party needs some fresh ideas." The educated persuasive voice rumbled on. Thatch had been standing. Now he sat. He listened to the voice and he saw the stacks of letters.

"Are you sure you have the right man? I've never been active in politics. Maybe you're looking for another John Thatch."

"I've got the right one," Bookbinder said. "One reason I'm talking to you is because you haven't been in politics. But your remarkable performance on that India-Pakistan bridge gave you a powerful and potentially persuasive public image—"

"Mr. Bookbinder," Thatch cut in. "I think you misunderstand the situation. That bridge thing was a flash in the pan. It produced a lot of letters and publicity but it was just a freak."

"Not quite a freak," Bookbinder contradicted him easily and

with command. "Somehow that episode touched a nerve in millions of Americans."

Thatch was irritated. But Carroll had said this Bookbinder character was responsible, so he listened.

"My colleagues tell me that the public reaction to you is quite unprecedented in polling history. For a person who is not a political figure to generate such a reaction is unique. One pollster, a Dr. Cotter, after examining the interviewers' questionnaires, told me he believed your decisiveness at the bridge was very reassuring to many Americans. Almost at once you have become a figure like Lindbergh in 1927 . . ."

"Interesting," Thatch said. He wanted to end the conversation.

"No, you don't find it interesting. Not yet," Bookbinder said. "But if you happen to be in New York, we'd like to pick your brain for ideas. We need some this year."

Thatch worked over the Zamboanga specifications and glanced through the letters. It was not a big project, but it could be expensive if they didn't get the machinery in on time. It seemed to him impossible that the Huks could actually be operating again.

He called Tom Carroll.

"Tom, I'm going to try and handle the Zamboanga situation by seeing the Philippines Ambassador in Washington," he said. "It might just be a local political upset or some crackpot."

"It didn't sound that way in Ferguson's cable," Carroll said.

"Ferguson has always stayed away from politics. The Ambassador could make a call to see if someone is looking for a little squeeze . . ." He was for some reason not completely happy with his reasoning, but it was a long trip to the Philippines. "Get tickets for us, will you, Tom? To Washington but route us through New York."

"We'll make this short, Terry," Thatch said as they went into Bookbinder's office building. It was on lower Wall Street where the powerful upward thrust of the buildings on either side of the narrow street never failed to excite Thatch. "They want to talk over some ideas." It sounded unreal to his own ears so he added, "Foreign policy, I guess."

"Are you a foreign-policy expert these days?" Terry said, smiling.

"Everybody is, so I'll thank you not to run down my reputation."

"Speak to them in Tagalog. Tell them a dirty joke . . . not too dirty . . . and say it's an old proverb and—"

He swore at her in Tagalog and ended with the proverb that too much talking makes a woman ugly.

Bookbinder's secretary took them into a large elegant study. A big, gray man, confident and at ease, got to his feet. This was Bookbinder. He introduced them to an older man named Levi, a young man named Curver, and a woman in a severely tailored suit named Dr. Devlin.

"Thank you for coming, Mr. Thatch," Bookbinder said.

"I was on my way to Washington anyway," Thatch said quickly.

"We're seeing a lot of people, Mr. Thatch, trying to gather some ideas that might go into the Republican foreign-policy platform at the Convention," Bookbinder said. "Mr. Levi and I have served on the foreign-policy committee before and we probably will next year. We hoped that with your experience overseas you might give us some fresh leads."

"I'm no expert, but I've spent a lot of time overseas," Thatch said. "Don't expect much, Mr. Bookbinder."

"We're pretty casual around here . . . would you mind if we called you by your first name or your nickname or whatever your friends call you?" Bookbinder asked.

"Not at all. Everyone calls me Thatch. It's just an accident. *Thatch* doesn't sound like a real name in India where I was raised, so the kids called me that and it stuck, so now my family name is my nickname."

"My last name and nickname are also the same," Levi said. "But for quite a different reason. My father was infatuated with the names of Rattigan and Pilsener, a famous brewery. It was spelled out in big elegant gold letters over every saloon. So I was named Rattigan Pilsener Levi."

"Mr. Madison Curver we call Mad, for several reasons,"

Bookbinder said. "Dr. Devlin we call Dr. Devlin. It gives class to the place."

Thatch smiled. He liked Bookbinder. The man was direct and quick and Thatch liked the way he so calmly accepted the elegance of his own offices.

"Dr. Devlin is a behavioral scientist," Curver said. "You can ask her later what that means."

"Thatch, what's going to happen in Viet Nam?" Bookbinder asked.

Now it had started, Curver thought. He settled down, watching Thatch.

"We're going to lose Viet Nam, Laos, Cambodia, Thailand, and probably Malaya," Thatch said.

"Why?" Levi asked.

"Because the only kind of warfare that will work out there is guerrilla warfare. We're not geared for it," Thatch said.

"What about the Special Forces Kennedy has been pushing?"

"You have to understand Asia. First, the Special Forces are trained only in military combat. That's not what counts in Asia. Mao Tse-tung knew that. What you need is propaganda and political agents out in front of the troops. We don't have them. The Vietnamese don't. So every village in Viet Nam, and most of Southeast Asia, is dominated by the Communists. The Special Forces may win a lot of battles, but they'll lose the war."

"But with those helicopters and control of the air and superior supplies we ought—"

"To land right on our back. Wars are won inside the heads of people. We don't understand that yet. Those helicopters go in dropping napalm and napalm is funny . . . it can't tell the difference between a Viet Cong and a six-year-old girl. So it burns them both up." Thatch paused. He stood up. His eyes, which had been calm and neutral, were now glittering. Terry watched him with surprise.

"What would you do about it?" Levi asked.

"I would send out Vietnamese who understood politics and get one of them into each village and if we *had* to drop napalm he would talk to the people and explain why," Thatch said. "And I'd teach Americans a bit of the language . . . enough so they could say 'thank you' and 'I wish to pay for this rice you are giving me.' And I'd tell them to stop kicking in the ribs of every skinny kid who is hiding in the reeds because he doesn't want to get killed. Also, I'd sit down with the Vietnamese military people and say 'Boys, the time has come. The Mickey Mouse war is over. Go out there and lead your men or we're getting out. Stop spending all your time in Saigon trying to get in on the next *coup*. Or we're leaving.' Levi, I don't like losing Americans out there, but I'm prepared to if the Viets see it as *their* war."

Thatch leaned back against the cold fireplace, looked out the window for a moment and then closed his eyes.

Jesus, he's got it, Curver thought. He's got whatever that thing called *charisma* is. He's sure. He's confident. He's got presence. Curver tried to suppress his own sense of excitement. He watched Thatch stretch his arms out on the mantle. Thatch's big chest heaved.

"Would you say that publicly?" Bookbinder asked.

Thatch weaved, like a boxer taking a punch on his shoulder. He hummed. He looked at Bookbinder and grinned.

"No," he finally said.

"Why?" Bookbinder asked.

"Because I'm not in politics." Thatch paused and then went on. "Here's another thing nobody'd listen to. I'd put a television set in each village with a hand-operated generator and make sure it got one station: Saigon. Then the central government would have a chance of getting to its own people. During the day you could use it for teaching. It would give the Vietnamese a sense of being *somebody*, a nation."

He paused. Curver had the impression of anger which was under strong control. He looked at Dr. Devlin. She was staring at Thatch. Thatch stretched and then quickly socked one fist into the palm of the other hand. It made a sharp popping noise.

"Those people have suffered out there," Thatch said. "Suffered so long and so much and for no purpose that they don't believe in anything. I knew a Viet who came to the States and educated himself to be a surgeon, a good one. For ten years the French wouldn't give him a certificate. After the Communists cut off one hand during the fighting in fifty-four, he learned to operate with one hand. Then the Viet Cong caught him operating in a village and shot him in a leg which he amputated himself. And now he is in a prison in Saigon because one of the

Nus doesn't like him . . . but he doesn't know which one or for what reasons."

Thatch snapped his fingers, calling himself back to attention. "About the TV sets. It sounds like a crazy proposal, but it would work and it wouldn't cost much. And if the Viet Cong shot up the TV sets they would alienate every peasant in the country. And if they merely captured them they would be listening to our side of the mess."

"Do you think there is any chance of holding continental Southeast Asia?" Bookbinder asked.

"Not much. Not until we start to propagandize on a big scale. And that's what it is, propaganda, though some people don't like the word. But no one in Washington is interested."

He paused again. He seemed to be thinking, hard, unaware of the others in the room. He bit his lower lip. The silence grew thick.

"What do you think about the integration problem?" Levi asked in a voice so soft it barely carried across the room.

Thatch slowly turned and looked at Levi. "I don't know much about it," Thatch said. He was puzzled. "You mean the Negro thing?"

"Yes."

"I guess I think part of America is crazy. I've lived overseas for so long that it doesn't touch me. Oh, maybe once in a while. I had a Filipino pile driver who got paid less than the American journeyman pile drivers on the job so I told Manila to pay him the American scale."

"What did Manila say?" Levi asked.

"They sent me around to someone in the American Embassy," Thatch said. He hesitated, put his hands in his pockets; his voice became softer. Curver made some quick notes in his heavy cabalistic scrawl. "Some man behind a desk said I couldn't pay 'colored men' the same rate as white."

He looked at Terry. She smiled, but he could see she was nervous. Thatch plunged on.

"I—uh—fingered his necktie, I guess, and I swore and told him a few things about color and then dropped him on the desk and left," Thatch said. He grinned, shaking his head. "I took the workers out on strike and in three days we got permission to pay the Filipino what we paid the Americans."

"We have not been invited to an Embassy party since," Terry said.

Thatch seemed relaxed, as if over some obstacle. He spoke easily.

"Well, I don't give a damn about the color or race or religion or shape or ideology of a pile driver," Thatch said. "I just ask that he be a good pile driver. Levi, you know it as well as I do, excellence is color-blind. Also, excellence is religion-blind."

"I wish everybody agreed with you," Levi said.

"You're a Jew, aren't you?" Thatch asked. He went on without waiting for an answer. "You believe there has been a conspiracy against you and your people and there may have been. Yeh, I suppose there was. In some places still is. But your problems will be over when a Jew who is ten feet tall, speaks twenty languages, and is as handsome as a Greek god applies for a job as a pile driver and the competition is an ugly, bigoted, snotty little Limey . . . who happens to be just a little bit better pile driver. And the Limey gets the job."

Levi looked quietly at Thatch, his lean head unmoving. He drew himself up out of his chair, uncoiling like a crane, and walked toward Thatch.

Slowly his hand came out. He reached for Thatch's elbow and his long thin fingers gripped tight.

"You are a man with a good heart," Levi said. "And a great deal of experience."

The two men looked to Curver like art forms demonstrating two different physiques and metabolisms: Thatch big and muscular and moving constantly, Levi thin and stationary and intent on conserving every ounce of strength.

"Would you give a Negro a job if he were as qualified as a white man?" Bookbinder asked.

Thatch slapped his hand against his thigh impatiently. Then he laughed.

"Book, I've slept, eaten, fought, and worked with men who were every color from shark-belly white to a black so deep it was purple," Thatch said. "I've only looked for one thing: competence. And I've found it in men of every color, just like I've found crooks come in every color."

"Don't you think we ought to be giving some special attention to the Negro here in the United States?" Levi asked.

"Special attention? I don't know just what that means," Thatch said. "If it means special attention just because he's a Negro I'd be opposed. The moment a man feels he is being treated as a member of a group instead of being treated as himself that's the moment something goes out of him. That's why I hate discrimination. Take the farmers. They want special attention and they get it." Thatch stopped for a moment and roared. "Oh, good God, the farmers. They are all so big on free enterprise. They are buccaneers and they want to do it on their own. Get socialism out of farming, give the land and its produce back to us, let us be Americans like Daniel Boone, let us go bankrupt if we can't cut the mustard, they say. Right?"

"That is what they say," Bookbinder said.

"And then they all vote for higher government subsidies and the country is up to here in warehouses full of stuff that these big buccaneers can't sell and they go crying to Congress to help them keep enterprise free.

"Levi, Marx never dreamed of a day when farmers could just file . . . now remember this . . . just file a form saying they would *not* produce a crop and automatically get a check from the government. That, good friend, is the living end: grave free enterprise driving up to their banks and cashing government checks for a good many thousand dollars because they promise to produce nothing."

Curver watched the look of guarded admiration grow on Levi's face.

"We should be going, John," Terry said. "These people have work to do."

Thatch blinked. Curver noted it and so did Dr. Devlin. He looked around the room as if seeing it for the first time. A flush started on his neck.

"I've talked a lot," he said. "I'm sorry I took so much time. I wandered all over the place. But I told you I'm no professional. I was just spouting off."

Curver watched closely, not sure what he was seeing. Thatch was, in the passage of a few seconds, awkward and shambling; his speech commonplace, the force gone from his voice.

Everyone stood up. Bookbinder and Levi walked out to the elevator with Thatch and Terry.

"This was very helpful to us," Bookbinder said. "I don't give out compliments easily, but this is one of the most exciting sessions we have had."

"I wonder if you would consider giving a talk to a group of people interested in politics but not experts or professionals," Levi said. "I would like to see how they react to your ideas."

"Call me in Washington about it," Thatch said. "We're at the Mayflower. I've never given a public speech."

"While you're in Washington, you might look up Bert Kelly at National Committee headquarters," Bookbinder said. "He's a pro who's also a statesman and he'd be interested in your ideas."

As Bookbinder and Levi walked back to the office Bookbinder said, "Do you really think he believes he has never given a public speech? What was that thing on the bridge?"

"He is a complex man," Levi said, "but I like him. So do you."

Bookbinder was alone in his study. He was tired. He would have liked to nap but was sure he could not.

Thatch excited him. The man was shrewder than he had expected and more tightly wound.

I will tell him about the political virus the next time, Bookbinder said to himself. He was confident that there would be a next time.

He had started the theory of political virus as a joke. Then, over the years, it had hardened into a private conviction that he took quite seriously.

He had seen men venture casually into politics, run for minor office and for various motives: publicity, the urging of friends, some notion of reform, a whim. Then the virus struck. A doctor with a $150,000 practice ran for Congress and won once and then lost and ran again and again and lost each time . . . but still wandered, now penniless, over the political landscape with the assurance he would win. A flourishing lawyer ran for a county central-committee position, won it, and disappeared into the dusty halls of courthouses and political rallies and frantic organizing and never again practiced law, sure in his heart that he would go to Congress some day. Some men, a few, cut into politics like a knife into cheese . . . with brittle determination and glittering mind and utter determination and made it.

But the casualty rate was high and the victims were horribly maimed. Puffed and fat, bitter, high on divorces and low on income, professionally smooth, internally shaking . . . the casualties circled the old places of glittering power, still in a fever. They would be back, they would find the hidden routes, they would hear again the masses howling for the hero denied them.

The virus made good men say evil things and evil men say good things and wives go hysterical and, after a victory, made impotent men walk like studs through the land. The disease was marked by a huge intake of alcohol and a great output of idealism. Parochial men, who ran a mean country store, became generous with a four-billion-dollar foreign-aid bill. Savage self-made millionaires were possessed by a desire to give milk to starving children in South America. Liberals, coming in like sheep full of pious bleatings, became hard-eyed and mean and cleverly gutted the very things they came to Washington to accomplish. They did it for a simple and awesome reason—they wanted to remain close to power. The marble halls, the rollcalls, the sweet eye of the television camera, the sound of applause, the call to the White House, the $100-a-plate dinner where everyone stood up and wept, the hard sharp deal in the caucus, the phone calls from the White House, the marvelous sense of looking a lobbyist in the eye over an expensive dinner and saying *no*, the intoxicating euphoria of the conventions, the feel in the fingers of the parchment invitation to the Indonesian Embassy dinner.

Bookbinder felt a moment of self-pity. All of these luxurious and prideful things he had not wanted. He had wanted only to study and persuade and labor and vote on the numbered bills which made his country great. And then he knew he was lying to himself. He wanted the power and he wanted all the rest of it, too. But with him the fever had run its course.

Curver took Dr. Devlin into his office, shut the door, and told his secretary to hold calls.

"Let's get it down systematically, Mad," Dr. Devlin said. She brought out a notebook. "Initial impressions are the best in an unstructured situation."

"Don't be heavy-handed, my dear Doctor," Curver said. And

I'm not excited, he told himself. "First, can he be persuaded to run?"

"Absolutely. I took some Birdwhistell notations on him when Book asked if he would make a public statement," Dr. Devlin said. Birdwhistell, she had explained, was a linguist who had made a study of people's gestures and the relationship of those gestures to what the people were saying. Often he found that the speaker's involuntary gestures precisely contradicted his words. Dev spread her notebook out and Curver looked at the line of words and symbols.

"Thatch made one of the most drastic metaincongruences I've ever seen. At exactly the time he was saying he was *not* in politics his posture indicated that he was experiencing an extreme excitement with overtones of definite interest."

"Okay. You're the expert. But if he does run, he's going to be hard to handle. He gets wound up, abstracted, lost in his own thoughts. My guess is that he is mildly paranoid . . . which is going to make him hard to control."

Dr. Devlin glanced down her notes. She reached in her brief case and took out another notebook.

"Mad, you're right about the paranoia," she said. "I watched the kinescopes of the bridge episode eight times. He followed almost exactly the Cantril pattern for the agitator: he scared them over the collapse of old norms, then suggested how to satisfy their real needs . . . finish the bridge and avoid bloodshed. He really was masterful." She leaned forward earnestly. "He gave those miserable people a sense that they could control their own destiny and then, when they were sighing with ecstasy he holds out a promise for the future. It was too perfect to have been conscious, Mad. The guy is a walking paranoid," she paused and laughed, "but no more than most of the people in Congress."

"He's already got Levi strong for him," Curver said.

Dr. Devlin said, "That thing about taking the miserable Limey over the heroic Jew was just about as flattering to Levi as you could get. And Thatch did it all intuitively. He sensed that the Jew has arrived, no longer feels defensive, and hates condescension. If he can do that kind of thing before an audience there might be no stopping him."

"All right, we've agreed that our candidate is a walking paranoid with great personal appeal, that Levi likes him, and that he can make a hell of a speech. But we have to go to Bookbinder with a bit more. For example, how do we get Thatch to run?"

Dr. Devlin drew a few lines on an empty page of her notebook. She glanced at Curver, then along the rows of lawbooks.

"Mad, there's something about Thatch I don't quite get," she said. "It's an intimation, a kind of suggestion. That's not very scientific, but I feel it. It's like he is very wary of exposing himself. As if he had secrets he was afraid of. It could be anything. But we ought to tell Bookbinder to push him about a public speech. Then we'll see how he really performs. This tendency to draw back has to be examined."

"That will be tough," Curver said. "Book hates to push people."

"Mad, it's important. For two reasons. First, we have to see how stable Thatch really is. Second, I'm sure he won't run under the normal circumstances. There is something about politics he doesn't like or is frightened of. But he is fascinated by his ability to dominate people by words . . . and he hasn't done much of it. I watched his wife and she was as surprised as anyone else in the room. But he won't run for President in the normal way of primaries and politicking. He will have to believe he has been 'called.' "

"No one 'calls' anyone in American politics any more," Curver said. "Rockefeller and Goldwater and Nixon are all out running and spending money and building organizations. If Thatch has to wait for a call it will be a long cold wait."

Dr. Devlin scribbled a few words down on her notebook.

"I guarantee you that even Kennedy thought his victory in 1960 was just a call from the people and forgot completely what kind of machine Bobby had working for him," Dr. Devlin said.

"All right," Curver said slowly, thinking aloud. "Book has to get Thatch to make a speech. And it must be a big success. If we have to 'persuade' him to run, a good rousing reaction to a speech might help some. Just the right audience, though. A group he respects and one which will probably like his kind of approach."

"And also a group which the potential delegates to the Republican Convention will respect," Dr. Devlin added. "Not a 4-H convention."

Curver looked at her and grinned.

"You really are becoming very political," he said. "What we'll do is a simulation of the convention delegates first and then just stick in a Fortran instruction for the profession they most admire. And if they all love different professions we pack our bags and go home."

"They'll be in agreement," Dr. Devlin said quietly. She was up and packing her brief case.

The report came back a few days later. On the first page it said "Copy #1 of the Confidential Report Prepared for Madison Curver, Esq. Four other copies of this report exist. They are in our security files and will not be released without client's consent."

Curver read it carefully. He felt the excitement rise. He put through a call to Dr. Devlin.

"Dev, I got the report from Simulations Enterprises. It's going to be easier than we thought. The average delegate is white, Protestant, around mid-fifties, high SES, college-educated. We knew all that. But the issues on which the delegates can be swayed don't have the remotest connection with what Gallup and Roper report about the average voter. The Republican delegates are most worried about income taxes, the possibility that medicine might be socialized, knuckling under to the Communists, keeping peace, a domestic Communist conspiracy. The professional group they most respect are doctors. Their idea of a winner is someone who can match Kennedy's flair . . . young, with a pretty wife, energetic, has popular appeal. Most of them don't personally care for Goldwater, but think he has 'flair.' "

"That makes it simple," Dr. Devlin said. "Let's get Thatch to speak to a convention of doctors. Bookbinder should be able to arrange it."

Thatch looked at the chaotic office, the massive lunch tray, the bottles of cold beer beaded with sweat. It made it easier not to look at the strange little man behind the desk.

Why do I think "little man," Thatch thought? He must weigh 250 pounds. There was something eerie about the man's physique, an odd asymmetry of bone and flesh which made Thatch think a smaller man lurked inside the bag of skin. Kelly's laugh was appropriately huge, but his hands were small. He kept them below the table.

"You talked to Bookbinder, eh?" Kelly said from behind his

sandwich of pumpernickel, liverwurst, Italian salami, Bermuda onion, mayonnaise, and Polish ham.

"Yes, I saw him in New York."

"He's a good man. Honest. Once someone said at a convention 'Book, you're too damned honest,' and the man may have been right. Have a sandwich?" He disengaged a hand and waved toward the tray.

"Ate late, thanks."

"You interested in politics?"

"No. Except in a very general way," Thatch said.

Kelly's head lifted, the teeth worked away at the sandwich. There was no surprise in his eyes. He merely stared at Thatch.

"I'm an engineer, a construction man."

Kelly's delicate fingers hesitated, the last bits of meat and bread at his mouth.

"Hoover was an engineer," Kelly said. He picked up a bottle of beer. "Engineers and generals are often intrigued with politics. They yearn to make politics as orderly and neat and manageable as the building of a bridge or the maneuvering of a regiment of soldiers. They hate the disorder of politics . . . and they can't keep their hands off disorder. They want to rush in and set things straight."

"Well, here's one engineer that doesn't want to get into politics," Thatch said. Irritation stirred in him. "But I thought I'd like to do something for the country, for the Party perhaps, if I can."

"Thatch, you're a curiosity. Like some kook that flew in the Lafayette Escadrille, made a million bucks, went over Niagara in a barrel, and then married Elizabeth Taylor with Burton panting on the sidelines. You've got a reputation, but a very peculiar one. You're not political."

Thatch did not know whether to be angry at the man or to laugh. "And you, Mr. Kelly, what's your role?"

"First, I'm a servant of the National Committee. In that capacity I'm neutral. Secondly, nobody believes that and they are right. The whole damned Committee is looking for someone who can win."

"Have you got a winner yet?"

The green bottle tilted up, caught the yellow sunlight, glittered in the man's hand. The eyes above the bottle were puckered with pleasure. Thatch knew this pleasure, this sense of anticipation, this involvement. He had seen it in others. Where the hell? He could not recall, but it was Oriental, something from Asia. With a sudden insight he knew what could buy Kelly's knowledge and ability: success.

"It's very unlikely that anyone can beat the President."

"Why?"

"I won't bother you with details. But the incumbent has a lot going for him. Others can tell you what it is." Kelly stopped and looked immensely bored.

"Thanks for your time," Thatch said. He stood up, walked over toward the door, picked up his brief case and, just as he reached for his hat, paused.

"If you come back I'll want some information," Kelly was saying. First, a very complete biography of yourself and your wife, including anything which might embarrass you or the Party if it were printed in the papers. Second, the amount of money you can afford to spend before, I repeat, before the Republican Convention. Third, how much money your friends will spend for you before the Convention. And remember that none of it is tax-free."

"I don't have many friends."

"Good. Maybe that means you don't have many enemies," Kelly said. "In any case look around at the prominent candidates. Almost all of them are millionaires. Nixon is the exception. These are determined and skilled men with the resources to assemble a staff, hire PR men, buy television time, charter an airplane— two, three airplanes. The day of the poor but worthy candidate went out about the time radio was invented."

"Would that money buy you?" Thatch wanted to insult the little bastard.

Kelly laughed. For the first time it was a small laugh. It sounded authentic.

"Thatch, I already have money, a lot of it. All inherited. Didn't earn a dime myself. No one could buy me for all the money in Fort Knox. I might work for a man, but it would be for free. I'm the cheapest thing in politics and, with all undue modesty, one of the rarest."

"So Bookbinder said."

"Thatch," Kelly drew out the pause, "they've got you. You're running already."

Thatch's big head snapped back and he laughed hard and, Kelly saw, honestly. He was really amused.

"Since I'm running already, do I have a chance?"

The two men looked at each other.

"For the nomination? A chance, yes."

"And the election?"

"I don't think you've got a goddam chance."

"Thank you," Thatch said and left.

Kelly, his physiology begging for nourishment, refused to make another sandwich. He eyed the green bottle like a talisman, an eye into the future.

Thatch had left, but in Kelly's mind he stood there still in the door—large, young (forty-eight?), handsome if you liked irregular features, tough, smart, self-made, independent, rich (amend that: medium-rich). He was the natural child of a *Time* cover story and a CBS documentary, yesterday's hero and tomorrow's nonentity. Thatch? John Thatch? The name is familiar but I can't seem to place him.

His qualifications for sacrificial lamb were superb.

10

It was a mistake, Thatch thought, as he looked down the head table with its vases of flowers, its place cards, the gleaming black podium, the glasses of water, the long row of coffee cups. He did not bother to look up at the ranks of tables in front of him.

"This is the biggest turnout ever for the internists' lunch," said the woman next to him. "I guess, in a way, Mr. Thatch, you are a kind of spokesman for the Free World. Really, I'm embarrassed, but it's the truth. You've been around the world and you stood up to the Communists in India and—well, it's a great honor."

Thatch looked down the table at Terry. She was sitting next to the president of the organization. She was scared, Thatch knew, because she kept looking out over the audience and then at him.

The doctors were enthusiastic and they talked a lot. In fact, their conversation before lunch had shredded most of what Thatch intended to tell them after dessert. It just would not make sense.

Thatch felt thick-tongued, a bit tired and, at the very edge of his consciousness, there was a sense of panic. He deliberately lifted his head and looked out over the ballroom. Faces. More faces than he had ever seen in one room. And all neatly adjusted in little tables of six or eight. Did he just imagine that they lifted their heads and sniffed the air and then, catching the scent, looked toward the speaker's table?

Ten more minutes. Fifteen at the most and he would have to start talking. He turned and looked closely at the mouth of the woman next to him. Slowly, like an acrobat trying a difficult stunt, he brought every energy to bear: Listen to what she says. He could not make out a word.

He had the sensation that he would soon go crazy. He thought of that silly speech about "flabby American businessmen" and "bankruptcy is health" and "excellence is color-blind." He could feel it rustling inside his coat pocket. They were too sharp for that, too discerning. They knew America. They'd been born here, raised here, educated here, worked here, interned here. And he was, like some big-assed bird, going to tell them what to think. Yet he knew he was right. Damned little good that did.

The pluck at his elbow was very gentle. He missed it at first.

He would quit. Just say that he was sick. Doctors would understand that. Maybe he could vomit for them.

He felt the pluck again, the slight pulling of sleeve cloth.

"Mr. Thatch, it's me," a voice said. It was the girl from Bookbinder's office, the psychiatrist. My God, psychiatrists were doctors. She probably engineered the whole thing. Halfheartedly he decided to hate her.

"I know it's you, Dr. Devlin . . ." he said and then stopped.

She did two things, but it was only later that he recalled one of them. First, her right hand grasped his left wrist and held very steady. (Later he knew she was taking his pulse.) The other hand gave him a packet of cards with very large printing on them, the kind done with a felt pen.

"Mr. Thatch, you were a dear to do this," Dr. Devlin said.

"I worried about what you might say, and I sort of outlined a speech you could give that would be just right for this audience."

"I've got one already," Thatch said. He knew his voice was unconvincing. "I wrote it myself."

"I'm sure it will be superb," the woman said. She looked quite different from how he remembered her in Bookbinder's office, better dressed or some damned thing. "But I just jotted a lot of crazy notes that occurred to me because I'm a doctor myself. Just ignore them if they don't fit in with what you wanted to say." Thatch was aware that her voice was steady and somehow authoritative. There was an emerging crispness in her manner. "The cards are arranged as notes for a speech using your own background, of course."

With a riffling motion, like a professional gambler, she ran through the cards, showed him the bold heads, the supporting sentences in smaller type.

"I've got a speech," Thatch said again. He looked down the table at Terry. She was staring out at the audience, making no pretense now of talking with the president.

Thatch was halfway through the strawberry parfait before he realized that the cards were a better speech than he could have written. He felt a calmness. He read through the cards again slowly, responding at the same time to the half-hysterical woman beside him.

He saw a chance to get home. All he had to do was to give this speech and he could leave them something and still get home alive. Then he would never have to give a speech again.

The thunder rose from the audience. They were actually on their feet. Hundreds of young doctors, the flesh and blood of America, the best there was. He focused on a few faces. They were squeezed into expressions of real pleasure. They meant it.

". . . and so the man who needs no introduction. None at all. Because by his actions he has made himself known to all of us," the toastmaster said.

Thatch walked to the podium, touched the microphone easily, spoke a few words of thanks, looked out over the audience. He felt almost serene. Except for the dread sensation that if he stepped back the smallest space he would fall into oblivion. Smiling, he reached for the cards. They were in the same pocket with his written notes. He brought out the stack of cards with the rubber band around them and laid them on the podium. He smiled once more, still mouthing sweet nothings of acknowledgment.

The look of the cards was as decisive as a sword-thrust. He picked them up, flicked off the rubber band. The cards merely organized what he had said in Bookbinder's office a few weeks ago.

"America stands at the edge of a great adventure, the most exciting ever faced by mankind—but America refuses to walk forward," Thatch said. There was a scattering of applause. Thatch was aware of an unsteadiness in his legs, a kind of faltering. "And it is, alas, a sad fact that many of you in the medical profession are among those who refuse to walk ahead, who refuse to take the first step."

Instantly the huge banquet room exploded with applause. Later Thatch puzzled over why they would applaud at that moment. He had, with regret, accused them of hesitation. But they were moved. Thatch was, by the time the applause died, filled with an exultant kind of confidence.

"The world is made up of people who are sick with hundreds of afflictions, weak with years of little or no medical care, desperate for the end to pain," Thatch went on. "You know that better than I. These people have heard of the splendid miracles of American medicine . . . of our drugs, our new techniques, our machines, our hospitals, our medical teams. And they wonder why these wonders of modern medicine are not sent to them rather than recoilless rifles and M-1s and tanks. The medical profession of America, if it were turned free, could start a revolution the like of which has not been seen in all history. Why do we not cut our bonds?"

There was a moment's hesitation and then the room rocked with applause. A few people stood up, their faces red with exertion, clapping their hands together with sharp popping sounds, whistling.

"My wife, sitting right there," Thatch pointed to Terry, "my wife was a practical nurse in the Philippines. She trained herself from books plus a few weeks' experience in a hospital in Manila. Yet she and others like her were able to work a revolution in an entire province, to give the Filipinos a level of care they had never had before. Think what the impact would be on the world if each year we committed all of the graduates of our medical schools to spend a year abroad. The Huk movement could be broken in the Philippines. In Viet Nam we could activate a dozen medical stations which the United States has committed itself to support, but for which it cannot find American doctors. Multiply this a thousand times and you would see the young doctors of America working a revolution which would end the fear of communism for all time. For the healing hand of the doctor is the way to the heart of a people. The hand of the politician or the soldier strikes a chill around the world. We have had enough of selfish politics and aimless war. Let us now strive for a tough-minded way to wage peace. And let doctors take their place in the front ranks of that army."

Thatch felt curiously detached. He knew his voice had taken on timbre, but it was almost as if he were talking to himself. He really did not care about the audience in front of him. At the same time he felt almost giddy with a sense of control over it. He moved his hand in a forward gesture, the sign of the platoon leader to advance and the entire audience applauded and whistled. Thatch felt that he had, somehow, learned the secrets of control long ago and was only now remembering them. He spread his hands and the crowd fell silent.

Thatch went on, his voice soft at first but gradually rising. The words were spaced out; he spoke slowly. He told of American failures in India and Pakistan and Indonesia, and how, in each case, the presence of American doctors might have changed history.

There was a hard subsurface of contempt in Thatch's voice. It was undirected, unfocused, but it was heavy. The crowd did not applaud when he stopped. They stared at him.

Thatch had the quick passing feeling that if he told them they were to blame, if he turned his contempt on them, that most of the women would faint, the men would weep.

"Why can we not cut our bonds?" he asked quietly. "Is there something weak in the American character? Have young doctors like yourselves and your young brides lost courage just when the opportunity is the greatest? Perhaps."

Thatch paused. He watched the confusion spread among them, the faces pucker and darken.

"But I think not," Thatch said, in a voice even quieter now. "I think that there has been a failure of imagination, a lack of vision on the higher levels of our national life. I am no expert on medical affairs, but you tell me—can we not do more? Can we not, for example, take one billion dollars—less than one per cent of our national budget, and pay internes and medical students a decent sum so that they do not have to wait until they are close to forty before they can lead a normal life? Apprentice plumbers make over six thousand dollars a year. Can't we afford to give to our future doctors eight or ten thousand dollars a year? Then we would not be lacking in doctors to go overseas and change the face of the world."

Thatch paused and after a split-second the applause came thundering in. Thatch understood why: they had been relieved of guilt. His eyes glanced down the rest of the card. It had some statistics and budget figures. He decided to ignore the cards and finish it from his head.

"We are told constantly, endlessly, until we sicken of it, that 'things are complicated,'" and the edge of contempt came back in his voice. "Of course things are complicated. We can, if we wish, infatuate ourselves with complexity. We can fondle it in our hands, adore it, dazzle ourselves with it. But, in the end, we must realize that every situation can be reduced to a simple decision: Do we act or not? If yes, in what ways? We need not be hindered by the fears of older and less daring men. Nor need we be fearful of our enemies . . . for it is only our fear that will make them dangerous. And so, to you who have given so much to the American public, I ask you to give again—and again—and again. And above all, you must give one thing: give thought."

He had not yet come to the last card, but he sensed he had talked long enough. He bowed his head and softly thanked the group. The applause started slowly, almost languidly, as if the audience were recovering. Then it grew and became more fierce and the smack of palm against wet palm became a solid undertone. The sound was shot through now with the tapping of spoons against water-glasses.

Thatch caught it all very precisely. The ferocity of the applause, the feeling that it veiled some revenge or intent he sensed but did not understand. Other smaller things he heard and remembered:

"Mr. Thatch, you hit it right on the nose. If those old bastards who run the AMA would give us a chance we'd be off and running." A very pink wife in a masculine suit reached for his hand from below.

"Christ, you don't understand what we have to put up with," a bespectacled hollow-chested young doctor said. "They tell us to get out there and serve the small towns, but we're in debt twenty-five thousand before we get there."

He remembered, too, the tone of Terry's voice when they were walking down the steps of the hotel and away from the crowd:

"I'm glad you remember me, sir, the practical nurse who worked a revolution in Negros Oriental."

He looked at her face and she wasn't smiling. He took her arm and it shook violently in his grasp.

"Mad, that was our speech he gave," Dr. Devlin said.

They were in Curver's hotel suite. The knot in Mad's tie was down on his chest and he had his shoes off. He had spent the morning circulating among the young doctors, talking about Thatch. But he stayed out of Thatch's way.

She looks happy, he thought, in fact quite handsome. And she hasn't a clue as to what happened.

"He did, you're right. But he didn't need it."

"What do you mean?"

"Dev, we gave him the lines, but that wasn't what made the speech," Curver said. "Thatch made a performance out of it, a real sidewinding Messianic speech. He was a demagogue up there. He could have read the phone book and they would have gone wild. It was the style, not what he said, that hit them right where they don't think."

"A political personality is part substance and part *charisma*. But he has to have both. You know that."

"Not this Thatch character," Curver cut in. "He swings with any kind of substance once he gets angry or excited. I wonder how Book would have reacted?"

"Mad, if you say a word to Bookbinder I'll tell Thatch about it and go to work for him for nothing," Dr. Devlin said. "He doesn't need you or Bookbinder."

"Does he need you?" Curver said. Immediately he was sorry. It was a childish retort. But her cheeks had flushed and her eyes

went hard and glittering when she spoke about Thatch, and
Curver could not resist the question.

Dr. Devlin stared at him and for a moment she was almost
beautiful. It was not only her face, suddenly alive, but something
had happened to her body. It was tensed and the tension somehow
made her more attractive, gave a tone of urgency to her. She
sensed it, sensed that he saw it, and wilted. The color left her face,
she became professional and neutral, her body folded back into
its well-tailored, colorless suit.

A dull anger swept Curver. But he was not sure who or what
he was angry with.

11

He had been summoned, Curver did not doubt that. Kelly had
called and said he would like Curver to come down to Washington to talk. About what he did not say. There was no need.

Thatch's speech to the internists had been featured in most
major newspapers, two television networks had run fifteen-minute
clips of the speech, and Senator Reddick had read the speech
into the *Congressional Record*. Both parties indicated they would
introduce legislation to help build a "medical corps" and, already,
it was being compared favorably to the peace-corps concept.

The fact that Kelly had specified they would have lunch in
his office was an indication of Mad's elevation. The huge lunch
was Kelly's acceptance ritual—it was symbolically like kissing a
Cardinal's ring or saluting the marshal's baton or toasting the
Queen. But Mad well knew that Kelly, with a sardonic perversity,
had vulgarized the reality. To eat with Kelly was like visiting a
Mongol chief or Viking leader and sharing a great meal and with
the grease still on your fingers and hard around your mouth
knowing that you had sworn obeisance.

"Mad, there is a chance we are going to do some work

together in the next year," Kelly said as soon as Curver came into his office. "There is also a chance that we are not. A lot depends on how our talk comes out today. I'm going to treat this talk as confidential. Are you?"

"What about Book?"

"Confidential."

"All right."

Each knew that whether they would treat it as confidential depended entirely on how the meeting came out.

"Mad, every man has got a right to think that American politics works in any way he wants," Kelly said. "Book has one theory. It happens to be the theory that most Americans believe. Book believes that the two parties scrap with one another over issues, watch one another like eagles, criticize when they are out of power, look for the best men to carry their banners . . . and that the American voter is watching all this with high interest. It's pure Jeffersonianism. It's also utterly wrong." He arched his eyebrows into a question.

"So far agreed."

He's not using his famous flair for jokes or gamy language, Curver thought. Book had mentioned that he was more than just a hack.

"Now, I'll tell you my theory. It's very simple. Most of the voters can barely remember what party they are in, but they tend to be 'regular.' They have very little interest in and even less information about politics."

Curver nodded. But we'll split pretty soon, he thought.

"Mad, did you ever see a sculptor put a statue together?"

"No."

"You're surprised I did, eh? Well, he starts with an armature, a kind of thick wire structure roughly the shape of the figure he wants. Then he begins to slap big chunks of clay over the armature. Now, Mad, if that statue ever came to life the thing that would make it move is the armature. It's like the human body. The rest is just inert flesh."

Mad nodded and said nothing.

Kelly finished trimming his cigar and shoved it into his mouth without lighting it. "In politics that armature is made up of the people who are interested, dedicated, active. Usually they are called ward-heelers or bosses or pros. Nobody likes them. Nobody

trusts them. The mere word *politician* makes most people sniff
like the sewer has burst. But these are the influential ones; they
make the system go. Most of them are working hard for one of
the two parties. They're partisan. They want their party to win.
Sounds pretty simple, doesn't it?"

"Only a little," Curver said. Give him credit for knowing
where he stands. "What about political issues?"

"They don't matter much," Kelly said. "They come swirling
up out of life. But let the party in power pick up an issue and
the opposition party will oppose it. The Negroes were freed by
Ole Abe, the first Republican, but now a lot of Republicans are
dragging their feet on a civil rights bill and most Negroes have
swung to the Democrats. One time the Republicans are for high
tariffs and a little later they are on the opposite side. Issues take
care of themselves, Mad. My job is to take care of that armature
of people who work day in and day out in politics."

"You don't make it sound very attractive," Curver said, "working with a bunch of hacks—"

"Go easy there," Kelly said mildly. "There are just about as
many hacks in politics as there are in any occupation. But there
are more dedicated men by a hell of a long sight."

"Dedicated for maybe the wrong reason?" Curver asked.
Kelly disturbed him. The man was more tightly organized intel-
lectually than Curver had anticipated. Also the switch from tough
political talk to philosophical discourse made him wary. "Going
for a free ride, sitting around the courthouse, drifting into the
Congress, or getting jazzed up about being a delegate to a
National Convention."

"Mad, did you read that Brookings Institution report on
delegates to the national conventions?"

"I'm not sure," Curver said. He had, but he wasn't positive
Kelly had.

"Well, read it sometime. It shows that the average delegate
is one hell of a lot superior to the average American. Makes more
money, has more responsibilities, is less swayed by emotion."
Kelly turned the chewed but still unlighted cigar in his mouth.
"Mad, I read some of that stuff you read. But most of it is too
petty to be useful. I don't need a goddam study to tell me what
I already know: American politics belongs to the few (call them
elite if you want), the few interested enough to really work at it.

Book's notion of everyone being steamed up all the time about important issues and the mysterious tension between the parties and the vast inarticulate electorate whom we must coddle and educate is a beautiful illusion. I don't try and talk Book out of it. I'm just amazed that he still believes it."

"So where do you fit in?" Curver said.

"I work with the influentials, the politicians. They are the ones who form the first bottleneck any candidate has to get through before he can even be considered at the Convention."

"Someone has to work with them," Curver said, his voice bland.

"Someone has to work with them," Kelly said and his voice was full of wonder. Then it turned savage. "Listen, you snotty bastard, I do it and consider it a privilege. I do it because someone has to organize these people, screen the candidates, give the Party a sense of unity. Someone has to plan the Convention. Someone has to run the campaign, raise the money, keep peace with the county leaders, get the rejected candidates back into line, arrange television time, keep Senators and Congressmen happy. It's messy work. But it just so happens to be the most important work that anyone in this country does. It happens to be the work of sovereignty."

Curver did not budge in his chair. The word *sovereignty* had almost jerked him upright. It sounded archaic, unbelievable, pompous, but the way Kelly used it the word had dignity and purpose and was uncannily apt.

"You through with your illusion?" Curver asked.

This was the breaking point if there is to be one, Curver thought. Kelly believes in what he says. He is as tough as I thought he would be, but smarter. Now I find out how flexible.

Kelly's small head turned, ferretlike, and he looked at Curver. He was not smiling, but there was no anger in his face.

"Yes. I'm through describing my illusion," Kelly said. "Let's hear yours."

"I don't care how you select the candidates," Curver said. He spoke fast and confidently. "You can do it by flipping coins, holding caucuses, primaries, conventions, or just picking the best-looking guy. But once you get the candidate, whether for Senator or Congressman or President, that's when I become interested. Then your influentials have done their job. All they can do now is keep the regulars regular. But there are a hundred million Americans out there eligible to vote and *why* they pick a candidate is what grabs me. That's when the horse race gets interesting."

"You can't predict how they'll react," Kelly said. "I've seen these pollsters kicked in the ass too often. I've read all those silly damn polls about who prefers the Flyboy for President. He still has to get past my influentials before he gets anywhere at the Convention, and what goes on in Arizona doesn't cut much ice with them. Understand one thing, Mad: ninety-nine per cent of the American people could prefer the Flyboy right now and if my people say *no* he won't even get on the ballot."

"Sure, I understand that," Curver said. "But your influentials are not about to pass up the Flyboy"—he paused—"if they think he'll win."

Kelly waited. He bit off a soggy inch of his cigar and dropped it into the brass spittoon at his feet.

This is crazy, surrealistic and unreal, Curver thought. Here we sit in a stage setting out of a cheap Tammany Hall cartoon and this wise fat and very shrewd character is trying to pressure me. And I don't know about what.

"They could," Kelly said. His voice was cold. "Sometimes they want to lose in the right way."

"Like this year?" Curver asked.

"Maybe," Kelly said. He looked again at the slouched figure in the chair, the expensive tweed suit with the bottom button of the vest properly undone. The kid was skinny and arrogant but not dumb. "But go on with your illusion."

"Bert, those pollsters are about as profound as Nostradamus or reading tea leaves," Curver said. "If you want to find out what sort of package sells dehydrated soup no doubt they're helpful. But in politics all they can tell you is that the Democrat has forty-five per cent of the voters for him and the Republican forty-two per cent and the rest undecided. How much good does that do you?"

"What's your answer?"

"Bert, I want to go far beyond my man's fifty-one per cent or forty-nine per cent of the vote," Curver said in a leisurely voice. "I want to know why. Why are they voting the way they do? That's the big mother of them all."

Kelly put down his cigar.

"Wait a second and I'll order up lunch."

"Count me out," Curver said. "I've got to get back to New York."

No one had ever put it to him like this before. He could order the lunch and see what Mad did. Kelly decided not to.

"Go on," Kelly said.

"To find out *why* you need tools that are a lot sharper, cut a lot deeper, and can be used more rapidly. In 1960 Kennedy used the Lou Harris polling outfit. Harris is one of the brightest, pushes the polling art as far as you can, pinpoints his targets. But Kennedy also used something called simulation."

"Simulation?" Kelly asked and laughed. "Boy, you talk about science fiction and a brave new world!"

"The name of the corporation is Simulmatics," Curver said. "You can buy stock in it now if you want."

Carefully Mad told him how it worked, moving slowly from the pollsters to the psychiatrists to the computing machines. He ended with his description of the 480 groups the electorate was divided into.

"How did they draw up the groups?" Kelly asked.

"Using the obvious—white or black; rich or poor; East, West, North, South; education level; urban or farm; the age factor; old family or immigrant. That sort of thing."

"That sort of thing, eh? Would you say they use eight or nine such characteristics?"

"Probably more."

"My dear Mr. Curver," Kelly laughed, and this time Mad knew he was really amused, "do you realize that these computing geniuses of yours have come up with more categories than there are people in the United States? Have you taken nine to the ninth power lately? If I'm not incorrect, you're dealing with over three hundred and fifty million categories." He boomed his deep political laugh and his little hands fluttered in delight, like butterflies.

Kelly had done it so quickly that Curver thought he was joking. He felt mousetrapped and annoyed with himself—and he felt at the same time a growing respect for Kelly.

"Bert, you didn't tell me you were a mathematical genius." Curver wrote Kelly's figure, 350 million, on a card and slipped it to the bottom of the pile. He would have Dev check it out later. "The point is that you have produced mathematically possible categories. Simulmatics produces empirically real categories."

Curver paused.

"Don't worry, I know what it means," Kelly said. "Categories based on actual experience. But how do they actually use this information—an example, Mad."

Curver talked more slowly, thought ahead, searched for the right problem.

"Okay. Let's take—should the US pull out of Guantanamo Bay? From memory now, it went something like this. As a flat proposition, seventy per cent of the people were opposed. If somehow it was done—uh—gracefully, through the UN—sixty-three per cent opposed. Of the four-eighty, the category one hundred per cent opposed was male, Southwest, middle-aged, oil-rich. One group the most in favor was female, urban (New York City, actually), middle-aged, highly educated, middle-income—well, social-worker types."

Kelly listened attentively. He had heard rumors that Kennedy had hired this Simulmatics outfit, or one like it, in 1960, to feed him voter information. He didn't know—or care. Curver's figures represented nothing more than his own practical knowledge. So maybe they could specify that all Afro-Jewish-Protestant-illegitimate quadroons in Boston with two million dollars were opposed to Nixon. All of the AJPIQBs Kelly knew were in that category and he didn't need a computer to remind him.

The whiskey Kelly was sipping made him mellow. Usually the whiskey was only preliminary to a hard discussion over lunch. Today the battle was over and Kelly relaxed with the whiskey.

"Mad, I don't believe a dammed thing you said," Kelly said. "Maybe you're right on a small point here or a fact there, but statistics will never win an election. By the time you get them all recorded and nicely laid out the election is over. . . . Mad, I'll bet you a case of the best bourbon made that I can tell you how the state of Minnesota feels about disarmament before you can. The one closest to the poll results wins. Okay?"

Curver hesitated. Then he knew Kelly would win. It would take time to set the thing up, to process the bits, to interpret them.

"There is a lot more to it than this, Bert. I just got started."

"I know there is. But please don't bore me with it," Kelly said. He poured himself some more rye. "The important point is that I think we can work together. Just a few things we have to clear up. First, short of a miracle, Kennedy can't be licked next year?"

"I assume that," Curver said. He paused; something bothered him. "I told Book as much. It's no secret."

"Secondly, you believe that Thatch has a chance for the Republican nomination?"

"Largely because no one else really wants it. It's a year of stale and tragically flawed candidates."

Kelly laughed and Curver wished he hadn't sounded so pompous.

"We won't pursue the tragic flaws. But just one more thing. Mad, someone has to be in charge of any kind of campaign. You can run a lot of things with split command and everyone playing Mexican general—the PTA cookie drive or the United Crusade or the World Affairs Council. There's no opposition. But a campaign means you've got opposition; an enemy; someone out there fighting against you. And that calls for centralized control." Kelly paused, looked directly at Curver. "I just want to make sure I've got it."

"Meaning what?"

"You can research and consult and advise as much as you want," Kelly said. "You can bring in all the head-shrinkers, Ph.Ds, statisticians, and pollsters you can find. But you can't commit one dime of our money for it unless I approve. And you can't instruct the candidate except through me."

"No private brainwashing sessions?" Curver asked and laughed.

"Sure. All you want," Kelly said. "But you can't give a draft of a speech or an official instruction except through me. I don't care what you convince him of privately. I just want public control of the man."

"If I agree, do you go to work for Thatch full-time? Is he your final choice for sacrificial lamb?"

Kelly sat back and swirled the brown liquor in the glass, watching it stick to the sides and come down in beautiful whorls. He smiled. He felt very warmed. It was a good day. Not one day out of a thousand did you meet Mad's caliber of friend–enemy.

Christ, how I hate the toadies and the incompetents and the buddy-buddies and the ingratiating ones. Mad is all right. Tougher than I thought. I was thrown off by that careful tousled Eastern-college-boy look. They all try to give that impression of great composure and leashed power. But usually they fold at the first hard jab and settle down to selling stocks or watching the family capital grow or marrying someone with wealth.

"Mad, you know who is going to be President in 1968?" Kelly said. It came out too fast for him even to calculate why he said it. Instantly he felt companionable, sure of Mad's confidence.

"Bert, I just barely know who is going to be President in 1964," Curver said. He watched the other man drink. Kelly could put it away. The guy must have downed half a pint already and was going hard on his second. The strange puffed flesh of his face, which seemed to surround no bones, was sweating slightly.

What animal is it that has no bones, the only one? Curver thought. It came to him. He sat straighter in the chair. The shark.

"Mad, this is the year," Kelly said, and like a slightly inebriated cherub he settled into his chair, the sun combing down his back. "This is the year we want to lose in the best way."

"Meaning what?" Curver asked.

"Meaning in such a way that the man we really think can win will have clear sailing in 1968. When there is no incumbent."

Curver sensed this was a time to learn. He nodded. He drew on his small Danish cigar.

"The Loser and the Millionaire and the Flyboy don't really matter any more. For their own reasons of vanity or pride or anger or revenge they want to run. But we know they can't lick the President. Right?"

"Right," Curver said, deep in his chair, careful to keep his face away from Kelly. He flicked some signs over the cards.

The room was warm. Kelly had a fine even voice and he knew how to tell a story. His voice droned, but in a surging way, coming to climaxes and then falling away. For Kelly the afternoon had taken on a fine tone.

"My man is going to win in sixty-eight," Kelly said, and his voice was almost delicious with anticipation.

His man, it turned out, was Dr. Bryant Clark. Dr. Bryant Ellsworth Clark.

Kelly had met him at Princeton. Bryant Clark, Instructor in Classics. His lectures glowed, were contained and reasoned and had reach. Plato, Aristotle, Democritus, Lycurgus, Aristophanes, Aeschylus, and the politics of the Aegean and the gleam of the marble of the Acropolis and the sheen in the air of Greece and the *agape* and *eros* and *lynen* and . . . with a crash of his palm on the desk . . . asking if any student could relate all this to Roosevelt's effort to pack the Supreme Court. The centuries were nothing to Bryant Clark; he swept over them and Marsilius of Padua was as Connally of Texas.

"Man is the same, century after century, and he faces the same problems and the same misery and the same hope and the same failures and same successes," Kelly intoned. He held his glass up to the sunlight and it glittered except for the dark pool of hundred-proof in the bottom. "Sweep is what he has. Everything is connected. Life is orderly. He is a generalist. He can synthesize, relate one discipline to another. You understand? Do you know the name?"

Bryant Clark, Curver thought. Forms flickered through his mind, there was a whirring and then . . . quite suddenly . . . he had it. Bryant Clark on an IBM card in his mind. He closed his eyes, waiting for Kelly to go on. But Kelly didn't.

"Of course," Curver said cautiously. "University president, Ambassador to Greece at one time. Big egghead. Administrator. I know the name."

Kelly was leaning back, holding the glass up to the light and remembering. Brown liquor, white-crystal glass, dirty Washington sunlight. . . .

The brilliant young instructor had invited the shy unpromising student to his apartment and ordered in a half gallon of red wine and some bread and cheese. There were two other undergraduates there, but most of the conversation was between Clark and Kelly. Clark had talked of vocations and what had value in an evil world. Kelly, usually quiet, found himself speaking up. He challenged Clark and Clark grinned. The wine took its hold and Kelly sensed that his time was short.

"You, sir, are antidemocratic," he said to Clark.

"But, of course. Everyone who is not *demos* must be *anti-demos*. The problem is to be elegantly antidemocratic," Clark said. He was very serious. "You, Kelly, are from the *demos*, the crude and arrogant people. But not *of* them. Your task is to lead them out of their ignorance."

Clark had stopped and looked hard at Kelly. Kelly never

forgot the moment. Clark appraised him carefully. It was the hardest, most honest look Kelly had ever known.

"You are not to be a warrior or a writer, but you are meant to be in the midst of the *polis*, that part of the *polis* which knows and leads. There is no higher profession."

Clark had never asked him to dinner again. But he had sent Kelly handwritten notes telling him of a new book by Sir Ernest Barker or remarking a style detail in Churchill or an obscure essay by Carlyle on leadership. When Kelly graduated Clark had sent him a small leather diary with a silver pencil attached by a chain.

"He was an ambassador, wasn't he?" Curver said. Two or three minutes had passed and Kelly's small hand had held the glass without moving.

"Ambassador? Yes. He was an ambassador," Kelly said. He told Curver more about Bryant Clark.

During the Greek civil war Truman sent Bryant Clark out there as a special counselor. He spoke both classic and modern Greek. He could walk. And he could talk. He walked with and talked to one hell of a lot of Greeks. By the time he left he was recognized as, next to Bowles, the best amateur diplomat of his time.

He went back to Princeton and lectured for a semester. Then he was asked to be president of a big Midwestern university. It sprawled in chaos. It was bankrupt. It did everything, but nothing well. It offered courses in baton-twisting and radio-announcing. But it had 20,000 bodies. Bryant Clark slid into the position easily. He cut off the fat so fast that 25 per cent of the normal-school teachers didn't know they were unemployed until their checks stopped. He tightened administration. He raised money faster than the state could grow corn. Always he wore a vest, his jokes were classical and wry, and he wrote at least two monographs a year in his field.

The faculty respected him. Kelly hesitated, glanced at Curver. The faculty *feared* him. Because he could outpolitick any of them and not look raw while doing it. The students were in awe of him and at his last lecture (yes, believe it, he kept lecturing) of each semester most of them wept. The alumni fought for a few months when he said that he was going to de-emphasize football, then were delighted at the Ivy League air that surrounded the campus. The trustees watched as Bryant Clark reduced the total cost per student by ten dollars a year and still attracted a superior faculty. Gymnasiums languished, libraries grew, the stadium was empty, the seminars were jammed, and the major in radio-announcing was dropped.

"Today the man is in marvelous shape," Kelly said. "Huge metabolic rate. Never has to sleep. Loses a pound a year. Trimmer now than when he was a freshman."

Bryant Clark could speak. Not just repeat words. He could make them come to life. He was the best money-raiser in the business and last year a book of his collected speeches—his collected *speeches*, for God's sake—received a front-page review in *The New York Times Book Review* and went into a second printing at a university press. . . . Kelly's voice droned on and on, rising in enthusiasm and falling away in revery.

The answers fell into place, the slots in Curver's IBM card were being filled out. Kelly was not cheating, not yet. But there were still a few slots unpunched. Curver decided to push a little.

"Why does he want to run for President?" Curver asked.

"Mad, he doesn't even think of running," Kelly said. The glass came to his lips, a few drops trickled into his mouth. "But if he's drafted he will run. Why? Because he knows he's the right man at the right time. He knows history and human beings and what today is all about."

Bryant Clark was no phony. Not even so much, or little, of a phony as Nixon or Jack Kennedy or Hubert Humphrey. He would run because he was sure. He had certitude. He knew what he was doing. There would be no posturing, no holding back, no wondering if he were really the "people's choice." He could do what was necessary and do it well. The man had the rare gift of selfless assurance.

Curver, sunk in his chair, felt something jar. His fabled memory was not working today. Some slots of Bryant Clark's IBM card he could not yet punch. It annoyed him. Something was missing.

Curver's pencil moved over one of his cards. Kelly hunched forward. Sure enough, the kid was doodling.

"I remember something about Clark," Curver said. He almost sat up, then controlled himself. He was in danger of losing an advantage. "Something about his early years. Something . . ."

Curver slumped back. Now he remembered. Christ, don't blow it, he told himself. Just stay cool.

"His early years, Mad?" Kelly was all attention, leaning forward.

That did it. It was the "War Record" part of Bryant Clark's IBM card that was blank. Slowly it came to Curver, his marvelous memory filled in the slots, the card was complete. Now he had to retreat, to invent.

"It was a book he wrote," Curver said, "something about *Education in a Pluralistic Society*, and it came out in the early forties. Great reviews."

Kelly's face cleared. Curver knew he had cut very close to something important.

"Mad, that is one of the best damn books written in our lifetime," Kelly said.

He described the book carefully. Very objectively.

Curver was not listening. He had found the punchout on the IBM card which had not been pushed. It was horizontal #13 under general vertical #2.

"Conscientious Objector."

Curver's pencil made another cabalistic sign. Kelly talked of old campaigns, of tricks, of jokes, of famous people. He told Curver of campaigns they had pulled out of the fire by sheer cunning and skill; the torments of building a political machine; the pleasures of victory. On and on he went, defining what was proper and what was improper, the written and the unwritten rules. His pride in the game and his knowledge of its limits were enormous. He had no interest in other things . . . everything bore on politics. Kelly was not smug; he was merely a man who could conceive of doing nothing but what he was doing.

On that warm spring day, in a gentle mood, he told Curver a great deal. Curver forgot none of it.

12

The moment just before waking. Sweet as honey, but quickly
retreating. Always he squirmed backward into the sweetness, away
from the yellow-white loom outside the eyelids, backward into the
fading sleep. But today something was different.

A smell. Cosmoline and paper. This was the day . . . maybe. It
was filled with a hard magnificent possibility: a gun was there and
the clip of 6.5 ammo and some spares. He had a quick vagrant thought
of that bulky gung-ho Marine sergeant who gave the cool instructions:
Squeeze off, don't pull. And a sudden urge to fall back into sleep,
to avoid the harshness of the room, the piles of books. But, twisting
through the weakness was a hard black line of necessity.

His eyes popped open. He was awake. Bright-eyed and bushy-tailed
(as they said in the Corps) and ready. It wouldn't happen. Things
like that didn't happen. *They* blocked him and would again. Always
they had, from the start. The agate eyes of the kids . . . do
wind-sprints or you can't play football, get personality or you don't
get invited to the parties; don't read those books.

He swung out of bed. . . . The Corps had been no better. AWOL,
they said, and swearing at the noncom who didn't have a goddam
brain in his head. His eyes stung with self-pity. Then the discharge,
as if they wanted to say you aren't a Gyrene, you're a green kid and
we want no part of you. They did the same thing to him in the
Soviet. He said it straight to the bastards at the American Embassy
in Moscow and walked out . . . and in a few weeks they were
after him again. Always the same.

He felt sick. Oughta roll back in the sack. But the black line of
necessity (sometimes in the books it said *imperative* or *inevitable*,
but he liked *necessity*) shot through him and snapped him to his feet.

Dressed, he reached for the long paper-wrapped object. The
cosmoline smell was strong. The heft of it made him feel better, like
a surgeon who picks up a lancet and walks toward a bug-ugly boil
and makes a little cut which saves the whole body. Lenin said
something once: "from the feverish body of mankind must be cut
the festering sore. . . ." Or Trotsky, no not *him;* maybe one of the
others. He had read so many.

A face tends to remain the same day in and day out, particularly the face that goes with duty. Charles' face was black and went with a duty. He was the waiter who had served Bookbinder and Levi at the Union League Club for thirty years. Charles took away the soup bowls and his face was the same as always. Two minutes later the face came through the door pushing the *steak tartare* and it had changed beyond the limits of possibility.

Bookbinder knew it was death. He had seen it before, played back on the faces of others. This was a death that mattered. He winced, turned away. He knew that he too would be involved.

Charles moved toward them, every gesture familiar, but so slowly that the gestures were grotesquely exaggerated. As he served the *steak tartare,* his motions precise and glue-slow, he was weeping.

Levi did not notice. He was running down a document entitled "Catholic Voters and the Democratic National Ticket." It was allegedly written by a Presidential Assistant and circulated during the 1956 Democratic Convention. Levi, his love of statistics aroused, pointed out to Bookbinder the statistical inaccuracies in the document. "It was an ingenious argument to prove that if Kennedy had been the Vice-Presidential candidate in 1956, he might have pulled Stevenson through," Levi was saying. "If he had been nominated, he would be dead politically today."

Bookbinder tapped his friend on the forearm and gestured with his head toward Charles. Levi looked up into the black face of despair.

They both said "Charles—" and pushed back their chains.

Curver knew that Dr. Cotter loved to watch the cards run through the machine and fall into slots. But Curver was bored. It was a necessary procedure but antique: one needed the polls as a check. They were useless for any other purpose. Dr. Cotter's simpleminded, unqualified love of the procedure made him uneasy, like watching an *idiot savant* who had no premonition of how soon he would be obsolete.

The machine stopped. The cards were sorted. Dr. Cotter lingered a moment, admiring the neatness of the whole thing. In each slot there was a stack, some much thicker than others.

"Emily, work up a quick percentage of Thatch-preference choices on this run," Dr. Cotter said to the girl sitting quietly on a stool.

They went into Dr. Cotter's study. It was book-lined except for one wall, which was covered with a blackboard. A long equation ran across the board. A television set was on in the far corner of the room. It was turned on, but the volume was too low to hear.

Curver and Dr. Cotter sat down. Curver looked at the television screen. A line of limousines jammed into a narrow space. Motorcycle cops in white helmets spun into hard turns. Hospital attendants in white jackets came out. Why in hell was Cotter watching this afternoon TV soap-opera, Curver asked himself.

He turned as the door opened and the girl named Emily walked in. He had hardly noticed her before, but now he found her attractive, with a kind of trembling beauty. He laughed to himself. She was afraid of Cotter—good Lord!

Emily looked at Dr. Cotter, who was looking at the television screen with a peculiar intensity. Curver was still looking at Emily. Then he realized he did not want to look at the television screen.

"Thatch gets eleven per cent on name recognition," Emily gasped. Jesus Christ, Curver thought, she didn't have to be that broken up about it. "When his name is identified as 'The man who built the bridge from India to Pakistan' the recognition goes up to sixty-three-e-e-e . . ." and it ended in a shriek.

Dr. Cotter said something, a primitive grunt, a rudeness.

Curver knew the meaning of what he would see on the screen before he turned back to it. He hated to swing around. He knew what he would see: not actors but real people on the screen. Real bodies, perhaps. Oh God, they'd warned him not to go down there. What did it all mean?

Friday afternoon and night and Saturday morning Dr. Devlin had worked in her apartment on the California primary. She took the phone off the hook, ignored the radio and television set. On Saturday afternoon she went to the New York Public Library to check the Bureau of Census publication on characteristics of the population of California. She was unaware of anything different in the streets. In the library she saw three librarians and they were all red-eyed and for a moment, only a moment, she was puzzled. Then she thought, Someone in the library has died and they all weep institutional tears.

She went back to her apartment excited by the material she had uncovered. California was going to be a perfect model, an exact experisituation. If they just had a candidate in June, the California primary would be an easy one to simulate. She worked all day Saturday and most of Saturday night.

On Sunday morning she pushed the television button to *On* and was halfway to the kitchen when she heard the sound. Regular, sharp, about the speed of the heart, strange and very compelling. She smiled and opened the can of orange juice. The machine sounds better when it is broken than when it works. She liked the muffled rhythmic sound . . . even though it probably meant broken tubes and a seventy-five-dollar repair job.

She took her orange juice and walked around to push the set off. A riderless horse was frisking on a broad avenue, a man in uniform walking steadily by its head. Both horse and man were in some kind of rhythm with the muffled sound. The Capitol showed in the background and a line of people, military men, she saw they were, and horses drawing something. She saw the flag and at the same time heard the words *the late President* and a deep black wave of understanding crashed over her and she sat down.

The young President's face emerged from the black wall and she felt a moment or two of deep, deep (and, for her, strange) sorrow, but the President's face quickly became another's—thinner, bigger-jawed, deeper-lined—and she was staring at Thatch and saying to herself "Now he's got a chance, now he's got a chance," over and over.

For a moment guilt engulfed her, but long ago she had learned to turn it aside. Guilt was not the stuff of science—only a sign of sentimentality.

As the cameras panned across the faces lining both sides of the street, she could see many were weeping. Others were granite-hard, staring straight ahead, or solemnly holding children in the air for a better view. Something inside her slipped and for a moment she wanted to be with those who had shiny cheeks.

She should be weeping. She had a sense of estrangement from the entire world: She was alone, tiny, isolated, without protections that she so badly needed. Then the moment was over.

She remembered the Emch and Blitzsten report on reactions to FDR's death in 1945. Now the controls were back and she felt better. The thing to do was to get the same sort of study going right away, but on a broader basis. They must find out right away what this would mean to the electorate in '64. She reached for a pad and began to make notes furiously.

Kelly watched the political hack dig into the famous Kelly lunch. The fat bastard was drinking beer so fast it spilled out the sides of his mouth.

The phone rang. Kelly listened. He knew. But he also knew it was too much for his mind and body to take. He felt as if he would be sick.

He told the hack. He told him the young President was dead. He didn't say the talented charming fantastically equipped candidate-even-though-he's-on-the-goddam-other-side but that's what he was thinking and also "Oh, God, what a political loss," and "How often do they come along?"

Around his salami, bread, and onion, the hack spewed little bits of food in the hard yellow sunlight and mumbled, "Well, that changes things."

"Get out," Kelly said thickly to the hack. The hack looked up, surprised, thinking he had misheard. "Get out."

Kelly pointed at him and then at the door.

The hack got out.

Kelly waited. Then he put his head down against the cool mahogany of his desk. In a few seconds he was pounding it on the dark brown wood and when he stopped there were tears on the desk. Kelly was surprised. He thought his tear ducts had dried up long ago.

Thatch walked out into the corral and jumped on the back of the Batangas mare. She skidded sideways, bucked twice, and then steadied down. Unchallenged, he slid off her and walked out to the guest house where the letters were stored.

Thatch thumbed through them and picked out one on heavy parchment. He read it and felt the waves of guilt wash over him again, almost as if he'd wished the man dead.

It was Sunday morning. The boys slept and Terry always had a late breakfast. Yet he knew they were awake, in their beds, looking at the ceiling. They had talked so little since Friday. Maybe because there was nothing to say. Maybe, and Thatch danced away from the thought, maybe it was because they felt Dad would be different because of Dallas. No, he told himself firmly; no man's family would believe that.

And yet around the country he was sure there were people who were making calculations of how this terrible event advantaged them.

Much later, Terry was at the window. She tapped with her fingernails. They stared at one another through the pane of glass. She beckoned and he saw a new terror in her face. It had grown worse—and yet that was beyond belief.

He followed Terry, not touching her, to the house. The boys were crouched in a corner of the room by the television set.

"Something else?" Thatch asked.

"Yes. Another murder," Terry said. "The boys saw it live. They saw it!" She looked at them in the corner. "And the television people say they will run it again."

The sweetness of sleep had moved into daylight and a new illumination: the bright lights set up for the television cameras. He looked sideways at the husky, well-fed, Stetson-wearing men. He could have laughed: *they* were finally baffled. He had not spoken to them. It was beyond belief that *they*, when he finally faced them, would be this gross. *They* made him right. It had been necessary. He put his hands to the scabs on his face . . . one over his left eye and another on the right brow. They were the stigmata of rightness and worth.

They wanted to know if he was a Communist, a Trotskyist, an anarchist, a follower of Fidel and a dozen other things. So he just looked at their round strong faces and said nothing. They missed the big question. He was a Universalist. He LOVED everyone. For hours he merely sat and watched them. He was silent. It was revenge.

He walked out of the cell, aware of how small he was between the big deputies, and the crowd parted. Something swelled in him. They were all there waiting to see him . . . and he was JUSTICE walking.

A movement flickered at the left edge of his vision. A man in a

black coat, wearing a black hat. He was respectable-looking, not a
bum, but he was lunging and he held something in his hand. There
was a crash of sound. Huge bodies swirled above him. Something
had happened to his side . . . his left side. Like a giant stitch. It
dulled and the bodies swirled away and he felt a liquid surge of pain
and then pleasure: THEY would not forget him.

The thrill was so great that the pain dulled and he did not feel
dread at the blackness which flowed across his eyes. He could still
hear. He slid easily onto the floor. Shoes kicked and shuffled about
him and someone shouted "Stand back. Let us see him." He smiled
as the blackness closed in.

Bookbinder sat at his desk in his study, out of habit pulled
over a pad of yellow legal-size paper and took a sharpened pencil from a Morocco holder.

For a moment he was baffled. He had nothing to write.
Usually at the end of a week end he had a few dozen ideas
which he noted in short sentences and took with him next morning to the office. Today the pencil did not move.

He had discovered two things about his body over this long
week end. First, the brain was a marvelous protective device.
After the first shudder of shock, the rending disbelief and then
confirmation, every new piece of information was translated into
political terms . . . the order of succession, the new alignments
in Congress, the consequences for the civil rights bill, the pros-
pects for new tax legislation, the 1964 election. He had stared
blindly at the kinescope of the Secret Service man beating his
hands in frustration on the trunk of the car, the face of the man
on the grass who had thrown his body over that of his child, the
unbelievable widow following the coffin in her bloodstained
suit, the frisky horse bearing the reversed boots . . . and while
watching he had translated everything into manageable terms,
into old familiar words.

Once he had thought, with something like amusement, that
he was like Dr. Devlin's 7094 machine . . . taking whole ideas
and instantly reducing them to bits of information on a tape
which flicked meaninglessly across his mind.

But on Sunday the second discovery occurred. He could still
weep. When Oswald was shot on stage, Bookbinder's eyes flooded
and it took him several racking minutes to know why. It was be-

cause these two shootings, taken together, spelled the end of the Constitution, the shattering of law and order, the end of a belief by Americans in themselves. He wept for people who had suddenly become animals, and the heavings of his big shoulders were like seismic waves of chaos pounding in toward Washington from across the nation.

Then on Monday he wept again when the pallbearers in neat, unfaltering, slow gestures folded the flag and turned to hand it to an official. The movement of the young steady hands was, somehow, the reknitting of the nation, the end of the ceremony which re-established order. The nation had pulled itself back from the edge of some black abyss. Bookbinder wept with relief.

By Sunday night, Thatch knew he'd had it. His office would be closed on Monday, the day of the funeral and a day of national mourning, but he felt he could not watch the flag-draped caisson, the black-garbed widow, the sorrowing crowds, for another minute without going mad. He appreciated the value of ceremony and the magnificent manner in which this particular ritual was being carried out, but instead of expunging his guilt and blotting out the horror, it reminded him over and over of the shame, the overwhelming national disgrace, and—obscurely— of his own part in it.

He did something he had not done for years. He went to his empty office and pored over the accounts; he lost himself in costs and prices, job estimates, material specifications. He studied lists of figures, making notes. He pulled out construction sheets and field reports. He buried himself in detail, refusing to stop, refusing to think or recognize any greater reality than these rows of figures.

By nine o'clock, still alone in the office, he felt cleansed. Later in the week he would go out to the Philippines to see what all the shouting was about. His visit to the Philippines Ambassador in Washington had produced nothing. Ferguson really seemed to need his help.

And as soon as he got home tonight—this black Monday Presidential funeral night—he and Terry would burn those goddam letters.

13

The small plane went down the runway of the airport at Cebu City and lifted easily into the air. Terry sat beside the young Filipino pilot. She started to gossip in Tagalog. The pilot was pleased. Later Thatch would ask her what she found out.

"Okay, Fergie, what happened at the pier?" Thatch asked. The channel below was blue, flat, and hot.

He had asked nothing of Ferguson during the wait at Cebu City. They had drunk a San Miguel, waiting for the plane to be gassed. One did not talk business in airport bars, not in the Philippines.

"Everything went fine until a month ago," Ferguson said. He was a tall lean man who had turned gaunt since Thatch had last seen him. "We were getting the pilings in fast and the cement crew was right behind us. We only had another fifty yards to go. Then one morning we came out and the pile driver was blown up. I mean really *up*. It was blown right off the dock and into fifteen feet of water."

"Who did it?" Thatch said.

"On the pile driver someone painted the word HUK in big red letters. You can see it through the water."

"Huk." Terry turned around. She had whispered the word; familiar, dreaded, the name of an old ghost.

Huk was a contraction of *Hukbalahap*, which in turn was a contraction of the Tagalog phrase *Hukbo ng Bayan Laban sa Hapon*, which meant National Anti-Japanese Army. The movement had started during World War II to fight the Japanese. After the war it had slowly become Communist-dominated. Few of the Huks knew the word *communism* and even fewer knew the name Marx. But they had a savage sense of having been deprived of land.

The Huks had taken to the hills and forest. They had embraced terror, and learned terror's hard discipline. They walked, grease-guns blazing, into the suburbs of Manila. It was a time of gunning down strangers, of fleeing, of putting surplus US mines under buses, of swearing Filipinos to obey "the law of class warfare," of working out new "progressive people's" notions. Then came the time of killing friends, then brothers and, finally, anyone. The bodies of both Huks and the Filipino militia started to fill the morgues of provincial towns. Then, under the leadership of Magsaysay, the movement had been destroyed. It was a bloody time and had cut deeply into Filipino life.

"The Huk movement was destroyed in 1952," Thatch said.

"Rizal Sipa was never captured," Ferguson said, "and the Balgos brothers were given a ten-year sentence. It was up a few years ago. They disappeared. I knew a year ago that something was up. Isolated military jeeps would be stopped by a log on the road and be jumped by a half-dozen men. They took only weapons and ammunition and let the soldiers go. The officials played it down. Said it was just hoodlums or hunters trying to get weapons. Then we lost one hundred pounds of plastic explosive out of the warehouse. Poachers or amateur hoodlums don't steal stuff like that."

"Is that what they used to blow up the pile driver?" Thatch asked.

Ferguson turned to him and grinned, nodding his head.

"About twenty-five pounds of it, I'd estimate," he said.

"What did the police say about the pile driver?" Thatch asked.

"Said it must have been an accidental explosion of the engine," Ferguson said. "I explained that you couldn't explode an engine like that, but they wouldn't listen. They said that anything that had that much power, that could drive *narra* logs thirty feet deep in an hour, must have enough explosive power to tear itself to bits. I didn't argue. They know it's Huks. But they don't want to go out in the bush looking for them. I don't blame them."

Ferguson had been born and raised in the Philippines. He

had been educated in the States, but had returned after the war to work for Thatch. Although the Philippines operation was called Thatch Inc., it was really a partnership between Ferguson and Thatch. Ferguson was married to a pure-blood Filipina and had five children. His family lived in Manila.

"What about the workers?" Thatch asked.

"They showed up for work, but they wouldn't touch the pile driver," Ferguson said. "They stood around and admired it in the water, but had a dozen reasons why they couldn't rig a winch to pull it out. And none of them could read HUK on the pile driver. They'd all giggle and laugh and do the Twist and scratch, but not one could read the word."

"Did you get the pile driver out of the water?"

"Sure. I flew in a couple of men from Manila, a rigger and a machinist, and we set up a winch and got it back on the pier. It's ready to go again."

"But it isn't going?"

"No. It isn't going," Ferguson said, his words bitten off. "The Manila men fixed it and left. That night HUK was repainted. And everyone just shuffles by and looks sweet and sick and can't work. Bellyache, toothache, trots, dead mother-in-law."

The plane was over the plains of Mindanao. Thatch looked down at the long reaches of tough *cogon* grass, watched the wind bend it into waves that rippled for miles, soft brown, beautiful and comforting. Thatch knew, however, it was pure hell to walk through. Blades of grass tore tiny slices from one's flesh, the heat was suffocating, and scurrying endlessly and tirelessly were the rats . . . teeth ready to snap at a dangling hand, snatch a sandwich from one's fingers, eager to eat nylon, wild for the salty sweat on a leg.

In the distance was a smudge of smoke. Thatch told the pilot to fly over it.

The smoke came from a *kaingin*, one of the small clearings cut out by landless peasants and planted with whatever crop would grow. The *kaingero* was standing in the clearing, a hoe in his hand, looking up at the low-flying plane. His wife was standing beside a fire which burned beneath several blackened five-gallon gasoline tins. Two children, completely naked, stood staring at the plane. The pilot circled slowly.

"Multiply that isolated *kaingin* by a couple hundred thousand and you have the reason why the Huks can operate," Thatch said. "Tough people but ignorant, living an isolated life and hating Manila."

"They don't have a clue about what is going on in the cities," Ferguson said. "They are suspicious of city people and that's what makes them a natural for the Huks. I talked to dozens of old Huks and not one of them had ever heard the word *Marxism*. They thought they were fighting for land. And oh, good Christ, did they fight hard for that! When they realized that they were fighting for something called communism and it was 'political' and maybe just as corrupt as any Manila political machine, the whole thing was over."

The *kaingero* and his family stood frozen. Their stillness made Thatch restless. He looked at Terry. She had tears in her eyes. She shook her head.

"The Huks are back," she said in a small sad voice. "Filipinos wave to everyone. When they don't wave there is trouble."

They flew over a dozen *kaingins* and each was the same picture of upturned quiet faces, heads turning to watch the plane, not a hand lifted. Thatch had the pilot come up fast over the hills which lined the Sulu Sea coast of Mindanao, where he had seen a thick cluster of smoke plumes. The smoke snuffed out as they approached. The fires had been burning in a long deep valley cut in the soft red soil by the monsoon rains. At the foot of the valley the water of the Sulu Sea was a huge fan of light red spread like some incredible and fecund bacteria.

"Fergie, that splotch on the water probably has enough soil in it to feed half of Mindanao," Thatch said. "Every monsoon washes away enough land to keep these poor bastards going for generations."

Ferguson gave Thatch a comic look. Then he wagged his head; the ancient sign of listening to nonsense.

Thatch's eyes were closed and he spoke very softly. In English. He knew, however, exactly what the room was like and who was there. It was a nipa hut with thatch sidings that ran completely to the ceiling. In one corner a Coleman lamp gave off a thin illumination. Across from him was a Filipino named Fernandez Rizal Bayan, who had the nickname Bull . . . a middle-aged man with a tough hardened body who was an expert pile driver and had worked as a foreman for Thatch Inc., for twelve years. Thatch and Bull were separated by a table which smelled of rice, sour canned milk, old coffee, and hardened layers of pig fat. Behind Thatch were Ferguson and an old Asia hand who was American but had spent so much time in the Orient that he blended into the background. He was a stringer for an American news service, but known as one who could be trusted.

The nipa hut belonged to the Bull, but his wife and three children had left three hours ago. Thatch picked his words carefully.

"You do not object to the presence of Allen?" Thatch said, jerking his thumb in the direction of the stringer.

"No. I do not object. I do not object for I have nothing to say or to conceal," the Bull said. "I do not even know why we are meeting."

"Fine with me. Also as you know there is another listening to all this," Thatch said. He was tempted to open his eyes to see the Bull's reaction, but he did not. "Somewhere, under the floor or at the end of a microphone line or leaning against this hut is someone from the other side."

He felt the Bull's powerful restless body shift in the chair.

"Of that I know nothing," the Bull said.

He lied badly. Thatch felt relieved. He also knew that it was dangerous to push the Malay too far, to stretch his dignity too much. The Filipino, although a remarkably shy person, could at some point lapse into the odd condition known as *latah*. In this mood the Filipino was, just because of his extreme shyness, likely to run amok, to fade off into a savage unreasoning and ravening kind of violence, a form of insanity.

"Of that you know nothing," Thatch said, and the Bull knew that Thatch meant the very opposite. "Very good, Bull, I want to meet with Rizal Sipa. Tonight."

"Mr. Thatch, I know nothing of Rizal Sipa," the Bull said. "I know him only as a name."

"Then send word out to the name that I would like to see him," Thatch said gently. "I know, Bull, that you have not dealt with him. But somewhere among your friends there is someone that does know him. I would consider it a very great favor if I could talk to him. There are, I think, things which we could discuss to our mutual benefit."

"It is impossible," the Bull said. "I do not even know anyone who—"

"Try anyway, Bull," Thatch said. "I ask it as a personal favor."

The Bull shifted in his chair. Thatch, the memory of the table still clear in his mind, reached for the bottle of Scotch he had brought. Without opening his eyes he poured two inches of the whisky into Bull's glass and an identical amount into his own glass. He did it entirely by feel. He raised his glass. He heard the Bull toss off his drink and then the Bull's bulk lifted from the chair.

"I will ask someone if they know of Rizal Sipa," the Bull said. "It is useless, but I will ask."

Thatch heard him move toward the thatch door, which led to a ladder.

"Bull, I would like him to bring his political-education committee with him," Thatch said. "Rizal Sipa says he is the spokesman for the people. The people should be represented."

The Bull grunted and went down the ladder. Thatch knew that a lot hinged on whether Rizal Sipa brought the political committee with him. It was a device of the Huks to form a committee of peasants who were supposed to have political control of the area, although the Communist cadre made the real decisions. But Sipa, caught by surprise, might not be able to avoid bringing the political committee.

The moments passed very slowly. Thatch seemed almost asleep. His eyes did not open. Ferguson stretched out on the floor and actually fell asleep.

What neither Thatch nor Ferguson knew was that Allen was no longer an honest stringer. He had been in the Philippines ten years and had lived well. So well that he had acquired a load of debts which were just at the point of being unmanageable. The government was asking questions about what they called "unreported income." A public trial, even the rumor of one, would instantly shatter the carefully built reputation for honesty on which Allen depended. Along with debts and delinquent taxes Allen had acquired a legal wife, two mistresses, and six children, three of whom were legitimate. He had recently developed a deep distaste for the Philippines. He wanted out.

He sensed, with the prescience of one who had lived long in the Orient, that the Huk movement was alive again. He had not appeared at Zamboanga by accident. He had heard of the blowing up of the pile driver and of the red HUK written on the dock. He had put the episode together with other rumors. When he found out that Thatch was flying to Zamboanga he knew the time had come. He was a wronged man, a poor stringer in need of a big break. Desperate, Allen had evolved an idea which was both irrational and quite brilliant. With the death of President Kennedy he felt there would be a search for new heroes, for signs of strength. Allen knew Thatch would not leave Mindanao without a decision. It was a thin beginning, but Allen was a desperate man who could make himself believe in anything. He approached Thatch and said he would accompany him on an "off-the-record" basis. Thatch had agreed, for he knew that Allen had as good a reputation with the Huks as any journalist in the Philippines. To have him nosing around would be more dangerous than to include him in.

Allen sat in the shadows, impassive and quiet, but his hands were busy. In his right pocket was a transistorized tape recorder no larger than a pack of cigarettes which could record over two hours of conversation. In the other pocket was a rubber bulb which when squeezed pushed air through a tiny tube which ran inside of his clothing to a camera no larger than a single cigarette. Its lens was actually in the center of one of the buttons which ran down the front of his *barang-tagalog*. The camera was self-adjusting, soundless, and could take fifty small but accurate pictures.

The doorway was suddenly filled with the Bull's muscular figure. He was breathing heavily and his face was set in a curiously hard manner. He stepped to one side and another man came easily up the ladder, paused at the door for a moment, his eyes quickly taking in the men, the room, studying details . . . the cooking slab with its pile of glowing charcoal, the San Miguel bottles neatly lined in the corner, the two mosquito-net-draped beds. It was the look of a man who is careful, of a man who has been hunted often but has not yet lost his nerve.

Rizal Sipa stepped forward into the hut. The simple act was a declaration. He balanced on his toes and was slightly crouched; not because he was apprehensive, but because it was the stance of the man who is ready to move. The man was a presence and part of his presence was danger. Ferguson woke up instantly and looked with unblinking eyes at Sipa.

The man's aura puzzled Thatch, even though he had heard much of Sipa. From the doorway he had seemed like any Filipino. He walked with the alert grace one associates with good boxers, but aside from that he was physically unremarkable. But as he came close Thatch sensed that the man was feverish, intense, almost electric. He emanated dedication and a hard-won purity and, Thatch suspected, bitter experience: experience of death and killing and torture and the cat-and-mouse hunt of the forest and the execution of former comrades and the days of self-examination and other days of starvation and long marches and ambushes.

The aura actually came from Sipa's eyes. The eyes of a man poised on the delicate edge between madness and saintliness. Sipa protected his eyes, keeping them narrow slits most of the time—as if they were a source of strength which should not be wasted.

The hair rose slightly on Thatch's neck.

"I am Rizal Sipa," he said simply.

"I am John Thatch and this is Eli Ferguson."

Thatch did not offer to shake hands. Sipa was motionless. There was a pause which became a silence. It was broken by a hacking tubercular cough from outside the hut. Sipa had brought others. Sipa turned his head toward Allen.

"That is Clark Allen," Thatch said.

"The honest reporter," Sipa said. He spoke without cynicism. Allen sighed. He would be permitted to stay. His hands went back in his pockets, sweaty fingers reaching for the delicate controls.

God, how I wish I could blow on that charcoal, Allen thought. These pictures need more light.

"What do you want of me?" Sipa asked.

"A conversation," Thatch said, and then added slowly "a conversation with you and your political committee."

"Some of my political committee are known to you or to

Ferguson," Sipa said. "How can they be protected from being revealed to the police?"

"You have my word of honor," Thatch said.

He paused, for Sipa's eyes had opened and gazed straight at him. Thatch knew that more was needed. *Honor* was a word Sipa had come to distrust.

"Also, you know that there are only three of us who can inform on your people," Thatch said. "All three of us will be in Zamboanga for a month. We will be unarmed. Your people can easily shoot us. It is not the usual situation you face, Rizal Sipa, of having to find who has informed. If there is a leak you will know it is us. And you will have the means to kill us. We all value our lives."

Sipa smiled. "We shall talk outside," he said. "There are too many people to bring into the hut."

Sipa walked to the doorway and spoke quickly in Tagalog, ordering someone to light torches. He stood aside and motioned to the three Americans. The nipa flares were already beginning to glow.

"I will search you for weapons as you pass through the doorway," Sipa said.

Allen did not break his stride, but his heart seemed to stop. His hands came out of his pockets, jamming a handkerchief around the bulb with his left hand. Sipa ran his hands lightly over Thatch, and then Ferguson. Allen moved forward mechanically, forcing himself not to think, only to move. Sipa's hands lingered for a moment over the tiny recorder, but a cigarette package crunched slightly and the fingers did not stop. The hands pressed against the left pocket and the handkerchief shielded the rubber bulb. The click of the camera was lost in the sound of feet moving down the ladder.

Allen lived again. His moist hands almost slipped on the ladder. The rest of his body seemed to be caught in a quick dry wrack of fever which passed by the time he reached the foot of the ladder. He looked around the clearing in front of the hut. Some twenty-five men were squatting on their heels, four of them holding nipa torches. The light was fitful and uncertain, sending tongues of shadow darting across clearing, but still it was light. Allen felt a great relief. The pictures would be adequate.

Sipa, the three Americans, and the Bull stood in front of

the squatting semicircle of men. Thatch recognized a few faces, but identified them only as people who worked for Thatch Inc.

"This man, who is a representative of both the capitalist class and of the imperialists, wishes to speak to you," Sipa said.

Thatch had never heard these words spoken seriously. He was surprised that they did not seem hackneyed or humorous, but somehow had a forceful original ring to them. He knew that this was another quality which Sipa had learned: the art of making a fresh statement out of a much-used slogan. It was an art that came only with complete conviction. The committee nodded at Sipa's words, their faces hard.

Allen moved slightly to one side. He pressed the bulb as the torches flared up momentarily. He knew intuitively that it would blow up into a magnificent picture. He had already started the tape recorder. When Thatch began to speak Allen turned slightly and got a picture of the semicircle of men. He sensed again how it would print . . . a line of hard-faced crouching men, most of them carrying carbines, but with one clerkly type in the center taking notes. This would be the secretary who would give a report at the next meeting of the political committee.

"I am a capitalist. We will let the discussion reveal if I am also an imperialist," Thatch said evenly. He spoke in Tagalog and glimpsed surprise on Sipa's face. "But let me make it clear that I represent only myself and my company."

"Subjectively you may think yourself an individual, but objectively you speak for capitalism and imperialism," one of the squatting men said.

There was a parrotlike quality to his voice. Thatch felt a quick relief. And then, overlaying the relief, a strange new sensation: He felt competitive toward Sipa. He wanted to be as persuasive as Sipa. *Quite apart from what happened to Thatch Inc. and the pier.*

An image, quick and fleeting and deeply etched, played at the edge of his mind: a bridge, a blood-red river, a clot of faces, the look of collective raptness as dirty teeth began to show in smiles of approval. Thatch cut off the memory.

He moved backward a single step. He did not know why. But it took Sipa by surprise. The curve of squatting men, Thatch sensed, bent forward.

"Subjective or objective?" Thatch said in a wondering voice.

"Is one's wife objective and his *kwalingking* subjective? Or is it the reverse?"

Most of the men laughed. *Kwalingking* was a Huk slang word invented to describe adultery which was permissible because a Huk was separated from his wife for months, the man in the forest, the wife in the *barrio*. There had been a fierce intellectual battle within the movement as to whether or not such affairs should be permissible unless the legal wife had first been notified. It had become a joke among the early Huk movement because a few couriers carrying letters to distant wives informing them of their husbands' intended infidelities had been killed on the way. The demand for wife notification had been quietly dropped.

"There is no *kwalingking* in the new movement," Sipa said, his voice very flat.

"Objectively or subjectively?" Thatch asked.

Sipa's eyelids raised. His eyeballs caught the glitter of a torch and were so alive they seemed independent of the man. Thatch stared straight back at Sipa . . . forced himself not to blink. Then he smiled. Sipa's eyes narrowed and he turned his head away. A sigh, soft and unintended, came from a man in the squatting semicircle.

"I know," Thatch said, "only myself. I know that I want my family to be fed. I want a house to keep out the monsoon or the wind or just the eyes of passers-by. These things every man should have."

"But few have them," a voice said. "Capitalism forces workers to the lowest level of subsistence. They cannot share in the profits of the capitalist, but are always at the edge of starvation."

It was a different man speaking from the semicircle, but the voice had the same parrotlike quality.

"I do not know about subsistence level of all workers," Thatch said. "But those workers who work for Thatch companies, wherever they are, share in the profits. Half of the profits at the end of each year are returned to the workers."

"And what happens to the other half?" Sipa asked. His voice was scornful, heavy with sarcasm.

Thatch decided to feint. He deliberately hesitated. He let the silence go on until Sipa had to speak.

Good God, Allen said to himself, let the tape recorder not

be damaged by the humidity. Let it get every word of this, every tone, every pause. He thought vaguely of how much, word for word, this dialogue would sell for. Maybe ten dollars a word.

"The other half goes to you and your family," Sipa went on. "So you can travel in luxury, eat rich foods, drink Scotch whisky, have five homes, go to race tracks, and have bourgeois *kwalingking* in endless number."

"You believe that?" Thatch asked.

Sipa paused. The eyes lashed sideways at Thatch and then swept over the semicircle of men. There was a shifting of feet, a reaching for new balance.

"Let me ask just one question," Allen said. He wanted to bring in a topic which most Americans would understand. "Why do you think a Marxist shot President Kennedy? Is that what the revolution is supposed to do?"

Thatch was angry, but he did not have a chance to break in.

"Don't take us for fools, Allen," Sipa said. "President Kennedy was killed by a Fascist in order to inflame the generals and indistrialists against the people's republics. The assassin Fascist was then shot by another Fascist to seal his lips. It was so cheap and obvious a plot. Kennedy favored disarmament. The imperialist war lords cannot stand that."

Thatch went cold. And he became very alert, aware that his anger had raged beyond the reasonable.

"Wait! I wish to ask the questions." He needed to regain control of the situation. "I asked permission to talk to your political committee and offered my life and that of two others as a guarantee of sincerity. So your question must wait," Thatch said. "Also there is another question still unanswered. What happens to the second half of the profits of my business? Correct?"

Sipa made the Filipino gesture, the upflung eyebrows of agreement.

"Say that I receive a hundred-thousand-peso profit," Thatch said. There was the sigh again. This time it was one of astonishment at the huge figure. "At once seventy thousand pesos go into new activities. Then ten thousand pesos to charity. . . . to the tuberculosis hospital at Baguio, to the University of Santo Tomas."

"And what of the other twenty thousand pesos?" Sipa asked. "That is still forty times what the *kaingero* makes."

"It is a thousand times what this *kaingero* makes," one of the men said.

"Does the rest go for your precious *kwalingking*, for more women, for more Scotch whisky, for more houses?" Sipa asked.

Thatch was aware that impressions, vague memories, rumors, newspaper stories were falling into place. They added to nothing. Not yet. But they swirled behind his consciousness, almost at the edge of crystallizing into something.

"Of the twenty thousand pesos half must go for taxes," Thatch said. "Of the remaining ten thousand I support one wife and two sons in a single house." He was aware of something coming together in his mind, seeking to mesh, like gears in an engine. He paused and without thinking he put a question to Sipa which he knew was crucial. "Since my marriage I have slept with no other woman but my wife. Can you say as much?"

Sipa turned and again his fully opened eyes burned at Thatch. Thatch stared back calmly, but his mind was quickly ordering things. Wild things. Desperate things. Some irrelevant things. Every saint is compensating for a flaw. Sipa talks too much of adultery. There was a time when Thatch had talked to Huk prisoners in Muntinglupa prison and he remembered something of what they said. He must push Sipa to the edge of *latah*, to get him to the point of amok.

"My life is pure," Sipa said very quietly. "I have no time for women."

"But there was a time when you did," Thatch said. He stared straight at Sipa. A sigh went up from the watching men. "There was a time when you loved a girl in Manila so much that you went down from a Huk ambush and in the confusion fled to the city to see her."

"Tell him *no*," the clerk said in a voice that cracked the silence as if it had been made of glass.

Sipa's fingertips were trembling slightly. His eyes were fully open, but they were slightly unfocused. He seemed to be looking at some distant object. Thatch knew he was still listening.

"That is the lie of the treacherous kind which only the stupid bourgeois could invent to split the people's movement," Sipa said. It was said in the vibrant sure voice, but the eyes were clouded.

"And when you were discovered in bed by the girl's father

you made him a proposition," Thatch said. "Lying naked in bed, the girl beside you, her father with a pistol in his hand, you made a proposition."

Thatch paused. Sipa seemed not to hear. Allen maneuvered for a shot of him; pushed the bulb.

"A bourgeois lie," Sipa said. "The people's movement cannot be split by counter-revolutionary agents."

The men sighed again and this time it was louder, more heavily suggestive of clogged throats and breathing made difficult by tension.

"You told the father about the next two operations of the Huks Economic Struggle unit which were aimed at robbing banks in the suburbs of Manila to finance the movement," Thatch said. The semicircle seemed very close. Their breaths were loud. Thatch did not take his eyes from those of Sipa. "For that the good father, because he hoped by such information to work his way into Malacanang Palace as an assistant, allowed you to stay with his daughter. How many days was it, Rizal Sipa? Two, three, four? Were they worth the pleasure you had with the girl? Could you tell us of the objectivity and subjectivity of all this?"

Thatch felt an exaltation. He was winning this strange battle.

Sipa was half gone into *latah*. His body remained steady, with some slight trembling of the extremities. But his eyes were misted over, the primitive gleam replaced by a kind of faraway look which caused him to smile. But the smile was grotesque . . . saliva gathered in the corners of his mouth and then dripped down his chin.

"Talk, Rizal Sipa," the Bull said. "Tell us the truth of this. You have lectured us of sexual purity and revolutionary cleanness of thought and dedication of the people's movement. Talk. Please."

Sipa swung his head and gazed at the Bull. His neck went limp so that the head swung out of control. He fought for control and the head stiffened, but only for a moment. A dribble of saliva fell away from his chin.

Thatch knew he could talk no more. He felt primitive and somehow magical, as if he had absorbed Sipa's aura. Suddenly, with no preparation, he remembered the phone call from the New York lawyer. It delighted him, but he could not remember precisely what they discussed . . . but the memory was pleasing. Thatch was standing in the half-light and he slowly swung his head looking at the committee. They were watching him. For a moment he could not interpret their look: then he realized it was the way they had looked at Sipa. Their eyes flicked away from his whenever he looked directly at a person.

Thatch did not understand the new sensation he felt. It troubled him, but it was also thrilling, a deep physical pleasure. He felt he should turn away from it.

He tried to remember where he had first heard the rumor. He could not be sure. Perhaps from a Huk defector. Thatch, with a strange kind of perception, knew that Sipa had gone back to the hills because the rest of the Huk ambush had been wiped out and Sipa could not live with the guilt. The flaw had made a saint of the man.

"Talk, Rizal Sipa," a voice said from the semicircle. "Talk," said a half-dozen other voices underlaid with hardness.

Sipa stiffened. His head snapped back. He screamed. A scream of pure and undiluted rage but too huge to be sustained. It fell away, blurred with phlegm, exhausted in the passages of his chest. Sipa was amok, a man who had borne too much and now wanted to die and to die in violence. With a quick leap he went for Thatch, like a tiger making its last attack. Thatch ducked, but Sipa's arms went around him. Thatch was aware of a quick pain over his chest and, at the same time, that Sipa's arms were locked around him hard as granite. He looked down and Sipa's mouth was gnawing at his shirt.

The Bull and three other men jerked Sipa's head back. His teeth were filled with particles of flesh and cotton. His eyes were distended like those of a child who first faces danger.

Thatch looked down at his chest. The wound was not great, but his shirt was red with his blood.

The rest happened very quickly. The clerk became the leader of the court-martial. He asked fast jerky questions and seemed to enjoy himself. The other men stood about, shouting casual questions, but mostly stating that they had known of Sipa's corruption all along. Allen moved quickly around the group . . . pressing the rubber bulb, praying that he had enough film.

He did. His film caught the execution. Sipa was tied to a tree, his body in wild contortions, straining at the ropes, with a kind of power that seemed strong enough to tear him into separate parts. His mouth foamed. His eyes were dead long before the carbine bullets tore into his body and the last convulsion snapped him against the restraining lines. Then he was free.

14

Clark Allen moved fast. With Rizal Sipa dead the Huk movement was over on Mindanao. Therefore, he explained to Thatch, it was senseless to wait out the month to which Thatch had pledged him. Thatch thought for a moment, looking down the long pier where the pile driver was throbbing, and agreed.

"But the permission must come from them," Thatch said.

He did not specify "them," but he sent for the Bull.

The Bull came in, a cigarette on the edge of his lip, the smell of *tuba* preceding him. He smiled. Not apologetically, not with embarrassment, not with arrogance. He merely smiled. He was happy to be working with the pile driver again. Its massive fundamental throbs were pleasing to him.

"Allen wants to go back to Manila," Thatch said abruptly, with no introduction. "He feels that the movement is through and that no one is any longer bound by our agreement to stay a month after the meeting with Sipa and his committee. Do you agree?"

"It is over. The movement is through," the Bull said. He paused. He looked at the edge of the cigarette, burning close to his lip. It was not a comic gesture. It was the movement of a frugal man. "For the moment." He paused again. "The movement dissolved itself two hours after you left my house. But it will come back together again."

No more was said. Allen left.

In the darkroom of his Manila apartment Allen finished the first enlargements. One showed Thatch facing the semicircle of Huks with the dark face of Sipa to one side, like a brooding presence about to pounce. The detail was grainy, the faces were not perfect, but the shadows and the flickers of torchlight gave it an arresting drama.

Allen turned to the tape recorder. Delicately, as if it were explosive, he touched its controls. This is crazy, Allen thought; I am like Conrad's insane professor who walks about with his hand always on the tip of a bulb which, if pressed, will detonate an explosive charge which will destroy everyone within twenty yards. No policeman ever approached the Professor.

The tiny recorder spoke. Allen waited patiently until it came to the scene depicted on the picture. He listened to the words spoken by Thatch and kept his eyes on the picture. When he heard clearly the sentence "We will let the discussion reveal if I am also an imperialist," Allen sucked in his breath.

It was enough.

In the Peninsula Hotel, Kowloon, Hong Kong, the big white fans churned the air of the main-floor lobby very gently. It was not enough to cool a man but it was cooler than the streets outside.

"I am going to show you one picture and play you the words which were said during that period," Allen said calmly to the *Time-Life* man. He had drunk two or three stengahs, but it made no difference. He was beyond intoxication. "You must take my word for it that this is the least dramatic part of the whole thing."

He handed the man the photograph. He pressed a knob and the tiny recorder spoke its diminutive words.

The man handed the photograph back. His face was expressionless.

"How many people have seen this?" he asked.

"You and me."

"Will you show it to others?"

"Of course. At once. There are others lined up behind you. You happen to be first."

"No possibility of a two-hour delay?"

"No," Allen said quietly. Suddenly he was no longer a man with grievance. Even his anger at the Filipino tax official was gone. "No two-hour delay."

The CBS man listened to the recorder and looked at the picture. He leaned back in his chair, looked contemptuously at Allen, and spoke.

"Another stengah?"

"No."

The CBS man was surprised. Stringers were always spongers. Something was wrong.

"Interesting stuff, but not for television," he said. "We need action. Remember? TV is about action. Anyone can look at stills. Read a magazine. Look through the family album."

Allen's slight smile disturbed the man.

"Good-by," Allen said.

The CBS man began to sweat. Along his ankles, inside his socks, where the flesh of his thighs pressed together.

"Sorry, old boy, but things like this are hard to manage," the CBS man said. He reached for the check. Allen's hand was already over it. "It's an interesting bit, but not really for us."

"So I'll buy the drinks," Allen said. And repeated, "Good-by."

The CBS man stood up.

"We're having a party tonight at Aberdeen," he said. "Be glad to have you join us. The usual crap. Some Embassy people, some amateur spies, some journalists from the States. One person might interest you. A Senator. Important . . ."

"A Senator," Allen said, and smiled. He felt a control close to ecstasy. "You don't realize what's happened, do you? Since the President was assassinated the American people are sitting there with a big emptiness. They wait and no hero comes. And now you have just heard the voice of the new hero and you talk to me about dinner with a Senator." He paused, a pity just short of contempt in his eyes. "By the time you've started cocktails tonight this deal will be finished. And so will you."

The CBS man stood up as one stands up in a nightmare. He could not speak to Allen. Not after that insult. And he knew that by not speaking to Allen he was bringing down a doom on himself.

"Kind of nutty stuff for television," the NBC man said. "How do you see it being used?"

"How do *you* see it being used?" Allen asked. He waited and then let the words go off his tongue as if they had been rehearsed. "You're in the business of things moving. All these are still photos."

He waited, almost revolted at his appetite for the abasement of others. "Maybe they are worthless."

"Oh, not worthless. Not completely," the NBC man said quickly. "It's a risk for us. But maybe we could do what we have done with some of the shows where we take stills and intersperse them with dialogue and make a kind of documentary out of them." He paused, greatly eased, sure of a deal. He glanced at Allen again. If he had met him before, he could not remember. "Christ, Allen, without consulting the home office I'll take a big chance. I'll give you a thousand-dollar option on the whole thing. Tape, photos, your time, everything."

The drinks arrived.

"I'd like an orange juice," Allen said, pushing the stengah aside.

The Chinese boy, who was sixty years old and had a white label over his jacket pocket which said *Main Bar Coolie*, looked at the NBC man. Without a word he knew it was useless to offer the man the extra stengah. He went for the orange juice, dumping the stengah into a squat jar in which he saved remnants.

"I'll tell you quick," Allen said. "I'll tell you about a TV documentary. TV is always trying to catch history, do the big thing, thrill the public, and please the FCC. Right here you are looking at real live history and hearing it. You are seeing what is something like the succession in England. The step that comes after the King has died. Do I make myself clear?" The orange juice was placed before Allen. "But this time it is real history. Do you like history?"

The NBC man was confused. He treated the remark as a joke. He raised his stengah and drank half of it.

"To history," he said.

Allen sipped at his orange juice. A few pips of Mandarin orange clung to his lips. He took the time to lick them off before he went on.

Allen bent forward savagely. He knew he did not have to sell, but he wanted to depict a vision.

"Everything on TV is faked," he said quietly. "Everything is invented, contrived, acted out, staged." He paused. "For the first time your fat-assed viewer will see a real Communist face a real American capitalist and hear them argue . . . and the scene ends in death. The death of the Communist. The pictures will be stills.

True enough. But along with them goes an actual recording of what the two said. And it is history compressed into a few moments. For at the end of it the Communist is killed by his comrades. They killed him because the American was persuasive, heroic. And America needs a hero today."

The NBC man was transfixed and tried not to show it. He lit a cigarette, nodded for another drink, looked bored.

Allen smiled.

"Would you like to hear the sound of a Communist being executed by his comrades and see the picture of how he looked?" Allen asked. "And see the American in the background?"

"Maybe," the man said.

"Good-by," Allen said.

The man did not hesitate. He knew when he was close.

"Show me," he said.

Allen laid out a blown-up picture of Sipa with the heavy ropes binding him to the tree. He started the tape and played it very low. A hyenalike scream came out of it and behind the scream the sound of carbines being snapped into firing position and men yelling. Then there was the sharp snap of rifle shots. Allen laid out another picture. Sipa hung against the ropes, part of his forehead carried away, saliva flowing from his mouth, the huge soft dead eyes staring down at the ground.

The NBC man sighed.

Allen tucked everything away.

He sipped his orange juice. The NBC man drank off the new stengah. He looked up at the slow white whirring of the antique fans, at the vast and distant expanse of the ceiling.

Oh Christ, he thought, this is very big.

"I will guarantee you, here and now, that NBC will pay one hundred thousand dollars for the rights to the tape and the pictures," he said. Then he added, "Exclusive."

"Not exclusive," Allen said after a moment, as if he had really thought about it. "I am selling it to the slicks, the movies, the publishers. I will entertain only an offer for an exclusive on TV. And it should be around two hundred thousand." He looked at his watch. "Others are interested. Can you reach your New York people?"

"Now?"

"Now."

"Yes."

"Will you hold for my reply? I saw the bastard from CBS at the Foreign Correspondents Club and wondered why he was so depressed," the man asked. He detected a hesitation, a tightening in Allen's posture. He knew he had made a mistake. Some day, he thought, let me strangle this little bastard alone in a park. But it would never happen. Allen was blessed. "What I mean is that they don't really understand TV reportage the way we do. Understand?"

Allen nodded. It was a very noncommittal nod.

"Say it again, but slowly," Thatch said into the phone. His voice was cold. Terry came out of the kitchen, where she had been talking about Zamboanga with the Filipina cook. "Tom, make sure you've got it right."

Thatch looked at Terry. His face was stony.

"All right, we're going to stop them from showing it," Thatch said. "Get hold of Bookbinder. He ought to be able to handle something like this. Tell the switchboard to put him through at once."

He put the phone back on the cradle. He looked at Terry and then out the window and then down at the stack of papers he had been working on.

"Clark Allen turns out to be a bastard," Thatch said abruptly. "He had a concealed camera and a miniature tape recorder on him the night we met with Rizal Sipa. One of the TV networks has bought it and intends to show it as a documentary or some damned thing right away. He's also sold the story to *Life* and some company in Hollywood has made him an offer on a movie."

"Where is Allen?" Terry asked. "Still in Zamboanga or Manila?"

"He is in New York making deals, the son of a bitch," Thatch said. "He can't show those pictures and play that tape of me talking. I'll sue him for libel or slander or whatever it is you sue for."

Terry watched him, saying nothing. She was quiet lately, turned inward.

The phone rang. It was Bookbinder.

"Thatch, Mr. Carroll of your firm phoned me about that Zamboanga thing and this reporter who got the pictures and the recording," Bookbinder said. "I'll get on it right away, meaning that I'll get a look at what he has sold the TV people and what he proposes to sell *Life*. But let me tell you right now that I very much doubt that you have a chance of stopping all this. You have to show that you have been damaged in some way and from what I hear of the material it makes you look like a hero again. Also, because of that earlier bridge episode you are a public figure. That means, generally, that you are fair game."

"I don't want to be fair game," Thatch said.

"I understand. I'll try and stop it, but don't hold your breath for good news. It's not likely to happen."

"When will you know?"

"By tomorrow. I've got someone else checking with the TV people and he just handed me a note saying we can see the pictures and the format for the program today."

Thatch put down the phone and felt confusion. A snare of some kind had fallen about him. But it was not unpleasant. After the first angry reaction he sensed, again, this alien pleasure. It was like an interest in himself . . . as if he were viewing himself from a distance.

That night he could not sleep. He buried his face in the pillow so that its softness might absorb the hard edges of his thought. But something stuck, stayed, and bit into his brain and he felt a sharp headache.

It came through, finally. Ferguson. They had made an agreement, all of Thatch Inc., and all the Huks and Clark Allen. But it had been broken. Not by him. By Allen. And Ferguson was still there. But with the Huks disbanding (Bull had said it) they wouldn't, not the good, friendly Huks, they wouldn't seek revenge. For some reason, deep and obscure, he felt the acid gather in his stomach. He was lying. But he did not know about what.

When Bookbinder called back the next day his voice was strange, lacking its usual toughness. "I saw the pictures and heard the tape, Thatch," he said. "That thing you did, Thatch . . . it was incredible. Since November twenty-second I haven't felt so odd."

"What about stopping them from showing the stuff?" Thatch said.

"It's impossible, Thatch. There are no legal grounds. Even if you threatened to sue, the network would go ahead and take the risk. For this kind of a performance they would pay a million dollars in damages."

He went on to explain that the privacy of a public figure was protected in only some areas. This was not one of them. "And frankly, Thatch, I don't agree with you that the public should be deprived of seeing that film. I hope a hundred-eighty million of them see it."

The television program got the highest Nielsen rating of the year. It was narrated by a team of famous voices. A Princeton historian commented that this was the first time in his experience in which a whole Communist movement had been stopped by one man. There was, he argued, a lesson here for the entire free world.

Terry watched silently. Thatch did not speak. Tony and Harry, their sons, were delighted with the program. They regretted that Thatch had refused an invitation from the president of the network to fly to New York and appear live at the end of the program.

The next day the telegrams began to arrive. The second day the letters came. For the first time in his life Thatch was recognized by a total stranger on the street. A trim-looking young man in a business suit glanced at him, spun on his heel, trotted after Thatch, and asked him to autograph his copy of *U.S. News and World Report.*

15

There was a note from Curver on his desk when Bookbinder returned to his office.

"I'm with the two analysts in the conference room," it said. "Come in when you're free. But not after three. By then I'll have all they've got and can give it to you faster than they can sum it up."

Bookbinder smiled. Mad had confidence. Some people in the firm had thought at first it was arrogance, but not after they saw the quantity and quality of his work.

The conference room was big and comfortable, furnished mostly in old dull leather. Even the top of the table was leather, burnished to an antique glow by endless polishings. Beneath the table, and just to the side of each leather chair, was a telephone and buttons which controlled amplification and a tape-recorder system. At the end of the table Mad was talking to two men.

A woman was sitting to one side. She had a classic profile with the firm nose and rich lips Bookbinder associated with the bas-reliefs on Rhodes. When the woman turned toward him, Bookbinder saw that it was Dr. Devlin and he felt a mild exasperation. He was surprised that anyone with so handsome a profile should be so plain when seen straight-face. He nodded to her and said her name.

"Dr. Donne and Dr. Alex, this is Mr. Bookbinder," Curver said.

"Welcome, gentlemen. I'm sorry I was late."

Dr. Donne was young, maybe thirty-two, and he had a crisp driving look about him. He looks like an up-and-coming stocks salesman, Bookbinder thought. Dr. Alex was older, maybe sixty-five, spoke with a German accent, and was something of a dandy. He wore spats, a blue polka-dot bow tie, and a very well-tailored suit. His rounded professor's face at first glance seemed naïve and open, but the moment someone spoke, his head tilted to one side and he became almost aggressively attentive.

"They have been very helpful, Book," Curver said. "They told us first of the reactions two Chicago psychoanalysts got to Roosevelt's death in 1945."

"It involved a total of thirty-two subjects," the young psychiatrist said. "All of them were remarkably uniform in their reactions. They expressed great relief that the analyst was there, almost as if they had expected him to disappear. They were very apprehensive. They had trouble recalling the name of Vice-President Truman."

"That is a rather common guilt reaction," Dr. Alex said. "One forgets the name of the person one is now dependent upon. It would seem disloyal to the dead person if one could do this."

"They all displayed gastric upsets," Curver went on, glancing at his notes. "They vomited or had diarrhea. They wondered what was going to happen to them and the country. 'Who will run things?' was the way they put it. They felt disoriented, out of touch, very frightened."

"Not exceptional reactions except that they are usually reserved for the death of persons very close upon whom one is dependent," Dr. Donne said. "That they would occur at the death of so distant a person as the President was surprising."

"They sound as if they were all a bunch of Democrats who were also ardent New Dealers and wild about Roosevelt," Bookbinder said.

"A majority of them were Republicans, in fact," Dr. Donne said. "And most of them had never mentioned politics before in their analysis."

"It's interesting, but I wonder if it is a reflection of any widespread feeling," Bookbinder said. He hesitated. "After all, people in analysis are sick people. They are in treatment."

There was a pause in the room. Dr. Alex, the older psychiatrist, took a pipe out of his pocket, made no effort to fill it, but simple put it in his mouth.

"Analysands, people in analysis, are not sick," Dr. Alex said pleasantly but firmly. "They are troubled, upset, they have anxieties. But they are not psychotic. Most of them go on about their jobs. The point is that they have troubles which are an exaggeration of what most of the rest of us feel. The person in analysis is in a special way the same as all of us . . . only more so."

"Also he has twenty-five dollars an hour," Bookbinder added.

"Ah, I can see a not-so-thinly veiled hostility to psychoanalysis," Dr. Alex said, grinning. Suddenly he was very charming. He wagged his pipe at Bookbinder. "Also a man who is out of touch with the art. We often charge much more than twenty-five dollars an hour. If the person can afford it we charge him as much as fifty or sixty dollars. The point is that it has to hurt."

"Mass Observation, a reputable research organization, found the same extreme anxiety, the sense of confusion, the impression that everything was in chaos and disorder among people *not* in treatment," Dr. Donne said. "I think it is safe to assume that even by 1945 the Presidency had impinged upon the psyche of Americans in a very deep manner. The man who occupies the position of President is some sort of parental imago to the average person . . . one feels resentment toward the President, sometimes a feeling of helpless frustration, sometimes blind affection, guilt feelings, and in a political crisis a high degree of dependence."

"They were just outlining how this involvement has intensified since 1945," Curver cut in.

"Probably due to television, a very personal medium," Dr. Alex said. "Everyone, even the nonpolitical person, gets used to seeing the President in all the dimensions of his role . . . as a real father and husband, as the leader, as the one who protects us from strange enemies, as the man who opens huge dams, as the one who gives awards to Boy Scouts, medals to soldiers, proclaims Thanksgiving Day."

"Also the President and his staff, either consciously or subconsciously, have played on this tendency to personalize the Presidency," Dr. Donne said. "Since Roosevelt, Presidential staffs have always worked closely with newsmagazines, newspapers, and all the other media. Not just in preparing news, but in human-interest stories."

Bookbinder had a sharp memory of reading a national magazine story on President Kennedy and his son published the week Kennedy had been assassinated. He recalled the sense of bewilderment he felt as he turned the pages, looked at the man's smile, saw him walking hand in hand with his son. During the funeral the son had been caught in a famous photograph, saluting as his father's body went by. Bookbinder had felt confused and very upset.

"What was the reaction of your patients to President Kennedy's death?" Bookbinder broke in so abruptly that Curver looked up in surprise. "I presume you made such a study."

"Between us we had sixty patients in therapy at the time of the assassination," Dr. Alex said. "We at once decided to pool our reactions and to direct the analysand's—excuse me, that's the word we use for the person in analysis. We decided to pool our information also to encourage the analysands to talk about their political feelings. Normally patients do little or no talking about politics, as I said. It is not one of the things that concern them much."

"The assassination of President Kennedy, however, changed all that very quickly," Dr. Donne said, smiling faintly.

"All of our analysands opened their first sessions after the assassination with a discussion of the President," Dr. Alex said. He sucked on the empty pipe. "We were astonished at the reaction. First, many of them canceled their next appointment. This surprised us, because after FDR's death analysands almost rushed to their analysts. This time most of them were watching the events on television. To go to the analyst when these things were happening would have been, to them, like leaving your family to go to a dance the day your father died. You will recall, Mr. Bookbinder, that the whole four days was the unfolding of a dramatic and very primitive ritual."

"What was primitive about it?" Bookbinder asked. He made no effort to keep the harshness out of his voice.

"The muffled drums, the reversed boots on the horse of the leader, the warriors from other tribes gathering to honor a hero fallen in battle, the show of troops, the intense regard for ceremony," Dr. Alex said.

"The custom of the reversed boots goes back to pre-Christian days, to the days of the Mongol hordes," Dr. Donne said. "Freud believed that even today we see the leader as 'the chief of the tribal horde.'"

"Mr. Bookbinder, it is clear you were impressed by the ritual and solemnity of those four days," Dr. Alex said. "That is understandable. Civilized man is used to responding in certain ways to such stimuli. Your reactions are appropriate, for you are a man experienced in politics. Did you not, for example, quite quickly—uh—once your grief was over, worry about the line of succession? Did you not think about what would happen in the elections of 1964?"

Bookbinder did not speak, but he nodded his head. Somehow he felt guilty, as if he had been exposed doing something indecent.

"For you that was quite appropriate," Dr. Alex pressed on. "But think of the politically unsophisticated person. He was stunned, he was unaware of the durability of political institutions. He had focused his dependence on the personality of President Kennedy and abruptly that was torn away from him. And then the alleged assassin was himself shot. It seemed as if law and order and stability were collapsing. Quite normal people, Mr. Bookbinder, were driven to mental illness during those four days. Psychoanalysts and psychiatrists were flooded with calls from old patients; people called their doctors to report a sensation of heart failure or violent ulcers or to request tranquilizers. Never in the history of man was so large a group of people put to such a severe emotional strain as during those four days."

"When did the patients start keeping appointments?" Dr. Devlin asked.

"At once after the funeral was over," Dr. Alex said. "A large majority, four fifths perhaps, reacted in the most extravagant manner. They not only suffered from diarrhea and vomiting, as in the case of Roosevelt's death, but they seemed actually in some sort of hysteria which in many cases bordered on mild to medium shock. They wept deeply . . . not superficial sobbing, but real racking weeping which made them inarticulate for minutes. In some cases we became so alarmed that we took blood-pressure and pulse readings. The blood pressure tended to be very depressed and the pulse weak and thready. A few analysands breathed in short quick gasps and were clearly hyperventilated. In a few cases we had to resort to the very unorthodox procedure of giving the analysand a heavy sedative."

Dr. Alex leaned forward as he talked, became tense and spoke more rapidly. His excitement, more than the words he uttered, impressed Bookbinder with the novelty of what had happened.

"Let Dr. Donne summarize some of the reactions we found," Dr. Alex said suddenly. He leaned far back in the chair, closed his eyes, and took his pulse.

"After each patient left we dictated our reactions immediately," Dr. Donne said. He took a notebook from his brief case and opened it. "Gradually, we were able to find certain strands that ran through most of the reactions. Now I am going to use layman's language here for a few moments, for Mr. Curver indicated that you were interested in the political implications of our study. In the final report, of course, we will be using psychoanalytical terms and it will be much more technical. We will be addressing ourselves to a psychiatrically trained audience in a professional journal."

Bookbinder felt a slight irritation. He disliked condescension and never indulged in it himself.

"I appreciate your consideration, Dr. Donne," he said.

"First, there was an immense confusion, a disorientation felt by each analysand. It was so deep that many of them felt physically dizzy, as if they were reeling. Some were afraid to drive cars or to do normal actions such as housekeeping or writing checks. It was as if their whole world had been shaken down and would never be the same. Secondly, there was a brief period where the confusion was so intense that the patient came to believe that it was impossible that the assassination had really occurred. For a few moments some of them believed they had just escaped from a nightmarish dream. They became calm on the couch, some even laughed. Then the realization returned that it *had* happened and the patient would weep again. At this point, and I am referring now only to the first session after the assassination, the patient started to react so quickly, abruptly, and in so many contradictory ways that he seemed to be flipping through emotional layers, as a person might turn the pages of a book. With the realization that the assassination had happened there usually came a cry of rage toward a society which could allow this to happen. 'Oh, Christ, what an awful country,' one patient said. Another said, 'My God, we have sunk this low. Like dogs they have turned on a courageous man.' "

"Upon later consideration we came to the conclusion that this was an attempt to divert guilt from one's self," Dr. Alex said. He seemed agitated and his words were punctuated by sharp sucks on the empty pipe. "The analysand instantly tried to divert guilt by referring to the larger and more cruel society. It was a desperate attempt to avoid the fact that each of them had, in petty ways, felt hostility in the past toward the President."

"Hostility about what?" Bookbinder asked. "Give me an example."

"Example: a stout, wealthy woman, exactly Mrs. Kennedy's age, had convinced herself that Mrs. Kennedy took reducing pills," Dr. Alex said. "Example: an ardent Republican had said after seeing the movie *PT-109*, 'I wish the Japs had got him.' The words came back to him during the four days and he experienced a pseudo heart attack. Example: an attractive twenty-three-

year-old girl spent all of November twenty-third racing to different friends, knocking on their door and then, starting to talk,
experienced total amnesia and wept. In later analysis we discovered she had gossiped with these friends about President
Kennedy and wanted expiation for her 'sins.'"

"In general those who had been the most hostile toward the
President experienced the most guilt," Dr. Donne said.

Curver said, "A Columbia study of the Truman-Dewey election in 1948 reported that those people most hostile toward Truman months before the election were the ones most likely to
switch over and vote for him when they got to the polls."

Dr. Alex nodded. "Those most bitter toward the President
are, as the election approaches, the most guilt-ridden about throwing him out."

"Is it possible that a widely feared President would be guaranteed re-election?" Dr. Devlin asked. The two analysts smiled
thinly. "If he did his job well, acted strongly, and was decisive,
he would probably be re-elected by those who were most bitter
toward him."

The analysts paused, not sure it was a joke. Dr. Devlin
smiled.

"After the guilt, there came an outpouring of the most aston-
ishing violence," Dr. Donne said. "Usually analysands will not
discuss violence. It is there and they suspect it, but it unnerves
them to expose it. Under this crushing impact of the assassination, the violence came out." He referred to his notes. "'They
ought to shoot the son of a bitch on sight,' a middle-aged house-
wife said. 'And then they ought to shoot all the Jews and Communists who did such a thing.' During this phase some of the
analysands squirmed on the couch, beat their heels, tore hand-
kerchiefs to pieces. 'Before, I was liberal. I loved everybody. But
today I'd like to cut the nuts off every Birchite and rightist I can
lay my hands on,' a young liberal lawyer said. 'We've got to take
things into our own hands. We've got to choke sense into them.'"
Dr. Donne paused. He smiled. "That was spoken by a minister.
A college girl said, 'He was murdered by a damned sex pervert.
Pervert. Dirty lousy pervert.' She became murderous toward Dr.
Alex when he asked her for any evidence that Oswald was a sex
pervert."

"Once the wraps of respectability were off, each analysand

selected his villain as the one who had killed the President," Dr. Alex broke in. "Some of the phrases used by quite proper people were unbelievably obscene. Those who hated Jews fastened on Ruby as an example of all that was evil. Those who feared Communists fastened on Oswald, and, behind him, Castro. Those who feared the right-wing attacked the Dallas police and the 'mood of hatred' in that city."

"The discharge of violence left most analysands exhausted, but more passive," Dr. Donne went on, still glancing at his notes. "At the next session almost all analysands spoke of the magnificent manner in which Mrs. Kennedy had conducted herself, the poise of the President's two children, the kissing of the casket, the little son's salute, the reassuring clip-clop of the horses pulling the caisson."

"How did your analysands react to President Johnson?" Curver asked.

"This calls for further analysis," Dr. Donne said slowly. "Remember that almost all of them saw pictures of his being sworn in on the Presidential plane with Mrs. Kennedy beside him. So they had favorable things to say . . . he is a good man, big and friendly, competent, experienced. But often there would be a pause then and the analysand would start to talk about some person he did not care for."

"Ah, yes. Remember the Texas thing," Dr. Alex said, smiling.

"We asked analysands where President Johnson was from and very few could remember he was from Texas," Dr. Donne said. "Ten days later it came to them. We theorized that it was a sort of fearful confusion. Most people fear graveyards, and the new President came from the graveyard—the place of death. We haven't developed that yet."

"What do you make of this in political terms?" Bookbinder asked.

"The President has become an integral part of the psychic life of Americans," Dr. Alex said instantly. "Indeed, the President arouses more emotion in most people than their real parents. Modern families have decomposed. The First Family is the family we can all adopt. If, in addition, the President has personality characteristics which are attractive, they are at once exaggerated by the citizen. Clearly we all hunger for the President to be infallible."

"The adoration of the led for the leaders is latent," Dr. Devlin said. The two analysts sat stiffly. "It reveals itself by signs barely perceptible, the tone of veneration in which the idol's name is pronounced, the perfect docility with which the least of his signs is obeyed, and indignation at the slightest criticism of his personality."

"That is very perceptive," Dr. Alex said.

"It is a crude paraphrase of a paragraph written by Robert Michels," Dr. Devlin said. "He was a student of trade unions."

Dr. Alex did not turn at once, but he said, "He was also a very intuitive student of human nature."

"All right, all right," Bookbinder said impatiently, "but what we need to know is how long it takes for the new President to become the incumbent, to pick up all this enthusiasm."

The analysts glanced at each other. Dr. Donne swung his head sideways.

"No one knows," Dr. Alex said cautiously. He looked, for the first time, fully at Dr. Devlin. "There has been no opportunity to study such situations before."

"You have no opinion as to whether or not President Johnson can take on the power of the incumbent between the time of the assassination and the election in November?"

"We're not in the political profession," Dr. Alex said. His mouth showed his distaste.

"No, but I am," Bookbinder said. "You haven't helped me a great deal, but maybe Mr. Curver or Dr. Devlin has been informed."

Both Dr. Donne and Dr. Alex tensed. They were not used to being either criticized or dismissed. Bookbinder had done both with a few words.

"Gentlemen, one moment," Mad spoke almost formally, choosing his words with considerable care, "did your patients—that is, your subjects—mention any other individual with admiration or intense conviction during this postassassination period?"

Dr. Alex thought a moment and then answered with some hesitation. "Yes—yes they did. One man's name came up with surprising frequency. This engineer who manages to get himself in trouble all over the world—Thatch is his name, I believe."

Dr. Donne nodded, "Yes, he is an attractive figure of strength to cling to, temporarily at least. His projection as a kind of king-sized hero twice in six months was an extraordinary thing." He smiled. "It probably won't happen again in a hundred years."

"I would like to ask one more question, Mr. Bookbinder," Dr. Devlin said. Bookbinder nodded. "What was the dream life of your patients during this period?"

"Do you know much of the analytical theory of dreams?" Dr. Alex asked.

"A bit. I have read about it and—"

"Then I shall make it simple," Dr. Alex said.

"I have also written about it," Dr. Devlin continued. Dr. Alex stopped. He glanced at Dr. Donne. "Not much, but a little book. A collection of monographs entitled *The Dream as Reality Substitute.*"

"I read it," Dr. Alex said. "A very provocative little book. With your background you can probably guess what the dreams were like."

"But I should not like to guess," Dr. Devlin said. She smiled encouragement.

"In each case there was the appearance of a dominant guilt-inducing figure," he said. "The figure varied, as you might guess, with each subject. Initially there was clear evidence of violence toward him. This was followed by censored knowledge of violence, a very quick transference of guilt to more conventional figures . . . usually an anonymous superego and collective figure . . . animals, a mob, a sublimated figure of one of the assassinated President's opponents."

"In one case, Dr. Devlin, a woman reported fleeing from some terrible danger and finding a cleansing river," Dr. Donne said. "She lowered herself into the stream and was calmed. Then she saw flecks of gold in the bottom of the stream. Suddenly the water was like acid. She leapt to the shore and woke up sweating."

"Did you explain to her that her prior feeling for Goldwater had induced the acid sensation?" Dr. Devlin asked.

Dr. Donne paused and then flushed. Dr. Alex cut in.

"We use a quite permissive form of therapy," he said. "She will discover that for herself in due time."

Dr. Devlin looked at Bookbinder. He seemed to be trying hard to control himself. "I dreamed one night not long after the assassination that a feller threw a rock at me . . ."

Mad swallowed his laughter. He had to look away. Solemnly he left it hanging.

The two psychiatrists stood up. Dr. Donne said he would send a copy of the report along, even if in crude form. Bookbinder nodded his appreciation.

"Gentlemen, we have enjoyed this," Dr. Alex said briskly, "but we consider it, of course, to be a professional consultation," he said.

"Of course, Doctor, of course," Bookbinder said. "You will find we pay our bills promptly." He led them out of the conference room.

Dr. Devlin and Curver stayed behind.

"Jesus, Dev, you get one more pair of nuts like that in here and Bookbinder is going to give us up for lost," Curver said.

"They are both good men, plenty of publications, excellent reputation," she said. "But you don't ask psychoanalysts to give you a political prognosis. We scared it out of them."

Bookbinder came back in. "Well, what do you two geniuses think? About Johnson and what will happen to his popularity, I mean."

"It involves a lot of things, but they add up to a pretty firm conclusion," Dr. Devlin said. "Take the polls first. Since polls have been operating, two Presidents have died in office: Roosevelt and Kennedy. When Truman took over after Roosevelt's death, his popularity went up to eighty-seven per cent, which was higher than Roosevelt ever got. When Johnson took over, his popularity went up to seventy-nine per cent, which is higher than Kennedy ever got. Conclusion: The Vice-President who takes the Presidency after a death is going to be more popular than the man he replaces . . . for a while."

"For how long?" Bookbinder said. It was the first time he had questioned Dr. Devlin with such interest and implied respect.

"A lot depends on how the new President performs," Dr. Devlin said. "His first surge of popularity is probably due to the fact that death is more interesting than politics. But it wears off. Johnson is already slipping . . . down to seventy-five per cent."

"Will he slip enough to lose in November?" Bookbinder asked.

"I doubt it. He'll go lower and by fall it will look like a real horse race, but he'll probably win," Dr. Devlin said. "Truman took the biggest plunge ever. He went from the highest popularity ever recorded, eighty-seven per cent, to less than fifty per cent just before he ran against Dewey . . . but he came back to beat Dewey."

"We need a hero, a miracle worker. No doubt of it," Mad said quietly.

They sat there in easy silence. For the moment anyway, they understood one another. Each was thinking of John Thatch. Dr. Devlin considered the transfer of Kennedy's shining image to another youthful hero and how it might be accomplished. Bookbinder ticked off Republican governors, important Senators, and the influential members of the National Committee and the susceptibility of each to a man like Thatch. Mad thought about a *Life* cover story—late afternoon pictures taken at the California ranch, two sons riding those Batangas ponies, Thatch (strong on father image here) with his arm around his handsome slender wife watching his sons with obvious pride.

No one mentioned his name.

16

Things and faces orbited about him, almost known but then whirling away or dissolving as the power of his eyes forced them to melt. To look hard was antimicroscopic . . . for the thing observed blurred at the edges, began to collapse, and then was formless. Focus was maddeningly impossible. His eyes bulged with the effort. He felt a vast terror at his loss of perception.

A large man wearing jack boots and some sort of uniform walked into the middle distance. There was something familiar about him, but Thatch knew it would be a mistake to focus too hard. The man was young but weary, hard-driven, a person who had sacrificed, but one of noble bearing. He stood, his legs slightly spread and his hands at his side, and waited for the attack. He had nothing but rocks in his hands and his head wobbled with fatigue.

There was a slavering noise from all sides. A din of howling. A roar of mucus-lined throats. And beneath, like a counterpoint, the smaller sound of paws running at great speed. Then he saw the bodies, quick-moving, fur-covered, converging on the man. The man's head snapped to an exhausted attention. He looked around. He was encircled. But it was not yet clear what the animals were—wolves or coyotes or dingoes. They scrabbled across a wild lunar landscape, streaked behind rocks, paused at stunted trees, and then came on with a rush. One creature passed through a streak of moonlight. It paused, lifted a foot. Its head turned. The animal was a dog with a human head . . . and Thatch knew the head.

It was his own.

The gray circle drew tight around the man in the jack boots. He pulled himself up and his hands held the rocks like primitive weapons. The man was sure of death . . . that was visible on his face. But he was also grinning or laughing or exulting at what would happen before he died.

The animals were very close now and one made a leap. It fell back with its head smashed. The beasts circled, their howling abated, but the teeth clicked and snarls came from their throats. Thatch was sure he knew other faces . . . he strained to recognize them, but then they were gone.

The clouds parted for a moment and the man looked up. As he did Thatch recognized him. The dead President. There was no doubt of it. And then the beasts closed in a wave of gray fur and snapping white teeth. For several moments there was the smash of rocks against skulls and the bellowing of the man. Then the man disappeared . . . he must have fallen. For a moment a macabre shape, covered with beasts, crawled along the strange landscape. It looked like a single animal. But the dog-men were snapping downward, ripping and tearing. Then the figure exploded upward and stood for a moment. White bones showed on his arms, his skull was clean of flesh. But he had a voice. He roared once more. The voice was not unhappy. Then the figure fell backward. In a few seconds it was over and the beasts were fleeing. They fled silently. And they did not leave even a bone behind them.

"John, just let go of the pillow," her voice said. Her small hands pulled at his shoulders.

He rolled his head sideways and stared. He was hunched in the bed on all fours. He had a foam-rubber pillow in his mouth and he felt that he could never let it go.

Her hands came to his mouth, ran over his lips. His mouth opened. The pillow dropped. It was wet with saliva.

"Terry, I think he knew he would be killed," Thatch spoke with a voice harsh with phlegm. "That's possible, isn't it?"

"I suppose it's possible," she said. "Every man who takes an office like that knows he might be killed. It's—it's part of the whole thing."

Another thought struggled to come out, but his lips would not form it.

"Don't try and talk any more," Terry said.

She pushed him over on his back. He was sweating. Not just on his face, but all over. Like no sweat he had ever known in the tropics. With his head back, the salt drops ran up his nose. Some kind of rottenness was being squeezed out of his body. He felt he was strangling on it. He sat and tried to cough it up.

Then she was back with a glass of water. His teeth rattled against the glass. The water went down in a single gulp. He no longer felt dizzy.

"Better?" Terry asked.

He nodded. "The dream was so strange. Now I just feel physically sick."

They listened to the Batangas horses moving. It was a foggy night which killed the wind, so there was no other sound.

"It's the letters, John," she said. "You shouldn't read them."

He did not respond. He was too tired, too exhausted by the new thoughts, drained by the effort to rearrange a chaos.

Ten days ago Bookbinder, Levi, and Curver had left. It was their second visit, and quite different from their first. This time they seemed intent on his running, determined, even passionately convinced of something.

Thatch had dismissed them from mind and had begun planning for a fertilizer plant in Kenya. It was challenging work and for a few days it went well. But a sense of restlessness had developed in him. His skin itched; he felt hungry at odd hours; he would stare at a page and discover that he had been watching a single word for five minutes. It was then he began to read the letters.

. . . for me a surrender to Jesus Christ was the only way of salvation. Now I feel that you have shown that the goodness of man can be known in this world and we can work in harmony. I am a widow and just a little over fifty.

I'm an old duffer and I only joined one movement and that's the Townsend Plan, but if you want help in banging heads of them Hindoos and Pakustans I'll help. Thatch, people have to be beaten into doing what they should do.

One man can take his place . . . you. For weeks after the terrible thing in Dallas I just stayed in bed and drank tea and felt worse. Then I saw you on TV and knew you had been sent to replace him.

No one has a plan for this country. I'm a veteran. I like plans . . . not just a lot of crap and a lot of stuff from Washington. I hate socialism and communism. They ought to get those pinkos out in the front lines and let 'em see. Please kick ass until they give us a veterans bonus.

Won't sign my name. They're after me and after you. They'll tear you limb from limb and rub acid (nitric, I think) into the wounds. But you bear up and I'll follow. They're snuffing around the back door now.

The Democratic Clubs of this state would like you to address us at our annual endorsing convention. We do not know your politics, but, since the Death of the President, we have watched your performance with great admiration. We would like you to speak on any topic you wish.

Would you care to write, either alone or in collaboration, a book on your experiences in India and the Philippines? Our firm, one of the best established in the trade-book business, will be glad to send a representative to see you and . . .

Run, you miserable nigger-loving bastard. Go like a thief because some of US AMERICANS KNOW. You're going to turn black . . . from lying down with dogs.

Our club gives an annual award for Americanism and would like to give it to you. Our dinner is on June 15. We're just fifty Gold Star Mothers, but we voted unanimous for you. You know how to handle foreigners.

His mind revolted, twisted back against itself, refused to go on. But he must push ahead to some kind of conclusion or the dream would come back. This he now knew: his mind could invent more awful variations of the dream than there were nights in his life. He had to decide something.

"Lots of the letters are very rational, very kind," Thatch said. "But when I sleep I only remember the ferocious ones. They come at me like . . . like . . . I don't know what. But like they want to eat me alive or have me eat them alive."

"Why does it worry you, John?" Terry said. "Some of the letters are from crazy people. But lots of them come from respectable groups . . . universities, political groups, church people. John"—she gripped his arm, for help, he thought—"you know I don't want you to get involved in this thing. I saw too much politics in the Philippines. I'm frightened of—of public things. But don't just sit there and misread the letters. You're beginning to think you're responsible for the President's death somehow. John, you can't go on feeling that way. It's dangerous."

The sweat was cooling on his body. Tremors ran over his skin, like the first cold-hot assault of malaria. He felt detached and somehow crafty and very suspicious.

"No, Terry. Even the ones with the proper spelling and the good stationery are wrong. They are written by people who are demented . . . even the ones that look sound."

"John, be quiet. Those people have turned toward you because you did something that took courage and they were afraid they had lost their own."

He shivered. Terry pulled a sheet over him. He reached over the headboard and fumbled for a moment, then commanded his fingers, and they picked up a letter.

"Read this one, Terry," Thatch said. "Read it aloud."

I am a psychiatrist who has, over the last ten years, come to specialize in social psychiatry. I am a *diplomate* within my specialty and I attach a bibliography as well as some names which you may wish to consult to establish my credentials.

I take these precautions only because I am sure you are besieged

by profoundly sick people, all of whom have a single plan for saving
you, themselves, the United States or the world. It becomes very
difficult to tell reality from soaring fantasy or downright psychosis.

I have only one suggestion to make to you. It may not have occurred
to you that an entire society can, quite literally, become sick. In my
opinion, American society today is either absurd or sick. As a
psychiatrist I am distressed for I realize that in most of my patients
I am inducing an individual accommodation to a culture which is ill.
In short, my patients may be well but their society is sick. However
paradoxical it may seem, the psychologically healthy ones are those
who appear for treatment and are, in the course of treatment, made
psychologically sick and socially proper.

I take the liberty of suggesting that you acquaint yourself with some
of the more recent developments in American culture. For reasons
which you well know you have become one of the few culture heroes
of our time. That role carries with it a considerable responsibility . . .
if you wish to take up the responsibility.

                                            Most respectfully, . . .

Terry put the letter back on the headboard. She looked at
Thatch.

"Do you believe him?" Thatch asked.

"I don't know. I haven't lived here long enough. But if he is
right, why do you take it so hard?"

Thatch twisted and for a moment felt that he was going to
be unable to answer.

"I've always thought I hated politics," he said finally. "I
resisted any responsibility for people I didn't know. But I remember those sermons my father used to give. Oh, hell, it's so
hard to say. But he used to preach about loving thy neighbor
as thyself and maybe it sank in deep and I've been ducking it all
this time."

Terry waited for a long moment.

"John, you didn't have the nightmares and the fevers before
those men came out from New York," Terry said. She put out a
hand and could feel his body stiffen against her. "Don't fight me,
John. Just listen. They came out and asked you if you'd like to
be President. You said no. Then they came again and you took
a long time about it but you finally said it again. John, I don't
believe you mean it now."

"That's crazy. I don't want to be a big public figure. I
just . . ."

"John, don't lie to me because you don't have to. Just stretch out and let things flow across your mind and don't worry about them. Think of being President or Senator or running Thatch Inc., or lying on a beach the rest of your life. But don't gulp and strain and have nightmares."

Terry's hands ran across his chest, under his arms, through the crisp hair on his neck. Thatch laughed. He could not relax but he could bend all his tension toward his still beautiful, brown-skinned wife.

The next morning Thatch called Bookbinder.

"How are you feeling, Thatch?" Bookbinder asked.

"So so. Need to get down to work, I guess."

"Get plenty of rest, Thatch," Bookbinder said. "That's going to be important."

Since Zamboanga Bookbinder's manner toward Thatch had changed. He listened carefully to what Thatch said, watched Thatch's face. Thatch could not precisely identify the new manner, but he suspected that it was a mixture of deference and fatedness. Bookbinder no longer talked to Thatch about politics, but his whole manner assumed that Thatch would make a judgment. Although he disliked Bookbinder's new manner, Thatch found himself calling him increasingly, but always on nonpolitical matters.

They talked for fifteen minutes about tariffs in Asia and Thatch asked if Bookbinder could send him some literature on the subject. For a sliver of time he knew Bookbinder almost said "Yes, sir," but the words came out "Sure thing, Thatch." Thatch asked if he could be switched to Curver. He had a question to ask him.

He talked to Curver for only five minutes. When Curver hung up he called Dr. Devlin.

"Dev, Thatch got the letter from your psychiatrist friend," he said. "How do I know? He just called and asked me if there were any books on 'the sick society' and did I think such a thing was possible. Where the hell else would he get such a line?"

"This is a lovely home, Mrs. Thatch," the woman from the picture magazine said. "It's very unusual. A sort of eclectic home . . . things from all over. Bobbie, get the boys with the Batangas ponies behind them. One close up and then a couple of long ones."

The photographer, a coolly arrogant little man, directed the boys toward the door. They walked out in the corral toward the small horses, the boys each going for a different horse.

"Tell me about the ponies," the woman asked.

"They are not really ponies," Terry said patiently. "They are a kind of small horse which is sometimes called Siamese. These are from Batangas Bay in the Philippines. They are very strong and will carry a full-grown man all day long over rough terrain."

"Did you enjoy your visit to the Philippines?" the woman asked, making notes. "How do you like the Filipinos?"

"I guess I didn't make it clear. I didn't visit there," Terry said. "I was born there. I'm part Filipino myself . . . so I guess I like them."

"I'm sorry. I didn't mean—" Then she gathered herself. "You don't look it. You look . . . oh like Spanish, real aristocratic Spanish."

"I think I'm part Spanish and part Portugese, but no one kept very good records," Terry said. "Some of the people from my town think I am probably part Chinese."

"Those boys," the woman said, "are just marvelous with those ponies."

Terry realized the woman was embarrassed. She felt badly, as if she had offended the woman, but she did not know how to talk around the subject. This awful necessity to tell a strange woman about her house and children . . . and then to dodge around about this Filipino thing . . . this was what frightened her. She would talk to John. Tonight. She had delayed too long.

The boys had two Batangas saddled and at once the horses started to buck. The woman reporter asked if it was safe. The photographer was taking pictures very fast.

"Yes, it's perfectly safe," Terry said. "The boys are making them buck. They tickle them with the spurs and the horses seem to like it." The boys were showing off and it irritated Terry.

They talked until the fog broke over the hills and came down in great billows, misting the distant houses, taking the tops from the trees.

"In our magazine we stress the family background of the women we write about," the woman said. "We know that it's not all peaches and cream. Did you see the article we did on the Italian actress? I'm sorry. You ought to see it. I'll send a copy. It told all about her really miserable childhood in Naples."

"My family owned a mahogany plantation down on Mindanao and later a sawmill," Terry said because she thought it was expected of her. "I was the only child."

"My notes say something about a sister," the woman said. "Those researchers can get the simplest things mixed up. I'll cross that off." She moved her pen across something in her small elegant leather notebook.

"I mean the only surviving child," Terry said. "I had a sister. Her name was Flora and she died." She was suddenly frightened of the book the woman held. How much of her would it contain when the woman left?

"Did you date boys on the island?"

Terry's head jerked around. She glanced at the notebook.

"No. We didn't have dates."

"Don't tell me Mr. Thatch was your first date? In prison camp?" The woman laughed. "That would be too marvelous."

"In a way he was," Terry said. She fought away from black memories pushing in on her. "I was very shy."

There was something hideously funny about what she had said. She wanted to laugh.

"Tell me about the things in this room," the woman said. "They're so marvelous and different."

They walked slowly around and Terry told, in a flat voice, where each piece came from. She knew the room was in abominable taste, she could see it in the woman's eyes. She had never thought so before. But recently there was so much she had never noticed which now seemed important. She hated the woman—and all the other women she knew would come trooping through the house. And the men too.

17

The thirty-day period of mourning stretched to sixty in its public moratorium on politics. It was a time of agonized and frenzied action, all carefully handled so as to remain invisible.

The staffs and assistants recovered quickly. They knew there was no pause in politics; it flowed on like a great river of lava, lapping up events, personalities, life, death. The assistants began the first cautious phone calls, the needlelike probes, the first loop in the snare, the beginning of the web. The principals could mourn, could remain quiet, could read and ponder, but the assistants could not—by their nature and the nature of their jobs—stop. They were, in some dark and secret place, exhilarated by the new game, excited by the new opportunities, carefully calculating new odds. Each used his own method, but all knew that new opportunity was present. Like men probing a strangely still landscape for valuable ore, each felt he must rush before the others might stumble upon the vein. Their conspiracies and counter-conspiracies were too intricate for any one man ever to untangle. But it was heady stuff.

"And for us the third objective entails a fourth," Dev said. They were meeting in her apartment. It was surprisingly feminine, with red ersatz-satin wallpaper, a small coal-grate, fragile antique furniture, a sherry decanter with a silver peacock for a stopper, and a piano in the corner. There was not a book in the room. It is too feminine, Curver thought when he walked in. Somewhere there must be a study, a wall of books, a filing cabinet, a calculating machine.

"Why the hell do you use words like *entails?*" Curver asked. "It's so unfeminine. It sounds dirty."

"If you have a prurient mind," Dr. Devlin said, and she smiled. "The fourth objective is to keep the aura or whatever it is from brushing off on the new President."

Notice the number of funerals he has gone to? Probably unconscious, but a desire to keep the country aware of the tragedy and himself as the inheritor."

Curver shook his head and said, "Sweet, gentle Dev."

"Mad, your humor is—"

Curver snapped her off with a brisk salute.

"Now, Madame General, be quiet for a while and non-Freudian and try to listen." He was joking, but his voice had a bite in it. He took out a large sheet of paper. "I am going to diagram for you how to win the nomination of the Republican Convention." At the bottom right-hand corner of the page he wrote $1308 \div 2 = 654 + 1 = Victory$.

"That's the end of the whole bloody battle," Curver said. "Whoever gets six fifty-four delegates and then one more is the Republican candidate for the Presidency. But the ordinary path to that figure, dear girl, is fraught with ambushes, deceptions, bloodshed, duplicity, wild chase, much booze, little sleep, elaborate organization, and dollar bills. We haven't got the horses to take that road. We take a byway."

Curver quickly sketched in the broad and complex strategy of selecting a Republican candidate for President. Fifteen states had direct primaries in which the delegates to the San Francisco Convention would be chosen by the voters. The rest of the states had their own conventions at which selection of delegates started in Pennsylvania in January and ended in Montana on June 20. New York had the most delegates, ninety-two, and the Virgin Islands the fewest, three.

Curver's pen flicked over the page, drawing up the columns of direct-primary states and of convention states, the number of delegates to each, and dates. He looked at it with admiration.

"It's a mess, isn't it?" he said proudly. "Senseless, idiotic, and malformed. What honest man aspiring to be President could wend his way through that maze and emerge sane? Not one. So we will take a shorter route."

Through the convention states Curver drew a thick black X. They were out. A man with huge sums of money and endless connections and political know-how might, just *might*, tie up those states. But not entirely. For these men delighted in going to the Convention to bargain, caucus, argue, drink, shout, swag-

ger a bit, and be wooed. Kelly would do well with these delegates from the convention states.

Dr. Devlin could add. She looked down his columns and
leaned back.

"This changes the whole thing, Mad," she said. "We've lost already. If Kelly can really get the convention states to go for his
man, he'll have eight hundred fifty-six votes and the nomination."

Curver explained patiently. Lots of the delegates would say
to Kelly they were for Bryant Clark but they wouldn't mean it.
The delegates from convention states could say *yes* to five or six
campaign managers and pick up room and board, a few drinks,
and transportation to and from the airport, and no one would ever
know where they stood. They could say they had hung in hard
for each candidate and there would be no way to check them
out.

Of the fifteen states with a direct primary, a few got the publicity, packed the weight, and were well observed. Most of them
were not worth a feather at the Convention. Pennsylvania would
be for Scranton, New York for Rockefeller, Wisconsin for favorite
son Congressman Byrnes.

Dr. Devlin watched the figures on the big sheet dwindle.
Illinois and New Jersey had favorite sons. No outsider could win
in Ohio. Nebraska had no sex appeal around the country. Florida
was interesting, but it was Southern. No one took Southern Republicans seriously.

Curver finally crossed out everything except New Hampshire and Wisconsin.

"With luck we have a grand total of forty-four delegates,"
Dr. Devlin said. "We're already licked."

"Wrong on both counts," Curver said. "We're not licked and
we plan to go into San Francisco with no delegates at all."

"No delegates?"

"Not a mother-grabbing one," Curver said.

He went back to the big sheet of paper. He drew a circle
around New Hampshire, Wisconsin, and California.

"We're going to bore in there like termites and keep very
quiet and make just enough of a show to impress," Curver said.

"Impress who?" Dr. Devlin asked.

"We impress the delegates."

"We go to the Convention with no delegates and Clark,

Rockefeller, and Goldwater maybe have a few hundred each. What's so impressive about that?"

"If no candidate has six hundred fifty-four plus one on the first ballot, the candidate without any votes might look good. Especially if his name is Thatch and he hasn't looked for any delegates or encouraged them. All the big boys will block one another. But if we have lost New Hampshire, Wisconsin, and California in just the right effortless way we look stronger than the boys who have marked themselves out for a few hundred delegates. That's an art, losing just right. Do you understand so far?"

Dr. Devlin nodded. "Politics is gambling. If you don't win on the first roll your friends look for someone else to shoot with."

"You've got it," he said. "But these delegates are not hicks. They want a party, some booze, some fun; more than that, they want to be with the winner. For the delegates this means a lot of prestige, to be a member of the winning team. So that's what we've got to create around Thatch—the aura of the winner."

Curver bent over his big messy chart. Dev watched him without comment.

"And so you see, *Ma Capitaine*," he said, "we run in New Hampshire and we lose . . . but with a big write-in. And the pros know all about it. And we run in Wisconsin, where they don't even count the write-in votes. But we get the newspaper reporters and county clerks to leak the results. Again we lose well."

"And what do we do in California?" she asked.

"We, Dev? You have it all wrong. You've got to give us a simulation for California that will tell us exactly what to say to whom, why, and when. That will be the big one."

Dr. Devlin saw it as two problems: First, to keep Thatch innocent and removed and, second, to reach out to the voters and make them think Thatch was their own-discovered hero.

"Dev, our problem is to tie up that convention. Now I learned a few things from Kelly. One is that it doesn't take a hell of a lot to make a delegate 'your' delegate. A phone call, his name remembered, asking him for advice, almost any little thing will make the Convention delegate believe that you are 'his boy.'

"But I've got to know what kind of people these delegates are." Curver reached into the brief case and came out with a piece of paper with a neat chart on it.

Dr. Devlin looked at it for a moment. It cut the likely delegates for the Republican Convention into ten different groups such as Urban, Jewish, high SES, wealthy, Eastern; Urban, Protestant, high SES, professional, Midwestern; Urban, Catholic, high SES, wealthy, West Coast (California); Rural, Protestant, medium SES, wealthy, farmers, South; Urban, Protestant, low SES, wealthy, professional, Negro, Eastern; and so on.

Dev nodded, "First, we analyze the delegates. Then we run a simulation on how they will react. Let's take a group"—she leaned over the chart—"urban, elderly, retired, intensely conservative, high on fantasy."

"Not many of them will be delegates, you'll notice. The regulars are too damned tough for that. The Flyboy is picking up most of his support from such people in Sarasota or Long Beach or some senior citizens' suede-shoe operation outside Palm Springs. They won't be well represented. Now, let's take the biggest group—High SES, urban, white, professional. We will go ahead and simulate their reactions and do a confirming poll. But you can guess how they will go."

"They'll go for someone who is economically conservative but sounds politically liberal."

"Right. That 'Bankruptcy is health' is a good line. They remember it."

"And they believe it applies to everyone except themselves," Dr. Devlin said. "But what about the big daddy of them all, Mad? Don't we have to assume that Thatch is the only one who can possibly win?"

Curver glanced up from his papers admiringly. He caught the fine face in profile and wondered if she had a doctored nose. Probably. It was too gentle for the rest of her. "I put down on my card 'Certitude our man is the only one who can win.'"

"The whole thing is to convince the delegates of what 'others' will believe, isn't it?" she asked. "The delegate thinks he is making history, but he knows he can't do it alone. He wants to be in on it."

She did not smoke, Curver thought, she drank very little, she didn't chew her nails. In frustration she merely takes her lower lip between her teeth. It was childish and, in a curious way, appealing. He wondered how many men had mistaken that gesture for helplessness.

Mad shook his head to clear it. "Better add one more in-gredient—basic anticommunism, at home and abroad."

Dev nodded approval.

Mad laughed, "We've got everything worked out—*everything* —except how to get our boy to agree to run."

Dr. Devlin's face was, for a fleeting moment, creased with a look of anger. The white teeth bit deep into the light-pink flesh of her lip. Then her face smoothed. "Who ever refused the Presidency? But tell me, exactly what does this Kelly do with his personal approach?"

"Phone calls, letters, slaps on the back, endless meetings. He gives people jobs to do until finally they get the feeling they are committeed to the candidate."

"Ridiculous and haphazard, isn't it?" she said. "Kelly's a dinosaur. A fat, cigar-chewing dinosaur. How can he run any-thing?"

The four men were tensed in a complex mood composed of silence, calculation, and hostility. Bookbinder stood watching the river. Curver was slouched in a chair, his eyes looking up like a scanning mechanism at regular intervals to watch Kelly and Thatch. Thatch was sitting behind Bookbinder's desk. He was smiling. Kelly sat spraddle-legged, fat, sweating, in a leather chair. He just looked straight ahead.

"So you're dumping Thatch because the new situation calls for an open mind," Bookbinder said.

"That's right. With Kennedy in no Republican was going to win," Kelly said. "Now all that is changed. I need an open mind, no commitment, no obligations. Now that there's a chance."

"You have a candidate in mind?" Curver asked.

Kelly turned his head, the hard refined eyes fixed on Curver. Kelly smiled and shood his head tolerantly. It was both a neg-ative sign and a warning.

"No, I'm open-minded," Kelly said.

The silence in the room was without tension, almost amiable.

"Fine, Kelly, you've got your principles and you're going to stick to them," Thatch said. He stood up. "That takes care of that. Will you shove off now?"

Kelly's face was puzzled.

"I mean leave, depart, go," Thatch said and smiled. "You're a political man. This is not the way you do things. But I'm an ordinary fellow and we're busy. So just take my thanks for your help in the past and shove off."

Kelly got up quickly, a monkeylike agility showing through his anger.

"I'll walk you out to the elevator," Curver said.

They went out. Bookbinder had not turned his head.

Kelly waited until they were in the corridor. He spoke without looking at Curver, walking with a grotesque stiffness straight down the middle of the cork floor.

"Mad, Thatch had a bad experience when he was young," Kelly said. "I don't want to bring it up, but it will come out. It's bound to hurt him. I can't tell you about it."

"The year in the loony bin?" Curver said.

Kelly was too experienced to show surprise.

"That's it. It will kill him, Mad. Deader than a doornail."

"Maybe. But maybe not," Curver said. "I think there are some grounds on which to believe it might be helpful."

Kelly laughed. It was a harsh, braying laugh which echoed down the empty hall. The laugh, the marvelous abrasive quality of it, was one of the things Kelly really enjoyed about his role. It was so blunt a weapon, so infallible.

He looked sideways. Curver was studying him and smiling, apparently unmoved.

"They'll kill him on that one thing," Kelly said.

"But then your man was a conscientious objector," Curver said, almost as if to himself. "A CO in World War II though he was in good physical shape and could not claim religious grounds. Can't you just see what the American Legion would do with that?" Curver hesitated, his smile deepened, he seemed to be regarding some internal secret. "Kelly, I wish you Godspeed and good luck and you just bring up that insane asylum issue whenever you want. I think it would be very educational for the American people."

Kelly got into the automatic elevator like a beaver crammed in with strange animals. He carelessly lounged back, pressing against a group of women, but his eyes glowered out at Curver. But in his face Curver thought he saw admiration, a sign of approval toward a student who had learned well.

At the last moment, just as the doors were closing, Kelly stepped out.

"Mad, when you get a chance to talk to Mrs. Thatch alone, ask her if she remembers a Mrs. Singleton from her days in Santo Tomas prison camp," Kelly said. "She was the older woman who wrote a great deal. She died a few years ago, but her diaries are very interesting."

"I've already talked to her survivors," Curver said quietly.

"She doesn't have any survivors," Kelly said.

"She has a nephew," Curver lied. He had never heard the name before.

"She does like hell," Kelly said and grinned. "Remember I told you, Mad . . . you're a good boy and you learn fast, but check that one out."

Don't expect any gifts from that baby, Curver said to himself as he went back toward Bookbinder's study, but don't expect him to knife you without giving warning. Like maybe one thirtieth of a second to move before the knife went in between the seventh and eighth ribs. When Kelly did it, Curver knew, it would be with an expert's skill.

He made a note to check on this Mrs. Singleton.

Madison Curver went back into the study quietly.

"Book, I won't change on that matter," Thatch was saying. "I won't go into any primaries on my own. Even in Oregon or any other state where I can't keep my name off the ballot, I won't visit the state or campaign or even make a statement."

"How do you expect to win, Thatch?" Bookbinder asked.

"I don't want to win unless the people want me. I certainly don't want to win by sucking up to party hacks and convention delegates," Thatch said. There was assurance in his voice. "That's Kelly's game. It's not mine. The American people will know where I stand. If I make it, it'll be over the heads or around the bodies of the pros and the delegates."

"Thatch, it's not that easy. I don't like this party infighting any more than you do, but it's part of the game," Bookbinder answered. "And don't think those delegates are dumb or badly motivated. Thatch, they are well above average."

"A candidate need only show them that he has the voters

with him," Thatch said. There was an implacable quality to his voice.

"How are you going to make this appeal, Thatch?" Curver asked. "Remember the moment you become a candidate for the Presidency, none of the networks is going to give you any free time. And a lot of those columnists who wrote nice things about you at the bridge and at Zamboanga are suddenly going to be reminded that they have a favorite of their own . . . some Senator who gave them a beat or the candidate their newspaper is supporting."

Thatch looked at Curver for a moment. His eyes were abstracted.

"I thought about that, Mad," Thatch said. "Right now I've got invitations to talk on every television program from *Meet the Press* to local disc-jockey shows in just about every major and half the minor cities in the US."

"But they'll withdraw those the moment you become a candidate."

"So I won't become a candidate."

Bookbinder turned slowly away from the window. His shoulders were hunched defiantly.

"You won't what?" Bookbinder asked.

"I won't become a candidate. I'm going to say exactly what I want wherever I am invited, but I refuse to play the party game."

Bookbinder looked dazed, but there was admiration on his face too.

"Thatch, politics isn't like that," he said. "If you want the job you've got to run for it."

"I won't run. It is not my duty to seek the Presidency," Thatch said. "Book, we talked about this. The people have to move, make choices. There has to be an end to all the politicians acting like medicine men and promising the world."

Curver slouched down in the chair. Thatch had a good idea. Curver could see it in action. Thatch the folk hero whom everyone wants to get into politics. The curiosity mounts. The pundits speculate. The Flyboy and the Millionaire and the Loser all throwing pokes at one another and no one is watching. What they are watching is the drama of Can Thatch the Lion-Killer Become President?

"That's not playing by the rules," Bookbinder said uncertainly.

"Book, during the last few weeks I've been reading up on those rules. I discovered that the Constitution doesn't say a thing about political conventions or parties. They just sprang up and made their own rules as they went along and anyway they change them so often that no one knows what they really are. Like the Democratic National Committee just decided to give a bonus of ten votes to the states that delivered the vote in 1960. What is the effect? The big states get more votes and Nevada and Wyoming get nothing. Now what is so sacred about those rules?"

"Thatch, I'm not talking technicalities," Bookbinder said, "but about a basic concept. You've got to get in there and make a race. Be an avowed candidate."

"Book, I don't agree," Curver interrupted. Intuitively he felt that Thatch needed support. "Look at those fools out there. The Millionaire buying TV time to explain about his divorce and his nice new wife and asking for public sympathy. And the Loser leaking the glad news that he can be had again. And the Flyboy saying our ICBM missiles are faulty and getting the headlines. And the Ambassador allowing a headquarters to be set up for him when everyone knows he could kill the whole thing with one flat statement. As long as bullets are whistling around his Embassy he knows he is making points."

"Granted, Mad, I see all that. But what we wanted was for someone to make a genuine acknowledged try for the Presidency against an incumbent," Bookbinder said. He turned to Thatch. "How are you going to do that running around the country saying you are not a candidate?"

"Book, I'm going to do it my own way," Thatch said. For the first time Curver detected something like hardness in his attitude toward Book. "I'm going to stay out of it. If I build up enough support among the voters, the delegates will take me. If they don't, I'll go back to building bridges and cement plants. Book, you wanted to lift the level of the political dialogue; you keep talking about your faith in the people. Well, what I propose is to rely precisely on those two things. I'm going to talk on issues and I'm going directly to your voters."

Curver stirred in his chair. Thatch swung his head and looked at him.

"Thatch, I know you're not big on the polls, but those are what the delegates are going to look at," Curver said. "So whether you believe in them or not is irrelevant; the delegates do. We want to make sure that your name stays toward the top of the list of the Republicans who have a chance. Right?"

Thatch looked at him calmly. He sat down, tilted the chair back. Thatch was, Curver realized with some apprehension, a very experienced negotiator. He knew when to be quiet. He also knew when to hang on hard.

"Depends on what one has to do to stay top dog on the polls," Thatch said finally. "What do you have in mind?"

"Nothing. Not yet. I just . . ."

"Mad, cut out that kind of crap. You had something in mind or you wouldn't have raised the question. Or you're a lot dumber than I think you are," Thatch said brutally. "Let's hear it."

"As I analyze the polls, you are weak with one group of Republicans," Curver said. "The group convinced there is a domestic Communist conspiracy. They aren't big, but they are active as hell and they are wealthier than most Republicans."

"Mad, the FBI and about five other agencies are running the Communist Party here," Thatch said. "They have so many agents in the Party that the poor Communists can't tell the agents from the comrades. And sometimes the agents can't. We've got Communist problems, Mad, but not in the US. In Viet Nam you don't have to worry about whether or not the opposition is Communist. You know damned well it is. If you want proof, just go for a ride in a jeep out to Soc Nimh and they'll oblige by putting a thirty-caliber slug in you as a demonstration of sincerity."

Curver made a quick note about the attractive possibilities of Thatch riding in a jeep in Viet Nam. Then he pursued his line of argument.

"Thatch, it isn't a rational question to these people. Almost everything is 'proof' to them," Curver said. "You've got to say something that allows them to read your position as being one of alarm about domestic Communists."

"I just don't think I'll do that," Thatch said. "First, I don't believe in it. Second, I think these way-out believers in conspiracy are a handful of people. Old disappointed frightened people."

Bookbinder gave a sigh of relief.

"I feel better," he said. "For a minute there I thought you had a bad attack of the political virus. You came in here sounding like a dozen men I know who have the virus in advanced stages. You may have it, but you've got it under control."

"All right," Curver said, "you have in your wisdom said that our noncandidate cannot take a stand on domestic communism. Good soldier Curver salutes and goes along. But if you think that you are going to build a steamroller of sentiment without setting up some kind of office or clearing center or some type of organization, you're wrong."

"You and I can do that, Mad," Bookbinder said. "We don't even have to ask Thatch. We just set up a Volunteers for Thatch in some office here and man it with volunteers and pass out pictures and biographies. We have not asked our noncandidate for permission. We'll just do it. Then we'll make a press announcement the first time Thatch talks on TV."

"When will that be?" Curver asked Thatch.

"I accepted an invitation to go on *Meet the Press* this Sunday," Thatch said.

"Fine. I'll make my statement on Monday," Bookbinder said.

"And I'll disown you the same day."

"Thatch, they're going to ask you about that year you spent in the mental institution," Curver said. A new element was loose in the room, like an invisible and deadly presence.

Thatch sat quietly. His right arm rose in a half-angry gesture and then fell back again.

"Who is going to tell them?" Thatch finally said.

"Kelly. He checked you out, but good, before he went along the first time," Curver said. "He's not neutral, Thatch. He's got a candidate—Bryant Clark, the university president. Kelly is going to do everything he can to cut you down before the Convention. He'll leak about that year in the mental institution. It'll come up on the *Meet the Press* panel."

Thatch's eyes blinked and his head made a weaving motion. He shrank in the chair, pulled his shoulder up in an oddly protective manner. In the silence the air came heavily in and out of Thatch's nostrils. He heard the sound and started to breathe through his mouth. Then, almost instantly, his posture changed, a flickering motion of the limbs, a straightening of the back. He came out of the chair in a long stride.

"It doesn't have a damned thing to do with politics," Thatch said in a thick, very controlled voice. "That little bastard doesn't have the right . . . no right at all—"

Most political people have that buried rage, Curver thought. They learn to handle it in various ways. Some, like McCarthy, seem to take everything as a joke. Some, like Vandenberg or Taft, develop a cool exterior. But it's there. Maybe it's the thing that gets them into politics. He remembered what Dev had said about the strong leader usually being afraid of his rage. But he decided to push a little further. Just a little.

"Look, Thatch, it's a perfectly legitimate question," Curver said. "If people are talking about a man for President, everything about his background is fair game—his parents, his childhood, his wife, his mental stability. Christ, you wouldn't want a paranoid in the White House with the ability to push the button and start a war, would you?"

"Mad, don't be crude. Thatch spent a year in a mental institution. Millions of Americans get help for mental illness at one time or another. That doesn't mean they're paranoid," Bookbinder said.

Curver watched Thatch. Thatch had taken a few steps from his chair and he wobbled slightly. Then he took a huge breath, fighting for control.

Curver pressed on. "What do we do about it?"

"Not a thing," Thatch said. His voice was even. His hard breathing had stopped. "I'll just tell them exactly what happened and read the report from the doctors who treated me. I won't answer questions about it. You're correct. They have the right to know. But they don't have the right to kick it around forever and bring it up again and again to me."

"All I'm trying to do, Thatch, is prepare you for the fact that you'll get the question," Curver said. "I'd like to work out some sort of statement you might make."

"I'll consider whatever you write," Thatch said. "And then I probably won't use it."

"Dr. Stephenson, this is Madison Curver in New York," Curver said into the telephone. "We met at the internists' convention. Yep. That's right."

Curver listened for a few seconds as the doctor tried to remember him. He would, but it would be a mistake. Curver had not actually met him, but who remembers names from a convention?

"Well, sir, a number of us have been talking about getting John Thatch interested in the Republican nomination for President," Curver said. "No. He hasn't approved and we haven't asked him to. We thought we'd just feel out some influential people around the country first. I noticed that you'd been a delegate to the nineteen sixty Republican convention and just wanted your reaction."

The doctor spoke for a few minutes.

"Well, that's better than anything I expected," Curver said. "I'll pass that along and you'll be hearing from us. We put great stock in your opinion, sir."

Curver hung up. He was tired.

Across the desk from him four young men sat quietly. They had been listening to him make phone calls for two hours.

"You've seen Mr. Curver make fifteen calls," Dr. Devlin said. "The list he called was carefully selected. They are all from high-SES groups . . . rural, urban, trade-union leaders, women. You will notice that no low-SES subjects were called. Why?"

"The low-SES person is not likely to be a delegate to the Republican convention," one of the young men said. The others nodded.

"All right. You are all graduate students. You know what is involved here, what we are trying to accomplish. You will, when you call, identify yourselves as Mr. Curver, Mr. Bookbinder's associate and, depending upon the person you are calling, say essentially what Mr. Curver has said. But keep in mind what the Bellengrath, Garrison, Sheldon, and Zeleny studies all indicate what Americans like in a leader: He is bigger physically, has a pleasing (but not pretty) physical appearance, is self-confident, is not too much smarter than they, is sincere, and has lots of energy. So keep hitting those things when anyone asks you questions."

"What about political issues?" one of the graduate students asked.

"Keep away from them," Dr. Devlin said. "If the person

persists, ask him what he thinks John Thatch's position *should* be. Say that Thatch is seeking the views of the electorate."

The four young men smiled. They had been carefully selected by Dr. Devlin from among the brightest graduate students she knew. They combined intelligence with a high interest in politics. Although they did not know it, on a social-manipulation test they had all fallen in the top 5 per cent of those who enjoyed manipulating people and situations.

The students walked over to a long table which held a half-dozen phones. Each had a list of names and at once they started to dial numbers.

Dr. Devlin and Curver walked into the other room of the two-room suite they had rented.

"They'll do all right," Dr. Devlin said. "It's silly to use your time and energy on phone calls."

"I know, but it's a little bit weird to have a bunch of graduate students all introducing themselves as me and then giving a spiel," Curver said.

"We'll be doing a lot more of this kind of thing in New Hampshire, won't we?" Dr. Devlin asked.

"Let's worry about New Hampshire after we get him by this first TV appearance," Curver said. "Kelly is bound to have planted that asylum bit with someone on the panel."

"Maybe Thatch's answer—to read from the doctor's report—is the right answer."

"There is no right answer to 'insanity,' and that's what people are going to call it."

"Mad, there is a right answer to everything except homosexuality—and maybe there is even for that. I've just never seen it tested."

Mad looked at her and suddenly roared with laughter. He collapsed his long frame into a chair and enjoyed her confusion.

The question came up toward the end of the hour-long *Meet the Press* program.

WRESTON: Do you intend to seek the Republican nomination for the Presidency?

THATCH: I do not.

WRESTON: Does that mean you would refuse the nomination if offered it?

THATCH: No man who thought himself qualified would, or should, refuse such an opportunity for duty.

WRESTON: Do you consider yourself qualified, Mr. Thatch?

THATCH: Not at the present time.

DYER: Does any part of your refusal actually to run stem from the fact that you spent a year in a mental institution?

THATCH: It was a little over a year, Mr. Dyer. When I went to college I had been raised and educated by my parents almost completely in foreign lands. They were medical missionaries, Mr. Dyer, in India, the Philippines, what was then Indo-China, and parts of Africa. . . .

DYER: I am not asking about your parents. I am asking about your mental collapse and its impact on your political decision as—

THATCH: This is the only way to answer your question properly, Mr. Dyer. When I went to Stanford I was not used to crowds and to university life. I suffered from what the doctors called "disorientation." It was not quite a collapse. On my own I went to a mental institution and for a year I worked in the gardens there and talked to a doctor several times a month and then left. I became a rather good gardener and—

DYER: But were you cured?

THATCH (reaching into a brief case): I have the final report of the psychiatrist if you would like to see it. I carry it as a memento. Unlike many, Mr. Dyer, I do not regard turning to medical science as a shameful thing even when the mind is involved. The report indicates that I never had anything more than a severe case of homesickness. Unfortunately my home was eight thousand miles away and I had no money to get there.

DYER: Well, assuming that is correct, let's get back to the original question. Does that affect your political decision now?

THATCH: I have no political decision to make. I have not held elective office. It would be presumptuous of me to offer myself as a candidate for the highest office in the land.

WRESTON: But if offered the candidacy you would not refuse?

THATCH: If I believed myself to be qualified I could not refuse.

DYER: Now can we get back to Rizal Sipa and that remarkable episode in Zamboanga. . . .

Dr. Devlin called the research director of the network two days after the program. The panel had gotten the biggest response in its history. More than three thousand phone calls, one third of them attacking Dyer for embarrassing Thatch. The rest were congratulations for Thatch.

"All right, Mad, I'll concede. Your statement was better than anything I could have invented on the spot," Thatch said. They were in Thatch's hotel suite at the Plaza, a tray of bottles behind them on the table. Dr. Devlin was talking to Terry.

"Most people think they can improvise on the spot and do better than if they prepare," Curver said. "It doesn't usually work that way."

Dr. Devlin heard part of the conversation. She carefully directed Terry's eyes to the two men and her voice rose slightly.

"A psychologist named Ebbinghaus who did the first work on retention and memory," she said, "discovered that extreme emotion tends to scatter the memory. The mind picks up odd bits and fragments here and there which may have no relation to the subject. You should *appear* spontaneous, but it is a very difficult thing to accomplish."

Thatch's head was turned toward Curver. But Dr. Devlin was sure he had heard. That was the important thing. He was not the sort to take kindly to a lecture from a woman.

18

"I don't really understand who is coming to this luncheon," Thatch said.

He was sitting in Bookbinder's sixteenth-floor suite of an Atlantic City hotel. Outside the ocean glittered and a few strollers moved along the boardwalk in the cold February sunshine.

"It's a meeting of the National Committee plus some important delegates plus whatever other influential Republicans want to come along," Bookbinder said. He glanced at his watch, noted it was noon and walked over to the bar. The decanters were exact replicas of the ones in his office.

"Their real job is to plan the primaries, but actually they are doing a lot of politicking. Especially the candidates for President, announced or unannounced. You'll see the Flyboy around and the Millionaire and they'll have cocktail parties in their suites. The Loser will just be here like it's an accident."

"They don't think John is an unannounced candidate, do they?" Terry asked.

"Some of them do," Bookbinder said. "Kelly is here and he will have planted the word with some people. By and large most of them don't think you're a candidate."

"My speech today is going to have the lowest political content they've ever heard," Thatch said. "Where is the speech? I gave you the only copy."

"Mad is having it mimeographed," Bookbinder said. "He'll have the original back here in a few minutes. You have to have copies for the newspapers or the reporters go nuts." Bookbinder saw that Thatch was tensing. "Thatch, don't worry about the speech being mimeographed. No implications. It's routine."

"Does Mad ever practice as a lawyer?" Thatch asked.

"Hell, yes, he does. He's one of the best in my office. It just so happens that he's overboard on politics and it's the season. But even when he's traveling on politics he gets up early and dictates for a couple of hours in the morning. He's a horse for work."

"Does he want to run for office eventually?"

"No. It's strictly a spectator sport for Mad," Bookbinder said. He felt a bit uneasy. It occurred to him that he had not seen Mad around the office much. Mad had gone up to observe the early phases of the New Hampshire primary campaign and had gotten in a little skiing while he was there. Mad just doesn't live like an ordinary lawyer, Bookbinder told himself. He might as well get used to it.

Bookbinder glanced at Thatch and knew the other man was nervous.

"This is a pretty hard-nosed group," Bookbinder said. "They hear speeches by the scores, so don't get nervous if they seem not to be paying attention. They're taking in the main points."

An hour earlier Dr. Devlin, in her fifteenth-floor suite directly below Bookbinder's, had read the speech. She threw it on the coffee table and looked at Curver.

"Mad, if he gives this he's through," she said.

"But this is basically the same speech that bowled over the internists," Curver said. He was genuinely surprised and a bit irritated. "It got more coverage in the media than anything since Thatch, boy hero, threw back the Huks in the wilds of Zamboanga."

"Which means that the people here will already have read about it," Dr. Devlin said. "So the speech will be stale. But it's worse than that. McClosky did a study on the differences between Democratic and Republican leaders. Republican leaders are more independent . . . even their rank and file don't go along with them. They are big on hard work, frugality, and believe that the government ought to stay out of things and let each man get his own reward. Any talk about government support for educating doctors and they'll be off and running—away. They're still half-convinced there's a Communist conspiracy in America and they're plenty cool on integration. That 'bankruptcy is health' bit will be okay because they'll all be thinking it's the other guy who'll go bust first. But most of this is awful for this group."

"There's nothing we can do about it," Curver said. He knew Dev was right. "Thatch won't change the speech. Not if I know him."

"If he won't change it we'll change it for him," Dev said. "You told him you were having it mimeographed so we've got some time."

"I didn't exactly tell him," Curver said, grinning. "I told Bookbinder I was having it mimeoed and ran like a thief."

"All right. We'll write in the changes, put them in the mimeographed version and hand it back to him at the last moment."

Curver groaned. "You may have an unemployed lawyer on your hands by this afternoon," he said. He kept his excitement down. It was mixed with a reluctant admiration for Dev's willingness to act quickly.

"We really should have had the speech two weeks ago. We could have made a rundown with Simulations Enterprises, done some pretesting, studied the characteristics of these political 'actives.' First, humor is out. No saliency for actives. Second, partisanship increases as information increases, so this group is going to be plenty partisan. Third, anxiety over solidarity of the organization. Fourth, . . ."

Curver watched and listened to her for a moment, then grabbed a pencil and started to write.

When Thatch walked to the podium, the mimeographed speech in his hands, he could sense this was a different group. They were not watching him. They were talking quietly and earnestly to one another. They picked at their food and there was the subdued tinkling sound of silver and china and glasses touching. The diners got up, walked to other tables, stood for a moment talking, and then moved away. The men were well-dressed, quick-moving, and their gestures were confident. There was, and Thatch knew this must be the difference, none of the mild flirtatiousness which often passes for good manners in a mixed group. The women were equals here and they knew it.

There were a few announcements as the dessert, a green crème de menthe parfait, was served. The toastmaster introduced Thatch as a man of courage, but said little more. Bookbinder, sitting next to Thatch, said, "Now that tepid introduction was, I guarantee you, suggested by our friend Kelly."

Thatch grinned woodenly at Bookbinder. He got to his feet and walked to the podium. There was a sprinkle of applause. A few incurious faces turned toward him. Most of the people went on talking. The crystalline hum did not diminish.

Thatch felt no tension as he began to speak. He also felt no involvement. There was an odd limpidity in the room, a lack of excitement, a quality of boredom. But, Thatch sensed, it was boredom only with him. The people below scurried like ants, whispered, conspired, touched one another. They were active and happy and could not care less about what Thatch had to say.

He noticed a gaunt elderly woman at one of the tables lift her lizard eyes and stare carefully at him. She was a composition of wealth . . . quiet expensive clothes, dull glitter of gold watch, fine pearl necklace, a small elegant brooch, flawless hairdo. It was the supplicating posture of the man bending over her that told Thatch the woman was also powerful.

The gaunt woman listened as Thatch mentioned "bankruptcy

is health" and she clapped her liver-spotted hands together. She was joined by the man talking to her and a few others. She listened intently for a few seconds and then put her hand on the man's arm and shook her head. His face melted with disappointment. He walked stiffly away and a few malicious smiles followed him.

Thatch droned along with his speech. He felt acid form in his throat. He recoiled from the pleasure the woman's attention gave him. He looked down the table at Terry. She smiled, and it was the most genuine thing she had done in months. He knew she was thinking that this was the last one. The last speech. The last strain.

He was boring people. He looked at Bookbinder and could detect nothing. He saw the figure of Kelly moving through the tables, chuckling to a person here, clapping another on the shoulder, standing always with his back to the speaker.

Thatch knew what quality the women here had—they were tough. And they were experienced. But they were not unsympathetic, they were merely bored. They listened, from time to time, and apparently they found nothing to intrigue them.

It was almost over now. He turned a page and although he had not been reading word for word, had been improvising somewhat, he suddenly was aware of error.

He did not recognize the next paragraph. It said something about "domestic Communist conspiracy."

Thatch stopped speaking.

Really it did not matter. No one was listening, so he might as well read the strange words. Someone mistook his silence for the end of his speech and clapped softly. A few others joined in and then stopped as they saw Thatch was still on the podium. He felt slightly unsteady. Maybe he had written these words and forgotten them.

Silently Thatch scanned the paragraph which said "All of us here are, because of the domestic Communist conspiracy, bound together into a battle against misunderstanding. I saw what was done to John Foster Dulles who, as an architect of peace, carved out a firm policy of massive retaliation. I saw this labeled brinkmanship. I saw columnist after columnist depict Mr. Dulles as stubborn and shortsighted. If protecting our national interests is stubborn, then we are stubborn. If banding together with our allies is short-sighted, then I am glad to join the ranks of the short-sighted."

Thatch looked up. The room was almost completely silent. In a far corner he saw Kelly talking rapidly to a table of men. Thatch felt, again, the old almost-forgotten sensation of being in danger, of being threatened by the crowd. But this time it was somehow different. He was threatened by their passivity, by their silent faces. He felt, suddenly, very powerful with the knowledge of what lay behind the masks before him: nothing.

Thatch chuckled.

It came out over the loudspeaker system as a distant rumble. The silence became alert. He sensed hostility, but he did not care. He was marvelously attuned to this audience he despised and he glanced slowly at them as he thought about the strange paragraph. The crowd wavered, the sounds dropped, silence spread, and then they had changed. They capitulated: They wanted the silence ended. It was, he knew, an exquisite agony. Thatch was astounded. All of these tough faces had capitulated: *They wanted the silence ended.* It was the one thing they could not endure.

The silence had lasted for forty seconds and was now complete.

The toastmaster shifted in his seat.

Somewhere a woman coughed and it sounded like a sob.

Thatch broke the silence only when he heard the sounds of people breathing, when every face had turned toward him.

"Domestic Communist conspiracy," Thatch said in slow round words. "How many of you have faced it? How many of you have ever seen a Communist? Not a college professor you think is a Communist. Not the trade-union leader who is organizing your plant. Not someone who is Communizing you with fluorides. No. Not that invented kind. I mean a Communist with a grenade in his hand and hate in his eyes and a firm desire to kill you. Is that what the Communists in this domestic conspiracy look like?"

"No," a voice said firmly. It came from the gaunt wealthy woman.

"No? Well, overseas they come this new way . . . with grenades and recoilless rifles." Thatch stood, looking at the fools. "And they come by the millions and they go right for the jugular.

They are not dreamed up and you don't have to have some pot-bellied Congressman to issue you a yearly report on who might be a Communist in your public school system. No, in Laos and Viet Nam and Burma they will step out of the jungle and tell you as they shoot."

He waited. The silence dragged out. Without thinking of effect, Thatch took off his wrist watch and put it on the podium. The febrile second hand jerked around in its endless circle.

No one spoke.

The second hand passed the thirty-second mark.

"My wife has seen the face of communism," he said, gesturing toward Terry. "I have seen it. In its real forms."

Thatch paused and looked toward Terry. She was staring at him, wide-eyed. The toastmaster was rapt.

"Marx was wrong," Thatch said. His voice, echoing within his own skull, seemed far away and precise and caustic. "Religion is not the opium of the people. In America communism is the opium of the people. All the miseries of your personal life you can blame on communism. And each time you inflate the power of communism, precisely as Marx would have wanted you to. Perhaps it is a special reality, the reality that brown and black and white Americans, banded together, can face international communism, perhaps that is what *you* cannot face. For perhaps you are unwilling to make the sacrifice, unwilling to hold a black hand in yours. The opium of domestic communism is so much easier. And so habit-forming."

Then from the corner of his eye Thatch saw the thing develop. It was like a smear across the eye, a wavering at the edge of vision. A man stood up. He shrieked and his rimless glasses glittered. He yelled words and he threw something. It was small at first but it grew in size. Grew in redness and roundness.

It was a tomato. To Thatch's internal eye it traveled very slowly, as if the air were thick. He could almost reach out and stop it. Then he knew it was impossible.

The tomato hit the water glass in front of Terry and went in a red splash across her plate. Terry stood up quietly with lamb chops and a white smear of potato and tiny green peas falling from her. She wiped them off, let them drop to the floor. She looked at Thatch as her hands moved. Thatch thought her very calm.

The moment the tomato hit, by some law of perception and recollection, Thatch knew what the man had said.

"Mulatto bitch," the man had said, his voice stuttering with anger. "Never had a nigger girl at a head table before."

That was what the man had said. Thatch got all the words precisely.

Thatch watched Terry finish brushing the food from her dress. Someone handed her a napkin. In Thatch's throat the pulse was brutal and jerking. He told himself not to look at the man who had thrown the tomato. *Amok, latah, juramendato;* oh no, not now. Oh no, not now! Not when he had fought this down and out of sight for so many years. He must do the civilized thing: speak rather than act.

"So she has seen it and she has fought it and she gets her reward," Thatch said finally. "A tomato thrown by a patriot. A man of courage. A man of valor. A man who has smoked the opium of communism."

The man had been trapped immediately. He stood in the rigid geometry of tables and white faces. He wanted to run, obviously.

"The threat of communism is not from within," Thatch said when the noise died. "All this poor creature could throw was a tomato. But in Viet Nam and Korea and Laos they throw hand grenades wrapped round with bicycle chain."

An ugly growl grew in the audience. Men advanced on the cowering tomato thrower. The toastmaster stood up. He cleared his throat. A university debater, a toastmaster, a charmer . . . he could not believe what he saw. He went to the fray with innocence complete.

"Now look, all you back there," he said. "Stop it. This is a meeting by Roberts *Rules of Order*. And I say stop."

The toastmaster looked at Thatch and said, "*Something!* Please. Please do something."

Thatch looked at Terry. She was watching with interest. She was not frightened by physical violence; she had seen too much of it.

Thatch waited and then replaced the toastmaster at the microphone.

His voice boomed.

"Stop," Thatch roared. It came through the loudspeakers like a command from heaven. The threatening crowd wheeled, gaped, stopped. Thatch watched while the man who threw the tomato was hustled out of the room.

The noise in the hall stopped.

"Stop. And be seated," Thatch said, quietly. "My wife has been abused. I feel no anger. Neither should you. One of the reasons we should be gathered here is to eliminate such feelings. How do we go about it?"

From the cynical, tough, experienced audience came a sigh of relief. Thatch knew they expected him to show the way. For a moment he disbelieved. Then he felt the odd pleasure he had felt only a few times before. Always it banished the fear.

"We eliminate such feelings by understanding what other people are like," Thatch said. Tears rolled down the cheeks of the gaunt woman with the pearls. "Violence is the pleasure of idiots. Anger is the drunken Saturday night of subhumans."

He sensed that he must pause.

He was not quite sure why.

Then he knew. For response.

"He's right. 'Excellence is color-blind,'" a voice called from the audience.

The whole banquet room seemed to shiver. Then the sophisticates gathered themselves to become hard and professional. But they failed. The room had a liquid and moving quality.

Thatch turned and he and Terry left the speakers' table together. The one face in the crowd Thatch fastened on was Kelly's. He was staring at Thatch, mouth open. No one left until they had gone through the door. The room was very quiet.

They were back in Bookbinder's suite. Terry was pale, color showing only on her cheeks. Thatch stretched out on the couch, looked up at the ceiling. Bookbinder poured himself a drink.

They had not talked since they left the banquet room.

"Thatch, you'd better be ready for a lot of pressure from here on in," Bookbinder finally said. "That speech got 'em."

Thatch rolled his head slowly sideways, looked at Bookbinder.

"They hated it," he said. "No one applauded, it upset their

meeting, it was just chaos. Book, you don't have to kid me. I'm a big boy."

Bookbinder turned away from Thatch. He was not sure what to do. Could Thatch really be sincere, he wondered? Was he, Bookbinder, being used by this big open-faced man? He shot a glance at Thatch. The man was staring at the ceiling and there was nothing but fatigue on his face.

"Thatch, I've listened to a lot of speeches," Bookbinder said. "Once in a great while a speech stuns people, catches them off guard so completely that they don't applaud. You did that today. That gang of professionals won't recover for days."

"Book, stop it," Thatch said. "It was a Keystone Kops episode. I acted like a madman. I'm not unhappy. It's the last damned speech I have to give."

Terry shook her head. "No it's not. I've heard you describe the political virus. It was not pleasant . . . your description of the walking wounded, broken by that virus. But John has your virus. I also think he would make a good President. Don't talk to me about duty or polls or speeches. I'd like John to stop." She turned to her husband. "John, I watched those people at lunch. You reached them. You shook them. Those people down there are going to be after you. But it's not too late to say no."

"Terry, please call me Book," Bookbinder said.

She looked at him coldly. Thatch did not see the look.

Thatch felt a kind of dull thudding relief in his bones and muscles. It was like a tonic, more so than any drink. Now, in some convoluted way, he was given permission to remember the victory of the speech. He listened to Book and Terry talk, but he thought of the uplifted faces, the rapt looks, the sense of possessing a power over the audience. It was indecent, he knew that. It was childish. He felt a low-pitched ecstasy as he recalled how they had surged toward the offender. And then how they had stopped, in midmotion, as his voice gave the order. And these were not ordinary people. These were the big ones.

Thatch laughed. He rolled over.

"Kelly is really a bastard, isn't he, Book?" he said. "I saw him snuffling around like a dog looking for bones. Does anyone take him seriously?"

"Don't get carried away, Thatch," Bookbinder said. "Kelly

packs a lot of power around. He does his homework. He lost today. So he'll come back at you. You'll hear more about your year at the mental hospital, Terry's Filipino blood—and anything else there might be."

Thatch did not speak. He nodded his head, staring at the ceiling.

"Mr. Thatch, I consider that a very remarkable speech," the portly man said. He had shouldered his way through the crowd and stood squarely in front of Thatch. "My name is Grove." He put out his hand.

"Governor Grove," Bookbinder said, "it's good seeing you."

"Good seeing you, Bookbinder," Grove said, his eyes still on Thatch. He had a slightly automated look about him. He was wound up and set forth to wander, Thatch thought, and beneath the flesh the wheels ground and meshed. That's your last drink, Thatch told himself. You're getting fanciful.

"In the Midwest, Mr. Thatch, we don't have any racial problem. Hope you understand that. None. None at all. Maybe it's because we're hicks. Provincial, the New York papers keep saying. One of the things we're hicks about is the race thing. Probably because we don't have it. I'm curious. Is your wife a Malay quadroon?"

Thatch laughed.

"I never heard of a Malay quadroon," he said. "Why do you ask?"

"Just curious," the man said. His round face turned to where Terry was standing talking to a group of women. His mechanical voice clicked off words. "I just wondered if a Malay quadroon was another name for Negress. I don't really know. Like I say, we're hicks."

Suddenly, Bookbinder was trying to break up the conversation, edging between them physically with his body. A familiar figure moved toward them from another direction. It was Senator Reddick. Thatch had only met Reddick a few minutes before, but he remembered him as the Senator who had made the ringing remarks about him in the *Congressional Record*.

Somewhere a glass fell. A tray of *hors d'oeuvres* passed and the light flickered off silver, black caviar eggs, thick wedges of cheese. Thatch felt very tired. But the fat man in front of him, the Governor, had said something and Thatch had to answer. Why did he resist?

"Say it again, Governor," Thatch said, smiling. "I'm tired. I must have missed something."

Senator Reddick stood beside the Governor.

"I just asked if a Malay quadroon would be a Negress by our standards here in the States," the Governor said. "We don't have any race problem in my state, but—"

"Governor, did you lay your wife before you married her?" Thatch asked. He was curiously cool. "If you did, Governor, you are a fornicator. I don't know if a Malay quadroon is a Negress by your standards or any other. You are deliberately being offensive; that I do know, but I do not know why."

The Governor's already opaque face went even more opaque. He became featureless, like a burn case who has a skin graft drawn completely over the face . . . no eyebrows, lips, nose. Only his eyes responded. The eyes grew, like grapes about to burst, and the man's ears were very prominent because he had no other features.

"Governor, that is a completely irrelevant and quite discourteous question," a voice said. "I was not aware that any of us harbored such thoughts or would put them so crudely."

Thatch turned his head numbly. It was Senator Reddick. The man had a Southern accent.

"Senator, you're from a Southern state, and it's one thing down there to just push it under the bed—" the Governor was saying.

"Governor, if you would just apologize to Mr. Thatch, I think that we could mingle with the rest of the delegates and enjoy ourselves," Senator Reddick said.

"I'm not goin' say 'scuse me for just askin' a question," the Governor said. "Look, Reddick, you—"

"Say 'scuse me and as damned quick as you can," Senator Reddick said pleasantly.

The Governor waited a long second. He worked his lips, tried once, failed. Thatch felt the world was mad. But he waited.

" 'Scuse me, Mr. Thatch," the lips said. But the eyes above the lips were bright with hate.

Senator Reddick took Thatch's arm and led him out of the group.

"You didn't win much, friend," the Senator said. "He'll be a bastard of an enemy. But the committee of which I happen to be chairman may, or may not, spend about one-half billion bucks on a canal-and-dam complex in his state. He's not forgetting that."

"We didn't exactly carry the day with our speech revision," Dr. Devlin said. She stared at her hands, clasped tightly in her lap. "He really went off like a rocket."

"Dev, you miss the whole damned point," Curver said. "Thatch has a quality that you and no one else in our lifetime is going to be able to research. He knows just how far he can drive a crowd. And he isn't afraid to drive them right to the limit."

"You sound like one of those crackpots who believes in ESP and spiritualism and the holy leader," she said caustically.

Curver spoke from the depths of his chair.

"Listen, sweetheart. I hired the guy to throw that tomato today. He was a Ph.D. candidate from Columbia and I had to pay him a thousand dollars. I also hired four other guys to get him out of there but quick, before the police arrived. But they missed their cue and got there late. The poor bastard just about got lynched. I was sweating blood. Our boy Thatch moved in and saved him. Neither you nor I could have done it."

Dev stared at him. She chewed on her lower lip.

Kelly waited until he saw Thatch's wife step off the board-walk down on to the beach in front of the hotel. She kicked off her shoes and left them at the edge of the boardwalk.

He followed her. She had an expert's appreciation for the beach which he envied. The waves came just to the edge of the scalloped path she made on the wet sand. She whistled at the gulls and they hesitated in their take-off scurry and then came curling back to examine her. She dug for tiny soft-shell crabs and then gently dropped them back and watched them scurry into the sand.

Kelly knew nothing about the shore or the sea. His shoes were wet and for a moment he thought of taking them off and walking barefoot as she was doing. He knew it would look silly. His skin was too pale.

"Mrs. Thatch," he said.

She swung around, her eyes still following three lazy gulls. Then she looked at Kelly.

"Hello. Out for a walk?"

"Just trying to get some exercise," Kelly said. They had never met, but she guessed he was a member of the convention.

"My name is Bert Kelly, Mrs. Thatch," Kelly said. She nodded. "We haven't met, but I've met your husband and Book and Mad and the rest."

"I'm sorry, but I just don't remember," she said. "It's because I'm not much interested in politics, I guess."

"I understand," Kelly said. "Mrs. Thatch, I want to apologize for that terrible incident in the ballroom." Kelly felt genuinely contrite, even ashamed. He was at a loss to understand it. "I can't imagine who that man was or how he got in. Nothing like that has ever happened before at a Committee function. The other members have asked me to convey their apologies."

"Don't worry about it, Mr. Kelly." She smiled at him and he was surprised to see that she wasn't upset at all. "I've had much worse done to me."

Kelly paused. God, she wasn't making it easy for him. He knew he had to plunge ahead anyway.

"Could we sit down a minute? I'd like to talk with you a moment." He took a package out from under his arm. "I think we have a mutual friend who was in Santo Tomas during the war."

There was no suspicion on Terry's face. She was delighted. She walked up the beach to where the dry sand began and sat down. Kelly sat down beside her and wiped his face with a handkerchief.

"I'll bet it was the Thacketts," Terry said. Kelly shook his head. "Dorn Stern? All right. I give up."

Kelly got to the point very quickly. He unwrapped the package. He had barely exposed the first page when he heard Terry sigh. He kept on until he had the diary completely exposed on his lap.

"It's Mrs. Singleton's diary," Terry said. "It was an obsession with her. She would trade chocolate for paper and pencils. She watched, scurried around, sneaked up on people who were talking. For a few weeks we thought she was spying for the Japanese. But she was just scribbling. She called herself the official camp historian."

"Did you ever see any of the things she scribbled?" Kelly asked.

"No. We had so little privacy that we didn't pry into other people's affairs," Terry said. "No one would go around reading someone else's diary."

"It's really quite complete," Kelly said, looking directly at Terry.

In that moment he knew she understood. The smile did not vanish from her face; it was simply underlined by gaunt lines that had not been there a moment before.

"I've marked a page or two you might be interested in reading," Kelly said.

At once, with an acquired deftness, he was defending himself. History, he thought, has always been full of people with great promise who have to be told they have some fatal flaw. As he went through the pages his fingers were suddenly fumbling and moist. He had done harder things before . . . someone had to do them. He hated the men who wanted the glory but wouldn't do the necessary things. Stop making excuses, he said to himself. His fingers steadied and he turned to the first marked page. He held his finger under a paragraph and Terry read it.

"Terry Whitehaus has, they say, gone over to the Japs. That is, she is sleeping with one of them and in return is given food. They say she gets three extra pounds of rice and some candy from the Jap. It may not be true. This place lives on rumors. The Whitehaus girl is in a strange situation. She seems to be some part Filipino, but she is from Mindanao and has no Filipino friends here. The Japanese will not even investigate her claim to be a Philippine citizen. The name Whitehaus convinces them she is a European. I cannot condemn her."

"Why do you bring this to me, Mr. Kelly?" she asked. She walked down to the sea until the water was just coming over her feet. Kelly followed, standing awkwardly a few yards from her, holding the diary in his hand.

"Partly out of consideration for you and your husband," Kelly said. "If he is nominated and runs for President this is bound to come out. It is the kind of thing which cannot be suppressed. It would be personally embarrassing."

"Yes, it would be, wouldn't it," Terry said. She looked very young, very slim, but, somehow, not very troubled. She drew with her toe in the wet sand. "Have you considered that it might not be true?"

"Of course, Mrs. Thatch," Kelly said. "I checked it with some of the people who had been in Santo Tomas."

"You went personally and checked it?" Terry said, and she looked at him with a surprised kind of loathing. "My God, I never thought people really did. . . . Do you make your living at that sort of thing?"

Her look was so ingenuous that he knew she was not attacking him, she was merely surprised. But in some part of his mind Kelly not only accepted, but welcomed, abuse on his political activities. It served to deepen his sense of dedication, of doing what no one else would do, of having a grasp of history which allowed him to see how the small, seemingly sordid, things ran like threads through the larger strands of history.

"Please don't answer, Mr. Kelly," Terry said. "It's just that I thought such things only happened in detective stories."

"I don't really do the checking myself," Kelly said. A moment before he would have gladly taken credit for anything, the more loathsome the better. "It's done by professionals. But I order it done."

"Aside from wanting to protect John and me from embarrassment, why else did you bring Mrs. Singleton's diary to me?" Terry asked.

Kelly looked at her, separated by several feet of wet glistening sand and hesitated. For years he had not thought much about sex. But now, for the merest slice of time, he had a vision of throwing the diary in the ocean, taking off his shoes and walking down the beach with this strange innocent woman. Then the moment was gone.

"First, I want to protect the Republican Party. Something like this, if Thatch got the nomination, could rip it apart," Kelly said briskly. He danced back a few feet as a wave sluiced in higher than the rest. "And, although I had supported your husband before November twenty-second, I did so only because I thought any Republican would lose to President Kennedy. Your husband was, and please understand this, was the ideal man to lose with."

"Did the others—Mr. Bookbinder and Mr. Curver—think that also?" Terry asked. She was glad this meeting had come at the beach. With the sea washing over her feet and the dreamy, rhythmic sea sounds in her ears, she felt boneless, without tension, and wonderfully perceptive.

"Of course. None of us expected him to win," Kelly said, and his voice was so sure, the response so instant, that Terry knew it was the truth. "Maybe Bookbinder, but he'd be the only one."

"Now that there is a chance for a Republican to win you have someone else?" Terry asked.

"Yes. His name is—" lost in a wave and she did not care to hear.

"You are kind," Terry said. In her detached and childish mood she liked this odd fat man. She ran on her toes toward him and his eyes bulged slightly. She kissed him on the cheek. Her face close to his, she said, "It was true, what Mrs. Singleton wrote. It was my way of staying alive. But"—she stepped back and looked at him—"you've never been hungry."

She turned and started to run down the beach. Kelly watched and saw that there was a style which sea people had. She ran in scallops, running up the beach as the waves rolled in, then down over the wet sand as they retreated, then coming almost to a standstill at the ebb between waves, and then picking up speed and swooping back up the beach. Once she stopped, looked quickly at the configuration of the beach, and stood far down towards the sea. A big wave came washing in, split just before it hit her feet, and spread out in two wings on either side of her. She had found a spit of sand slightly higher than the rest of the beach.

Kelly walked back to the Boardwalk. From far down the beach, toward the Iron Pier, he could smell some sweet confection . . . it was hot and fresh and cheap. He wheeled away from it and walked a few steps. Then, in midstride, he turned his fleshy body around and walked back toward the source of the sweet smell.

19

Bookbinder loved the massive rhythmic swing of politics. It was reassuring, this four-year cycle that held everything else together. Right after the election there was a period of quiet for the defeated. They examined themselves and were puzzled and waited for the hurt to disappear. And it really hurt. The victors swept into Washington sometimes rudely and sometimes with bad taste, but always with enthusiasm and the wild chaotic excitement that new unused power always brings. The victors were generous, they made mistakes, they reformed, they innovated—and know bone-deep they would be there forever.

That was the beginning of the cycle: Defeat and victory seemed absolute and complete. The swearing-in and the State of the Union Message and the great rituals made the victory appear seamless and of the victors dignified. The sudden anonymity of the losers shattered their identity, rendered them private citizens again, and they were lost and feckless.

Bookbinder liked the finality of the Presidental decision. Even when his party had lost he had taken a deep satisfaction in the absoluteness of the victory. To some it had the cruel swish of the guillotine blade, but Bookbinder saw it as the abrupt rendering of a judgment. It was a political invention which told the people that they were, in fact, a people and were bound together.

Then the political juices started to flow again. It did not take long. The defeated came back and observed and then began to criticize and finally to attack. And the winners had the first warnings they might not have power absolutely and forever. Then the cycle turned up and started to rise again toward the Presidential year.

Bookbinder looked out the window. He did not deceive himself. He knew that most of those antlike people out there, the swarming millions of them, did not think of politics from year to year. The knowledge did not bother him. That was as it should be. Soon enough the big unheeding mass would be aroused by the thin quick-growing nerves of politics . . . they would not feel or sense it at first, but as the four-year cycle rose to a crest, the political nerves would come alive and make the mass twitch and take notice.

Kelly glanced at the card again, read the last few lines. "Retailer in hardware, substantial interests in real estate. Gives canned lecture on 'Salesmanship! America's Salvation in a Troubled World.' Overweight, but good health. Nickname: Sam."

"Sam, I understand you perfectly," Kelly said into the phone. "It doesn't matter to you or me that Thatch spent a year in a mental institution, but what about the voters? After all, Sam, they make the big decision. The President is our salesman, Sam. Our Number-One salesman. He sells the American way of life to other countries. It's his job. I just don't think the American voters will turn over the Number-One salesman job to a nut."

Sam interrupted. Kelly rolled his eyes. He had twenty more calls to make this morning.

"I know he's not a nut," Kelly said. "But the voters won't know that. We can't back a loser. Sam, we have to win this time. It may be our last chance for eight years."

Sam spoke.

"Good, Sam. Just keep an open mind and see how he does. If he picks up strength I'll be with him. I'm not opposed to Thatch. I like the guy."

It's true, Kelly thought, as he put the phone down. I'm not opposed to Thatch. I just like Bryant Clark better.

Kelly was bold and excited. This was the contest he loved, the thing he had trained for, where all his skills were used. He hummed, pushed a button, and told the secretary to get that big-eared hick in Keene, New Hampshire.

Thatch was surprised. It hurt. He had known it would come. He had felt ready. But as Terry read the words aloud they struck on a very tender spot.

We have nothing but admiration for John Thatch and his splendid achievements. As we have said before editorially, we applaud him as a courageous American. But we think the record of his mental instability is enough to stop the rumors that he will run for the Republican nomination for the Presidency. We would be just as disappointed if John Glenn were to run for the United States Senate, another rumor which persists. Neither gentleman has the political experience for such high elective office. They should be recognized as inspiring Americans in engineering and in air exploration, respectively, but they should confine their activities to those rewarding fields.

"More?" Terry asked, looking up.

"That's enough," he said. Terry showed nothing. Somehow he wanted her to be angry, but she only looked up at him.

Thatch dialed Bookbinder's office. It took a few minutes to get him.

"Book, did you read that editorial in the *Dispatch*?"

"Yep. I also read one in a Buffalo paper which said you were a hero to bring mental illness out in the open and as public-minded as the politician in Massachusetts who confessed to being an alcoholic."

"Oh, Christ. Can't we sue them for something like that?" Thatch said. "I'm not running for public office. Isn't there some law that protects the privacy of an individual?"

"There are, but you have to be a private individual," Bookbinder said. "You're not very private these days."

"You mean I'm political."

"Not necessarily, but until the Flyboy, whom the *Dispatch* is backing, gets past the primaries they'll whack at you or any conceivable candidate."

"But I'm not a candidate," Thatch said.

"I know that, Thatch, and I respect that," Bookbinder said. Again Thatch was aware of how gently, almost reverently, Book had talked to him since the television show on the Huks. He was careful not to talk as if Thatch were a candidate and warned him, again and again, not to be trapped into "political talk." "Just forget things like this. I know it's hard, but history is working for you, Thatch."

Thatch felt a flush of embarrassment, said good-by, and put the phone on the cradle, realized he was pressing very hard on it.

"Baby, baby, baby," Terry said, speaking the soft pliant country Tagalog. It was the way a woman talked a man out of a rage. "You don't have to do it, baby. You don't have to do anything. Come here."

Her fingers ran through his hair and she continued the old senseless but very comforting chant. It was an incantation and it reversed responsibility. Into Terry's slim body the responsibility poured.

"But Thatch has never concealed the fact that his wife is part Filipino," Mad said. "So how the hell can anyone think it's a secret, Dev?"

"It's not the reality. It's how a thing looks or can be made to look that counts."

"So how do we make capital of the fact that Thatch took himself a Filipino wife and found God while working for the FBI?"

"First, the way in which the thing is presented," Dr. Devlin said. "It doesn't call for any simulation. There's a whole literature on prejudice. We have to bring the parts together in a sensible way. One study showed that the Southerner is really only excited about the American Negro. Put a turban and a robe on a Negro and introduce him as African nobility and he will be accepted anywhere."

Curver was out of his chair.

"Myrdal has something about the guilt of the Southerner," he said softly, with excitement. "Dev, what we need here is a drama which lets the Southerner off the hook." He snapped his fingers. "A situation where there is no appearance of secrecy. Thatch has to talk easily about it. Then there has to be the implication that Thatch and his wife are being persecuted, because ignorant people think she is part Negro. Then someone from the South, like Senator Reddick, has to gently tell the public that Mrs. Thatch is not a Negro, that every Southerner knows that and that a fine woman is being persecuted—by the North. At once the Southerner is going to feel superior to the Northerner, and that hasn't happened for a long time."

"Only one thing," Dr. Devlin said. "How do we avoid having the American Negroes think that Thatch is going along with the Southern attitude?"

"Dev, you told me the answer to that one. That selective-misperception thing. Everyone sees what he wants to see. All it calls for is the right staging and the right lines for Thatch and enough ambiguity so that everyone can believe what he wants."

"Okay. I'll work on that," Dr. Devlin said. "You're doing the projection on the New Hampshire voters?"

Curver nodded and was out of the room, almost running.

Kelly listened, but not carefully, to the Chancellor's rich voice coming through the receiver. His pudgy hands were turning over some cost sheets on his desk.

"Kelly, I saw a piece of literature someone is circulating in New Hampshire and it's a disgrace," the Chancellor said. "It keeps asking if Thatch's wife is Malay and is a Malay a Negroid type. They tell me there's another one circulating in New Hampshire which says flatly that Mrs. Thatch is a 'nigger.' "

"That's a pity," Kelly said.

"It's a lot more than that and I want it stopped. I don't mind trading punches with Goldwater and Rockefeller and answering the questions which the Lodge and Nixon people plant at all the meetings, but something like these throwaways is a public disgrace. It will ruin the image of the Party."

"Bryant, there isn't a thing I can do about it," Kelly said. "Those things happen all the time. There are always some nuts around you can't control."

"Well, there is one thing you can do. Have the National Committee put out a statement repudiating the throwaways. I'll do the same."

For a moment Kelly felt like chuckling. Clark was more innocent than he had thought.

"I'll be glad to do it for the Committee, Bryant, but if we put out a statement like that it will only give the thing national attention," Kelly said. "In addition, Thatch and all the other candidates would think you had made your statement for precisely that purpose."

There was a long silence on the phone. Then the Chancellor sighed and hung up.

Kelly turned to the cost lists on his desk. They were from a small printing shop in Lyme, a nonunion one-man operation. Cost for an additional twenty thousand throwaways came to just less than a penny each. Distribution included, the price came to two cents each.

Kelly scribbled an OK on the page, but did not add his initials. Nothing on the paper described what the throwaways would say. All that Kelly handled verbally.

He thought for a moment of how ironic it was that he was promoting the interests of the purest man he knew by methods which that man hated. But the Chancellor did not understand, Kelly told himself. Throwaways like this were a legitimate part of the game, and, with his rigid, hard-won morality, Kelly had studied them to make sure that they did not say anything which was false. To ask "Is a Malay a Negroid?" was not dishonest. It was merely a question. What was Goldwater saying in New Hampshire now about Rockefeller: "I don't believe in calling a man a liar or a wife-stealer. I run my campaign aboveboard." Bryant Clark could take that approach, of course. He could move about the country saying, "I don't believe in calling a man's wife a Negress. I'm above all that."

Kelly laughed aloud. You pays your money and you takes your choice.

Q. Mr. Thatch, one of our panel members is from Alabama. He is a former Nieman Fellow at Harvard and is very interested in— I don't know just how to say it . . . but family background. You care to elaborate, Mr. Hudgins?

A. I'm on now?

Q. That's right, Mort. You're on. Just ask anything you want.

A. Well, Mr. Thatch, my question is simple. Lots of people in this country are worried about miscegenation and crossbreeding and that sort of thing.

Dr. Devlin looked at Curver. They were sitting in the sponsor's booth. The studio below them was brilliant with undimmed light. The moderator sat in the middle of the curved table. Senator Reddick sat next to him, Thatch at the end of the table. On the other side were Hudgins and a female member of the White Citizens Council named Mrs. de Martine.

"My God, Dev, you staged it like the Inquisition," Curver said. "Sure you've got it under control?"

She shrugged.

Curver forced his body into the usual slouch. Hudgins had to put his questions just the right way. Everything hinged on that.

A. I'm not sure I'm being asked a question.

Q. I'm sorry, Mr. Thatch, but Mr. Hudgins does have a question, I think.

Q. Yep, I do. It's this. Do you think that mixing colored blood with white blood results in children that are inferior to both parents?

A. Say that again.

Q. Mixing blood, Malay and Caucasian, you know, that kind of thing . . . might it result in kids that are inferior?

A. [SENATOR REDDICK] This is a profoundly stupid question, if I may interrupt. Every civilized person knows that a Malay is not a Negro and no Southerner would ask such a question. Not only is it stupid, but it is most offensive and ungentlemanly for Mr. Thatch happens to have a wife, a very lovely wife, who is part Malay. Are you aware of that, Mr. Hudgins?

A. [HUDGINS] I guess so. But it's a proper question. People are worried about it.

A. [REDDICK] No one in the South is worried about that question.

A. [THATCH] Let me bring in some expert witnesses.

Silence. Thatch moved easily out of his chair and walked off camera. For thirty seconds the other members of the round table fidgeted. Then Thatch came back with two boys in their early teens, holding each by the hand.

THATCH: You ready for my answer?

HUDGINS: Not really my question, Mr. Thatch, kind of the question of the American people and what they . . .

THATCH: Hogwash, Mr. Hudgins. You have some direct line to the American people on this subject? These two boys might be mulattos, mestizos, Coloreds, half-breeds, Eurasians, gooks, mixed blood. You know why? Because they have some Malay blood in them. Now they look just like you and me, don't they? But if someone wants, I guess he could call them all of the things I just ran off.

HUDGINS: Mr. Thatch, I don't want to be rude to anyone. Down South we don't look for trouble. There's no sense just . . .

THATCH: Ask the kids. They are my sons. They have maybe one-sixteenth Malay blood in them. I'm not sure. But ask them how miscegenated they feel.

MRS. DE MARTINE: I don't think those sweet boys ought to be asked what Senator Reddick has called a stupid question. I agree with the Senator. We in the White Citizens Council don't think that Malay blood has any connection with our problem in the South. To ask these nice boys, with their lovely mother maybe watching, to ask them an ignorant question [breaks off, sobbing] . . .

THATCH: Ask them, Hudgins. They're more direct than you. They can recognize a question and answer it.

HUDGINS [to Moderator]:   I don't think this is quite fair, to ask young boys what they think about these things.

MODERATOR: They are Mr. Thatch's sons and if he wants them to speak I see no reason why they should not.

"This is it," Curver said. "This will get coverage like you haven't seen since that dog Checkers was trotted onto the scene."

Q.   Well, what do you think about mixing blood and religion and that sort of thing, boys? Nothing personal. Don't answer if it frightens you.

A.   Mr. Hudgins, I'm Tony Thatch. I'm fifteen. Your question doesn't frighten me. I just don't see why you ask it. Isn't the whole American thing, you know the Puritans and Unitarians and all the rest, kind of trying to let everyone do what he wanted about blood and religion and things like that?

Q.   Mr. Hudgins, I'm Harry Thatch. Tony's older. About two years. I'm thirteen. Have you ever been outside the United States, I mean, for long?

A.   Yes, Harry. I've been to Europe.

Q.   Well, if you went a little further you'd know that most of the world is not white. I mean not pure white and all . . .

A.   [TONY THATCH] What Harry wants to ask, Mr. Hudgins, is—do you think you're a member of a pure-white, superior, minority group? See, Mr. Hudgins, most of the people in the world are all mixed together and they have bigger problems than what color a man is. Like getting food and medical care. Things like that. Do you understand that, Mr. Hudgins?

Dr. Devlin looked at Curver. Behind the half-smile and within the relaxed slouching body, she detected intense pleasure.

MODERATOR: Mr. Hudgins, I'm afraid I'll have to cut you off. Thank you every one for your frank comments. Next week we will discuss the question of genetics and culture . . . the place where we left off tonight. Professor Clarence Wainwright of New York University will be with us . . .

Terry Thatch wept after they put the boys to bed in the hotel rooms. She could not tell Thatch why. She was neither apologetic nor angry. She merely wept.

"Thatch, it was extraordinary," Bookbinder said into the phone. "I watched it with some friends and every woman in the room was crying and I think some of the men. I apologize really for that fool Hudgins and I think most of your audience would agree. Thatch, there is a maturity among Americans that is often overlooked. They have a feeling for your promise and your sincerity and dedication. Time is flowing with you. I hope Terry understands that Hudgins is just an isolated damned fool. Tell her. And the boys were marvelous."

"Mad helped a lot," Thatch said, speaking slowly. "It was his idea to have the boys there in case it came up. I frankly didn't think anyone would have the guts."

"It's a pretty gutsy game, Thatch," Bookbinder said. "Keep above it."

They hung up.

The nation's most prominent and oft-quoted (and usually critical) TV columnist devoted all his space to the program three days later.

Quite easily the most dramatic television drama of the year appeared Tuesday night. It was unwritten, unrehearsed, and a much-needed tribute to television's power to make the contemporary and immediate thing a great drama.

The encounter, already famous, between Mr. John Thatch's two teen-age boys, named Tony and Harry, and Mr. Hudgins aroused one of the most frenzied reactions which has been seen in many a year.

Some of the results are in. Every large daily paper in the South ran an editorial supporting Senator Reddick's comments during the program. Viewer response was overwhelmingly in sympathy with the Thatch boys. Over ten thousand letters and telegrams have been received . . . and only fifteen of them were favorable to Mr. Hudgins . . . who now appears as one of the great villains of our time.

All major networks have under consideration ideas for programs which would deal with subjects in so forthright a manner.

"John, don't show the boys that clipping," Terry asked. They were sitting alone in the cluttered ranch house living room. She went on: "I can't stand the idea that they were speaking other people's words. Did you listen? Tony and Harry don't talk like that. Somebody gave them those lines."

He stared at her as if he had not heard.

"Don't worry about an editorial in *The New York Times*," Kelly said into the phone. He was irritated, his even sense of control slightly frayed. "In the South and in a hell of a lot of the Midwest and West that thing of a Negro wife—" He paused, listened.

"I know that a Malay is not a Negro, but who the hell else does?" Kelly cut in.

He listened again, drummed his fingers on the desk, looked at them with distate, and then let his eyes roam over the pictures on the wall. His face softened.

"Gus, just keep your people lined up for Bryant Clark," Kelly said. "Don't get into a fight on the color thing. It'll work against Thatch eventually. Forget about those editorials in the big metropolitan papers and the excitement about those Thatch kids. Now, Gus, you know New Hampshire better than anyone else." Except me, Kelly thought. "Tell me when we ought to peak this campaign for Clark. Gus, he'll have some great national coverage on this report he's done for a big foundation on higher education. TV, radio, columnists, that sort of stuff. But when do we pull out all the stops?"

The tiny voice crackled in the phone.

"Ten days before?" Kelly asked, his voice unbelieving. He respected Gus. The man had run a lot of campaigns, some of them pretty dirty and some respectable. He was only respectable when he knew he was going to lose anyway. "That's shaving it close, Gus."

The voice started again.

Kelly listened, suddenly feeling much better. Over this thin electronic thread of sound, they were balancing the fortunes of an entire country, each man intuiting the experienced judgments of scores of delegates, anticipating wavering opinions and collective anxieties and hopes. Gus and I know, Kelly thought. His irritation faded.

Bookbinder had called. When Mad and Dr. Devlin got to his office he was pacing and he was obviously angry, his shoulders hunched.

"Let's make it quick," Bookbinder said. "One of Kelly's boys came to me and said that Hudgins' question on the TV program was planted."

"Planted isn't the right word, Book," Curver began. "I suggested to Hudgins that because Terry has the sort of Spanish look and there has been a little talk about her that we ought to get it out in the open and—"

"That's enough, Mad," Bookbinder said. He was white across the mouth, but his forehead was flushed. "The two of you are through with the campaign as of now. I don't want you to see or talk to Thatch. Mad, you have the cashier arrange to pay Dr. Devlin off. Then you get back to your legal work. I'll handle the politics from now on."

"You'll what?" Dr. Devlin said, and gave a sharp, bitter, lashing laugh. Fascinated, Mad watched her gather herself for the attack. "Bookbinder, if you meddle with this thing you are going to break Thatch's life, your own reputation, whatever feeble power the Republican Party has, and disgrace a few people along the way." She stood up and walked around the table, close to Bookbinder. "You are a fool in a special way. You don't have the facts and you can't understand them when someone else puts them before you."

Bookbinder drew back from the bowed tense body of the woman. Her words whipped out of her mouth with a ferocity he had never heard even from passionate trial lawyers.

"Dr. Devlin, get out of here and don't bother me again," Bookbinder said. His voice was trembling, uncertain.

"Oh, no. Not yet," she said. "You ran across John Thatch by mistake. You wanted, you said, to get some fresh blood in the Party and give the Democrats a good race. And then that second heroic act of his hit you and his performance at Atlantic City hit you and you fell under the most primitive kind of spell. You began to believe that Thatch was touched with something holy. Right now you think he is a man with a divine spark. And it strikes you as sacrilegious that someone would trick the great man . . . that Mad would plant a question with a reporter."

Curver had, when she first started to talk, meant to stop her. Now he listened, speechless. Bookbinder, when Dr. Devlin mentioned Thatch, had gone limp, the muscles in his shoulders relaxed. He leaned back against his table and stared at the woman attacking him.

"Like a caveman looking for a leader, you have to endow Thatch with supernatural powers," she said. "Now anything he does has the magic touch. Were it not for your tailored clothes and your fine office and your reputation and your facility with words . . . all those protective things . . . you would be an ape shivering in front of a bigger ape who has done some remarkable tricks. Your eyes rolling, hopping from one foot to another, praying that this big ape is the appointed leader. Please, you wail, send me a sign. And Zamboanga was a sign. And Atlantic City was a sign."

She looked at Bookbinder and shook her head as if he were a hopeless student.

"Go on with it, get it out," Bookbinder said.

"It's no use. You are hopeless and all your noble talk of political tension and the majestic sweep of the American way is disgusting," she said. "But I will go on because it makes *me* feel better. I don't think it will inform you a bit. Thatch's speech on the bridge was a mistake. Some would say it was the result of a defect in his character. No matter. Once he was told that it was a success and he could lead, a man who felt deeply that he could *not* lead, all the rest is not hard to understand. But Bookbinder, he is a sick person, like most of us are sick people, with all of the capacity to chew the rug just like Hitler if fools like you prance slowly in front of him and moan when he talks. Manipulation you accuse us of. Don't you see, you rich self-indulgent fool, that *you* are manipulating him also. Every time you praise him or your voice goes soft with admiration you are manipulating him. No . . . you don't see that, do you?"

Dr. Devlin turned to Curver. She was quite relaxed and the overcontrol she usually exercised was gone. It made her seem much younger and it aroused a new sensation in Curver . . . different from that night long ago.

"I would like you to finish," Bookbinder said. He had moved into a chair. "Some of what you say is correct. Go on."

"I will, but not gladly because I'm not enjoying it. Oh, I did the first few seconds, but not after that. I think now that in your way you have manipulated Thatch. Mad and I have manipulated him in a deliberate way . . . thinking out what we want to achieve before we do it. We want to get Thatch the Republican nomination."

Bookbinder held up his hand. He smiled thinly.

"I have manipulated Thatch," he said. He closed his eyes. "I confess to that. And I did it in the name of big and wonderful things like patriotism, and that is the most vulgar excuse for committing a wrong that I know of."

Curver thought that Dev's mood would change. Bookbinder had been generous and he seemed still genuinely interested in advice. He stiffened when Dev lashed out again.

"Don't confound stupidity with morality," she said, and her voice had the original biting quality. "Most social contacts are a manipulation. The not-so-sly suggestion in your last remark that Mad and I were thinking evil and you were thinking good while we both did the same thing is marvelous solace . . . if you are thirteen years old or on your deathbed and want to regain faith in God."

Bookbinder's eyes opened but he stayed calm. "I did not mean to imply—" he started to say.

"But you succeeded," Dr. Devlin cut in. "I am not hurt by such things, for I know something of what causes them in people. Mad will have to handle his own feelings. But before I go I want to be certain that you know you're manipulating Thatch and that you're doing it for personal reasons. Please don't bore me with what they are, but just don't masquerade them as civility."

She stopped suddenly.

Bookbinder sat in his chair. He nodded his assent. Dr. Devlin hesitated a moment and then left the office. Mad stayed with his employer. For the moment he couldn't think of anything comforting to say to either one.

Bookbinder broke the silence and reasserted his old control.

"Go after her, Mad. Rehire her, if that's the word. Just keep her the hell away from me!"

Dr. Devlin knew something about moaning in the great man's presence and endowing him with supernatural powers and shivering in front of him, eyes rolling. She knew from experience.

Toward the climax of the New Hampshire campaign, Bookbinder had scheduled a big Boston speech for Thatch. The night before Dr. Devlin went up to Boston with some speech material just in case. She met Thatch in his hotel suite after dinner.

She spread the reports and graphs out on a table for Thatch to see. At the end of the table was the neatly typed speech which she had drafted.

When Thatch came in from the bedroom he was in shirt-sleeves and sweating. He looked around the room with a single sweep of his head, seeming to catch every detail, and then sat down at the table. As Dr. Devlin explained the research behind the speech, she glanced at his neck and shoulders. He was a muscular man and, quite automatically she assumed he would not really understand. Then Thatch's hand came out and the fingers pressed down on a graph. He spoke without turning his head.

"Do you believe all this?"

"It's not a question of believing. These are facts."

He laughed a warm laugh full of disbelief. Dr. Devlin looked at his neck and shoulders again and found nothing to say.

"But do they really substantiate the conclusions in this speech?" Thatch asked. She knew he did not want an answer. "Not worth a damn they don't."

She started to speak but something about the big powerful hand, the certitude of his voice stopped her. The man perspired but he was not nervous. The moisture was like the thin coat of oil on a high-performance machine.

Then her hand, as if belonging to another person, moved. Fascinated, she watched it come to rest on Thatch's shoulder. She was aware of his skin, his warmth under the shirt.

Her vision was suddenly constricted to an unfamiliar focus. She could see the hairs on his neck as if they were tiny steel wires . . . and the minute beads of sweat gleaming separately below the hair line. The muscles in his shoulder moved beneath her fingers. She tried to give them Latin names and failed.

"Why aren't the facts worth anything?" Her voice was remote, thin and unnatural.

"Because you have to have a policy first," Thatch said, "and then you gather facts to support it."

She could *feel* the words pass through his shoulder. To her hand the man's flesh was more than warm. It was hot.

In ways not clear to her, this man answered some deep need. She fought not to remember—the father she never had, the domineering, dependable larger-than-life, authority figure she never knew, the tweeds that smelled of pipe smoke she only read about in novels. Then she heard her own childish voice, a whining voice directed at her mother. It whined through easy tears and it asked the same question over and over: Where's Daddy? . . . Too much came flooding back now and she fought against it.

She stared down at Thatch and she realized she was going to kiss his neck. At the last moment she closed her eyes. Her lips barely brushed the stiff hair on his neck and then her head was moving through empty space. She jerked her eyes open.

Thatch had pushed aside the research papers and was looking at the speech now. He turned over the first page. He was quite unaware of what had happened. He had felt neither her lips on his neck nor her hand on his shoulder.

Rigid and unbelieving, Dr. Devlin suddenly felt she was safe from herself, and thus assured, she became angry at his composure. Her lips drew back with a faint disgust at the man's perspiration.

"Any kind of statement made without a factual basis is nonsense," she said and her voice had a lash to it. She was quivering but she assured herself that it was only from anger. She left the room under rigid control.

20

Kelly looked at the folder on his desk. He did not want to open it. Instead he glanced around the office. Then he grinned his quick, sharkish private grin. The office looked a mess, but it was a still life of politics. On the desk there was a letterhead with only the White House imprint showing; a telegram with the name of a Texas millionaire visible; a plain yellow sheet with the scrawled name *Dick* below a short letter. He came in each morning, arranged the desk, and then walked across the room and enjoyed it.

Magazines were scattered carefully around the room. They caught the odor of the times, told the subtle message that Lord Home was not doing well and Jomo Kenyatta was, that Israeli bonds were not moving. There was a current book on thermonuclear war and another on race relations. The *Manchester Guardian* was open to an article on "The Sources of Democratic Party Strength in the States," and this morning's *New York Times* had a few articles circled with a red felt pen-marker.

Kelly sighed and turned away from his carefully arranged chaos. He picked up the folder with distaste. Across it, in bold letters, were the words *New Hampshire Primary, 1964.*

The first page in the folder was a breakdown of the vote, which had occurred only a week earlier. Around 100,000 voters had turned out. Kelly put a question mark after that. It was too high. The turn-out for the primary is always low, but that day it snowed in New Hampshire. Why the hell such a turnout for a primary?

Kelly's eye ran down the page.

Kelly was not surprised by the Lodge victory. After all his people had run a clever campaign . . . concentrating on an old film clip of Lodge saving the world from the Nazis and the Communists and being blessed by Ike. They had spent around $25,000, which was one quarter of what Goldwater and Rockefeller had spent, but Lodge was helped by the fact that he was from Massachusetts and was in Saigon. Every time Rockefeller or Goldwater opened their mouths they lost votes. Lodge's victory just about sank the Flyboy and the Millionaire and Lodge himself did not worry Kelly. He would prove to be a favorite-son type, not a national candidate.

But what baffled Kelly was the size of Thatch's write-in vote. Thatch got five hundred more write-in votes than Clark and without a campaign . . . or at least not a campaign that Kelly could see.

Kelly felt the sweat of curiosity, not anxiety, start under his arms. Something was wrong, skewed, funny. Usually he knew what it was just by looking at the figures and matching them with reports from his people in the field. This time was different; his man had, to the eye of the pro, been clobbered by a newcomer, Thatch, and it was not clear how it had happened. He turned the page over. There was a letter of congratulation from Bryant Clark. Handwritten on university parchment and very precise. "For a candidate who merely filed and did not run a campaign, we did remarkably well in New Hampshire. Inasmuch as we spent nothing and got so fine a result I . . ."

Kelly turned the letter over without finishing it. Did Clark really believe that nothing had been spent in New Hampshire? Kelly quickly added it up to about $70,000. No doubt Clark was sincere in his belief that he had done well in New Hampshire. Later, Kelly thought, I'll have to tell him about Thatch. The pros knew. They had called and Clark's name had barely been mentioned. Each had remarked especially about Thatch's amazing write-in.

On the next page two objects were Scotch-taped to a sheet of paper. One was an emery board which said on one side *Thatch —an American Hero* in red, white, and blue letters. The other object was a high-quality card. On one side it said *Thatch for President;* the other side was a lacquered 1964 calendar. Kelly shrugged. They were good tricks, but old. No one would throw away anything valuable . . . a book of matches with your candidate's name on it was better than a simple card. Hell, Mad may have learned fast, but everyone in politics knew that.

The next item was a throwaway, a piece of paper about six by eight inches. The paper was thick and expensive. At least five cents each, Kelly thought. He read it again. He had puzzled over it six times now, and each reading left him confused and irritated.

Dear Neighbor:

I am writing you to ask you to write in the name of John Thatch as your Presidential preference in the March 10 election. Recently I moved to a suburb outside of Manchester. I cannot name it, but it is much like Goffstown or Allenstown or any similar place. The reason I cannot mention it is that the BOSSES who have controlled Manchester are forcing all of us who have worked, made a success of ourselves and moved out of the city, to vote the way they want. I REFUSE. I MOVED TO GET AWAY FROM THEM.

New Hampshire is a model for the whole of this fine country. Tourists flock in to see our attractions. But the bosses insist that we must vote the way they have always made us vote. We are a proud state. We are proud of our good senior citizens who have worked hard all their lives. We have more skilled workers than any other state in the Union . . . not crude laborers, but skilled and dedicated workers.

What is the proof of this? New Hampshire families, proud of their tradition and sure of their ability, are far above the rest of the Nation in family income. One more thing: Many of our respected senior women continue to do productive work. In California and Arizona and Texas older people spend their time in beauty parlors and getting suntans.

JOHN THATCH is one of us. He is a fighter against Communism. He lives in a suburb of San Francisco similar to your town. He employs people in his far-flung business whom others regard as "senile." Please join with me in writing in JOHN THATCH's name on the March 10 ballot.

A Patriot

P.S. Also, I'm sick of men with inherited fortunes coming in here and telling us how to vote.

Kelly read it slowly and then went through it again. He would never write such a throwaway. It was insane.

But these three things beat us, he said to himself, turning the pages over again.

Clark doesn't know it, but we got our ears pinned back. In the year of the tired stale Republican candidates Thatch's write-in vote was a signal flare in the sky . . . though it was only seen by the pros.

The sweat under his arms was still there, but now it was the sweat of anxiety. Mixed with the sweat of hope.

The thing nagged at him. With the President gone, it was a miraculous year for the dark horse and his dark horse was stumbling. There was something odd he didn't grasp about all this. Kelly felt pity for himself.

Curver sat at a desk in the unlabeled Thatch headquarters. Three of the college boys were busy operating the automatic typewriters, signing Curver's name to the letters that came off the roller and then stuffing them into envelopes.

Curver wondered what Kelly thought about New Hampshire. Kelly would hardly believe the emery boards and the calendars had done it. He and Dev had commissioned a Ph.D. candidate in Berkeley (keep things away from New York and Washington and prevent leaks) to simply show a number of cheap objects to a wide number of people and let them choose what they wanted. The emery board and the wallet-sized calendar card were the winners. But these gimmicks were really just to keep Kelly off balance.

"They weren't a loss, Mad," Dr. Devlin said. "The middle-class person will hold onto something that has value even if it carries a slogan he doesn't like. A few of them will even come to believe in the slogan. It's part of the acquisitive aspect of the American personality."

"Don't let's kid ourselves, Dev. It was the simulation that won for us. And it had better work in Wisconsin and California." If they could manage a big write-in in those two states, the timing would be perfect. They would have shown strength in a March primary, again in April and then the last one, California, just a month before the Convention. That way the country would see Thatch, without running a visible campaign, steadily building up steam.

"We've got to win big in California, Mad."

"I know, I know," Curver said. The California one had to be the climax. "The Simulations people have been trying to simulate California for months. It won't be as easy as New Hampshire."

Curver got out the worksheets on the New Hampshire. He smoothed out the computer reports and then the interpretations he had made of them. First, he had told them to find groups that could be persuaded to cast a write-in vote and, second, a write-in vote for someone other than Lodge. He had assumed that Lodge would get close to 10,000 with a moderately successful campaign and more if his people really poured in money, just because he looked like a favorite son.

The instructions to the computer were few and simple: Locate people who had moved into the state recently, people who had moved out and then back to the state, people with low political information, people who were hostile or at least resentful of the regular Republican Party.

The results had been interesting. The newcomers lived mostly in the urban fringe around Manchester and a few other cities and the urban-fringe population had increased by 104.1 per cent in the ten years between 1950 and 1960. The group with low political information and some evidence of past hostility to the regular Republican Party were the blue-collar workers and there was a higher percentage of them in New Hampshire than in almost any other state. There was a solid group of women over sixty-five who were working and a substantial percentage of these would probably have a residual dislike of the rich-people image of the Republican Party.

The next instruction card was more difficult to formulate. Mad had wanted to find groups who felt deeply about some particular issue. This meant feeding to the computer information which was not directly political . . . how many people were unemployed, how many unwed mothers, how many people sought a better mental-health program, and so on. A good deal of the information, fortunately, was available right from census tapes, government records, and specialized polls.

As the answers started to come in, the strategy became clear. One segment of people disliked the fact that both Rockefeller and Goldwater were millionaires but were trying to talk folksy. The anti-Communist anxiety still ran high. The older people were both suspicious and envious of the frivolous life in the hot Western states. A streak of Calvinism ran strong through the people and was reinforced by a long tradition of driving hard deals with the summer tourists. Mad concluded they had approved the state lottery because they thought most of the tickets would be bought by visitors from other states.

"I'd hate to have to show that throwaway to Bookbinder. He would not only think it was crazy, but he'd wince at the crudity of the whole thing," Curver said.

Dr. Devlin was glancing at the throwaway.

"It doesn't matter what Bookbinder likes," she said. "I don't think he'd know a typical voter if he met one on the street."

"What if Kelly analyzes that letter and starts to add things up?"

"No," Dr. Devlin said. "Kelly's like Bookbinder. He never really gets out and sees a voter. He deals with the influential people in the Party. They like style in a speech or a letter. But style isn't what gets some blue-collar worker with a seventy-two-year-old mother who is working in a shoe factory to write in someone's name. Your letter had something in it for a number of groups we thought might be pried loose from their traditional voting habit.

"They just picked out the sentence or two that applied to them and let it go at that." She glanced at him almost admiringly. "And it worked. The pros know Lodge won't carry weight outside of New Hampshire and the man they are watching is Thatch."

"Unless Lodge wanted to come out and run and it's already too late for that," Curver said. "By June New Hampshire will be only a faint memory."

They watched the fog pile up over the hills above San Mateo. It rolled slowly, so slowly that it took hours for someone watching to detect a change in shape. At some critical point, it would over-come a resistance and come flooding down the hot dry valleys. As it moved over the Peninsula the temperature would drop and the April warmth would change to a moist chill.

It was the first time in weeks Thatch had been home so early. He was traveling a great deal, speaking to groups all over the country, attending dinners in New York and meetings in Washington. Often his office knew his whereabouts but Terry didn't.

"It's good to have you home, John," Terry said. She looked down at her drink. She had been sipping it for an hour. "Not that we talk a lot, but at least I see you."

Thatch was sitting far back in the big leather sofa. He was staring at the fog.

"I'm sorry, Terry," he said. He shook his head as if to clear it. "It's not fair to you or the boys. It will be over soon. But as long as there is a chance, even a small chance, that I'll be called I have to wait."

"Called? Called to what, John?" Terry asked.

"To service, duty, country. Hell, I really don't know. Maybe it's just raw ambition that I like to call by some nobler name. But I have to get the answer. Terry, believe me, it's not fun. But I try to be consistent. I will not campaign or become an official candidate."

"But that doesn't stop others from campaigning for you," Terry said. "What about all that excitement over the New Hampshire thing? You didn't set foot in the state, but I noticed you made half a dozen speeches in surrounding states.

"Bookbinder's office arranged those," Thatch said. There was a slight irritation in his voice. "I didn't."

"That's the point. You say you're not in politics, but you do what those people tell you to do."

"No," Thatch said. "I make some of the speeches they line up, but I say what I want."

The fog broke. The big marble shapes became an avalanche of silent white mist.

"You're disappearing from me, John. Further away each day . . . until one day you'll be gone," she said. She said it very softly, and Thatch seemed not to hear. He did not move, but stared at the soft advance of fog. A panic rose in her throat. She gulped at the drink.

His eyes had glazed over, and he was miles away from her.

April 7; the day was fine, the primary was unrolling in Wisconsin and Kelly felt expansive. He had stayed in Washington because as a member of the National Committee he could not publicly take sides. But he had used the telephone carefully and this plus a few meetings in his Georgetown house had been enough to shape up the surprise. Tomorrow would be a day to remember among Republicans.

Wisconsin was, for Kelly, a happy trackless political jungle where he was the only one who knew all the footpaths. The La Follettes, in a reforming fit, had laid down a fantastic electoral code which made political parties almost useless. The state was ripped by feuds and factions, pointless ideological wars. Large sweeping visible power was impossible. Goldwater and Rockefeller, suspicious of the strange terrain and aware of the political ambushes which had taken place in the state, had a private agreement to stay out. The Republicans were running a favorite son, Congressman Byrnes, and no one expected him to have difficulty.

But Kelly knew differently. With an exquisite hand he went to work. With the purest pleasure he called old friends, dropped hints to one, picked up an old debt owed by a second, played competing small-town bosses off against one another. He wove and nipped and trimmed and was dreamily happy. What he constructed was a write-in campaign for Bryant Clark. It was, on the face of it, a most unlikely thing. Write-ins were technically illegal in Wisconsin, and would not be tabulated. But a substantial write-in vote for Clark, if somehow it could be tabulated and publicized, would seem to the front-running candidates a howl from the jungle, a shout of close pursuit and a crashing publicity victory for Clark. With great care and very privately Kelly had arranged for a number of the more prosperous areas to report their write-ins innocently. Certain friendly reporters would be ready to receive them.

Only two things marred the day. One was the recollection of the slim woman on the beach at Atlantic City and the piece of information she had carried away. It should, he felt, have achieved a result by now. Also he was waiting for Curver to use the CO thing. He did not really worry. The CO story was getting cold. After Wisconsin it would be useless. That was the beauty of fighting with amateurs . . . they did not appreciate timing.

Bookbinder was exuberant. On the day after the Wisconsin primary he had called Mad into his office. He slapped the *Tribune* and roared.

"Look at it," he said. "Lippmann calls it a stunning surprise. Teddy White says it's 'the portent of possible revolt within the

Republican ranks.' For some damned reason they counted the
write-in votes and Thatch got sixteen thousand and Clark got
seventy-five hundred! It's a spontaneous revolt against the stale
candidates, Mad. It's incredible!"

Mad looked up and managed a smile. Book was giving his
secretary instructions to call Thatch in California.

Spontaneous, Mad thought. If Book only knew. He did not
know because it was beyond his comprehension. It would have
been impossible ten years ago. It should have been impossible
today because even the IBM people were staggered at the
materials he had wanted put into the computers and the complexity of the information returned. They had fed in information
on first- and second-generation Polacks, the Catholic vote, the
Protestant vote, members of radical Socialist groups, precincts
which switched in 1952, 1956, and 1960, saliency of Democratic
Party among farmers, saliency of Republican Party in all groups,
cross-pressures among dairy farmers, name identification of Joe
McCarthy, percentage of college graduates, number of nonfic-
tion books sold per capita, foreign-language newspapers, attitude
toward foreign aid and a dozen other items.

Mad had known what Kelly would try in Wisconsin. It was
the perfect state for Kelly's kind of operation. He had also
known that Thatch must beat Clark decisively.

"Thatch, it's Book. What do you make of those Wisconsin
results? Surprised? You and half the people in the country. Without doing a thing, without even appearing in the state, you set
the Republican Party on its ear."

The talk made Mad nervous. He felt as if he had entered a
long corridor which was gay and sunny at the entrance, but which
was rapidly growing narrower, darker, and trickier and down
which he must for some reason run faster and faster. New Hampshire had been a lark, a kind of casual experiment. Mad could
have pulled out after that. But the thing had gotten out of hand.
He couldn't pull out now.

And now the Wisconsin result actually alarmed him. Using
the "two-step flow" method and sifting through names, they came
up with 1600 influential people in Wisconsin who received spe-
cial-delivery letters from a firm called Attitudes Research, Ltd.
Curver and Dev were the only members of the organization. The
letters simply reported the alarm among prominent national Re-

publicans at the "secret and insidious conspiracy" which was being organized against Congressman Byrnes. The letter would make the hair of a small-town politician who thought he was in on a private deal turn white.

They had also mailed 50,000 copies of five different letters to five carefully selected groups that shared only one quality: they were likely to turn out to vote and they had a special grievance. The groups were old Progressives, the unemployed, trade-unionists, Goldwater and anti-fluoridation people, and members of Americans for Democratic Action.

It had worked, but Curver felt misgivings mixed with the glow of accomplishment. After New Hampshire he and Dev had gone to Chambord, drunk two fifths of champagne, had an elegant dinner, and had thoroughly enjoyed their hangovers the next day. But there could only be a first time once. Now Curver's elation was marred . . . he felt boxed in by the damned computer, Book's enthusiasm, Dev's uncluttered dedication, and the fact that it would go on. And, more and more, he was having to make decisions which were *not* coming from the machine.

"We're not planning anything for California," Bookbinder was saying. "Not a thing official." He looked at Mad.

Curver had to hold back from twitching. Jesus, what if they managed to pull something big in California? Then what? He felt a sharp glitter of pleasure. Maybe someday he would go to National Security Council meetings. Mad Curver, the Ted Sorenson of the Thatch administration. He stopped thinking of it. The present was too much. Just yesterday Thatch had asked him for appraisals of two practical political situations about which he had not a clue. Thatch was careful not to indicate what his plans were, but he listened attentively to whatever Curver said. A few times he asked Curver to write him memos.

"Sure, Thatch, he's right here," Bookbinder said. "He'd love to talk to you."

Bookbinder held the phone out to Curver. Curver took it and made his voice hearty and enthusiastic.

"Look, sweetheart, Kelly called me weeks ago and I didn't take the call," Curver said. He looked across the desk at his calendar. It was April 15, a week after the Wisconsin primary.

"But this time you put him through," Curver laughed. He heard the line click open. "Mr. Kelly is one of my best friends in the whole world."

"All right, Mad, save your wit," Kelly said. "I want to see you. In person and alone."

"Bert, there's nothing to talk about. Or is there?"

"There is. They are going to knock Thatch off. I don't want it done the way they'll do it."

"If they can, they surely ought to," Curver said. He felt the thick glut of victory starting in his viscera. "I don't want to back a bum. Or a loser. You go ahead and we'll commiserate after the election." He was careful not to ask who "they" were.

"Mad, I can't hold these people back. They're going to blast Thatch on a TV network program the Sunday before the Convention opens in San Francisco. It's called 'High Public Office and Mental Health.'"

"Sounds interesting. What network?"

The lungs, sunk in the huge mound of flesh, wheezed. Five seconds passed.

"NBC. It's all over for Thatch. Mad, it's all over for you. That's the only reason I called. We got along pretty well. There's a future for you, but not if you stick with a loser."

"What kind of a future?"

"Just a future," Kelly said.

For a moment Kelly felt he might have won. He decided to be tougher.

"Mad, you've had your fun," Kelly said. "But now it gets serious. The big boys don't want Thatch and in the end they may not want Clark, but they've decided to eliminate Thatch and then go on from there."

The sound in the telephone was garbled. Then Kelly chilled. Curver was laughing.

"Kelly, you are the greatest character around," Curver said. "I mean you've got style. I like it."

"Mad, don't kid with me. I've been around a—"

"And you've developed a nice sense of humor," Curver said in a flat voice. "You're trying to keep NBC off our back and we're trying to keep the Legion off yours."

Kelly jerked in his seat. He did not ask about the Legion. This was the very thin, bright, dangerous edge. Kelly knew it. Only one piece of information separated them. He thought, for a part of a second, what he would write in his diary: I walked the edge of danger today and I won. He didn't want to make the walk. But he must.

"I've warned you, Mad," Kelly said. His eyes blurred with anger. This imperious young bastard with money and his phony science and his assured slimness. "NBC is a public corporation with a duty. I didn't start the idea with them and I can't stop it." It sounded erratic even to Kelly.

The sound of real sympathy came over the phone.

"Hell, Bert, don't worry about that," Curver said. "We tested the insanity issue early in the game. Remember when Thatch talked about it on TV? How did you think it went? Don't guess. I'll tell you. Ten per cent of the people in this country have been in nuthouses, have stretched out on the pad for the shock treatment, or have been down the twenty-five-dollar-an-hour route with the analyst where you get the leather couch and no talk-back. Those ten million each have about five friends or relatives who think they understand. That gets you about fifty million people who think that being in the looney bin is not bad. In fact they sort of admire a guy who's been there, survived, and succeeded."

"Mad, the American people wouldn't stand still for a madman."

"Of course not. But they happen to prefer a man who has been through some hell and turmoil to one who has slid through life on a waxed path of success," Curver said, and added, "and once upon a time was a conscientious objector."

Kelly cut off first.

"Who does he say he's with?" Kelly said into the phone. His secretary's voice came back small, whispering. The man must be standing in front of her.

"From the American Legion. A research man from the Legion," she said.

The man came in with a bland assurance. He was big and had a powerful look and one of those bone-crunching handshakes. He gave Kelly two sheets of paper.

"Should a 'Conchie' Be a Presidential Candidate?" Kelly saw in caps at the top of the page.

So this was it. Kelly sat down and read.

"Chancellor Bryant Clark will appear at the Republican Convention in July as a candidate for the nomination for President. A college president as our Chief Executive may well be a fine idea. What does give us pause, however, is the fact that Chancellor Clark was a conscientious objector early in World War II. This raises some difficult questions. As Commander-in-Chief of the Armed Forces could Chancellor Clark order our troops into action in time of national emergency? Or would his conscience stand in his way? Could a 'conchie' work out a tough guerrilla strategy in Viet Nam or order the invasion of Cuba . . . a thing which must surely come to pass?"

Kelly stopped reading. He looked up. The big man watched him blandly; obviously a messenger-boy type. Kelly finished reading. "And even if he has changed his views on this particular subject, how can we ever be sure? The American people must ponder Chancellor Clark's candidacy with the greatest care."

"Why are you bringing this to me?" Kelly asked.

"They say you're a friend of the Chancellor's and I wanted to quote you in the article," the man said. "You're a big name on the National Committee and we'd like your opinion on—"

"I wouldn't have a thing to say about a muckraking, lying article like that," Kelly said.

"Lying? It's true, isn't it?" the man said. His surprise was genuine.

"Get out," Kelly said thickly. "And be careful. You can get sued for libel if you print something like that."

The man looked back at Kelly as he opened the door.

"We usually take our chances," he said.

"Book, what the hell brings you down from New York?" a short energetic gray-haired man said. They were pushed together by the crowd. "Don't answer. Let me get my breath. Every time the Spanish Embassy has a party, by God you can be sure they'll fill the place."

The short muscular man was Eb Fork, a lawyer Bookbinder

had known for years and respected. With Tommy the Cork and
Ben Cohen, Eb had been a very big boy in the FDR regime. He
was one of those New Deal lawyers who had stayed on in Washington, built himself a successful law firm and watched, fascinated, from the sidelines. Bookbinder had asked Eb to go on a
foreign-aid commission during Eisenhower's first term. Eb had
refused. He would not work for Eisenhower and he had said why.
Rumor had it that Eb had practically moved into the White
House with Johnson a week after the assassination as "executive
coordinator" of presidential assistants, speech-writers, liaison men
and even, it was said, members of the Cabinet.

"Eb, we've got a case coming up before the Supreme Court
and the junior partner who is going to argue it needs a little
backstopping," Bookbinder said. "Hell, I don't even fully understand the case. This SEC stuff is getting very complicated."

Bookbinder did not like parties and he did not like the kind
of remark he had just made. He was down here for just one
purpose—to get John Thatch an invitation to speak at the Republican Convention. It would be a delicate thing to pull off,
but Mad had convinced him that it was the only way to bring
the Thatch campaign to a real climax. Senator Reddick was the
man who could arrange it, and Bookbinder wanted to see him
and then leave.

"Isn't that like sneaking him in under false pretenses?" Bookbinder had asked Mad. "A candidate isn't supposed to appear,
much less speak."

"No," Curver had answered quickly. "Thatch hasn't said a
word yet about his willingness to run. He believes he can be
drafted. To be drafted he has to be seen and heard. No one is
going to draft a ghost."

"You're correct," Bookbinder had said. Not right in the
ethical sense of the word, but correct. He wasn't sure any more
that Curver's generation knew the difference. Attacks of political
conscience were coming fewer and further between for Book.
Since Dr. Devlin's angry but not entirely unjustified attack, he
had worried some about it. But he had come to Washington
to do the job.

"Don't I know, Book," Eb Fork was saying. "I've fought
these SEC cases, usually lost—and didn't know why I lost." He

was a chain smoker, nervous but very controlled. He managed not to dart his eyes around the room, a feat which in Washington was considered the ultimate in control.

"They say you're running the White House," Bookbinder said. One drink and he would be out of here. But he had to catch five minutes with Reddick. He saw the Senator across the room.

"No. Just part-time job. The kind of thing you've done for two or three Presidents," Eb said. "LBJ knew I was available."

Available, Bookbinder thought. He smiled at Eb. Eb was losing perhaps a hundred thousand a year in income and the prestige wouldn't carry over. It never did. Not enough to repay someone like Eb.

"Book, someone said that you know this Thatch man," Eb said. He opened casually enough, but Bookbinder tensed. He looked blankly at Eb. "You know, the one who performed the miracle on the bridge in India and then raised hell with the Huks in the Philippines?"

"I know him."

"Does he speak Vietnamese?" Eb asked. He took a sip of his drink.

"Yes. Not as well as Tagalog or Hindi, but he speaks it," Bookbinder said. "Not fluently, but enough to get along."

"Get along on what level of conversation? They speak a dozen different dialects and use different grammar. But the educated ones, the ones who run the government, speak the same language."

"I don't know about that."

Eb finished his drink. He shifted his position as someone walked up to join them so that he was standing between Bookbinder and the crowd. Bookbinder sighed. Here it came. He recognized the gentle jockeying position which signaled to everyone that privacy was desired.

"The Chief is looking for someone to take over Viet Nam and really give us representation out there," Eb said. "It's a killer of a job and the Chief feels someone who could speak the language would be helpful. Apparently they sit around at meetings and talk French when they want to mystify the American ambassador. Then they switch to Vietnamese when they want to gut us—and later blandly say our Ambassador went along with everything that was said."

"Why not have the Ambassador take his translator along," Book said. He saw Reddick move toward the door and he started toward him.

Eb's hand was on his shoulder.

"They won't let a translator in," Eb said. "They say it's too secret and there are too many leaks to the Viet Cong." He paused, whirled the ice in his glass. "Maybe Thatch would be just the man for the job. He's got a big reputation out there. Hell, they think all our Embassy boys are pinkos or fags or nuts. After that Huk thing, Thatch is one of the big anti-Communist heroes in the East."

"I can't speak for Thatch," Bookbinder said.

"They've got him cleared," Eb said quietly. That meant it had already been approved by the President, Bookbinder knew. It was a firm offer. Thatch could be ambassador to Vietnam.

Eb Fork grew impatient. The only reason he had come to the damned cocktail party was to find out if Book could contact Thatch. Now Book was playing footsie. It was silly. Eb had been interested when Kelly had suggested Thatch to him. They lunched together occasionally and, although Kelly was a Republican, he was helpful at times. Both of them knew there had to be a few Republicans in high appointed posts. It would be smart to replace Lodge with another Republican. All the talk about Thatch running for the Presidency, Kelly had said, was ridiculous.

Kelly had suggested that Eb go directly to Thatch, but Eb had heard of Bookbinder's connection and decided that was the way to go about it.

"That damned spot is killing off a dozen Americans a week and the rate is going up fast. But maybe it's the kind of challenge Thatch would like. The Huk thing on a bigger scale."

"I'll talk to him about it," Bookbinder said finally.

"Right away?" Eb interrupted.

"Right away," Bookbinder said. He turned and pushed off into the crowd. Even before he reached Reddick he knew he would not mention Eb's offer to Thatch. Thatch wouldn't know enough about the game to realize he was probably being used. Bookbinder felt stubborn, crotchety, and resentful. He'd brought Thatch a long way and now the Democrats wanted to send him into a pesthole which they had created themselves. To hell with it.

Bookbinder called Eb in three days and without deliberately lying made it clear that Thatch would not go to Viet Nam. Eb took it well.

21

June 1, the day before the California primary. Curver swung out of bed five mintes before the switchboard of the Palace Hotel called him. He had not slept more than a few hours. He looked out the window at the white San Francisco fog. He looked at his fingers. The thin, slack flesh seemed to hang from them, blue veins prominent. He stood up, not quite trusting his senses. He pulled on his pants and had to take the belt two notches past where it had been before Wisconsin.

This had been the most terrible month of his life. All that could be said for it now was that it was over. Amen to that!

He shaved without managing to look at his eyes. They would be red, with pouches of flesh under them that made him look older and confused. It was the confusion he hated.

The phone rang.

"Good morning, Mr. Curver. It's eight o'clock," the operator's voice said.

"Christ, I've been up for five minutes. I'm shaving and—" He stopped and held the phone away from him for a moment. "I'm sorry. I know I left the call."

"Thank you, sir," she cut off coldly.

Curver walked back to the bathroom. He was not getting through to people these days. He mistrusted himself, felt he was catching the wrong clues and misreading the right ones. The control, the easy sense of swinging slightly ahead of the others, had vanished shortly after Wisconsin.

He remembered the exact day it vanished: the afternoon Kelly had found him in California. On April 10, three days after

Wisconsin primary, Curver had been sitting alongside the pool of the Beverly Hills Hotel watching the strange etiquette of Hollywood unroll. There was not a person there he recognized, but he could tell the powerful ones . . . the waiters had a way of cringing up with the Bloody Marys, a bellboy walked over to them and whispered their messages rather than paging them over the deafening loudspeaker system.

On the tennis court a camera crew was shooting what the lifeguard said was a television commercial for mascara.

Curver looked over and Kelly was sitting beside him in one of the brilliant plastic-covered chaise longues. He held a brief case on his lap and he was sweating. He was also smiling.

"You look familiar," Curver said.

"I should," Kelly said. "You dream about me at night. Now I'm here, in broad sunny daylight."

"Bert, you're marvie—that's a Beverly Hills word for marvelous—but I don't really dream about you," Curver said.

"Well, now you will start fast," Kelly said. He crooked a finger at a waiter. "A double Tom Collins." Kelly turned to Curver. "Damn, I'm glad I don't have to drink that bourbon and branch for a while. A nice sickening sweet drink with vitamins and lemons and oranges and gin in it is what I need."

Kelly put his brief case down beside the chaise, took off his jacket; Mad saw that sweat had already darkened most of his shirt.

Curver tightened a bit. He ran over the past few months. What could have gone wrong, what weapon might he have unwittingly handed Kelly?

Kelly took some papers out of his brief case. He placed them so Mad could see them. The top sheet was a list of the state primaries with the results and then a total at the bottom. Kelly pointed a pencil at New Hampshire.

"That was the first surprise. I didn't know you were running a write-in campaign for Thatch until a few days before the primary," Kelly said. "I looked at your emery board and your quality calendar and that nutty letter and figured there was nothing to worry about. I was wrong."

"Agreed. Thatch did well in New Hampshire. So?"

"Not sensationally, but well enough that the experts and the ones who think they are experts felt Thatch was doing well,"

Kelly said and looked at Curver ". . . for a boy who didn't have a campaign going for him."

Mad remained silent.

"Then Wisconsin. You win again." Kelly's pencil skipped down the page. His drink came and he downed half of it with relief. "That's good. Really good. Some day I'll give up bourbon. It gives me a sour stomach."

The balance had changed. Kelly was jocular, sure, deft, in control.

"So far, Bert," Curver said, "Thatch doesn't have one delegation pledged to him."

"And look at Clark," Kelly said. "He's picked up over a hundred fifty delegates. But they're all from states where the delegations are chosen by conventions. In the two primaries where voters pick the candidate Thatch looks better than Clark. In the convention states Clark did well because I could control them. The trouble is, Mad, that the big contributors, the pros, the columnists, know exactly where, why, and how Clark got his hundred fifty delegates. Because they're from states like Utah where they were so damned dumb in 1960 they thought they had to vote the unit vote when the convention actually forbids it. Clark got his delegates one way. They won't stick with him past the first ballot unless he does big in California."

Curver looked down at the first sheet. At the bottom was an artificial tally. Curver's eyes flicked over the totals and although they were all guesses they were too close to his own. No one knew for sure how the uncommitted votes would go because the majority of the votes were tied up by "favorite sons." But Kelly had been sniffing around. He had found out how the delegates would go once they cut away from the favorite son.

Rockefeller was doing well on Kelly's totals. Goldwater was strong but had too many uncertain delegates in states he had to carry. What was startling was that the artificial tallies put Scranton, Nixon and Clark very close together. For a nonpolitical figure Clark's performance was incredible and the papers had been saying it loud and clear.

"You've done pretty well, Bert," Curver said. "If any outsider is going to knock off the tired old pros, your boy looks like he's going into the convention loaded."

Kelly went on as if he hadn't heard Mad. "After New Hamp-

shire and Wisconsin I said to myself, there's going to be a third
one, later on, nearer the Convention. Here in California. And if
Thatch beats Clark in all three of those direct primaries, where
the 'holy will of the people' is made clear, and Clark wins only
in the states where they have conventions which any well-con-
nected professional can fix, the ball game is over. Your man
Thatch is the 'comer'—and, friend, in this race momentum is
everything."

"Bert, if the people like Thatch, there is not a damn thing I
can do about it."

Kelly looked at Curver, and his eyes were affectionate little orbs of glittering intelligence. His skin was turning slightly
pink in the sunlight.

"Mad, I really have to trot. See some people on the other
side of town," Kelly said. "But I want to tell you about a little
gumshoeing around I did, and how I found some interesting
stuff."

Kelly opened another folder. Curver took one long look and
then looked away at the deep blue of the pool. Perversely he felt
a sense of pride.

"To make it fast, Mad, I found out about this nutty thing
with the IBM people and the computer and I reread the New
Hampshire throwaway and then I looked over the letters that
went out in Wisconsin and it came to me. You're going to pull
the same stunts out here."

"Did you actually gumshoe the Simulations Enterprises reports?" Curver said, making himself laugh.

"I did," Kelly said and then stood up, stuffing papers back
into his brief case. "Mad, I was wrong. It was a wonderful idea.
You could have snuck that hero of yours into the Convention,
and with everyone sitting on their ass and bored stiff and confused you could have rammed him through just by using the
stuff you've got so far . . . if you could keep your campaign out
of sight and get a big write-in in the California primary. A much
bigger write-in than Clark."

"You've got it, Bert," Curver said. He tried not to be con-
temptuous. "With all your experience you figured out our strategy. So good-by." Curver felt almost serene, the early alarm gone.

"I'm on my way," Kelly said, snapping the brief case shut.
"But Mad, you should know one thing. We're going to beat you

in the California primary. We're going to leak the story of Thatch, the Computerized Candidate to five or six big writers. We're going to give them photostats of the emery board and the calendars and the throwaways and the letters you sent to the five groups in Wisconsin."

Kelly saw Curver move in his seat, deliberately switch his eyes to an oiled woman and a pot-bellied man taking tall frosted glasses from a white-jacketed waiter.

"Mad, it's a dull year," Kelly went on. "You concocted an image of a sweet innocent guy who could be tough as a US Marine when he had to be but didn't give a damn about politics and had a beautiful Filipino wife and wasn't ashamed of her, and talked about the great adventures we could have overseas. And when this stuff breaks about the machine-made, Madison Avenue candidate, you're going to find out what political anger is really like. Those delegates will kick his ass from here to Sunday. Hell hath no fury like a delegate misled."

Curver knew he had to speak. He turned his lean face up, found some solace in the discomfort of the perspiring, fat, overdressed, pink-faced man above him.

"You go ahead and do that, Bert," Curver said. "You'll walk right into a buzz saw. For every canned story on Thatch the Computerized Candidate there will be five on Clark as the conscientious objector who fell into clover while the rest of the boys were over there getting shot up."

Kelly's fingers tightened on the brief case handle. The man seemed to be getting more sunburned by the minute.

"That's going to be hard to make stick, Mad," Kelly said. "Clark never was a CO. He just wrote a letter asking about what it took to be a CO."

"That's enough right there to kill him. You know that. You can be anything except a homosexual and a CO and still get elected President."

"Probably right," Kelly mused. He picked up the brief case again. "But a month before he wrote the letter Clark had already been turned down as a 4-F by his board. Bad eyes. He just wrote the letter to find out what the general philosophy of the thing was. A man of many interests, Mad." He shifted his weight from foot to foot, glanced quickly over his shoulder at the sun.

"Mad, Clark is going to run as a regular candidate here in

the California primary and one of his main arguments is going
to be that Thatch is mischievous, dishonest, and misleading the
American people."

Kelly grinned and left, a penguin waddling down the edge
of the pool. Yet he had a kind of dignity . . . living by an obsolete ethic, he still had a kind of dignity.

Curver came up out of the chair and threw his body into
the pool in a neat, clean dive. But the water was so warm. There
was no shock to wipe out the inescapable fact. He had lost.

He could not believe it, yet he had to. He had lost.

Curver had finished telling them the whole story. They were
sitting in Book's huge green-white-and-yellow suite in the Beverly Hills. Bookbinder and Levi were quiet, Levi looking down
at the floor. Dev had been left in New York and Mad found
that he missed her. From the tennis court there was the sharp
repeated ping of tennis balls.

"We'll run Thatch as a candidate in the California primary,"
Bookbinder said. "I'll handle it."

He moved to pick up a phone.

"Book, it's impossible," Curver said. In the twenty-four hours
since he had called them in New York and they had arrived he
had not eaten a bite, although he ordered meals sent up to the
room. The food congealed on the wheeled-in tables and was
eventually wheeled out.

"Why?" Book asked. He was starting to dial a number.

"Because in California the candidate has to agree to let a
delegation be formed for him," Curver said. "Thatch won't do
that. We all know it. Even if he did, it would be the end of
him because he would look exactly like Nixon and Lodge and
the rest . . . wanting the call, not even pretending he doesn't.
Thatch's only chance—and we all agreed to this—is to remain himself: stubborn, aloof, and repeating his one phrase, 'I will do my
duty. It is not my duty to seek the Presidency.' Book, if Thatch
runs as a formal candidate it's the end of the whole thing."

Bookbinder looked hard at Curver, his finger still over the
phone. He dialed a number.

"Thomas, this is Book," he said. "Can you make it to the
Beverly Hills Hotel in the morning?" He paused. "No, no. I'll

explain everything in the morning. Nine-thirty. Room two-thirteen. Okay?"

The next morning at nine Levi and Curver walked into Bookbinder's suite to find that breakfast had already been ordered. It would not be served until Thomas Lander arrived, he told them.

Thomas Lander was seventy-two years old, publisher of the most successful paper in Southern California, and to Mad a relic from the dim days when someone had nicknamed him The Old Lion and made it stick. He had been US Senator from California for one six-year term. He lost his bid for re-election because as a Republican he was for most of the New Deal and he wanted America to go into the war against Hitler before it was fashionable. He was once nominated for a Nobel Prize because, over the years, he effectively exposed and eloquently opposed a long series of extremist groups which he thought were killing the chances for peace . . . all the extremists in the West, from Communists on the left to right-wingers running campaigns against fluoridation because they saw it as a Jewish plot, had felt the sting of Lander's wrath and heard the thunder of his oratory.

Curver felt bowed in, crushed by strange forces which he had dimly feared after Wisconsin, but which now had him by the throat.

"Mad, snap out of it," Bookbinder said. "If you want to mourn, do it on your own time. Head back for New York. We've got a lot of cases piling up."

"I blew it," Curver said. "Somehow I blew it."

Bookbinder went on as if he had not heard.

"Lander has the old political virus worse than any man I ever knew," Bookbinder said. "He also has principles, and when he half tries he can be a hell of an orator. He writes me letters complaining about making too much money, having too much sunshine, wailing about the lack of political guts in the country."

"I remember him, Book," Levi said. "No one ever raised so much hell in the Senate as a freshman. Made a speech his first day on the floor alternating between attacking Roosevelt and supporting him. He never got an important committee assignment while he was in Washington."

Lander was a surprise to Curver. He came in quietly, dressed in conservative clothes except for a big rancher's hat. His walk was still springy. He was jovially affectionate toward Bookbinder, very courteous to Levi, and nodded abruptly at Curver. He was a huge man—over six feet two and bulky. He wore soft Indian moccasins.

"Start from the beginning, Book," Lander said. He stretched out on a couch and without a trace of self-consciousness closed his eyes.

Half an hour later he opened them. He looked at the food which had been placed on the coffee table beside him. He scooped three slices of bacon and some scrambled eggs onto a piece of toast, clapped another piece of toast over it, and bit into the sandwich.

"And Clark is going to run in the primary too?" he asked. "That'll make Goldwater and Rockefeller and this Clark fella." He munched thoughtfully for a moment. "Goldwater will get the Southern California and Santa Barbara right wing . . . all the antifluoridation, anti-Semitic, let's-cut-taxes-and-blow-hell-out-of-Castro types. He'll get those smart slick new lawyers who are trying to take over the Republican Assembly because they think the state is sliding right and they want to be there when it happens. Rockefeller will get some of the regulars. Clark won't get much of anything. Now this Thatch won't run, and he shouldn't." He laughed; it was a big sound. "All he has to do is to stand aside and he makes Rockefeller and Goldwater look like two kids wrestling in the mud for a bone."

"If he did run, how would he do, Tom?" Bookbinder asked.

Lander brushed it aside.

"All right, maybe all right. He's from California, but it would ruin the whole feel of the man, Book."

"If we showed those pictures of him at the bridge and in the Philippines it would be like Kennedy on live television at the helm of PT-109," Bookbinder said, glancing at Levi.

"The man's got heroic proportions, and he can lead," Levi said.

"I've seen the films and I've read the articles," Lander growled.

"If there was some way we could get you and Thatch linked together," Bookbinder said. "The young hero and The Old Lion."

"Don't kid yourself, Book. I haven't made a political speech for ten years and I wouldn't do it for a million dollars," Lander said. But he was leaning forward, the sandwich dangling from his big hand.

"I wasn't exactly thinking of you stumping the state. I was thinking of a few big occasions. Hell, you could fill the Coliseum . . ."

"If I was hitting .410 for the Dodgers I could," Lander said. His eyes, fastened on a palm tree outside the window, glazed and he spoke slowly.

Bookbinder knew that the man had not made a speech in ten years because no one had asked him. Bookbinder had seen him at a dozen political meetings, shunted aside by younger men, watching the proceedings with a hard resentful fascination. The virus had not diminished with the years.

"But we can't run Thatch," Lander mused. He waved a hand in Mad's direction. "Sonny, order some whisky. Some Scotch. And some milk. I have to drink it in milk because I had an ulcer once and . . ." He stopped talking, his hand still gesturing. "But if we *could* run him, we'd pick up the Bay Area. They don't like Nixon 'cause of what he said in the sixty-two gubernatorial speech and 'cause he's from the wrong side of the Tekachapis Range. Rockefeller is the man to beat. The regulars and the liberals will go for him."

"Hell, they'd go for you first," Bookbinder said. "It was the lunatic fringe that beat you last time."

Lander looked up, his eyes gleaming. He pointed a finger at Bookbinder and stood up slowly. Mad could see the excitement rise in him like water coming to a boil.

"Book, I'll run on the ballot as a candidate. That's state law. But the moment I'm qualified I'll make it clear that I'm running for Thatch and I'll show those hero pictures of him up and down the state and tell how those Eastern crooks have been keeping an honest California boy from doing his duty. And the minute I get to the Convention we'll have one delegation, the second biggest, solid for Thatch."

Curver felt physically ill. Three months ago, even a few days ago, it had all been neat and scientific and well thought out. He and Dev had been close to doing the impossible . . . running an unknown for the Republican nomination against a gang of millionaires. And they had done it silently, cheaply, scientifically, and—almost—successfully. Now, because of Kelly, they were

going back to the messy, old-fashioned, haranguing days he had
read about in books and winced. It was too late to program anything about this new situation through the 7094. They would be
flying on intuition and snap judgments from senile old bastards
like Lander.

"Tom, that's exactly it," Bookbinder said. "We tie your reputation and influence to Thatch's hero image and youth and tell
the people the truth. And later we'll just have to persuade Thatch
to run."

Lander stopped in mid-stride and looked sharply at Bookbinder.

"You mean that?" he asked, and his look made it clear that
he did not believe it. "We have to convince him?"

"That's God's truth, Tom," Bookbinder said. "You can talk
to him if you want."

"Oh, no." The thought that Thatch was *truly* undecided
seemed to excite him more. "I don't even want to meet the man.
That would be bad. I want to say I have never seen or talked
to him, but I know my duty to persuade this fine young hero to
lead us out of the wilderness."

Lander drank off a glass—equal parts of excellent Scotch and
homogenized milk—and Curver gagged.

That night Curver couldn't sleep. He had a nightmare about
stomping the state with Upton Sinclair for his End Poverty in
California Party. He awoke and picked up one of his "background
reading" books on California law and discovered to his surprise
and then immense relief that to run in a primary election a candidate had to file at least six weeks before said primary.

He felt reprieved. Thomas Lander would have to go back
to writing editorials for his San Diego sheet. They would find
some other solution. Preferably a twentieth-century solution.

Early in the morning he called Book's room and in appropriately sorrowful tones told of his discovery. To his amazement
Bookbinder laughed hard.

"Don't sound so broken up about it, Mad. I had Tom Lander
file quietly with the Secretary of State—a friend of mine who can
keep his mouth shut—three months ago. I had a hunch that these
write-in campaigns of yours might run out of gas. Now go back

to bed and get some sleep. You're going to need it. You hit the road with Lander starting Monday, and The Old Lion is going to be hard to keep up with!"

Tom Lander turned loose on the State of California was a thing to behold. Somewhere he found a huge old Dodge touring car, had *Thatch for President* painted on it, and blew into every town like a medicine man. He was followed by a caravan which converted into an open-air theater and ran films of Thatch speaking on the bridge and arguing with Rizal Sipa and talking about "bankruptcy is health." Lander would finish with a sidewinding speech about the "invading millionaires who wish to buy our vote" and "it is time for the old to pass on the torch to the young" and "let us breathe life into the dead carcass of American Republicanism."

In the early crowds there was a fringe of older people, and the fringe started to grow as Lander moved south through the state. In San Diego Mad began to count the gray heads. He mingled with the older people and heard them talk about Upton Sinclair, Technocracy, the evils of the Southern Pacific, and Hiram Johnson in tones of undisguised yearning. The younger ones came to see the films of Thatch and enjoy the show. But they stayed to listen to Lander thunder at the inequities of an economy in which the stock market stood at 800 and still had "tens of thousands of young people pouring forth from our sacred halls of learning only to face the stark, black bleak prospect of unemployment."

The Los Angeles *Times* ran an old cartoon and an editorial in which they revived "Lander the Lion-Hearted." Lander promptly ordered new bunting which used the old phrase. Reporters came to watch, expecting to go home and write satirical pieces, and went away somehow impressed. An Eastern observer wrote that "Lander the Lion-Hearted is no joke in the valleys and towns and suburbs of California. He is only a joke when you have not seen him. He is a voice of an earlier and more dedicated and less calloused California. In some way he gives people who have been in California only a few months or a few years a sense of history. It is hard to judge the effect of all this on the Republican primary. But clearly Lander the Lion-Hearted has, by some trick of political optics, made Goldwater and Rockefeller seem like timid middle-aged men. Thatch, who has not spoken publicly in weeks and refuses to see reporters, meanwhile gathers something of the freshness and appeal which Kennedy had.

"One would guess that so odd a political technique could not upset the well-financed and professionally managed campaigns Goldwater and Rockefeller have mounted in this state. Clark's campaign is also well run, but in a quiet orthodox manner. One sign that Lander is scoring is the restlessness among the regular Republicans. They are starting to react against him and that, in a primary, is always a sign of the opponent's strength."

In May a Senator and an ex-Senator representing the Rockefeller and Goldwater delegations requested of the Secretary of State that Thomas Lander be stricken from the Republican primary for he was in fact not a legitimate candidate, but was already committed to someone else.

The legal situation took a week to untangle, but by that time the regular Republicans knew it had been a mistake. Lander, now magnified by the aura of a man persecuted by powerful interests, roared at "leaders who think only of the entrenched power of party regulars" and talked of the days when a man was judged on his merits and not on whether he was "a political lackey, a conformist who spends dull years in dusty courthouses so that he can finally finish his days in Washington, a sleepy do-nothing Senator . . . do nothing, that is, except to stagger to the public trough."

Through all of this Curver saw himself as Alice in a political wonderland. There was no scientific way of knowing what impact Lander's campaign was having. He grew to like The Old Lion. And he worried. He kept waiting for Kelly to mount his attack on Thatch as the "computerized candidate." Then he found out, quite by accident, that it wasn't going to happen.

He and Lander were driving out of Bakersfield in a Cadillac. The old touring car had gone on ahead the night before.

"We've got 'em off balance, Curver," Lander chuckled. "That's the biggest part of politics. Keep the opposition guessing. They're getting desperate, I think. A fellow named Kelly came to me the other day—"

Curver stiffened. Lander described the meeting with obvious relish, told him what Kelly had said. Lander had listened politely.

"You mean," he had answered when Kelly finished, "that I'm being victimized by a Madison Avenue computer, which is served by twenty dumb Ph.Ds, who feed tapes into an IBM machine which spews forth bits of information at the rate of one million every four seconds and then gives orders to Thatch." He had fixed Kelly with what he liked to consider his baleful stare. "Young man, I knew Tommy Watson when he was a boy. He didn't know a thing about politics then and I told him so and if he were alive today I'd tell him the same thing and that company of his, that IBM outfit, the whole shebang doesn't have as much political know-how as I carry around in my head. Then I stood up and pointed to the door and said 'Leave.' And he left."

Mad didn't know whether to laugh or cry. The picture of Kelly skulking out of The Old Lion's presence convulsed him. Now he knew why Kelly had abandoned the computer-candidate charge. It would never have penetrated the medieval armor of The Old Lion; his very presence at the wheel of Thatch's band-wagon refuted the charge and made it idiotic. The Old Lion simply could not be made into an IBM image.

Book had been smart. Very smart.

And yet, Mad knew, they were going to be clobbered in California. In 1964, you just couldn't win the race in a horse and buggy.

Curver finished shaving. He went into his bedroom and dressed. At least it was over now. The next time, 1968, it would be different. He and Dev would start earlier and they would keep everything under control. No loose ends.

He picked up the morning paper and smiled. He was not the only confused person. The latest Lou Harris poll admitted that the California primary was up in the air. They expected Rockefeller to win, but admitted that people were so evasive on the Lander–Thatch issue that it was impossible even to phrase a question in a properly scientific way.

That night at ten o'clock, Curver was technically drunk for the first time in his life. Rockefeller and Goldwater had gotten substantial votes but trailing only slightly was the Lander-Thatch ticket, leaving all the other candidates hundreds of thousands of votes in the rear. The news defied description. Lander's campaign, a caustic commentator was saying on television, had been "madness after madness, appeals to Prohibitionists (not on the ballot this year, they had switched their last hope to Lander), a careless lauding of technocracy, a salute to Willkie, praise for the welfare state and equally for the free-enterprise system, soaring oratory and, each night, the crowds growing bigger and bigger. We newsmen, trying to make sense of the campaign, imposed more order on it than it actually had. What can one say? The results of this primary are symptomatic of our times: confusion reigns. Long live confusion!"

Now in Bookbinder's suite Curver watched them. Lander was calm and poised, as quiet and assured as the worker of a miracle should be. Bookbinder excitedly interpreted what the victory meant to a group of reporters. Rockefeller could never make it on the first ballot at the Cow Palace and Tom Lander would swing the huge California delegation to Thatch on the second and the stampede would be on. Thatch wasn't there; he had continued to refuse to make a public appearance and, for reasons Curver could not understand, the people who had assembled in the Lander headquarters in Los Angeles and San Francisco were delighted with this further proof of purity.

The phone rang for Curver. It was Kelly.

"That was some job, Mad," Kelly said. "I'd congratulate you, but I know that you didn't have a thing to do with it. It wasn't your kind of campaign and every time I saw you on television you looked like you were dying by inches."

"I was, Bert. And I'm damned near dead now."

"You're celebrating and you should be," Kelly said. "But, Mad, ask Thatch once more what he's going to do about that Mrs. Singleton matter."

"What's it all about, Bert?"

"Just ask him, Mad. For your own sake."

Thatch had talked to Terry, but he hadn't listened to her responses. Not for weeks. Maybe it was months. This political thing had become all too complex just to sit down and explain.

He hadn't thought much about Terry's mood until Mad had mentioned her just a few minutes before. After the congratulations, Curver had yelled into the phone, above the noise, "Did you ever hear of a Mrs. Singleton? In Santo Tomas with Terry. Something like that. Our erstwhile friend Kelly mentioned her."

Thatch did not know the name. He asked if Curver thought it important. As he walked back to the living room he tried to review Terry's attitudes. At first she had been firm in her opposition to his getting into politics. But if he wanted to run she would do anything . . . I'll be a proper American wife, she had said and laughed. Later she didn't laugh any more, grew strangely silent. After the Atlantic City week end she had, for a few weeks, seemed like a Filipina who was in *latah* . . . shy, jerking around at a question, spending long periods staring at nothing. A sudden sound would make her whirl and stand still, holding her breath until the noise was identified.

Now she was reading. As he bent and kissed her on the forehead, he remembered Mad's question. "Terry, does the name Mrs. Singleton from Santo Tomas mean anything to you?"

Terry put the book on the floor. She turned, and her face was suddenly relaxed. She seemed very young, a slight smile on her lips.

"Yes."

"Mad asked about her just now. Wasn't sure what it meant."

"I am. It means that you're never going to be President of the United States."

Thatch sat in a chair across from her. He wasn't sure of her mood. He didn't want to speak until he knew. For the first time he realized how, for months, events had bent her and bent her some more. Now, with the tension released, she looked calm and easy. But he didn't know what had released her.

"What is it, Terry?"

"There's not a lot to tell," Terry said. Her look, calm and bemused, frightened Thatch. "There was a Mrs. Singleton in the camp. Very nice Englishwoman. Her husband was killed in the fighting. She took up writing a diary about the camp. Her father had been a historian, I think, and it took her mind off her husband's death. She kept very detailed notes about everything that went on. Including the fact that I was a whore for the Japanese. Your friend Mr. Kelly has that diary."

"How did he get it?" Thatch asked.

Terry shook her head. "I'm not sure. I think a private detective or someone like that."

For several moments Thatch felt nothing. He knew that the diary could be used, but he did not want to think about the details.

"Terry, we talked about this just once years ago and I told you what I thought," Thatch said. He reached out and took her hand, and felt a kind of sick terror. The hand was as light as feathers, cold and without life. "I still believe it. A woman is not a whore who sleeps with a man to save her life. A whore is a woman who has a choice. You had none. It was your only way to survive. I loved you then and I love you now. That is the end of it. Kelly can do whatever he wants with the diary." He paused. "The goddamn diary."

The slight smile was still on Terry's lips and the strange look. Thatch sensed she was beyond tears. If she would cry he could deal with her. Right now she remained remote, beyond words or appeals or gestures.

"He'll use it to ruin you," Terry said. She licked her lips. Her voice had a faint musing sound and the Tagalog accent was stronger. "Even if he threw the diary away, someone would still use the information against you." She was silent. Thatch had both her hands in his. "It happened so long ago. It seemed so small a thing . . . life so much more important."

He couldn't find the right words. He could only sit and hold her cold hands and stare his love into her eyes.

"John—John—I want all this to end. I want you back, our old life back again. But not because of this," she said in pure Tagalog.

Still she did not cry. She had the coldness of the child who did a reasonable thing and sees it grow huge and terrifying— and can neither understand the terror nor change it.

Thatch knew this was why she had reverted to the old language.

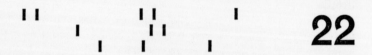

22

The day had been blazingly clear in the morning, foggy by noon, and filled with gales by the afternoon. Around Nob Hill the fog was alternately thick and then very thin. It altered the light and gave a bewildering sense of instability. One knew that other climates were more reliable. Such a July day as this in San Francisco brought to the mind of the newcomer a dim story of the 1906 quake, a haunting sense of instability, the feeling which comes from being on islands and sailing vessels.

"I suppose," Thatch said quietly, "that you want to hear what I'm going to say tomorrow night?"

Bookbinder leaned back for a moment and looked out the big fog-smeared windows of the Fairmont Hotel. Far away, just at the edge of vision, he could see the sweep of lights reaching very high into the black night. It must be the Bay Bridge. Then he heard the moan of the foghorns. They were not heard with the ear, he thought. It was a sound so deep and pressing that it vibrated in the marrow, shook the hard bone of the skull, reverberated in the body.

"The sound of those foghorns is the most animal-like sound that a mechanical device ever produced," Bookbinder said. "Makes you want to get out and see what is making it."

"I like the sound," Thatch said. He listened. The suite was quiet. Terry sat in a big chair and looked down at a cup of coffee in her hands. Mad was in a corner, sitting on a barstool. Dr. Devlin was in the shadow of Mad. Two days ago, Mad had informed Bookbinder that Dev was coming on for the convention. Bookbinder, realizing that he was being told, not asked, had merely grunted.

"Because the foghorn is a sound of danger and when you hear it you know you are secure and that gives pleasure," Dr.

Devlin said. "Someone out there has to grapple with the tides and winds and currents or whatever it is. But you, safe and warm in this hotel room, are listening to the warning directed toward others."

Thatch looked at Devlin and then smiled. "A clever analysis, Doctor. I accept it."

"The sound of the foghorn arouses pleasure in all of us," she went on. "It tells us that others are in danger and we are not."

"Cut it out, Dev," Curver said quietly.

"No, she's right," Thatch said. "We get pleasure from the torment of others."

"Thatch, we've got to move tomorrow," Bookbinder said after a few moments passed.

Thatch stopped and reached for something. Dr. Devlin watched his big hand go into his pocket and shivered. There was a muted assurance about the man which was sensual. Her mind spun off . . . good God, she could stand him forever as long as he was that sure and that decisive and that—that *what?* She forced herself to go on: that sweaty and disordered and strong, in a simple brutal way.

Thatch pulled a sheet of folded paper from his pocket. He spoke quietly, without moving.

"There's the usual introductory stuff about the chairman and the delegates and . . ." His voice faded. He stared at the sheet of paper. "I'm lying. There isn't that stuff at all. It's very short: 'I thank you for your attention to the views I have put before you. It is my belief that an energetic struggle between the two parties is absolutely necessary to keep our democracy vital and tensed. To those of you who have urged me to lead the Republican Party in this struggle I have nothing but thanks. But I have not the qualifications to take on the task. I will support whomever you nominate as your candidate. Not because I am opposed to the incumbent President, but because I believe in the necessity of stress in our system. I shall not offer myself in nomination nor shall I run if you offer me the candidacy. This is not, I assure you, an act of arrogance. It is, much more, a cold appraisal of my abilities, my inexperience, and the needs of my country. Good friends, I am not the man for the job at this time."

Bookbinder cleared his throat, looked at Thatch and then away. The foghorns moaned. He thought he saw the window glass quiver under the pressure of the dull far-reaching sound.

"Thatch, if you want to do it that way, I won't say a word against it," Bookbinder said.

Terry sat, hands folded tightly in her lap. Then she whispered, "I don't understand."

Dr. Devlin felt a rip of anger burn through her that finally came out as a phrase somewhere in her head. *He has to run.* But even more powerful was her unreasoning rage at Terry. For a moment she luxuriated in the spasm of random thoughts: slothful bitch, uneducated, lazy, too beautiful, all sexy body, so very quiet about it, sucking the spirit from a man, bleeding him white. Dr. Devlin calmed herself . . . what had Terry whispered? *I don't understand.* Of course not, she never would.

Dr. Devlin stared at Curver, willing him to look at her. When he did, she arched her eyebrows and glanced down at his brief case. Curver was puzzled and then, understanding, quite fearful.

"Mad, if you'll hand me the speech we did in rough draft, very rough draft, for Mr. Thatch I'll read it," Dr. Devlin said. Curver hesitated and his tongue came out, licked at his lips. He went carefully through the brief case. She saw him go past the orange folder which bound the speech. She almost laughed. They had worked on it for so long, had analyzed the Checkers speech, had pretested the Negro and pacifist and UNESCO-member and League of Women Voter and Birch Society and ADA reactions . . . and so many more. But Mad just flicked past it as if it didn't exist.

"I don't see it," Curver said.

"Let me look," Dr. Devlin said.

She walked over and knelt down before him. He was white around the nose. He eyed her warily. And yet she knew that to the others she looked merely like an academic type doing her job, enthusiastically, for Thatch. She pulled the orange folder out.

"I'm sorry, Mad, but I had the stenographer put it in a new folder," she said.

"Read it to us," Thatch said. He was in a corner of the room, his face in shadow.

Terry stirred from her trance. "Why? Is it necessary?"

"Maybe Mad ought to read it. He . . ."

"Read it," Thatch said. "You've got it in your hands. Go ahead."

The order made her shudder. She felt almost sick and, at the same time, exalted. It was the first time that Thatch, or any man in her memory, had been so final. Her mind cleared. She almost whimpered—and knew, instantly, that she was a million light years from whimpering.

"Mr. Chairman, friends, and fellow Republicans. . . . I thank you for the opportunity of appearing here today as your guest," she read. The words were huge, they swam before her eyes. And yet each word had been put there after hours of thought and days of research. It was like reading a monograph to a scientific society, but the audience was not scientists. She was not quite sure what they were. Then she knew the audience was one person. Immediately her language became smoother and she stopped shivering.

"I put Republicans last because the time has come to put mere party affiliation behind us," she read. "We stand in the world as Americans. *Americans*. Think of that for a moment. To be an American is to be privileged in a number of ways."

"I can't say that," Thatch said clearly. Dr. Devlin knew she must not stop.

"Americans have the opportunity to thrust back the most evil conspiracy the world has known: communism. We may count on the English or the French, but we should not count on them too heavily. They have their own interests, as we have ours. In some ways we stand alone. Let me repeat: We stand alone. The waves of conspiracy wash up against us and we must push them back by our own efforts. Not NATO or SEATO or the United Nations, but our own efforts will keep freedom alive in the world of tomorrow. With our bombers ready in the air and our rockets ready in their protected sites—and, most important, our citizens ready in their minds and hearts—we need not fear the Soviet Union or Communist China or Castro's Cuba. All of these threats can be handled. What they call for is a firm hand at the tiller of the Ship of State."

"What do we do about Cuba?" Thatch asked, a slight edge in his voice. Again Dr. Devlin did not respond.

"Americans originated the art of guerrilla warfare," she said. This one had been tested so well she knew it to be infallible.

Ninety-five per cent of Americans felt that they were better at guerrilla fighting than any other people in the world. "So we shall use it, not the big bombs, to support our friends and to humiliate our enemies. *Humiliate!* I use the word deliberately. For we have been humiliated by extremists in Panama. *[Pause here. Take a breath.]* We have been humiliated in Viet Nam. We have been humiliated in Cuba, and without reason. *[Slowly.]* This we shall not long endure.

"We are surrounded indeed by a monster conspiracy. We must gather our forces. We must focus our energies on the powerful enemy we face. We must take the red rats of communism, the rodents of internal subversion, and smash them against the nearest pole which flies the American flag."

"Dr. Devlin, that's more than a little inconsistent," Thatch interrupted. "You say the enemy is big and powerful one moment and the next you propose smashing him like a rat. Is he big or is he little like a rat? We can't have it both ways."

Dev heard the *we* like a clap of thunder.

Curver broke in. "Let us explain the reasons for the particular wording after the speech. For now just listen and see what you think." He nodded at Dr. Devlin. She started to read again.

"Within our country we are torn by the wrathful claims of minority groups to be treated as equals. No one wishes to deny them what they can earn. If any person discriminates merely because of another's race, color, or creed he violates the best that is in the American tradition. At the same time we know that many minority groups need and deserve our help in attaining the skills and levels of education which others have had for generations."

Dr. Devlin paused. This was one of the most delicate paragraphs in the speech. It was based on the polling result that most Southerners thought Negroes were not earning their way—and the sure knowledge that most influential Negroes knew they needed help in training their people. The paragraph was a device by which Southerners, Negroes, and liberals could all selectively misperceive, each taking out of it what they liked.

Thatch was looking at her. She glanced up and then quickly back at the pages. She felt a terrible burning sensation at the back of her neck and resisted a deep desire to scratch at it. She did not know how he was taking it.

"Some professors contend that we must learn to live with

permanent unemployment of close to five million people," Dr. Devlin read. She found herself swinging with the words, caught up in their rhythm as if she were speaking through Thatch's mouth. "I have employed many men all over the world and I do not believe this. There is nothing that condemns well-motivated and hard-working people to live without employment . . . except the short-sightedness of some big businessmen. I do not call on big government for more dole. I call on big business to stand up to its own responsibilities, to lick the so-called problems of automation. In this way, and in this way only, shall we have abundance for all."

Dr. Devlin thought back on the research that had gone into that passage. Most Republicans were wealthier than most Democrats, more hostile to taxes, more property-conscious . . . and they ignored what the Republican candidate might say of a liberal nature on such matters simply because they thought he was saying it only to win "swing votes." Negroes and Mexicans and Japanese and other low-SES groups would respond in small numbers to such a statement. Not enough to win the election, but a small slice which could be added to other slices.

Thatch sat far back in his chair, only his head pushed forward. Occasionally he would glance up at Dr. Devlin. His eyes were narrowed but his face was expressionless.

"I have not, nor shall I, attack the motives of any candidate for this high office. There have recently been public statements about the personal background of one of the candidates," Dr. Devlin read.

She glanced at Curver. They had worked this passage over, pretested it, simulated it, talked to the psychoanalysts about it, put each word in place with a deliberate intent, and then polished and repolished.

"Specifically the charge has been made that Chancellor Bryant Clark is unfit for office because he was a conscientious objector during World War Two." Dr. Devlin went on. Her voice had slowed; she gave emphasis to each word. "The decision not to fight in defense of one's country, if made on religious or ethical grounds, is a purely personal matter. We should be committing the most outrageous invasion of an individual's privacy if we asked whether a sincere conscientious objector could serve as Commander-in-Chief of the Armed Forces. Chancellor Clark is aware of the powers and the responsibilities of the Executive and what the Constitution has said the President shall do. If he decides that he will run he has, within himself, settled the matter of how he will act in time of national military emergency. How he has resolved the possibly inevitable use of military force with his convictions about war I do not know. What I do know is that we have no right to ask him."

Thatch swung forward and put his hand up.

"Hold it there," he said. "Who has objected to Clark's being a CO?"

"The American Legion has questioned his competence," Curver said. "An ex-FBI agent who runs a confidential newsletter has raised the matter. Once the Convention gets moving it will come out in the open."

Thatch said nothing.

Curver nodded to Dr. Devlin. She went on.

It was a short speech, timed for exactly ten minutes, allowing for five intervals of anticipated applause. When she finished, Dr. Devlin hesitated a moment, a passing sense of bewilderment on her face. Then she sat down. Curver could see the sheets of paper tremble in her hands.

Thatch stood up and walked over to the marble fireplace with its large antique-gold-framed mirror above it. He looked in the mirror, rubbed his hand over his chin. There was no vanity in the act. It looked as if he were feeling his skin to see if he needed a shave.

Thatch glanced at Dr. Devlin and then at Curver. Curver did not move from his deep sprawl. He looked straight at Thatch and waited.

"Mad, I'm pretty slow about some things and I'm new at politics," Thatch said, reaching slowly for the words. "So it took a while for me to put it all together. But eventually I managed. The changes in the speech to the internists could have been an honest misunderstanding. But then I see a boy in your office one day and he takes a look at me and is off like a rabbit. Two days later I remember he's the guy who threw the tomato at Terry at the luncheon. And after that luncheon when the Governor asked me if Terry was a Malay quadroon it took a while for me to realize he was too stupid to use the word *Malay*. Someone had prompted him. And you also briefed the reporter on *Meet the*

Press to ask the question about my year in the mental hospital. And you saw to it that my boys were there and fed them their lines. I don't know what all you did in New Hampshire, but it must have been plenty."

Thatch paused. Bookbinder had come out of his chair and was standing in a corner. He had a mixed look on his face, but no part of it was shock.

"That's right, Thatch," Curver said. "I did all those things."

"So the write-in vote in New Hampshire was not spontaneous like it was reported," Thatch said. "It was just as crude as an old ward-heeler rallying his boys. And the only one who didn't know was me."

"Just a minute," Curver said. "It wasn't crude. It was pretty damn clever, in fact." With considerable relish he told Thatch about his and Dev's activities in New Hampshire, about simulating the primary and isolating various groups of swing voters, about carefully developing an effective approach to the urban fringe group, the older working women and others. "I'm proud of it, Thatch. It was a very professional job."

Thatch smiled. He shrugged his shoulders. "Why didn't you tell me about it?" Thatch asked. "Or Book?"

"Book knew—or half-knew. And you didn't want to hear it," Curver said. His voice was casual, very sure. "You wanted to believe that goodness and courage and heroics would be recognized and like a fairy-tale knight the people would sweep you into office. But you wouldn't face the fact that the Flyboy and the Millionaire and the Loser were out there using all the tricks they knew, which, thank God, were based on some old notions of Boss Crump or Mayor Curley. Kelly was in there slashing away for his man Bryant Clark. Thatch, all those people, while they were making their nice speeches, were fighting the invisible dirty battle. We stayed out of it. We had a different plan. And we won. That eleven per cent write-in vote you got was one of the most sensational events in modern Presidential politics."

"So they tell me," Thatch said. "And I thought it was because everyone loved John Thatch, missionary's son and boy hero."

"Thatch, you and Book are living in a dream," Curver said. "A genuine 'draft' of a nonpolitical person is impossible. The hero has to give it a push. You wouldn't. So we did."

"A very professional job you did, too." Thatch meant it hard but he couldn't keep the admiration out of his voice.

"Let me add one more thing about that reference to Chancellor Bryant Clark in the speech," Curver said, "just to make sure we all know where we stand. This year the only person with a chance to beat Johnson is going to be a fresh face, a nonpolitical person who catches the public imagination. The only two in sight are you and Clark. He is a university president and he has a lot going for him—including Kelly, who is no slouch. We simulated a big university president as Presidential candidate and the idea comes across strong and clear to both Democrats and Republicans. He would pick up a lot of high-SES liberal-Democratic votes . . . at least three million. If his own party stands firm, that might be enough to win right there. But a university president who is a former CO wouldn't have a chance of getting by the Convention . . . they just wouldn't believe he could win the election. So we leaked it to the American Legion and to the ex-FBI character. It's an act of charity. He would have been cut down anyway by the Convention."

Thatch took a deep breath. His hands came together, the fingers locked, and he bore down hard. The sound of knuckles cracking reached across the room.

"So I kill Clark and do it in terms of friendship and tolerance," Thatch said. "That part of the speech reads well," he laughed. "You worked hard on it."

"You're not killing him, Thatch," Curver said. "You're pushing him out of the race before he gets hurt."

"Thatch, if anyone is at fault it's me," Bookbinder said. "I authorized Mad to spend a considerable amount of money in ways he saw fit. I suppose I didn't want to know what he was doing with it, but I think I had a pretty good idea." He turned to Mad. "What did it all cost?"

"Up until now, Book, it's been cheap," Curver said. "You and Levi and your friends put up a hundred twenty-five thousand, and we've spent eighty thousand. We owe a few thousand to Cotter and something to Dev."

"John," Terry said, "I'm tired." Her small voice fell into a complete silence or no one would have heard her.

Dr. Devlin felt the anger again. It surprised her, this strange bitter dislike of Terry, so motionless, slack, apparently exhausted.

Thatch looked at Terry and shook his head. He rubbed his eyes with his fingers.

"Not yet," he said. "I'm learning something. You see, Mad, what I've always been afraid of is being controlled by forces outside myself. Maybe it's common to all men, but in me it's a real fear. That's why I wanted to be independently wealthy; that's why I have few friends, why I hire people to run my business. In a way, I guess, that's why I wanted to be 'drafted'—because if I were drafted I wouldn't owe anyone a thing. Then, a bit at a time, I discover that you're manipulating me. You really took me over, Mad. I was your creature. When it dawned on me I could have strangled you—and you too, Dr. Devlin."

Bookbinder sighed. "While you're in a strangling mood, Thatch, you'd better get a good grip on my esophagus, too. I turned down an ambassadorship for you—Viet Nam—without even telling you." He described Eb Fork's approach at the Spanish Embassy and his own annoyance at what he considered this crude attempt by the Administration to remove Thatch from the political arena.

Thatch looked genuinely surprised. He opened his mouth to respond, shut it, and rubbed his chin.

"Thatch, I'm afraid none of us is in a very apologetic mood tonight," Curver said. "We didn't hurt you. You've got the itch to be President. You've showed it in a dozen different ways. That's your ambition, Thatch . . . not mine or Dev's or Book's. We took your desire and worked to advance it by means you neither understood nor approved of. But none of it hurt you."

"Except the knowledge of it," Thatch said. "And what it told me about myself. That I am ambitious for political power and I've been calling it a dozen different things except that—duty, patriotism, dedication." Thatch sighed and it was a sound no one except Terry had ever heard from him before.

Then he went on, his voice firm and loud again.

"You all think this probing and measuring and analysis of the electorate is pretty great stuff," Thatch said. "You say it will help me to win. In your godlike hands these new tools are safe. But what if someone like old Joe McCarthy came down the turnpike and decided to use them? How would you feel then? If the computer tells me to accuse and point a finger and find 103 Communists in the State Department, it's in the cause of virtue. But if it tells McCarthy to do the same, then he's serving evil. Why? I don't know. I believe a person ought to say what he thinks and not what a machine tells him some large group of people fear or some other group of people love. Let a machine write the cute speech Dr. Devlin just read and why couldn't it write a cuter speech for McCarthy or Huey Long or Hitler . . . I'm ambitious, sure, but I also want to be principled."

"Thatch, in politics it's hard to separate ambition from principle," Bookbinder said. He sounded suddenly very old. Curver wondered if in these few minutes the last lingering traces of the virus had been seared out of Bookbinder. His voice carried authority. "Does ambition make you seek for certain principles to advance your own position? Or does your love of the principles make you seek high position to advance the principles? Don't ask, Thatch, because there is no answer. The two curl around one another until it is impossible to tell whether the origin of any single act is ambition or principle. But without ambition—I mean real self-seeking—politics would crumple into a gray bureaucratic mess. It would be the sanctuary for everything dull and mediocre and, ultimately, mean."

"Mr. Thatch, ambition is a thing which every functioning man in our culture must have," Dr. Devlin said. Her voice was reassuring, professional. "Don't torture yourself over things which are natural, in fact necessary."

Thatch looked at her, nodded. The room pivoted on Thatch; everyone waited to see what he would do. This is the *charisma*, Curver told himself. Even if he never ran, Thatch had it . . . the kind of personality meant to command.

Thatch was very still. He looked out at the fogbound city. He listened to three moans from the Embarcadero foghorn. Then he moved.

"All right, Terry," he said. "Let's go."

"Take a copy of the speech," Curver said. He handed Thatch an envelope. "And if you use it you'd better know what's going to happen. About one thousand Thatch supporters have been given tickets to the Cow Palace. Don't ask how we got them. The moment you finish the speech, if it's the speech in the envelope, they are going to start a demonstration. Signs saying *Thatch for President* and *There's No Match for Thatch* and a half-dozen other slogans are going to appear. They will look as if they were made in hotel rooms last night or right on the spot, out of pieces of paper, programs, cardboard. They were made weeks ago. And a bunch of people outside who couldn't get tickets will storm the gates as they get carried away by the demonstration and the cops will let them in. The TV cameras will pick up the supporters outside as well as the demonstration. After five minutes of demonstration some of the official delegates with their badges on will join in and then it will form into a serpentine and will wind around the floor picking up delegates from states where we know we have supporters."

"That sounds like the best-prepared spontaneous demonstration in modern times," Thatch said.

"A little better than Stevenson's in 1960," Curver said. "Just like we simulated the speech, we simulated the convention. We found out a lot of things about the delegates, but the big things I just told you. The delegates want a show, a feeling of excitement, the sensation of being swept off their feet . . . most of all they want to be with the winner. And they like to believe the winner emerges spontaneously. Even when they know it's a fake, they persuade themselves that a new hero whom everyone loves has descended from on high." Mad laughed, but tiredly. "There are some other touches, including TV interviews with at least ten delegates, four of them Negroes, who will announce then and there that the demonstration has convinced them that Thatch is the people's choice."

He stopped. Then he said two final sentences. "The key is the speech. I don't care whether you give it or not."

Thatch's mouth twisted up bitterly for a moment and then he shook his head. He smiled. He looked down at the envelope Curver was holding out. He took it and put it in his coat pocket.

Thatch and Terry turned and left the room.

The lobby of the Fairmont was crowded and several people recognized Thatch. He waved at them, but did not stop to shake hands. He asked Terry if she would walk to the Palace with him. He needed air. She searched his face for a moment and then said no, she was too tired. He patted her arm absently, put her in a cab and turned to walk down California Street.

Someone called his name before he had left the pool of light in front of the hotel. He waved and went on quickly. Footsteps sounded behind him and someone was pulling at his sleeve. Thatch turned and looked at the man without stopping. It was hard to make out the man's face in the gray fog. But the voice was familiar.

"It's me, Thatch," the man said. The face came toward him, presenting itself for identification. "Clark Allen. Tom Gulligan of AP has put me on a special assignment to cover you. Gulligan's big on you. Thinks you ought to be the candidate and that you've got a good chance."

They had turned and were moving down the sharp incline of California Street. Thatch was not listening to the rapid talk of the other man. Instead he thought of what Bookbinder had said about ambition and principle. Crudely, he tried to arrange the events of the last months, but they would not fall into categories. Faces; stacks of letters; phone calls; faces again, turned toward him as he spoke; the applause (Oh, God, the sweetness of that applause . . . he could admit to the pleasure of it now); the feeling of power over others, the sound of his own words "Excellence is color-blind" biting into people, the vastness of the country, the noble-pillared buildings in Washington.

The cable hummed in its groove and, as they came to a corner, rattled as it went over rollers. The hill seemed too steep and Thatch's feet had to reach to regain contact with the sidewalk. Maybe I should have stayed in the mental hospital, Thatch thought. Certainly I should have stayed out of this political thing. He felt vulnerable to everything and everyone. He tried but failed to impose an order on all the things that had thundered at him from every side since that day on the bridge.

"That was some time at Zamboanga," the voice at his side was saying. "Guess I should have tried to clear some of the things with you, but big scoops like that move awful fast. I had to get it done in a hurry. Anyway I was sure the coverage couldn't hurt you."

Thatch's shoulders tightened. He turned and looked at the man. Clark Allen, the "honest" stringer.

Instantly Thatch felt again the awful sensation of physical unreality. The colored fog was now threatening, its laciness hiding something ominous. The Chinese looking out through the moist glass windows seemed very small.

"Did you hear what happened to Ferguson?" Thatch asked. They were the first words he had spoken to Allen, and his voice was thick.

"No, what about him?" Allen said.

"They've got TV sets and movie houses in Zamboanga, Allen. Did you know that?"

"Sure. Most Filipino villages have a movie house and I guess Zambo should have TV. It's a big enough city."

"They ran your program out there, Allen. In fact they ran it several times. It was very popular. Especially with the police."

"I didn't know that," Allen said. He was walking more slowly, as if he had abruptly tired. "I never thought of that."

"You never thought," Thatch said wonderingly, "that the pictures of the Huks would be valuable to the police? You never thought that with those pictures they could round up the ringleaders? Did you also forget that we promised to protect the Huks if they would call the meeting?"

"Did we promise that?" Allen said. His voice was a disingenuous sigh. It all seemed such a long time ago.

"We promised that. But we didn't keep our promise. *You* didn't. So the police rounded up eight of the Huks they could identify from the pictures. But before they got to Bull—remember Bull, the big fellow?—well, before they got to him he got Ferguson."

"Ferguson?"

"Yeah, my engineer. The guy we left behind. Bull apparently felt we hadn't kept our agreement and he went *juramentado*. All wrapped tight in Moro death shrouds he came down the dock swinging a machete and screaming so loud they heard him a block away. One of the American pile drivers had a thirty-eight he wore under his shirt and he opened up on Bull, but the Bull ran right down the stream of bullets. All they did was bring out red spots on the white shroud. Later, during the autopsy, they found four bullets in him, two in his lungs."

Allen had fallen behind. Thatch stopped and looked around. Allen came shuffling along the cement, his shoes very loud in the smothering quietness of the fog. He walked slowly up until he was even with Thatch and they went on down Grant.

"They say Ferguson didn't move," Thatch went on. "He stood and watched Bull and he shook his head like he was sad. And the next second his head was off his shoulders and rolling on the dock. They say the Bull picked up Ferguson's head and roared for someone to shoot him. And the pile driver finally obliged and shot him through the eye."

They had come to an intersection. A small Chinese stood behind an outdoor newspaper and curio counter. Thatch turned and looked at Allen.

"None of that's my fault," Allen said. His face was puckered into a childlike mask, but his body was bent—either for escape or combat.

Thatch felt an enormous relief. His left hand swung across and hit Allen in the stomach. His right came up and the last moment he snapped his body in behind it. A straight line ran from his heel to his fist. For Thatch, it was as if he were striking back with the pent-up fury of months at all his tormentors. The blow caught Allen on the cheek and he collapsed against the Chinese newsstand. The Chinese moved very delicately away from the counter, slid around the end, and watched with a slight smile as Allen carried the whole counter down. Newspapers and rubber dolls and chopsticks fell around Allen. He didn't move.

"How much?" Thatch asked the Chinese.

"Twenty, thirty dollars, about that. I'll save most of the stuff," he said. "You've got a nice right hand. Like a professional."

Thatch took out his wallet and gave the man two twenties. The Chinese wanted to go on talking about fighting. He was apparently very well informed. Thatch shook his head and walked away.

The Chinese watched him go. He tried to place the man, to remember the familiar face. A retired heavyweight he'd once seen on TV, perhaps? A classy college-type fighter like Gene Tunney. That satisfied him. He bent to pick up the newspapers, careful not to touch the victim. He'd come to soon enough.

Thatch walked, rubbing his right knuckles gently into the palm of his left hand. He felt rested, no longer in need of sleep. Somehow a decision had been made—and not by him.

23

Whatever convention comes to San Francisco the Fairmont Hotel lobby gets the action. The high-domed lobby with red velvet chairs and the big empty stretches of old-fashioned rug can accommodate hundreds of people. The convention may name whatever hotel it wishes as official headquarters, but the Fairmont lobby is the real headquarters. When it is too crowded one can always back into one of the bars or the soda fountain or one of the conference rooms. For the Republican Convention the television networks had all set up permanent cameras which could sweep over the lobby, seeking out targets of opportunity. They had caught Goldwater talking to a group of frenzied students from the University of Arizona; Nixon with his hand on the shoulder of Tom Dewey, the pair hunched forward like two boxers so that no one could hear their words; Eisenhower had walked smilingly through, applause spattering the lobby; Scranton came in and no one recognized him and he stood for a long moment, observed only by the omnipresent eye of television.

The cameras caught Clark Allen because it was late when he came through the glass doors and the lobby was about as empty as it ever got. Also, the cameramen knew he was doing the big story on John Thatch and reflexively they covered him. Ever since the big Philippine story, Allen had had plenty to say and write. It was always about Thatch. It took them almost a minute to realize Allen was holding a handkerchief to his mouth and his right eye had a big bruise over it. They assumed quickly that he was drunk. They killed the shot and went back to a long view of janitors cleaning up the Cow Palace in preparation for tomorrow's session.

The reporters spotted Allen and moved in. They had seen him leave a half-hour ago with Thatch.

"What happened, Clark?" One of the team from the Los Angeles *Times* asked.

Allen looked at them and knew he had made a mistake. He should have come up the California Street entrance and gone right to his room. Go easy now, he told himself. Go softly.

"I slipped on the slimy sidewalk," Allen said. He took his handkerchief away and grinned at them. "This fog is a menace."

"Slipped and split your lip and got a contusion on the forehead?" Abelman of the San Francisco *Chronicle* said. Allen kept grinning. Allen knew he had to make the explanation right. It came to him from a murder trial of a Filipino politician he had covered in Manila. It was the defense's chief argument. "I fell in front of one of those apartment houses. Went sideways onto the cement steps. Caught my head on one, bounced and then the lip got it."

Abelman looked at Allen closely, nodded, and walked away. The rest of the reporters went back to the endless exchange of gossip, hard fact, rumor, official statements, and unofficial denials which made up their business. Allen walked to the elevators.

Curver had a small room in the back of the Cow Palace which normally was used as a horse stall. The room was not labeled and had been arranged by Bookbinder, who had told the Arrangements Committee that it would be a courtesy to Thatch . . . nothing more. They were not the kind to ask petty questions about accommodations when the request came from Bookbinder.

It was early, not yet 10 P.M. and, although the Cow Palace was filling, all that would be heard was the perfunctory oratory necessary to fill the air while the big-four committees—credentials, rules, permanent organization, and platform—were meeting.

Someone was standing in the door, casting a short dark shadow. Curver glanced up. It was Kelly. He was holding a small package under his arm.

"Mad, you've done well by your boy," Kelly said. "I congratulate you. Also, allow me to believe that part of the technique you learned from me."

"All of it, Bert. All of it," Curver said.

They shook hands. Surprisingly Curver was pleased to see Kelly. There was something hard and bright behind those layers of fat . . . a strange morality.

"I wanted you to look at something," Kelly said as he unwrapped the package. He looked up innocently. "Did you ever find Mrs. Singleton's nephew?"

Curver laughed.

"We've become best friends," Curver said. He had an uneasy feeling that he should have checked this thing out.

"I'll bet," Kelly said drily.

Kelly stood back and Curver could see a stack of handwritten pages. Kelly turned them over to a yellow marker. He pointed with his finger at a paragraph. Curver bent forward and read it.

"The world is full of nuts who write crazy things, Kelly," Curver said. He felt sick.

"Four other people who were in Santo Tomas confirm that Mrs. Thatch was a very strange girl, quite friendless, very quiet, and that she was the first woman to become a whore." Curver looked at Kelly. He knew he could not bluff past this.

"Go ahead and use it, Kelly," Curver said in a voice which had an edge of contempt in it.

Kelly's mouth did not stop smiling, but his eyes went serious.

"Mad, Thatch shouldn't be in this thing," Kelly said. "He doesn't have the experience, the background, the know-how. Also, he hasn't earned it. He's been an engineer who just happened to stumble into a couple of heroic situations. That doesn't qualify a man for President, Mad. It's a job a man has to be prepared for."

"Like the Chancellor?" Curver said.

"That's right," Kelly said evenly. "The Chancellor is qualified. And in the year of stale candidates he is the only dark horse who might—just might—make it in November."

"Do you think the Chancellor has a better chance of beating Johnson than Thatch?"

"No. If Johnson can be beaten, which I doubt, either the Chancellor or Thatch can do it. The others don't have a prayer."

"Kelly, I don't know whether Thatch is going to run or not," Curver said. "But one thing I do know. I'm not going to show him this diary. So use it any way you want."

"He may already know about it. I told his wife. She might have told him."

Bizarre scenes raced through Curver's mind. The last one was of Terry sitting, small and deadly quiet in her chair, saying "John, I'm tired."

Mad could only shake his head.

Kelly's small hands were tying the package back up. He did it primly, with a kind of exaggerated neatness. He leaned back and admired his work. Then he looked at Curver and smiled.

"Mad, you disappoint me," Kelly said. "Did you think I would really use this against Thatch?"

"Why did you show it to me?"

"Because I want the Chancellor to get the nomination. Even if he loses, he will become the titular head of the Party and will have a damned good chance in 1968. I just showed you the diary because I wanted you to know that someone else, not me, might use it against him in the election. In short, Mad, the Chancellor has a future. With this kind of stuff in his background, Thatch doesn't. Someone should tell him."

Curver felt a sudden surge of relief, so deep it was almost a spasm. Both Kelly and he knew that this kind of weapon would probably not be used. Once the two Conventions had picked their candidates a strange psychological mechanism set in; certain kinds of scandal were simply not printed. The candidate acquired part of the protective aura of the President. Alcoholism, lechery, a bad temper, even dishonesty were not mentioned. If they were, the gossiper was violently attacked and usually not believed.

"What are you going to do with the dairy, Bert?" Curver asked.

"I'm going to walk around to the incinerator behind this building and pitch it in and watch it burn," Kelly said. "Want to come along?"

"No, Bert. I don't have to watch. I believe you'll do it."

"There aren't any other copies, Mad. And the woman who wrote the diary is dead."

Mad nodded.

The little fat man walked out of the room, his back stiff. Curver admired him.

Dev came in briskly, all business, a few minutes later. "Where are those extra hundred tickets that the Flyboy people promised?" she asked.

She was glancing down a long list of names with numbers after them. She checked off some and moved rubber-band-bound stacks of tickets to one side as she did.

"Dev, you've become a ward-heeler," Curver said. "I thought we were going to do this all with science."

"Shut up," Dr. Devlin said. "Where are the tickets?"

"In the lower left-hand drawer," Curver said. Her hand reached down; her eyes did not move from her checklist and she picked out a packet of tickets. She made a check mark and looked up smiling.

"They're all there," she said. "Are you sure you've got enough bodies to go along with the tickets?"

"Guarantee it, absolutely guarantee it," Curver said.

"Mad, you've held back a few times on me," Dr. Devlin said. Her voice had a flat finality about it. "This time I want to know what to expect. You kid me about becoming a ward-heeler, but you know it's necessary to get past this bottleneck. After this we have the great American public to operate on and we don't have to worry about these circuses. Until then I'll be a ward-heeler, but I have to know what is going on."

"I told it all to Thatch last night," Curver said.

"You did not," Dr. Devlin said. She tore a page off her pad of yellow paper, poised her pencil above it. "Tell me what else you've scheduled."

Curver knew there was no sense in hesitating. She would know what he had been up to soon enough.

He told her about the Cow Palace guards he had bought, the ushers who were in fact Berkeley graduate students, and the rest of the arrangements.

Bookbinder watched the TV technicians setting up the camera and cables in his suite at the Fairmont. He glanced over at Levi. They had agreed there was nothing they could do except say what they knew.

The interviewer glanced over his shoulder. The cameraman nodded. They tested for voice level. Then the interviewer went on. Later his voice would be replaced by Huntley or Brinkley or some big name. If the interview produced anything worth putting on the network.

"Mr. Bookbinder, you are supporting John Thatch as a dark-horse candidate. Is that true?" the interviewer said.

"I am supporting him," Bookbinder said. "I don't know that he's a dark horse exactly . . ."

"Mr. Thatch has not allowed his name to be run in any primary, although he has done well in some. If he does have a chance it would be as a genuine draft by the Convention. Do you think that might happen?"

"There haven't been many genuine drafts in our history," Bookbinder said. "In 1868 the Democrats really did draft Horatio Seymour and then adjourned before he could refuse it. Seymour knew he would lose to Grant. In 1916, we drafted Hughes and he resigned from the Supreme Court and then got beaten by Wilson. In 1952, the Democrats, in my opinion, really drafted Stevenson. And that's about it. It's not something you count on."

"And you are still for Mr. Thatch, after what you have just said?"

"I am. I don't expect miracles. But if one happens I hope it happens to John Thatch," Bookbinder said.

The interviewer smiled and cut the camera. Only the last reply would make the interview newsworthy, but there might be a blank spot to fill. The television crew backed out of the room, cables and cigarette butts and bits of paper behind them.

"You know, Mr. Thatch, the Cow Palace ain't really in San Francisco," the limousine driver said. He had told this to a dozen people and it had become routine. "It's just outside the city limits." He turned his head and looked seriously at Terry and Thatch. "So the Convention isn't really in San Francisco."

He seemed to think the story important, as if the Convention were a gigantic hoax which San Francisco had perpetrated on the rest of the country.

The traffic started to thicken as they turned off Alemany. He could see the big low shape of the Cow Palace and streams of people walking toward it. Many of them wore badges; some had banners and placards. Thatch could not resist trying to make out the names. He saw GOLDWATER twice, NIXON once, and then, with a relief he disliked, he saw a girl carrying a sign which said THATCH . . . NO MATCH. He turned away and looked at Terry.

"Did you sleep all right?" he asked.

"No. Did you?"

"Yes. Better than I expected."

They looked at one another and then quickly away. Thatch sensed how far apart they were.

"Sir, they told me to deliver you to the back of the Cow Palace," the driver said stiffly. "One of your people made that emphatic. He gave me the gate number and passes and the rest."

Four motorcycles swung out from the curb and moved into position in front of the limousine. At once their sirens went on. It happened so fast Thatch thought there had been an accident or they were being arrested.

"An escort," Terry said. She stared at the motorcyclists with their round white helmets.

Already heads along the sidewalks were turning and staring at them. There were some shouts of encouragement. Thatch grinned and raised a hand. Instantly the sound seemed to him to double in volume.

Curver watched the limousine swing into the gateway. He had ordered Thatch brought there because it was remote from the speaker's stand and close to a parking lot that would not fill until later. He could watch the college kids with Thatch buttons and banners and see that they were well spaced out and following directions: They were to stay on the curb so the people behind them seemed part of the demonstration. Curver turned and nodded to the boy with the bull-horn.

"Thatch is here. Over by Gate Sixteen," the voice came booming out. It sounded somehow official, though the voice was young and excited. Around Gate 16 the group Curver had posted began to chant. "Thatch, Thatch . . . he has no match." "Go, Thatch, go." Curver had told each group separately (for none of the college groups were supposed to know that other groups were similarly employed) to avoid joining into a chorus. Just make up something and keep yelling it.

Inside the Cow Palace, now almost full, the sudden noise rose above the drone of the chairman reporting on a preliminary statement by the platform committee. Someone walked to one of the floor microphones and, miraculously, it was on.

"It's Thatch," the man's voice boomed. "He just arrived at Gate Sixteen."

Figures ran in from Gate 16. They were antic, convulsed, excited. They yelled and pointed back down the entryway. The chairman rapped for order, but he did not speak. The big hall was full of bored people and suddenly something was happening. In waves they came snapping out of their lethargy. A few moved toward Gate 16.

Outside the limousine had come to a halt. It was instantly surrounded by people who were chanting slogans, waving banners, jostling. Curver watched closely and was astounded. Even the ones who were paid, and there were a handful, had become infected by their involvement. The face of a middle-aged woman, red and flushed, bobbed up and down with delight. Curver had interviewed her two days before and paid her taxi fare and five dollars and she had been cool and neutral.

People walking to the Cow Palace pressed in to see what was happening at Gate 16 and became a part of the demonstration. Far down the street Curver saw some high school kids come running, whooping and yelling, ready for any break in the monotony.

Curver nodded at the motorcycle officer who had led the limousine in. The officer viewed the crowd once more, saw the high school kids coming, and walked over to his cycle and picked up the radio speaker. A dollar a second that officer would make, Curver thought. Sixty dollars for himself, twenty each for the other three . . . but the money would be paid only after he called in that a riot was starting around the Thatch limousine. It would take about a minute to make the connection, call for reinforcements; then his job was over.

Curver saw Terry and she looked frightened. He imagined what she must be seeing . . . a welter of faces, banners, shouts, ferocious-looking people, gestures which could be threatening, strangers with unknown intentions moving toward her. Thatch sat stolidly, not smiling. He looked straight ahead. Somehow the posture, the refusal to glance at them, delighted the crowd.

"Boss, that man is boss, like no man is boss," a Negro yelled. "That man no chicken. He don't back down when he say somethin'. Hey, Boss, look over here, Boss."

The police reinforcements arrived. They poured in with a smooth efficiency, sirens muted, but loud enough to be heard, a kind of authority to the sound.

Everything hinged on timing. Curver looked toward the gateway. If things were going well inside, a few hundred of the delegates would start moving toward Gate 16. They would see that the riot squad had had to be called out.

"There is no match—" a voice said, loud, clear, and overpowering. It sounded supernatural. The mob froze for a delicious moment. Then, for the first time, they spoke in unison.

"—for Thatch."

One of the college kids swung at one of the riot squad. There was a quick ruffle of violence, a bobbing of heads, a lurching of bodies, a voice choked off in mid-obscenity.

Curver was frightened. It may be too much. The delegates from inside were pouring out for a look and the riot squad was just a handful of cops. Christ, it was one thing to have a demonstration. If it turned into a riot they would lose the effect. By now there were over two hundred delegates in the parking lot, craning their necks, shouting. He glanced around and saw the television cameras were scanning the scene. It was so perfect . . . exactly the way he had wanted it. And now the whole damned thing was getting out of control.

Thatch was out of the car and standing on a fender. He was still not smiling. He lifted his hand and pointed a finger and swept it around the crowd. The noise dropped. The riot squad turned the college boy loose. Thatch waited. The radios on two of the motorcycles were giving off static and, occasionally, words. Someone walked over and turned them off.

"We are here as citizens," Thatch said. "Let us act like citizens. Let us obey." Then he smiled. "Mrs. Thatch and I thank you for your attention, but please don't break up the car . . . not while we're in it."

The crowd laughed, then cheered. The ebbing of tension was almost a physical thing to be measured by a delicate instrument.

Thatch helped Terry out of the car. Curver led them to the room in back of the Cow Palace. He shot a look back at the television cameras. He had told them separately and in confidence that they had an exclusive. That was why each had a camera at Gate 16.

They sat down in the small room.

"Your speech is scheduled in about ten minutes," Devlin said.

Thatch nodded. He looked at her and then back at Curver.

"That was a little tense out there," Thatch said. "Makes me nervous. Those people close up and yelling."

"And they spat on the window," Terry said. Then, when she

spoke again, her voice had faded. "It's dangerous. They could get hysterical."

"Mrs. Thatch, don't worry," Dr. Devlin said. "Those were well-disposed people. There's a difference between a mob and a crowd of supporters. That's what you had out there—"

"John doesn't need support for anything," Terry said, her voice suddenly shrill.

There was a long embarrassed moment.

"Mad, that crowd looked awfully young," Thatch said. "Where were the delegates?"

Curver managed to look preoccupied in some papers. Here we go, he thought. Thatch grows up in San Francisco beside the Bay.

"They were there," Curver said. "About two hundred of them came out to see what the hell was going on. It's all over the Cow Palace by now. You caused the first riot call to go out. But don't jump for joy, Thatch. Not one of the delegates thought the big hearty demonstration was spontaneous."

"It was, though," Thatch said. "I could see it in their faces."

"The people close to the limousine were gone on you," Curver said. "They were not faking it. They may have started cool, but they got spontaneous. But the delegates will conclude just one thing: It was faked, but it was good. And that makes you a big new man in their eyes. A hero with a sense of tactics, knows how to deploy the troops."

"Was it a hoax?" Thatch asked.

"You define a political hoax and I'll give you an answer," Curver said. "But one thing I can tell you, Thatch, old friend; a lot of people are running screaming through hotel corridors, into caucuses, bursting into press rooms, hunching together to 'beat Thatch' and thinking you're a natural, a walking genius."

The phone rang. Dr. Devlin answered.

"They want you to go in now, Mr. Thatch," she said. The phone gave off the thin whine of a closed circuit.

Thatch, Terry, and Curver left together. Dr. Devlin watched and something welled up inside her. She refused to examine what she felt. She looked at the phone. She listened to its small scream. She smashed it neatly against the edge of a metal file cabinet. It screeched louder, as if defending itself. She hit it again . . . and then five more times. Finally it broke in half. She threw the debris on the floor and walked toward the door. She could watch the Thatch party moving toward the main building. The mess of black plastic and wire which had been the phone receiver still gave off a diminutive mechanical howl of anger.

Thatch's group grew as it moved, picking up a person here, a reporter there, adding to its bulk in the curious geometrical way in which crowds grow. Dr. Devlin realized that at a certain point the people joining a crowd lost their identity, became expressionless, were like identical units which only added mass but no individual to the crowd. Only Thatch, big and unsmiling, stood out . . . a nucleus around which the scurrying senseless faceless units moved.

Dr. Devlin remembered one of her fantasies. She possessed the magic-ray gun seen in the comic strips, but she also had the power to grant immunity from its lethal power by touching a person. When that person was surrounded by enemies she swung the ray gun over the crowd, burning them off in sharp puffs of smoke that left only a mound of ash where each person had stood. She could feel the gun in her hand, imagine the people around Thatch falling away, and then he would be walking alone. Not really alone, for she could catch up with him. They would go into the Convention together.

"Mrs. Thatch, I'm Walter Cronkite of CBS," a man said to Terry. "Your husband has created a lot of commotion. It's the first real excitement of the Convention. Some people downtown are betting that if he indicated he will accept a draft nomination that he'll get it." Terry looked puzzled. "What do you think Mr. Thatch will say when he gets up there?"

"I don't know, Mr. Cronkite," Terry said. Her eyes were frightened, and she made no attempt to hide the fear. "I really don't know." Cronkite did not doubt her for a second. He moved out of the crowd with a piece of news that would be dramatic if he could make the television audience believe it. But he knew he could not. Everyone was so used to the denials, feints, ambiguities, and double-edged statements of politics that they believed only what they wanted to believe.

"I hope Mad knows what he's doing," Levi said. Bookbinder noticed his hands were shaking. "Remember the Democratic

Convention in 1960, when most of the Kennedy family discovered their tickets had disappeared just about the time the Stevenson demonstration was started? If Mad gets carried away by that kind of thing he could land Thatch in a lot of trouble."

"He wouldn't do that," Bookbinder said. "The boy is honest. He told us everything last night. It's all part of the game; we both know that. Mad learned the game well and quickly and he's playing within the rules."

The mood of the Convention came to them through the television set. They were both restless, pacing the room, glancing at newspapers and then throwing them aside, switching stations. Irritable, the way the crowd at a championship fight is irritable. Anxious for the combat to be joined.

"Book, he really never told you what he's going to do?" Levi asked.

"For God's sake, Levi, do you think I'd hold out on you!"

Curver was nervous but not uncertain. He had studied the limits of the game and had decided they were flexible. He also knew that only a few of the men at the Convention understood how to stretch the old limits, to give them a new twist, but still make them look traditional. For just a moment he thought with relief about the time when the Convention would be over and he could start to work outside the shaky edifice of the Party and its Victorian mores and gabby old-timers and ancient habits.

The officer in charge of the motorcycle police came over to Curver. The other three motorcyclists were drawn up in a line across Gate 16. Behind them the Convention ushers were hunched in a circle, sullen and uncertain, but knowing that this was not what they had anticipated . . . being outmaneuvered by the police. They had the petulant childish look petty authority always has when it has been frustrated.

"The man inside says the chairman has called twice for Mr. Thatch," the officer said.

"Tell him to send Senator Reddick up with the news that the spontaneous demonstration outside has delayed him," Curver said.

The officer picked up the radio microphone and spoke into it. Curver knew the order would get through. He had read carefully about the walkie-talkie sets the Kennedy team had used at the 1960 convention. It had struck him as both clumsy and obvious. And expensive. He had simply used the motorcycle police as a communications system. Inside the Cow Palace there were three officers who would relay the messages. They were being paid triple-time for this additional duty which, they thought, had been given them by the National Republican Committee. Total cost $450. The cost of just one of Kennedy's walkie-talkies was more than that.

"Thatch, they want you to wait a few more minutes," Curver said. "There is some trouble clearing the aisle. When those three officers with the helmets step aside it will be time to go in."

Curver knew precisely what was happening inside. All of the people who had received tickets from him also got a card instructing them to go to Aisle 16, which would allow them to shake Thatch's hand as he walked to the speaker's podium. The National Committee had, in its wisdom, shuffled the thousand tickets released to Bookbinder so that the recipients would be scattered around the Cow Palace.

The people, anxious to shake the hand of a man who might be President, would cause a congestion that looked like a riot. When they dispersed and went to their seats they would be muttering about "police tactics," a "frameup," or simply raising a doubt—"Who the hell is running this show?" They would be feeling manipulated, but not by their hero. By whom, then? By the ushers, the police, the official organization, the oppressive kingmakers—by Thatch's enemies.

A roar came from inside the auditorium. It hit the exits, was funneled into the narrow passages, bounced down the hard concrete walls, and came out a confused and angry blast. By some odd quality of acoustics, in the midst of the howl of sound, Senator Reddick's words came through very small and precise.

"Mr. Chairman, could the aisles be cleared so that Mr. Thatch can enter? I understand that outside there is a demonstration for Mr. Thatch, but he is unable to enter because the congestion is so great. His friendly supporters will release him, I am sure, if the ushers or the master-at-arms can merely prevail upon those in the aisles to return to their seats. I have no objection to anyone expressing himself, Mr. Chairman, but those who are blocking the aisles merely to prevent the entrance of an authentic American hero are acting contrary to the whole tradition of the Republican Party."

The people around Thatch started to shout a protest and press forward. They became what the Senator had described—a demonstration. They had not known they would be involved, but once instructed they behaved in appropriate ways. Not because they were members of a conspiracy, but because they were, in a flash of time, part of a crowd . . . a crowd with a purpose. The purpose could be defined later. Right now the presence of Thatch was enough.

"Thatch, a lot of things can be faked and I've faked some, but enthusiasm like this has to be real," Curver said. He spoke into Thatch's ear, his hand boxing the words in, treasuring them.

Thatch turned and looked at him. Thatch's eyes were opaque, slightly glazed; his face had no expression. Thatch did not reply.

"Good God, why doesn't the Chairman clear that aisle?" Bookbinder asked. The cameras had zoomed in on Aisle 16. It was a long avenue of confusion. "Things like that can get out of hand."

Levi did not speak. He was curled in a chair. He not only disliked confusion, it frightened him. As the confusion grew, he found it the more unbearable. Perhaps the lingering shadows of pogroms in long-forgotten ghettos or the small tribal meetings of SS men before they descended on a Jewish household. . . .

Aisle 16 foamed with people. The ushers moved ahead and very reluctantly the people in the aisle retreated, becoming more congested as they pressed together. Bookbinder heard a sentence or two. "We just want to shake his hand." "We got a right, goddam it." "I know he'll shake my hand." "Take your paws off me, mister, or you'll get busted right in the lip."

Staring at the television screen, Bookbinder could see the thing spread. He felt a sense of congestion in his chest, a kind of deepening conviction.

"It's madness," Levi said. He was not looking at the television screen.

"It's not madness, Levi," Bookbinder said instantly, too quickly to have considered. "It's popular enthusiasm. It's what I said could happen. A single man getting through to the people."

"If they don't tear one another apart before he gets to them," Levi said.

Senator Reddick had seen more conventions than the Chair-

man. After making his announcement he watched the confusion
with a shrewd eye. Curver hadn't told him everything . . . just
enough. The standees in the aisle were not, he realized, opposed
to Thatch. They were *for* Thatch. And yet, at the other end of
the Cow Palace, the delegates and spectators, growing impatient
and wanting to be involved, were beginning to chant "We want
Thatch. We want Thatch."

The Senator moved up behind the Chairman.

"This can get bad very fast," he said. "Let's cut them off by
having the organist play 'The Star-Spangled Banner.' That'll
freeze 'em all and then Thatch can come in."

The Chairman bit. He called an aide. A few seconds later
the National Anthem began to pour out of the loudspeakers. The
action in Aisle 16 became slow-motion. The voices died. Abruptly
everyone was still.

Thatch blinked. The huge auditorium was decked with flags
and it was full of people. Powerful spotlights sought the place
where he stood. The rest of the Cow Palace was dark and very
still. The only sound was the airy majesty of the organ playing
"The Star-Spangled Banner."

Curver, a foot behind him, spoke softly into his ear.

"Thatch, they've never done this for anyone before. Maybe
Ike will get the National Anthem when he arrives, but no one
else."

Curver was not sure this was true. He only knew that, by
some accident, they had stumbled into a magnificent entrance—
all the lights focused, the crowd at attention, absolute silence,
the wheezing organ playing the majestic music. Curver had not
the remotest idea how it had happened.

When the organ stopped Thatch took a step forward, put
his hand under Terry's elbow and started down the aisle. It
stretched away like a path that came to a narrow point above
which grew a structure covered with flags, bunting, a spread of
cobra-like necks that ended in thick microphones. On the stand
were faces, small and luminous, but all attentive. It seemed a
long way to walk.

The path was lined with people who were standing or squatting. As Thatch advanced they stood up and began to murmur.
The first few people put out their hands . . . a cluster of older

men, wearing some veterans' badge and quivering with excitement. Thatch shook as many hands as he could, but still moved at a regular pace.

He sensed that Curver had left his side.

"Terry, shake hands with the ones on your side," Thatch said. "We've got to move along."

He let go of her elbow and was dimly aware that it was like a thing released. Her arm jerked away. Thatch shook hands, giving each of the waving hands a brief quick shake. He stumbled, caught himself; the crowd sighed and then, for no reason, applauded. For a moment he knew what it would be like to be in high office: Every sneeze would be admired.

He could not see Terry. He looked around. She had vanished in the crowd. Or with Mad. Someone would take care of her, he thought. There was so much affection and enthusiasm that surely it would spill over onto Terry and take care of her.

Terry slipped back down the corridor. She had looked at John's face during the playing of the National Anthem and knew she had to get out. She came out of the passageway and into the night. She walked over to the limousine. The chauffeur was not there. The whole expanse of cement and fence and doors was empty. A roar came from inside. Terry reached in her purse and drew out a pen. There was no paper. She looked around. On the inside of the limousine was a yellow placard Scotch-taped to the windshield. It said *Official Car*. She reached in and pulled it off, took it to the hood of the car, and began to write.

24

From the steps of the little office, Dev watched the woman in the parking lot. Then she recognized her. What was Terry doing here? She should be with Thatch pushing down the aisle. She listened for a moment to the announcer describing the riotous scene. A bitterness welled up in her. This woman, this wife, this mother, so undeserving of the man in there. She watched Terry leaning over the hood of the car. Like a scarab, Dr. Devlin thought, caught in the yellowish light and obviously helpless. But at the same time an ornament and safe; so damned protected and safe.

Why did she have to stand there, right under the light, looking up, fluttering her hands as if she were lost? Dr. Devlin hoped no one would come for her. This would be good for Terry, in the therapeutic sense, help her to develop self-esteem. Dr. Devlin's mind reached for a citation and, with the mental tick which was habitual, she found the name of a monograph: *Is Grief a Disease?*

But Dr. Devlin felt somehow attacked and from many sides— pleased by Terry's evident distress, ashamed of her pleasure, frightened by Terry's strange presence in the parking lot. Terry was writing furiously on the placard . . . jabbing at the yellow paper, drawing back and then slowly running her eyes around the pools of yellow light and the black patches of oil-streaked cement. She was not looking for anyone, she was *scanning* the place. As if she wanted to remember it.

Dr. Devlin came off the steps quickly, running toward the other woman, not sure why she was in motion.

"Hello, Mrs. Thatch," Dr. Devlin said.

Terry twitched around. Her face was quiet, without animation, but one hand came down quickly and accurately on the paper.

"Please call me Terry," she said.

Dr. Devlin nodded. Even in this yellowish fog-streaked light Terry was beautiful. So unearned, Dr. Devlin thought, some random mixture of genes and a face was well-formed and a figure lithe and a good husband waiting . . . even if the woman didn't have a brain in her head.

"It's very exciting about the demonstration," Dr. Devlin said. "Now we wait and see."

"I'm not waiting," Terry said. She turned back to her writing. She spoke without looking up. "I mean I'm not waiting tonight to see what happens." She turned and faced Dr. Devlin. "That's all I meant."

She began to fold the yellow placard. She folded it again and again until it was a tiny packet. Then she put the Scotch tape around it.

"Dev, would you give this note to John when he comes out. Also could you call me a cab?" She leaned against the car. "I'm terribly tired."

Dr. Devlin took the note and walked back toward the office.

Something was trying to come to focus in her mind and she was resisting it. At the same time she felt a nagging self-pity. Then her rational mind, the trained mind, the part she valued so much began to run off a series of statements:

—Terry quiet at the meetings. Even quieter recently. Hands clutched in lap.

—She had wept at the television show when the boys were taken from her to go on camera.

—The story in the women's magazine about Terry losing her parents and her sister.

—Quick glances, frightened eyes, her tension when Thatch spoke, her pleasure when they escaped from a meeting together, her fear of crowds.

The self-pitying part of Dr. Devlin's mind was angry with that part which was sharp, analytical, logical. She should stop this endless examination of people and their motives. It was Terry's problem, Terry's inadequacies, *Terry's life* . . . The phrase hit so hard that she stumbled. In the office she dialed for the cab and slit the packet open with a letter opener. The handwriting was large and clear, but it sloped unevenly across the page.

Dearest John:

The diary in Kelly's hands makes my life unbearable. I shall not be a burden to you and a disgrace to the boys.

I love you very much. And it was so clean and wonderful when we were alone. But you must do what is necessary for yourself and your duty although . . . [Here a sentence had been crossed out. The words still showed. . . . *although duty may be a monster.*]

Watch the boys carefully. Spend time with Tony. He is the lonely one these days. Take them to Zamboanga for a vacation and teach them to fish and sail.

The next Batangas foal should go to the Johnsons. We promised. I am so relieved.

Love,
Terry

She ordered the cab and stuffed the note in her pocket. As she went down the steps she saw Curver walking fast toward the office.

"Mad, I've only got seconds," she said. "Tell me about this diary Kelly has."

Curver looked at her carefully, hesitated a moment and then spoke.

"I just found out about it," he said. "The diary was kept by an English woman, a prisoner with Terry in Santo Tomas. It says Terry slept with a Japanese guard for over a year."

"Is it true?"

"Yes," Curver said. "How did you find out?"

Dr. Devlin saw the lights of the taxi cab. "I haven't time . . ." She thrust the note into his hands. "Read it."

Thatch had known, Dr. Devlin thought, as she ran through the patches of yellow light, felt the chill fog swirl by. He had known and he had married her anyway. Dr. Devlin felt a quick disgust with Thatch and it was followed instantly by a sense of delight. They were both filthy and, of course, this is why they were so remote, so jealous of their privacy, so . . . so . . . unbearable. Both of them.

The taxi, its lights blurred by fog, had swung into the parking space.

Terry opened the door and turned back to say good-by. Dr. Devlin climbed into the taxi with her.

"Dev, I'm not going to the hotel," Terry said. "You shouldn't miss the excitement. I'm just going to ride around."

"I'll ride with you," Dr. Devlin said. She wanted to slap Terry. And yet she felt the other woman's pain. "Where do you want to go?"

"Towards the Presidio," Terry said, loud enough for the driver to hear.

Dr. Devlin had snatched up a small transistor radio from the office as she ran out. She couldn't leave Thatch behind. Now, holding it in her lap, she turned it on. Walter Cronkite, speaking from the Cow Palace, was still describing Thatch's tortuous approach to the dais. He sounded tired. Terry glanced at the radio and then out the window. They rode otherwise in silence.

The taxi swung out onto the concrete ramps which went by the Presidio. The driver turned his head.

"There's the Presidio, lady," he said. "Want to go in?"

"No. We want to go on to the Golden Gate Bridge," Dr. Devlin said. As she sank back in the seat Dr. Devlin wondered, with a kind of weariness, why *she* had ordered the cab to go to the Golden Gate Bridge. The answer came so easily, so professionally, so completely that she knew she had known all along.

San Francisco and its magnificently arched bridge beckoned seductively to the would-be suicides of America. The City had the highest suicide rate in the nation and a big fraction of them went off the Golden Gate . . . jumping back toward the city and continent that had rejected them, screaming their rage or fear. The Coast Guard sailors came to know the screech, and the bone-crunching sound when a body hit solid water. For each one that actually jumped, perhaps 500 came and looked over the edge and were tempted, Dr. Devlin knew. But the other 499 fled, horribly frightened, back to their cars or continued their hysterical stroll, thrilled with how close they had come to their black freedom. San Francisco was the bright glittering mecca of the dedicated suicide, and each thought first of the Golden Gate. And that, she said savagely to herself, is why I ordered the cab to go to the Golden Gate.

The riotous sounds from the convention hall blurred and pulsed and faded in the background. Mad read and re-read the note on the yellow placard. He had watched Dev and Terry drive off together in the taxi. The idea of Terry leaving Thatch and her two boys was preposterous, incomprehensible. The woman must be out of her mind. . . .

Then he realized that what he held in his hand was a suicide note. He felt sick and dizzy and cold. Dev was riding around in the night with a woman bent on killing herself.

He had to get to Thatch. He left his little office on the run.

Kelly watched and admired what he saw. He also knew that no one could have planned it this well, so he felt little envy. The standees in Aisle 16, whom everyone else in the hall had thought were John Birchers or just crackpots suddenly underwent a miraculous conversion: these people, thought to be obstructionist and ugly, were shaking Thatch's hand. A few women, in their late fifties, actually kissed Thatch's hand. Around the Cow Palace Kelly could feel the thing grow. It was almost religious. Thatch's enemies had been struck down and now were like lambs, Kelly said to himself. Oh, this was going to be a day. If Thatch gets it, we'll have a battle and I'll pull in all the big people and the Party leaders and the fur will fly and blood will flow and mayhem will be done in the name of politics and the American way. And I'll be there by his side along with that clever young son of a bitch, Madison Curver.

Still it hurt. It hurt because he could not practice his art exactly as he knew it. And he had perfected it so well since 1960. In Chicago he had watched Nixon come oiling into the Convention with everything for him . . . and a staff so sadly organized that they almost managed to make a crisis of a shoo-in. Len Hall and Bob Finch had breakfast together and that was supposed to be coordination. Chuck McWhorter, one man, Kelly groaned to himself, had been in charge of contacting delegates . . . and he remembered the Kennedy machine in L.A. which functioned like some marvelous self-balancing mechanism and had a card on every delegate at the Convention and where the poor stupid bastard stood from hour to hour. It hurt because Kelly had a machine ready to go which would beat Nixon, Goldwater, Rockefeller, Lodge, or Abe Lincoln. If it had a candidate. And, in the last two minutes Kelly's candidate had gone up in smoke.

Kelly put down the bile in his stomach. There would be another time. He was certain Curver would be contacting him before the night was out. Kelly would play it hard and tough, but he knew, and Curver would know, that Kelly would go along.

Kelly knew, the way poor McCarthy *hadn't* known, that he was a political man. To be isolated from the game would kill Kelly. Just as it had shrunk the meat off McCarthy's bones, sunk the eyes in his skull, made him beg and whine at newspapermen he had thrown out of his office two months before, and finally the simple fact of isolation killed him.

Thatch moved slowly against the crowd in the aisle. He told the policemen with the white helmets and the ushers not to worry.

A woman kissed his hand and Thatch almost snatched it back. She looked up and her face was melted fat, rouge, tears, and happy ecstatic black eyes. Thatch said something to her and the woman's eyes rolled in her head. He could not remember what he said. Probably "Thank you, ma'am."

When he was halfway down the aisle he became aware of another rising sound, different from the voices along the aisle. It came from all directions, fell on him like a wave. The sound came from a thousand voices, and it said many things. But one thing was in all of them: *Thatch*.

Thatch felt the hair rise on his neck. He felt a dizziness, but no unsteadiness or fear came with it.

They don't know me and they like me, he said. It's real. Not faked. Not Mad or Book or anyone could fake this.

The sound from around the auditorium grew, became an assault on the ears, and Thatch could no longer distinguish words. He looked ahead at the standees. They were almost to the end of the aisle. Then the strange thing happened; the standees seemed to be growing smaller, to be actually diminishing, as if by trick photography.

By the time Thatch got to the stairway leading to the speaker's stand, he was physically bigger than most people on the platform.

Thatch shook hands with various people, made the right comments, apologized for the commotion outside. But he was listening only to the sound in the auditorium. It was deafening now and it grew. He looked at the Chairman and at Senator Reddick and Thatch knew that he *was* bigger . . . not physically, although he looked down at them, but in some other more important way.

"I think, Mr. Thatch, that you're the only one who can stop this demonstration from getting out of hand," the Chairman said.

"No need to introduce me," Thatch said. "They seem to know who I am."

Senator Reddick looked sharply at him. Thatch was aware of it and did not even try to analyze what it meant.

"I guess so," the Chairman said. "Why don't you just go ahead."

Thatch half turned, remembered something but was not sure what.

He had lost Terry. That was it. He did not know where she was. Thatch walked to the battery of microphones. The cobranecks were swaying, they were quivering from the battering of sound.

"Remember, only ten minutes, Mr. Thatch," the Chairman said. There was a note of gloom in his voice which delighted Thatch. Probably the poor bastard had just lost a whole book of Brownie Points for what had happened. Thatch felt a quick and passing rage toward the people who had tried to frustrate his appearance here.

The bridge came up out of the foggy night. First there was only the lighted cubes of the toll booths with the blurred arrows blinking STOP . . . and the word seemed harmless in the dark. Then the big shoulders of the southern bulwarks took shape and raising from them the massive cables, swinging up until they merged with the fog and were lost. The bridge was eerie and dangling, the whole fragile structure incapable of holding up the thick wet strip of black asphalt which reached out over the water. Dr. Devlin felt the seat cushion move and knew Terry had pushed back into her corner.

"We'll stop on this side and walk out," Dr. Devlin said to the driver.

Remorselessly, against her will, pieces of Terry's "case" fell into a pattern in Dr. Devlin's mind. The total picture she could not see. In many suicide cases there was a record of parents who were suddenly lost and to Terry it must seem that Thatch was being removed from her. And then the boys had been taken from her at the television show and turned over to the world. Often suicide notes left practical instructions, dealt with ordinary things, had "neutral units" in them . . . like "Give the next Batangas foal to the Johnsons."

Dr. Devlin had done a lot of reading on suicide. She knew that a majority killed themselves because they felt they were a burden on others. All were in some way lonely, in many cases having suffered a recent sense of rejection. Lost, bewildered, thinking herself abandoned, Terry—and now Dr. Devlin forced herself to acknowledge she might have sensed this building in

Terry weeks ago—a person like Terry, driving herself to the final conclusion, would take her life in the quietest possible way . . . silently off the bridge or with sleeping pills behind a locked door. The pseudo suicide slashed his wrists and screamed for help or threatened to jump from a building with wide-eyed crowds below or walked into a crowded bar holding a pistol and threatening to put it in his mouth and pull the trigger. These were the exhibitionists, the retrievables. Terry was the other kind and Dr. Devlin was surprised to feel a quick flash of admiration for her.

Dr. Devlin paid the cab driver. She still clutched the muttering little radio. The two women walked out onto the bridge. Car wheels hissed on the wet. Drops of water fell softly from the invisible steel matrix high above them. Dr. Devlin, walking carefully on the outside, glanced at Terry's face. It was set in a rigid calm.

"Terry, when you're gone it will be impossible for Thatch to be nominated," Dr. Devlin said.

"What do you mean 'when I'm gone'?" Terry said. Her voice was toneless.

Dr. Devlin turned the radio up.

"John Thatch has made his way to the speaker's platform, but now there is a mob of people around him. The air is full of crude hand-made placards and flags. Some of them are Rockefeller or Goldwater placards turned over and with the word "THATCH" written on them in lipstick. Senator Thomas Lander, the venerable leader of the California delegation, is trying to pry Thatch loose from the crowd . . ."

She turned down the volume.

"No convention could ever select a man whose wife just committed suicide."

"I didn't say anything about suicide," Terry said.

"I did."

They walked another hundred yards and stopped. They could feel, rather than hear, a ship pass beneath the bridge far below: a pressure against the eardrums. Then the sound of its foghorn came up to them, throaty and elemental.

"There is nothing else to do," Terry said suddenly. "I've brought John so much trouble. He took me . . . took me . . . picked me up when I was dirty and contaminated and knowing what I was he still took me. We lived quietly and we had the boys and I forgot the other thing—I never thought of it. But I was once filthy and low and John and the boys can never lead a decent life so long as I am around."

Dr. Devlin knew the pattern. If I am gone they will be free. So simple. I just disappear and everything will be made well again.

They stopped and Terry leaned over the rail. There was nothing below except steel rods and then white emptiness. Dr. Devlin sensed that the fog would make it easier . . . one would be jumping into softness and invisibility and would be gone without pain.

Why had she brought Terry here to the bridge? Because, the textbooks said you must not restrain a suicide who is in no immediate danger. Allow free will to operate. Otherwise you merely postpone the inevitable and for only a brief period. Persuade but don't restrain . . . She wondered whether this was the truth. Back in the parking lot she had hated this woman, this undeserving wife of John Thatch. Had she planned, on some level or other, to encourage the suicide, to make it easier. She shuddered.

"Terry, nothing you *have* done will ruin him," Dr. Devlin said. Suddenly she felt a quite foreign ache of her own. She had the weird sensation that she was not controlling the situation, but was living in it. She was frightened.

"You don't know what I have done," Terry said. She was staring down into the mist, speaking over her shoulder. Dr. Devlin knew this was no time to touch her.

"I know what you want to do. You call it suicide, but you really think of it as revenge. You want to believe you are sacrificing yourself but actually you are out to punish someone. That's why you left a note which you know will rend the hearts of Thatch and your boys. How many pills have you saved up?"

"About fifty," Terry said. She swung around, her face puzzled. "I don't want to punish them. But they're going to be taken away from me. Just like before."

"Like before?"

Terry nodded. "My father and mother and sister."

The little radio in Dev's hand suddenly stopped its muttering and she turned it up.

"Political ambition is the vice of American life." These were, she knew, Thatch's first words. "The Presidency is not an object of ambition. It is something given by the people to an individual. It should not be sought, for in the seeking lies the corruption."

Mad came out of the office with his head down, running full tilt, still clutching the letter. He bounced off a policeman who said, "Steady, buddy," and looked curiously at Mad's badge.

Curver plowed into the crowd in Gate 16 and his tall lanky figure had worked its way three ranks deep before he realized it was hopeless. The crowd was getting denser. Mad was not moving at all. Curver slipped past a few more people and then the crowd was impenetrable, locked together and motionless, staring ahead, impervious to his elbows.

He turned and worked his way out. By now he was sweating although the night was cool. He could call the speaker's platform, but there wasn't the chance of a snowball in hell of the Chairman stopping Thatch or passing him a message. Still running, Curver sloped leftwards, moved by some old piece of knowledge.

Long ago he had memorized the plan of the Cow Palace, the entrances, the exits, the positions of the rest rooms, the hot-dog stands, the plans for seating the delegations, the security plans, the posts of the policemen. Normally the three lanes in front of the speaker's platform would be open, but he had himself arranged to have them jammed with Thatch supporters. He had seen enough inside to know that they would be full. He felt a quick frenzy and put it down.

He slowed to a trot, calling the plan of the Cow Palace back to mind.

He should take the trickiest route that no one would think of. Two passages in the diagram came to his mind and intersected. He started running. He went past two gates and ducked into a passageway in which a group of white-coated janitors were standing. The place smelled of cleaning oil, old mops, brooms, all overlaid with a heavy tobacco odor. He trotted down the passageway. One of the janitors, a lanky man, put out a languid hand.

"No use, buddy. Door at this end is locked. They only open it when there's been a demonstration and they want us to sweep the aisles clean." He spoke to Mad's back. "Paper in the aisle is a fire hazard."

"Thanks," Curver called over his shoulder and kept going.

Halfway down the passage was a door on the left-hand side. He opened it and went into a large room. The smell of cleaning supplies was thicker than before and Curver was sweating hard. He could see the outline of the door behind some brooms, a heavy gray-metal door. He reached for the handle and someone spoke behind him.

"Even if that door is open you're going to walk right into the special security cops," the lanky man said, watching him without interest. "Since Dallas, you know . . ." he shrugged his shoulders.

"I've got permission," Curver said. The janitor turned away. He took out his pen and in large letters printed some words on the outside of the yellow placard.

He tried the door and it opened. A line of San Francisco police, leaning against the wall of the passageway, eyed him and then came to the alert, fanned out and made an arc that blocked both ways. To the right he could see the arena, the flags around the speaker's platform and he could hear Thatch's voice. And the passageway behind the platform was open.

"It's okay. I'm with President Eisenhower's party," Curver panted. He waved the note at the sergeant who was standing slightly in front of the other men. The sergeant did not take his eyes from Curver, but moved forward, his hand out. "Can't read it. Personal from the President to the Chairman. Urgent. Deliver by hand. Dwight D. Eisenhower."

"Don't you have any identification? Rest of the Washington security people are wearing those special badges," the sergeant said.

"After Dallas, sergeant, some of us try to look as inconspicuous as possible." Curver turned quickly and jerked the placard from the sergeant's hand. He started off down the corridor. He had seen the flush start on the sergeant's face.

"Go with him, Wilson," the sergeant said. "Lend him a hand."

Once he was in the cleared lane Curver started to run again, the faces of the delegates flashing by him. He was drenched with sweat now and had no idea of how long he had been running. He could hear the cop running behind him.

He came to the stairs at the edge of the platform, a hand reached out to stop him and he turned with exasperation to the cop who had followed him. "Tell him," he ordered the cop. Wilson nodded and the hand fell away. Curver trotted out into the blazing lights, saw the thousands of heads suddenly turn toward him. He put down his panic, slowed, walked over to Thatch and handed him the note.

"Your disappearance will be revenge for all you have suffered," Dr. Devlin said. She stared at the mist below, trying to see through to the river. She felt something crumbling within herself, a collapsing of thin but very strong shields . . . the shields of intellect, and statistics, and monographic details, which she had built into an impregnable internal fortress. She was astonished. There was no time to understand what was happening to her. One thing was clear: She was remembering and it was without pain.

"Terry, let me tell you a thing that happened to me," she said. Now it was as clear as a white line drawn through pure blackness. "I have never told this to anyone because I did not want to remember it myself. Until now. My father just disappeared. Not killed, not a suicide, just gone. And my mother started to drink red juice out of a bottle and told me it was for her cough . . . it must have been cheap wine." She paused and remembered the white gaunt neck stretched up and the bottle gurgling and red drops on her mother's chin.

"Then, mother left a note that said she couldn't give me a decent education," Dr. Devlin went on. "She hung herself in the kitchen and I remember . . . I remember . . . she wore her worst old dress and pinned the note to her skirt. I unpinned it and read it and I remember one line, 'Now maybe you'll take decent care of my child . . . the way you never did me!' I marched over to show it to a neighbor. I didn't realize Mother was dead. I don't know how old I was. Everybody called me 'that *poor* little girl.' "

"Oh God, Dev, why are people caught like this?" Terry said.

"I went to the orphanage," Dr. Devlin went on, "And I don't remember a face. I didn't want ever again to become dependent on anyone . . . unless it was a person who was indestructible. I guess I loved college work just because I disliked people so much. I became an M.D. but didn't practice. I said it was because I was more interested in research. Maybe it was because I didn't trust people. So I learned all about bodies and minds and muscles and nerve systems and that way I turned people into simple machines. Later I built this marvelous artificial notion of man . . . from monographs, polls, studies, reflex times, body chemistry. It was my form of suicide and my form of revenge."

Dr. Devlin stopped and leaned against the cold steel of the bridge. She felt a great relief. Terry's arm came around her shoulder. Dev looked around in surprise.

Terry's eyes were still unfocused. "I know, I know, Dev. Can't you see the headlines, PRESIDENT'S WIFE A WHORE?"

"No one will say that, Terry." She paused as she heard Thatch's voice, tiny and distinct on the quietness of the bridge. He was getting to the part about Bryant Clark being a CO. She cringed. How could she have written such a paragraph?

Dr. Devlin made herself turn up the volume.

"Now comes the thing about Clark," Terry said. "It's not John. It's not."

They both listened now fearfully.

"I have not, nor shall I, attack the motives of any candidates for this nomination. There are excellent men seeking the nomination and you must study their credentials carefully." He paused. "I shall say no more on this subject."

"On the domestic front I have stated often that the problem of racial tension is a sickness of our life. Excellence is color-blind. Those who deny a black or brown man the chance to show his excellence are, in the truest sense, being inhuman, and do the gravest injustice to their country."

"He didn't use the CO thing," Terry said. "He didn't attack Clark."

The radio fell silent. Dr. Devlin turned up the volume. There was the curious scuffling, hawking sound of a mass of people. But Thatch had stopped talking.

"There is something going on down on the platform," the announcer's voice said softly. "A man came out of a side door and raced across to the platform and handed Mr. Thatch a piece of yellow paper. No one here in our booth knows who the young man is, but the message is obviously of some importance. Mr. Thatch is talking with him."

Terry turned slowly and her eyes were wide with fright. "It's my letter. How could he have gotten it? I gave it to you."

"I'm not sure, Terry," Dr. Devlin said. It was difficult to put things back together. "I gave it to Mad. But I'd already read it, Terry."

"Oh, God, what am I doing to him?"

"Mr. Thatch is looking up now. The young man is running back the way he came," the announcer said. "Mr. Thatch is standing in front of the microphone."

"And now I must leave you," Thatch said, his voice fast and urgent.

Some delegates, thinking the note had told him to cut his speech short, began to chant "No, no . . ." but Thatch cut in swiftly.

"Some have associated my name with the purpose for which this convention was called, the naming of a Presidential candidate," Thatch said. "The result of this speculation has been so painful to someone I love that I cannot allow my name to be put in candidacy. Thank you."

There was complete silence on the radio for a few moments. Then the announcer spoke softly, "The Convention is stunned. Mr. Thatch is running out of the Cow Palace by the same path taken by the young man who handed him the note. Mr. Thatch was scheduled to speak for ten minutes and has spoken only five. There is great confusion. On the speaker's platform the Chairman is conferring with Senator Reddick and the Senator is approaching the microphones. He glanced down at something, apparently the same yellow paper handed to Mr. Thatch."

Terry moaned. She leaned against Dev. She was shaking. Dr. Devlin put her arm around the girl and held the radio so they both could hear.

"Fellow Republicans," Senator Reddick said. "In politics, as in everything else, there must be limits. It is no concern of politics what the racial or religious background of a man's wife may be. Yet some of us, in the heat of battle, have so tormented the wife of this man who was speaking to you that he is no longer available as a candidate . . ."

The radio exploded in a crash of sound. Dr. Devlin was not sure whether it was static or the audience. She heard a few individual voices shouting, "No. Bring him back." She snapped the radio off. Terry was running down the bridge toward the toll plaza.

A cab was waiting at the end of the bridge and Terry was already crouched in the corner of the back seat. Dev climbed in and said, "Cow Palace" to the driver.

"He gave it all up," Terry whispered. "He gave it all up for me."

"Don't blame yourself, Terry. Don't—"

"I'm not, I'm not. But he wants me more than all that, more than the Presidency. I had to know."

Dev felt a wave of loneliness wash over her. She knew it was because the girl no longer needed her. Terry had re-established contact with her own tight little world.

"But he's got to run. He mustn't give it up for me. He's got to accept."

Dev thought she hadn't heard correctly. Then she knew she had. A powerful, shocking emotion started in her knees and swept up through her body. Her head snapped back hard against the seat and she was laughing, laughing loud and hard and hysterically.

Terry reached over and took her hand. She patted it. No one in Dev's memory had patted her hand before in exactly this comforting way. She felt her loneliness again.

Curver sat at the desk in the little office. The three portable TV sets against the wall were still turned on, each channel showing a different angle of the convention floor.

Kelly sat stiffly in another chair. They did not speak, waiting in some peculiar vigil. A few minutes before just outside Thatch had broken away from Mad, saying he would call the police and then go wait for Terry and Dev at the gate. Mad had wanted to stay with him but Thatch had brusquely shaken him off. Mad had wandered back to his little office and minutes later Kelly had come in. Mad started to tell him what had happened but Kelly didn't need a road map. He sat rigidly, remembering Terry on the beach: "Do you make your living doing that sort of thing?"

Mad looked down at a yellow pad of paper on his desk. Earlier, to pass the time, he had been scribbling on it. At the top of the page in neat letters were the words "Convention to General Election."

1. Get Kelly on personal staff at once. Salary? Maybe nothing.

2. Big issues for Simulations Enterprises and depth interviews:
   a. Cuba . . . make the Flyboy support T. but forbid "expeditions" and Marine assaults . . . Keep right-wingers active . . . can we find out how many will follow the Flyboy even when T. is going opposite direction???
   b. Salve right-wingers by oblique statement that Eastern Seaboard, fuzzy liberals, Harvard, etc. all killed the Flyboy. Might build his saliency and then transfer it to T.
   c. Johnson's vulnerable. Hit the Bobby Baker thing. The hi-fi set and TV station. Just repeat in nice way.
   d. Research all polls and survey for info. "Dems are War Party. Won for Ike in '52 . . . Also Dems "lost" Vietnam, see how much saliency it packs for voters. Like Dems "lost" China.

3. Avoid T. and Kennedy image meeting head-on. Concentrate on LBJ trying to ride on JFK's coattails.

4. Can Warren inquiry JFK assassination drag on until November? Big help if ambiguity surrounds subject?

He looked at it with detachment now, as if someone else had written it.

Dr. Devlin walked into the office. She was still clutching the little radio. Mad and Kelly stood and looked at her and said nothing.

"Is she all right?" Kelly asked.

She nodded and the tight muscular agony went out of Kelly's face.

"Thatch was waiting at the gate and when she got out of the cab they just walked off together."

Mad stared at Dev. He felt empty, as if he had nothing to say and no way to say it. Kelly slumped in a chair, talking to himself.

"I wouldn't have used that goddamn diary. You know I wouldn't, I told you. I just wanted her to tell Thatch and take him out of the race. But the whole thing got out of hand. I lost control."

Dev looked at Mad. "I should have known weeks ago that she was in a suicidal depression. All the signs were there but I ignored them. I ignored them because I hated her."

Kelly looked up questioningly.

Mad nodded. He took Dev's cold hand and held it gently. "You stopped her, Dev. Whatever went before doesn't count now."

"No, Thatch stopped her." Briefly she described the scene on the bridge. "I had the little radio and she heard everything—first his omission of the attack on Clark and then his withdrawal. That was enough. He came back to her."

She felt a strange sensation in her chest and sat down. She reached back through the years into childhood trying to identify it. Suddenly she knew. She was going to cry. But she managed one more sentence before the tears came.

"And the last—the last thing she said in the taxi was 'He wants me more than all that, more than the Presidency, so he's got to run, he's got to accept."

Mad reached for her as she crumpled into the chair. Kelly watched for a moment and then walked into the passageway where he stood resolutely before the door like a sentry.

Bookbinder and Levi sat limply before the television set in their suite at the Fairmont. Neither had moved or spoken for ten minutes. Bookbinder's hand found Levi's shoulder.

Bookbinder's mind was torn with conflicting emotions. For a few minutes, watching the near-riot on the television screen, his enthusiasm for Thatch (and, yes, his belief in the man) had soared to ecstatic heights. Entirely forgotten was his distrust of the techniques that had helped bring Thatch this far, his growing reservations about Mad, his dislike of polls and behavioral scientists and simulations, his basic belief that fine old traditions were being perverted. The old virus had flared up in him again and made him feverish. Then, even as he watched the Thatch demonstration come to a boil on the television screen, Thatch's own voice of the night before interposed—"what if old Joe McCarthy came down the pike and used your new political methods?"—and McCarthy's hyena face and nervous laugh and evil eyes invaded Bookbinder's mind and he imagined the dead Senator standing with him at the Simulation Enterprises office on Madison Avenue and watching the tapes and spools and lights and buttons and planning some masterful manipulation of the American public so that it would embrace his kind of madness.

He shuddered, pulling himself back into the present. His hand reached out and found Levi's shoulder.

"It's over, Levi. All over. But did you notice, he didn't use the

C.O. stuff against Clark? It was in that speech but he skipped it. At least we're not such bad judges of character."

Levi did not respond. Bookbinder looked at him closely.

His old friend smiled weakly and nodded. The phone rang and, painfully, Bookbinder stretched his stiff legs and went to answer it.

Kelly had been standing in the passageway for fifteen minutes when the phone rang. He heard Mad answer and he stepped inside. Dev was seated quietly in the corner.

Mad spoke around the telephone, "It's Thatch," but his face showed nothing. He said "Yes, sir" a couple of times and then hung up.

"Where was he?" Dev asked.

"At the hotel."

"How did he sound?"

Mad sat there, saying nothing.

Kelly closed the door behind him. "Well, answer the lady's question."

"He sounded . . . ," Mad searched for the right words . . . "he sounded just like Thatch. Decisive, forceful, full of beans." He paused. "He said Bookbinder is coming to his suite and he wants us to join them right away, Dev. To talk . . . to talk about tomorrow's strategy."

Kelly was at the door. "He won't want to see me—yet. But I'll get hold of Reddick and call you at the hotel." He left.

Dev remained in her corner. Her habitual rigidly controlled expression of calm had been replaced by a look of real tranquility —or perhaps it was emotional exhaustion, Mad thought.

Her voice was low, almost a whisper. "What sort of man is he?"

"You, Dr. Devlin, are asking me? After six months of telling me all about him?"

"Mad, I haven't a clue. Do you know that? I haven't a clue."

He took her hand and patted it. For a second time tonight someone was patting her hand in this comforting protective way. She wanted the patting to go on and on.

"What sort of a man?" Mad repeated the question. "Let's go over to the hotel. We may find out."

Appendix

The following are the 480 groups into which the American electorate has been divided by the Simulmatics Corporation. I am indebted to that company for allowing me to reproduce them here.

NOTE: All types that are single-starred (*) DO NOT include Urban, White Collar and all types that are double-starred (**) DO include Urban, White Collar. The designation SES refers to social-economic status.

1.	Democrat	Eastern	Protestant	Male	Rural	Professional & White Collar
2.	"	"	"	"	"	Blue Collar
3.	"	"	"	"	Town	Professional & White Collar
4.	"	"	"	"	"	Blue Collar
5.	"	"	"	"	Urban	Professional
6.	"	"	"	"	"	White Collar
7.	"	"	"	"	"	Blue Collar
8.	"	"	"	Female	Rural	Professional & White Collar
9.	"	"	"	"	"	Blue Collar
10.	"	"	"	"	Town	Professional & White Collar
11.	"	"	"	"	"	Blue Collar
12.	"	"	"	"	Urban	Professional
13.	"	"	"	"	"	White Collar
14.	"	"	"	"	"	Blue Collar
15.	"	"	Catholic	Male	Rural	Professional & White Collar
16.	"	"	"	"	"	Blue Collar
17.	"	"	"	"	Town	Professional & White Collar
18.	"	"	"	"	"	Blue Collar
19.	"	"	"	"	Urban	Professional
20.	"	"	"	"	"	White Collar
21.	"	"	"	"	"	Blue Collar

22.	Democrat	Eastern	Catholic	Female	Rural	Professional & White Collar
23.	"	"	"	"	"	Blue Collar
24.	"	"	"	"	Town	Professional & White Collar
25.	"	"	"	"	"	Blue Collar
26.	"	"	"	"	Urban	Professional
27.	"	"	"	"	"	White Collar
28.	"	"	"	"	"	Blue Collar
* 29.	"	"	Jewish			Professional & White Collar
** 30.	"	"	"			Blue Collar
* 31.	"	"	Negro			Professional & White Collar
** 32.	"	"	"			Blue Collar
33.	"	"	Protestant			No SES rating, Non–labor force families
34.	"	"	Catholic			No SES rating, Non–labor force families
35.	"	"	Other relig.			
36.	"	"	No relig.			

These first 36 types all refer to DEMOCRATS

Types 37 to 72 are identical to types 1 to 36 except for the classification REPUBLICAN

Types 73 to 108 are also identical to types 1 to 36 except for the classification INDEPENDENT

Now you have 108 types, all referring to EASTERN:
Repeat three (3) times, changing only the regional classification:
Types 109 to 216 are SOUTHERN
Types 217 to 324 are MIDWESTERN
Types 325 to 432 are WESTERN

The last 48 types fall in the BORDER STATES and are as follows:

* 433.	Democrat	Border States	Protestant	Male		Professional & White Collar
** 434.	"	"	"	"		Blue Collar
* 435.	"	"	"	Female		Professional & White Collar
** 436.	"	"	"	"		Blue Collar
* 437.	"	"	Catholic	Male		Professional & White Collar
** 438.	"	"	"	"		Blue Collar
* 439.	"	"	"	Female		Professional & White Collar
** 440.	"	"	"	"		Blue Collar

* 441.	Democrat	Border States	Jewish	Female	Professional & White Collar
** 442.	"	"	"		Blue Collar
* 443.	"	"	Negro		Professional & White Collar
** 444.	"	"	"		Blue Collar
445.	"	"	Protestant		No SES rating, Non–labor force families
446.	"	"	Catholic		No SES rating, Non–labor force families
447.	"	"	Other relig.		
448.	"	"	No relig.		

Types 433 to 448 are repeated two (2) times, changing the party description only, so that:

Types 449 to 464 are REPUBLICAN
Types 465 to 480 are INDEPENDENT

Professional and white collar levels were not separated outside of cities because there were too few professional in the rural areas and towns.

The criteria for community sizes were:
Rural—population of under 5000
Town—population of 5000 to 100,000
Urban—population over 100,000

The regional division of states was:
East—Maine, New Hampshire, Vermont, Massachusetts, Rhode Island, Connecticut, New York, New Jersey, and Pennsylvania

South—Virginia, North Carolina, South Carolina, Georgia, Florida, Alabama, Mississippi, Arkansas, Louisiana, Oklahoma, Texas

Midwest—Ohio, Michigan, Indiana, Illinois, Wisconsin, Minnesota, Iowa, Missouri, North Dakota, South Dakota, Nebraska, Kansas

West—Montana, Arizona, Colorado, Idaho, Wyoming, Utah, Nevada, New Mexico, California, Oregon, Washington

Border States—Maryland, Delaware, West Virginia, Kentucky, Tennessee

About the Author

Rhodes scholar, political scientist, world traveler, lecturer, writer of best-selling novels, Eugene Burdick represents American versatility at its most startling. An associate professor of political science at the University of California, he is also a skin diver of more than local fame. He has written political science texts on one hand and famous novels on the other. His first novel, *The Ninth Wave*, was a Book-of-the-Month Club selection in 1956 and his second, co-authored with William Lederer, was the internationally famous *The Ugly American*. His third novel, *Fail-Safe*, co-authored with Harvey Wheeler, was another Book-of-the-Month Club selection and another world-wide best-seller. He has published short stories and articles in *Harper's*, *The New Yorker*, *Collier's*, *The New York Times Sunday Magazine*, and many other periodicals. Mr. Burdick was born in Iowa, raised in California, educated at Stanford and Oxford, and lives today in Berkeley with his wife and three children.